Marina Fiorato

Marina Fiorato is half-Venetian. She was born in Manchester and raised in the Yorkshire Dales. She is a history graduate of Oxford University and the University of Venice, where she read for a master's degree in Shakespeare. After university she studied art and worked in the film and music industries, creating visuals for U2, The Rolling Stones and the Queen musical We Will Rock You. Her novels *Daughter of Siena* and *Beatrice & Benedick* were shortlisted for the Romantic Novelists' Association Historical Fiction Award. Marina was married on the Grand Canal and lives in north London with her husband, son and daughter. You can find out more about Marina and her writing at www.marinafiorato.com. and follow her on Twitter @marinafiorato

The Glassblower of Murano
The Madonna of the Almonds
The Botticelli Secret
Daughter of Siena
The Venetian Contract
Beatrice and Benedick

The Double Life of
Mistress Kit Kavanagh

MARINA FIORATO

HODDER

First published in Great Britain in 2015 by Hodder & Stoughton

An Hachette UK company

First published in paperback in 2016

1

Text and illustrations copyright © Marina Fiorato 2015

A CIP catalogue record for this title is available from the British Library

ISBN 978 1 473 61049 1

Typeset in Dante MT Std by Palimpsest Book Production Limited,
Falkirk, Stirlingshire

Printed and bound by Clays Ltd, St Ives plc

Hodder & Stoughton policy is to use papers that are natural,
renewable and recyclable products and made from wood grown in sustainable forests.
The logging and manufacturing processes are expected to conform to the
environmental regulations of the country of origin.

Hodder & Stoughton Ltd
Carmelite House
50 Victoria Embankment
London EC4Y 0DZ

www.hodder.co.uk

In memory of Joshua Bennett
who had his own battles to fight

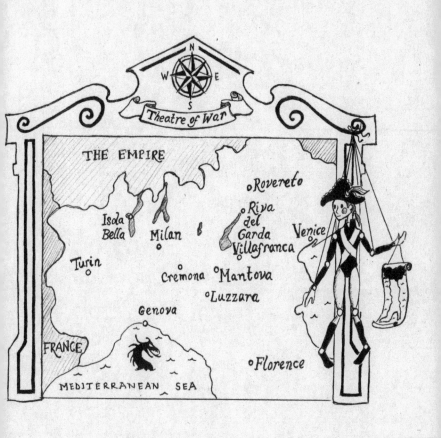

Theatre of War

THE EMPIRE

Rovereto

Riva
del
Garda
Villafranca

Venice

Isola
Bella

Milan

Turin

Cremona Mantova

Luzzara

Genova

FRANCE

Florence

MEDITERRANEAN SEA

Prologue

Aughrim, Ireland, 1700

The red-headed girl was the bravest.

She went higher up the green hill than all her fellows, and rolled down head over heels, breakneck and reckless. There might have been half a dozen girls with her, but it was hard to see the others. She drew the eye like a comet.

She seemed to have no mind for her modesty. Her petticoats flew anyhow about her bare legs. Nor did she heed her safety; more than once she knocked her head on a tussock or clod, fit to break her crown. And if she did? There would be no king's horses or men to put her together again. Nine years ago they were plentiful here, for this place had been a battlefield where Jacobite rebels had been put down by the forces of an English king. They had bled into the ground, those renegades, melted away like the Jacobite claim itself, and now Killcommadan Hill was a playground for their daughters.

The red-headed girl scrambled to the top of the hill, and tumbled again, egged on by her less courageous fellows. As she fell this time, pitching and turning, her universe contracted to a rolling drum of green earth and blue heaven. Snowy clouds flocked in the sky, sheep grazed in the fields. Sheep floated in the sky and the clouds grazed in the fields. No – the sky was the one with the sun; a golden coin, too bright to look at, a coin that left a white round ghost on the back of her eyes when she blinked.

This time, in that spinning scene, a coach and four drew across the earth-sky. Not Phoebus's carriage or anything fanciful like that, but something solid and tangible and wooden. She practically rolled into one of the great wheels. The quartet of horses whinnied and stamped, unsettled by this missile.

A fancy gentleman, plump and bewigged, leaned from the carriage. His beckoning hand wore a glove, and the snowy fingers spun a gilt coin dexterously between them. A little golden sun in a glove as white as cloud. He looked at the redhead, close to. At the top of the hill she had just been a petticoat with a hank of red hair; now he could see her properly she stole the breath. He took an inventory; a slipwillow of a girl with copper curls falling to a handspan waist, bottle-green eyes in a pearl-pale face, full rose lips and a brand-new bosom.

'Well done, Bess,' said the fancy gentleman.

The girl frowned as she scrambled to her feet. Her name was not Bess. But the protest clotted in her throat. She was spellbound by the golden coin. He seemed to have plucked the sun from the sky.

'It's yours,' said the fancy gentleman. '*If* you roll again; from the very top.' He leaned farther from the carriage window, lowering his voice, so close that she could feel the breeze of his whisper. 'And this time, show me your *tail*.'

Her frown deepened. She had come to the hill looking for a little excitement. Now this man held adventure in his hand, and his admiration warmed her like the sun. That little coin meant freedom – freedom from a mother who had beaten her every day for nine years, ever since her Da had died on this very field. That little coin meant she could go to Dublin, to live with the aunt she had heard of but never seen.

Kit turned and climbed the hill, marching higher and higher, with an almost martial step. When she reached the top, with her eye on the distant carriage, she tilted and launched herself. She could feel her skirts rising – the winds rushing between her legs and across her bare rump. The fancy gentleman would get his wish.

Down at the carriage again she righted herself. She half-expected him to drive away, but he handed down the coin to her. Now it lay in her hand, warm and heavy. It was gold, and it was stamped with the head of William III, the English king who had murdered her father.

'Well earned, Bess,' called the fancy gentleman at her retreat.

She turned back. 'Why do you name me so?'

He leaned towards her again, the curls of his wig spilling out of the carriage window. 'Bess was a red-headed queen; and when she was by, no one could see anyone but her.' He nodded to the other girls, specks and smears in the distance. 'Those others are nothing to you.'

'My name is Kit,' she said, with a conqueror's confidence. 'Kit Kavanagh.'

'That's your given name?' The man frowned, his eyebrows appearing below the piled fringe of his wig. 'But it is a gentleman's name, surely. Are you not Katherine or Kate?'

'My mother named me Christian. It was my father who called me Kit.'

He smiled. 'No love for Mama, eh?'

'I would not care if I never saw her again.'

He snorted. On another day he would have bundled her into the carriage and then, of course, the redhead would never have had to see her mother again. But he was a man who lived on his whims – it was a whim that had made him stop in the first place and a whim that made him leave again. He knocked his cane on the driver's box. 'Kit, then,' he said. 'Goodbye, Queen Kit.'

She did not stay to watch the carriage away but turned for home at once, the coin hidden in her bosom. Six months ago she had been as flat as a board and the coin would have fallen to the ground. Now her new landscape cradled it. She felt powerful as she walked; so drunk with the tumbling and the coin and the prospect of freedom that she forgot the fancy gentleman long before he forgot her.

And not once did Kit Kavanagh imagine that she would ever meet him again.

PART ONE

The Sword

Chapter 1

Dublin, Ireland, 1702

For a soldier he leads a very fine life . . .

'Arthur McBride' (trad.)

There was nothing unusual about the day that Kit Walsh lost her husband.

There were no dark portents drawn on the sky by the flight of the Dublin sparrows, nothing to be read in the leaves of the tea, nor in the eyes of the little plaster virgin behind the bar who beadily watched the sinners drink. All was as usual in Kavanagh's alehouse, also known as 'The Gravediggers' – set as it was between the teeming lively city and Glasnevin cemetery. 'Noisy neighbours one side, quiet the other,' said the locals.

Kit stood behind the bar in her Friday gown, ready to serve the regulars. Aunt Maura sat at the far end of the bar, smoking a pipe for her health – she suffered with a canker in her breast – taking the beer money in her fingerless gloves. Dermott Shortt and Martin O'Grady sat in the snug laughing the skeletons of the week away, their grave-digging spades propped outside the half-door. Old Eamon Pearce propped up the other end of the bar, telling toothless stories to anyone who'd listen, passing the time until he too would lie under the diggers' dirt. It was quiet for a Friday, and Kit took a moment to look around her. She loved Kavanagh's, she loved Aunt Maura for taking her in with the beer barrels two years ago, but most of all she loved her handsome new husband, Richard Walsh.

She watched Richard fondly, as he rolled the beer barrels into the cellar on a long tilted plank, the muscles bunching under his cambric shirt. He looked up at her, direct green eyes through a nut-brown fall of hair, and smiled. She had been so *right* to marry Richard. Kit and Aunt Maura had had their first and only quarrel when Kit had announced her intention to marry Richard Walsh, a humble potman who'd worked at Kavanagh's since he was a boy. 'I *like* the lad,' her aunt had said, 'Mary and Joseph, I almost raised him – but with your looks and Kavanagh's to go with it you could have any man in Dublin.' Maura waved away her niece's protests and the pipe smoke together. 'To be sure, he's a good man and a solid one. But . . .' Maura sucked her pipe as she sought the words. 'He'll do whatever you expect of him every day of his life. He's *safe*.'

Of all the objections Kit might have expected, she had not foreseen this. Maura, kindly sensible Maura, had seen that seed of adventure in her, had known that Kit was a girl who would always choose to roll down a hill instead of walking. Perhaps she had been a girl who would roll down a hill instead of walking, too.

A second too late, Kit returned her husband's smile; but he'd turned away and she found herself smiling fiercely at his back as he rolled the next barrel. The smile froze a little. She could see a long way ahead in that moment; her life with Richard – home-keeping Richard who had lived in the alehouse since he was a boy and would most probably die here. There would be children in between perhaps, and christenings and Communions and weddings, but one day Kit too would move from one side of the bar to the other. She would go from serving customers to counting money at the end of the bar, while her son or daughter took over. She would wear Maura's fingerless gloves, smoke Maura's pipe, and mark the days until she too 'went next door', as the regulars said, to the cemetery.

And just for a moment, she wanted something *more*. The impulse

Maura had detected in her, the impulse that had made her roll down Killcommadan Hill, had not left her. She longed, in that instant, for adventure.

As if in response, from somewhere above the bar came a sound, hardly discernible above the low chatter. She looked up at her father's sword, hanging horizontally above the ranks of bottles. Her first act as the new taverner had been to hang Sean Kavanagh's blade over the bar, and there it had stayed, silent and silver from that day to this. But now it was singing in its bracket, vibrating with a barely perceptible ringing timbre, sweet with threat. Kit put a single finger up to still it. It felt alive. As she took her finger away a tiny red line appeared across her fingerprint. Then the line beaded like a rosary and she saw that it was blood. She sucked at her finger and flipped up the wooden top of the bar. 'Mind the bar, Aunt?' she mumbled around the finger, moving to the doorway, hitching her gown and repinning the heavy copper coils of her hair as she went.

Old Eamon said, 'Expecting company, Kit?'

'Only the King of Spain's daughter, Eamon, come to ask for your hand,' replied Kit with a smile.

She went to the doorway, and looked up at the inn sign, softly swinging – in, out – familiar as breathing. 'Kavanagh's' painted on a red ground, with the family crest of one red lion and two red crescents on a white shield. And the Latin tag below which no one, even Aunt Maura, knew enough to read.

Kit looked right to Prospect Gate. The sun was setting over Glasnevin cemetery and the cross-shaped shadows lengthened. The stone angels folded their wings and looked down, the stone doves roosted on the headstones, and the dead settled in for another eternal night. All was peaceful in grey-black and green, framed under Prospect Arch. No dead walked, no earth was overturned – but the sound, that regular pulse that shook the very ground, began again from somewhere distant.

Kit looked the other way towards the city, and that's when she saw it: a great swathe of red flowed down the Dublin road, red as the blood on her finger. Hundreds of boots struck the cobbles in time, marching nearer. The rhythmic heartbeat of the drum, the martial pipe of the fife. She fled back inside, telling herself the excitement she felt was fear. 'Best roll the barrels back up,' she called to Richard. 'The regiment is coming.'

It was the most profitable night that Kit could remember. It was also the busiest, sweatiest, bawdiest and loudest. Aunt Maura could barely count the shillings as they slipped like silver fishes through her gnarled hands. Kit, running hither and yon with three tankards in each hand, smiled, nodded, avoided grabbing hands, whirled from one table to the next. She was exhausted but elated; never was there such a hostess as she. There was a kind greeting for each polite officer, a scathing put-down for every drunkard, a witty riposte for every flirtatious ensign, and a smile for the drummer boy. But she was jolted, too, by their presence. She listened to their general chatter but could not make head nor tail of it – there were words she didn't know, countries she'd never heard of, cities and campaigns that were foreign to her. Fort Maurepas, Kaiserwerth, Cadiz, Klissow. But one snippet she did understand. The king, apparently, was dead.

The king is dead . . . now that the king is dead . . . of course, that's all changed now that the king's dead. Kit was confused. The only king she'd known was William, the king who'd killed her father, the king whose head had been on the sovereign she'd been given, and he'd died in the spring, fallen from his horse. There was a queen on England's throne now, for the shillings Kit took over the bar had gradually changed from William to Anne.

'What king?' she bawled to Maura over the row. 'Who died?'

'King of the Spaniards,' her aunt shouted back. 'Never fret. He's nothing to us. But Old Eamon won't get his daughter, I'm afraid. He died with no child.' She laughed, showing her pipe-stained teeth.

Kit turned back to the throng. She was half-frightened, half-excited by these red-coated devils. For they had other words too. She had thought that two years of working in an alehouse had made her deaf to curses, but she heard oaths that she had never heard before, words that made her blush. They seemed larger than life, these soldiers – something more, something extra than other men – their colours vivid like stained glass after rain. Just for a moment she pictured Richard in a red coat, with a guilty thrill of longing. The longing turned to a sick lurch in her stomach, and suddenly they seemed too much, those militaries: their vitality, their gaudiness, their number. They were so male, so . . . alive. Had her father been this way too, among his fellows? Did they live so loudly because they knew they would die?

Overwhelmed all of a sudden, Kit escaped down the stairs to the cool cellar and laid her hot cheek on the damp cold stones of the wall. The noise receded to a muffled hubbub. She breathed in the peaty smell of stone, then a warm circle of arms closed around her. A jag of fear – had one of the devils followed her to the underworld? Hot lips pressed to her neck, nuzzling the tumbled curls at her nape.

'Can you serve *me* now?' A low-voiced growl, a fair imitation of raucous army tones.

She didn't turn, but smiled at the wall. 'What are you doing down here? Get gone, and be quick about it; my husband is above. He will fight you to the death to protect my honour.'

'What honour, you wanton woman?'

He turned her round, and pressed his hot body to hers. 'They all wanted you,' he whispered fiercely. 'How many of them touched you here?' Hands on her breasts. 'Or here?' Hands on her buttocks, the buttocks a fancy gentleman once paid to see.

She arched against him and kissed him back hard, tasting ale on his lips. Her assailant had been drinking, heavily. She made to push him away, her arms suddenly as weak as her knees.

'No, I want you *now*,' he protested, 'for I have to ride tonight.'

'Where to?' She could barely speak through the sweetness, his lips now moving lower.

He mumbled into her bosom. 'Over the hills and far away.'

'I have to go back,' she protested. 'I must serve the regiment. But,' she smiled till the dimples came, 'come to my room after closing time. Then you can have all you desire.'

'And your husband?'

'He'll never know.'

A final kiss. 'He's a damned fool to take his eyes off you for an instant.'

Then he straightened. Groaned. 'Would to God they would all go,' he said in his normal voice. 'I would close the bar right now if you'd let me.'

Kit smiled at her husband. 'Not when they are so free with their shillings. It won't be long now till closing.' She laid a hand on his hectic cheek. Richard turned his head, kissed the hand and was gone.

Without him, she was suddenly ashamed of their game. Her cheeks flamed. Little *fool* to have her head turned by a red coat, like any camp-follower. Like her mother. She did not want a soldier, didn't want to keen and cry every night wondering where her man was. She wanted Richard – safe, sweet Richard. She forced a smile and followed her husband upstairs.

Then the smile died. A snatch of song floated down the stair, wreathed her ribs and stopped her heart.

> *Oh, me and my cousin, one Arthur McBride,*
> *As we went a-walkin' down by the seaside,*
> *Mark now what followed and what did betide . . .*

She had to lean on the wall. She had to listen.

'Arthur McBride'. It was a Jacobite song, and she had heard it at her father's knee every night of his leave. She had not heard the song for eleven years, had not known that she even remembered it. But she felt her lips moving as she mouthed every word.

> 'Good morning, good morning,' the Sergeant he cried.
> 'And the same to you, gentlemen,' we did reply,
> Intending no harm but meant to pass by,
> For it bein' on Christmas mornin'
> 'But,' says he, 'My fine fellows, if you will enlist,
> Ten guineas in gold I'll stick to your fist,
> And a crown in the bargain for to kick up the dust,
> And drink the king's health in the morning.'

She was ten years old again, watching her father leaving their farm on a frosty Christmas morning, his boots making perfect footprints in the rimed grass. Her father turning once to wave, the sunrise igniting his red hair, her father smiling at her with dimples like her own. She'd followed in his footsteps, as her mother had screamed at her in French to come back, that she'd catch an ague. Unheeding, she'd fitted her little footprints into his huge ones, until he'd outpaced her, and left her behind.

Kit mounted the cellar steps and faced the crowded bar and the song. Every mouth bawled the words of the song from every direction, with drink-fuelled enthusiasm.

> For a soldier, he leads a very fine life,
> And he always is blessed with a charming young wife,
> And he pays all his debts without sorrow or strife,
> And he always lives pleasant and charmin',
> And a soldier, he always is decent and clean,

In the finest of clothing he's constantly seen.
While other poor fellows go dirty and mean,
And sup on thin gruel in the morning.

Kit's ears were ringing, and she had to lean on the bar. Just as she thought she must fall, the song ended and another began. A faster song, one she knew, but one that did not have the power to chill her blood.

She looked for Richard. Suddenly exhausted, she longed to lie down – it was gone midnight, and some of the soldiers were melting away. Richard could close up, Richard and Aunt Maura. But, just for the moment, she could not see her husband. She went on serving, by rote, and answered the soldiers' bidding with the ghost of her former smile.

Another hour passed, and the soldiers became increasingly rowdy. One of them shot at a wine barrel, making a neat hole – the wine sprang forth like blood and each redcoat held the great cask above his head in turn, gulping at the scarlet gore. Kit looked round for Richard once more – the regiment had to be curbed, before Kavanagh's lost all their stock. She crossed the red lake to Aunt Maura at the bar. 'Make sure you charge them,' she mouthed, nodding to the wrecked barrel. 'And where in the world is Richard?' Maura, pipe in mouth, shrugged.

Kit bit her lip with irritation. Richard liked a drink, and had the gift of mixing easily with their customers, but she could not believe he had gone carousing with the regiment when there was so much work to do. It was another hour before the last redcoat had finally gone; the doors were locked, the shutters were put up and Kit began to collect the tankards to wash. 'Where can Richard *be*, Aunt?' she asked. 'Drinking with the regiment some-where,' she snorted.

Aunt Maura eyed her. 'He must be drinking from his shoe, then,' she said, 'for his tankard is over there.'

Kit walked across the bar, her feet crunching on crusts and broken glass, to where Richard's tankard stood. The tankard shared its time between a hook behind the bar and her husband's right hand. She did not think she had ever seen it set down. She picked it up. It was empty. No; not empty.

She tipped the thing upside down and something fell into her hand.

Something round and heavy.

For the second time in her life Kit Kavanagh turned over a single coin in her palm, a coin which would change her life. But this time the imprimatur was a queen's head, not a king's, and the coin was silver, not gold.

The Queen's Shilling.

Suddenly she was sitting on the floor, amid the detritus, without knowing how she got there. Numbly she looked about her, and all she could think about in that moment was what a mess the regiment had left, and that now she would have to clean it up on her own. How could Richard leave her to clear up by herself? Such a mess! Crusts, buckles, scuffed playing cards, the blood-red puddle of wine, nutshells, papers, broken glass, even a horsewhip. Yes, the regiment had left a high old mess.

But it had taken her husband.

Chapter 2

As for their old rusty rapiers that hung by their sides . . .

'Arthur McBride' (trad.)

'Kit.' Her father stooped near, his red hair and hers entangled, the threads close. He put something into her hand, a heavy something, wrapped in canvas. She opened the cloth. 'A paring knife,' he said, 'so you can help your mother in the kitchen when I'm gone.' Little Kit looked at the knife unenthusiastically. The thing was small, with a wooden handle. The curved blade looked sharp enough but it was not the blade that she craved. Her father's sword, that he hung high out of reach when he was not campaigning, was the stuff of legend to her; it held, in those three feet of tempered steel, the song of all the tales he told her at night-time. Gathering her interest, her father had taken her to the meadow and taught her swordplay, month by month and year on year. He taught her with a hazel switch, and the hazel switch grew as she did, but she was never allowed to touch his sword. Then the hazel switch became a stave, so that she could know the weight of a blade, but still she never held his sword in her hand. Her mother had sneered at her, jealous of their time in the meadow, asking what use swordplay was to a maid, telling Kit she was second best to a son.

And now, now her father was called to battle, he would go and the sword would go, and she would be left with her mother and a paring knife. Vegetables and fruits would now be her adversaries. 'Learn to wield *that* knife,' spat her mother, 'and you'll actually be of use to me while Sean is gone.' She never called him 'your father' to Kit, as if she could not bear to share ownership.

It had been the day before her father had gone that he had held her white hand in his freckled brown one. 'Now be brave,' he said, 'I'm going to make you and the knife friends.' And he drew the blade across her palm; gently, but the flesh parted one iota, the breadth of a red hair. He kissed the cut. 'No need to fear it now,' he said. *For a blade that cuts you once can never hurt you again.*

Kit sat suddenly upright in her bed at Kavanagh's. Her hand throbbed from the dream-cut. Her father was gone, Richard was gone and the dark was silent.

Kit was alone, and awake, as she had been alone and awake at night for the three months since Richard had been taken.

Maura had sent a fast rider to follow the regiment to Dublin, but of Richard there was no trace. When Kit glanced across the bar expecting to see him, or across the pew in church, or across the coverlet, acres and acres of space seemed to yawn where he had been. Kit, groping through the black bereavement for some sort of sense and logic, felt that it was all, somehow, *unfair*; that she had been cheated. For he was only a man. How could a man, a man of middle height and weight, take up so much space, leave such a hole? She saw in her mind's eye the barrel of claret which had been shot by the redcoat on the night Richard was taken – the wine spilling forth, the red lake on the floor. She became obsessed with the image. The smallest breach of a castle wall could let the enemy in; a single cannon shot in the midships could sink the greatest galleon. And even a small bullet hole could empty a barrel.

Worst of all, her grief had a racking familiarity – the hole Richard left, so vast and cosmic, so small and domestic, was the same shape as the hole left by her father. Her body remembered this pain – she woke with the same sick, churning stomach, and lived her days with a constant, dull ache of unhappiness caged behind her ribs. Her mouth was dry and tasted metal, as it did when she held her hairpins in her mouth. Eating became a functional necessity, not a pleasure, for food was dust in her dry mouth. Her clothes ceased to fit. Her hair fell dark and lank. She felt herself emptying, that leeching, bleeding loss she had felt as a child. Sometimes her father's fate and Richard's became so muddled and entwined that she forgot that Richard was alive. It hardly seemed to matter; he was gone.

Aunt Maura tried to comfort her – she had sent letters to the magistrate, to the mayor, even to Kit's second cousin, Padraic Kavanagh, who had gone for a soldier. Kit would hear word soon. Richard would get leave eventually and return from wherever he was with a healthy commission. But Kit could not be comforted. She wandered around the gravestones of Glasnevin, reading the names on the headstones. The words *beloved husband* etched themselves into her mind as firmly as into the stone. She would stand for long moments, glassy eyed, before the tombs where husband and wife were buried together, envying them their eternal, night-black embrace under the earth. She would calculate how long they had been married, those brides of bone; then count the days she had been married to Richard. Then she counted the days he had been gone; marking them neatly with a stub of pencil on a piece of paper, as a prisoner might mark the walls that held him. Dreading, living through, then passing day thirty; the day which marked a dreadful milestone. Day thirty, the day when he'd been gone as long as they'd been wed. She kept the dreadful little tally of pencil marks folded in her bodice, where her sadness lived.

Day thirty-one without Richard. Day thirty-two without Richard. She had to remind herself constantly that he wasn't, as far as she knew, dead. Now he was gone she was sure that Richard was all she had wanted, that moment of doubt forgotten. Now she was left with the old folks and the regulars she realised how much she loved him and missed him. She would replay their first kiss, their first coupling, their every minute interaction. Even the time when he'd smiled at her, that last day, and she'd been too slow to smile back until he'd turned away. And this brought it home to her. The guilt. For of course, it was her fault Richard had been taken. That one, idle moment at the bar, when she had wished for more and missed his smile. That instant when she'd imagined Richard in a red coat, when she'd acted that sick little scene with him in the cellar, had she cursed him then and doomed him to the pressing? If she'd taken Richard upstairs to bed after they'd kissed in the beer cellar, if they'd left Aunt Maura to close up, he would not have been pressed. But the lure of those silvery shillings, those tinkling tempting coins, had been too much. And one, just *one* of those shillings they'd so greedily craved, had been his undoing.

Sometimes she was angry with Richard himself – could he not escape? But she knew too well from her father's tales that to escape from the army was to be flogged to within an inch of your life, or shot for a deserter. But surely he could *write*? Maura had refused to have a dolt in her house, so had taught the young Richard his letters as she'd taught Kit – so Kit interrogated the poor post rider each day of that first month, before he'd even dismounted his lathered, dancing horse, for letters from her husband – but every time the answer was the same: no word. The mayor could not aid them, nor the magistrate, and the missive to Padraic Kavanagh simply came back marked 'Gone Away'.

Gone Away. Like Richard. Of course, it occurred to her that she could go after him. That she could plant her footsteps in his, just as she'd once planted her childish footsteps in her father's in that frostbitten field. Her father was dead but Richard was alive; some-where and *alive*. And she was no longer a child, to wait by her hearth for a soldier to come home. But she could not leave Maura – Aunt Maura who had given her a home, a profession, a husband.

Kit realised now how little she knew of her aunt. Oh, she had heard snippets of tales from the bottle washers; Maura Kavanagh had killed a feral dog in the alleyway with a single blow of a blackthorn shillelagh. She had brained an ancient suitor with a bottle. She had chased a debt collector from Kavanagh's door, shouting after him like a fishwife that she owed 'no such sum'. 'No such sum! No such sum!' chanted the pot washers, full of admiration and fear. Kit did not know whether the stories were true, or when in a long life they had happened. Maura was free with other people's stories but she kept the silvery onion skins of her own histories tucked inside her, one within the other, secret and safe. And she would certainly never share the severity of her condition with Kit. 'We're all dying,' was all she would say. Kit was Maura's heir and queen of Kavanagh's and must rule it even if she ruled alone, like Queen Bess. Lonely, powerful Queen Bess.

Now Kit listened carefully to travellers' tales of the army. There was trouble between Spain and France – she remembered it had been the Spanish king who had died – but such distant conflicts could have nothing to do with Richard. When she closed her eyes she saw him bleeding, dying, on some battlefield, mouthing her name. But in her brief dreams he was always on Aughrim field, bleeding into the grass which once had swallowed her father's blood. And that is why she no longer slept, in the bed which had been hers at fifteen, and theirs at twenty, and now hers again. Hers alone.

She must have cried out in her dream, for the chamber door opened and someone was in the room. A bulky black shadow on the wall, a bite out of the candlelight. Kit could not see; the tears had sprung to her eyes.

A weight on the bed, on the cambric coverlet. Kit blinked and the tears fell on the weave. Aunt Maura placed her hand on the coverlet, twig-thin bones wrapped in papery skin and tethered with blue veins. Kit covered the hand with hers, and found a smile from somewhere. 'Are you come to tell me a story?'

When she'd just moved to Kavanagh's Maura had told her stories at night; no book in hand, timeless stories that lived in her memory. Kit had been too old for stories, but she'd had no one to tell her one since Da had gone, and had found comfort in the ritual, as did her childless aunt. The candling shadows had been peopled with wicked stepmothers, benign faeries and obliging giants. In that deep darkness that lived in the corners of rooms and the nooks of beams, Kit found capital letters that looked like animals, animals that looked like capital letters, boars, elves, imps, sacred hinds, many-headed serpents and nameless creatures that dwelt under bridges. And queens, of course, there was always a long-haired queen. These queens would employ their useful hair for multiple purposes. They would use it to tether a dragon, climb down it like rope, or cast it on a sea loch to net wish-giving fishes.

'Yes,' said Aunt Maura. 'I'm here to tell you a tale.' She smoothed back Kit's hair with those frail hands.

'Is it about a queen?' asked Kit, playing the game. If she had been too old for stories when she'd come to Kavanagh's, she was certainly too old for them now.

'Just an ordinary girl,' said Aunt Maura. 'No: not ordinary. She is an extraordinary girl, who doesn't know it yet.' She sighed and settled, wincing and moving her bony elbow away from the tender breast. 'This girl married her man. They were as *happy* as a queen and a king. But the man was taken for the army. And the girl started to die.' Kit stilled, her breathing suddenly shallow. 'Her aunt saw it,' the peat-soft voice went on, 'because her aunt knew how dying felt.' Kit clasped the old hand, but the bones pulled away and scrabbled in a nightgown pocket. 'One night, the girl got up from her bed, because she wasn't sleeping much anyway. She cut her hair and put on her husband's clothes. Then she went to Dublin harbour to find the sign of the Golden Last, there to enquire after an ensign by the name of Herbert Laurence.' A scrap of paper, with a direction upon it, was pushed into her palm. The bony fingers were now under her chin, and she met Aunt Maura's currant eyes in the candlelight. 'I was wrong about Richard. He did something I didn't expect. But Mary and Joseph, Kit, you don't have to wait to be rescued. Go and rescue *him*.'

It could have been one night later, or many nights, when Kit stood before the oval of her looking glass. With a paring knife she hacked off her waist-length hair just below the chin. Kit felt a shiver of misgiving. How would she net a talking fish now, or tether a dragon? How would she escape from her tower? 'I will walk out of the door,' she told her reflection, 'the same way I came in.'

She tiptoed down the stairs into the bar, and looked to her father's sword, where it hung above the tankards. She took the sword by the blade, in both hands, and yanked it roughly from its bracket above the bar. She did not fear for her flesh, for she remembered the night Richard had gone, when the blade had sung to her of the regiment's approach, and had laid a hairline cut across her palm. *A blade that cuts you once can never harm you again.*

In the morning, when she rose to lay the fires, Aunt Maura found the red hair on Kit's hearth, stirring in the door's draught. She wanted to laugh, to applaud; and to cry. She took up the locks and tucked them in her bodice, next to the wretched breast. Hair shirts were no longer the fashion, but this would do well enough.

Chapter 3

My fine fellows if you will enlist,
It's ten guineas in gold I will slip in your fist . . .

'Arthur McBride' (trad.)

Day forty without Richard had not yet dawned, and Kit had not walked a hundred steps down the Finglas road before she saw a cooper's cart heading into Dublin, and flagged it down before she changed her mind. 'Are you going near the harbour, sir?' called Kit.

'Directly there. Jump up.'

The cooper, who already had another passenger seated between his barrels on the back, offered a hand up for her to sit beside him on the driver's box. He gave Kit a wink and his horse a slap on the rump with the reins, and the cart set off with a jolt that nearly threw Kit back on to the cobbles.

The cooper did not seem inclined to talk, for which Kit was grateful, for there seemed to be some kind of obstruction sitting like a stone in her chest. She listened to the clatter of hooves on cobbles, and looked at the country about her and the city ahead. The sun peeped over the Wicklow mountains, buttering the downs and gilding the roofs and spires of Dublin. Beyond the city she could see the golden spinnakers of the tall ships in the harbour. The stone in her chest rose to her throat.

The countryside receded and the cart turned into Cabra road, and the city proper, down to the Liffey and down the Quay past the wharfs and the Customs House. The passenger among the barrels began to whistle an air, the city bustled about them, and Kit began to feel more cheerful. Perhaps she would find Richard at once, and be back at Kavanagh's for sundown. Then she felt a pressure on her knee, and her heart plummeted.

She looked down at the cooper's vast hand, with hairy knuckles and square nails, where it rested on her knee. She looked at the cooper but he kept his eyes steadfastly ahead, fixed upon the road. Carefully, determined not to give offence, she lifted the hand off her leg, heart thudding. Now and again she'd had to deal with wandering hands in the pub, but in the safety of company she would deal with such importunities with sharp words or even a blow. More persistent suitors could be left to Maura's tongue or Richard's fists. Here on this cart she was defenceless; but she was less concerned for her honour than for her disguise. Her disguise, the costume she'd been so proud of before the looking glass in her chamber, had lasted all of five minutes. The cooper had seen at once that she was a female. She had failed in her masquerade and she had failed Aunt Maura, who, she was sure, had suggested this disguise expressly so that she could avoid these kinds of attentions.

What had she got wrong? She was fairly tall for a girl, had been exactly the same height as Richard in fact. (It had been something she'd liked, that when they faced each other they stood eye to eye and lip to lip.) Her hair now curled just below her chin, with a heavy fringe across her forehead to mask her long lashes. She'd worn a deliberately baggy shirt, bloused about the chest to disguise her curves, and a jerkin with leather facings to further flatten her down. Breeches, boots and her father's sword completed the illusion. She'd even rubbed some cinders from the fireplace on her chin, to imitate the ashy morning shadow on Richard's cheeks before he shaved. And yet the cooper's hand came back, like a bothersome fly, and settled even higher on her leg. The square fingers began to burrow into her soft inner thigh, creeping ever upwards to her groin, so now she slapped it smartly. 'Leave me be!' she spat, but the cooper laughed and the hand went higher still.

She was actually on the point of drawing her sword, when the other passenger leaned over from behind and pulled sharply on the reins.

'What the devil . . .?' exclaimed the cooper.

The horse clattered to a stop, hooves sparking on the cobbles of the wharf.

'That's far enough,' said the passenger; and Kit was never sure, afterwards, whether he was speaking of the cart or the hand. The passenger jumped down, grabbed his pack and handed her out of the cart.

She stood meekly beside him, hanging her head. She'd not even reached her destination and she'd already had to be rescued, like any silly damsel. 'I meant the lad no harm,' wheedled the cooper. 'We'll call it a penny each, since the journey was short.'

'You'll not get a penny from me, nor him,' declared the passenger shortly. 'Get on your way, you coney-catcher.'

The burly packman stood his ground, fists on hips; and, given no choice unless he wanted to descend and physically extort the money, the cooper slapped his horse once more and clattered off, cursing.

Kit breathed out for the first time, it seemed, since the hand had settled on her leg. 'Thank you, sir,' she said, sure the passenger was going to ask what a maid like her was doing on the road at dawn; or worse, elicit his own particular payment for rescuing her. But he did neither.

'The harbour's down that way,' he said gruffly. 'Get yourself into decent company, and soon,' he went on, more kindly. 'You're a pretty lad, and there's many more of his type round the harbour, I'll be bound.'

Kit turned and walked in the direction he had indicated,

trying to make sense of what had happened. The cooper had *not* known she was female, and neither had the kindly passenger. So why had the cooper placed his hand on her leg, *as if she were a maid*? What had he been seeking with that burrowing hand? What had he been hoping for, that a *boy* could give him? And what, by all the saints, was a coney-catcher?

Shaking her head to slough off the nasty little episode, she forced herself to focus on the matter at hand. She took Aunt Maura's direction from her pocket and read it over. *The sign of the Golden Last. Ensign Herbert Laurence.*

Kit wandered the wharf, peering into every higgledy warehouse and down every slipway. At length she came to a fine inn, with 'The Golden Last' lettered in gold over the door. A dragoon stood easy at the door, chewing noiselessly. 'Your pardon, sir.' Kit made her voice as gruff as she could. 'Is Mr Herbert Laurence within?'

The dragoon spat a gob of tobacco at her feet. 'He is,' he said in a strong Cork accent. 'He's beating up for recruits, so take my advice and make your mark at once.' He leaned close, and she remembered the cooper. 'For a soldier, he leads a very fine life.' Kit recognised the phrase at once – a line from her father's marching song, 'Arthur McBride'. She felt a chill as the dragoon laughed too loudly. She could see his tobacco-stained teeth, and she took a pace backwards, gulped a deep breath as if about to swim, and entered the house.

Kit found herself in a long oak-panelled assembly room with a pair of doors at one end. She joined the long queue and stood, rehearsing what she would say. The men ahead of her, an assorted bunch of farmers and sailors and foreigners, went in the double doors, and then came out again almost at once. Before long it was her turn – she heard a muffled 'Come!' from beyond the doors and entered the inner sanctum.

There sat a sandy-haired officer writing in a fat ledger, with a sergeant at his elbow.

'Are you Mr Herbert Laurence?'

Sandy-hair nodded without looking up. 'Name?' he enquired brusquely.

'Kit . . .' Kit cursed herself – she'd been practising 'Christian' all the way down the queue. 'That is, Christian.'

'Christian what?' He had a clipped English accent and a harassed manner.

'Walsh, sir.'

'Chris-tian Walsh,' he repeated, stretching the name out as he wrote it down. Kit thought: my third name in three years – Kit Kavanagh, Kit Walsh, Christian Walsh.

'Well, Mr Walsh. Welcome to the English Army.' There was a long silence as he scribbled further. She shifted from one leg to the other, not sure what to do.

'Is that it?' Her exclamation slipped out before she could prevent it. Surely enlisting could not be that easy. 'That is . . . Will I not need some training?'

Ensign Herbert Laurence was clearly not accustomed to questions. He looked up for the first time, and laughed, not pleasantly. 'They will keep sending these fucking bogtrotters, Mr Coley,' he remarked to his deputy. Then, to Kit: 'How many legs have you?'

Kit was bemused. 'Two.'

'Arms?'

'The same.'

'And eyes in your head?'

'Two, sir.'

'The full complement of fingers and toes?'

'Ten of each.'

'Got your own sword?'

'Yes.'

'Then I commend you,' said Sandy-hair. 'You've just passed

← 27 →

your basic training.' The ensign nodded to his deputy, who sprang forward with a little leather bag.

'Here's your guinea pay, and a shilling from the queen.' A coin was pressed into her palm, the twin of the one she'd found in Richard's tankard a month ago. 'Mr Coley, a drink for our new recruit. I give you Queen Anne.'

Kit was handed a jorum of rum, which she could see, with her practised eye, was half-measures. No one else had a drink – seemingly she was to toast alone. 'Queen Anne,' she repeated, and downed the tot in one. A line of fire ran down from her throat to pool and burn in her belly. She felt a little better.

'You now have the honour to be enrolled in the regiment commanded by the Marquis de Pisare. The lieutenant of your company is Mr Gardiner, your ensign Mr Walsh.'

'Mr *Walsh*?'

'Yes, boy. Walsh. I should've asked you how many ears you had. Report to Mr Walsh on the dock. He'll give you your orders.'

Herbert Laurence had clearly had so many men under his pen that day that it didn't occur to him that Ensign Walsh was her namesake. But Kit didn't care. The name was the sweetest music to her ears. Mr Walsh! Richard was *here*, he had *not* been shipped to the ends of the earth; someone had recognised his talents, and he had been made a recruiting officer right here in Dublin! She could have kissed Herbert Laurence, and when he indicated the door with his quill, she fled gratefully. By the time the next recruit entered, the ensign's eyes were again on his pages, and it occurred to Kit that Laurence must have recruited dozens of men to the queen's service that day without once seeing their faces.

'Arthur McBride' would not leave Kit's head, but now she was so near the end of her quest she sang the air quite cheerfully under her breath. She boldly asked everyone she saw for Mr Walsh, and followed pointing hands to the waterfront. Now that her reunion with Richard was at hand, her colour mounted and her palms began to sweat. Could she embrace him at once, if he was so busily employed? What would he think of her hair? Why hadn't he written if he was but an hour from Kavanagh's door? Tugging nervously at her blunt locks she spied a red coat and a tumble of brown hair below a tricorn. She knew just how she would greet him.

'Mr Walsh?' said she, lowering her voice, trying to keep the joyous laughter out of it.

He turned.

It wasn't he, but a man much older. He shared Richard's height and colouring but that was all. Winds and weather had chased the youth from him; wrinkles were etched on his face like scrimshaw, and his teeth were broken and discoloured. Her disappointment was so keen that she could not, for a moment, speak.

'Well, boy?'

'If it please you, sir,' she whispered, 'I am newly recruited.'

'Christ, they just keep getting younger.' An Irish accent this time; harassed, but friendly.

'What's your name?' He riffled through a sheaf of papers, licked his pencil.

'Walsh.'

He looked at her keenly. 'Of the Kerry Walshes?'

She had the spark of an idea. 'The very same, sir,' she lied. 'In fact, I am seeking a kinsman of ours: Richard Walsh. He came through here about a month ago.'

'Walsh.' The ensign tapped his teeth with his pencil. 'Yes – I remember him. Pressed, wasn't he?'

'Yes!' She nodded keenly, her heart thudding.

'Wait a moment.' He looked through his sheaf of papers, turning back and back through reams of names. Stopped. 'Yes,' he said, 'he joined Captain Tichborne's regiment of foot, and sailed a month past. Why?'

Sailed a month ago. 'I need to contact him. A . . . about a bequest. His Uncle . . . Padraic died and left him some money.'

The ensign snorted. 'Lucky fellow. Nothing for me, I suppose?'

In time, she recognised a jest. 'Could I get a message to him?'

'Whatever it is, you can tell him yourself; for we're sailing to join Tichborne's regiment tomorrow.' He produced another paper, businesslike once more. 'Use the day to get yourself the things on this list. There will be time enough – you seem a clever brisk young fellow. Collect your uniform from the tent yonder. Find yourself lodgings for the night. Report here at dawn. We sail with the tide.'

It was all said and done with such dispatch that Kit's head began to spin. She latched on to the most pertinent problem to steady herself. 'Please, sir, where might I find a room?'

'Good God, I don't know, boy. I'm not your mother.' She looked so crestfallen that he relented. 'Try the Red Lion in the Liberties.'

Kit turned back towards town, and it didn't occur to her till much later that she hadn't even asked where they were sailing to. It did not matter; Richard was there; so she would go there too.

She collected her uniform in the flimsy canvas tent, flapping and ragging in the keen wind from the Liffey. The army tailor took one practised look at her and handed her a bale of heavy red clothes and a pair of boots which looked distinctly second-hand. She had no great hopes of them fitting well, for she was dismissed almost before she could take hold of her garments.

Her spirits were much depressed by her encounter with the wrong Mr Walsh, and she could only hope that after tomorrow's voyage she would soon be in the arms of the right one. As she headed to the Liberties her natural optimism began to surface.

She had been to the Liberties before – a lively ward of Dublin which was exempt from the city's laws. She had come to buy hops with Maura, but always in the company of Richard or one of the potmen, employed to keep the ladies safe, with a stout shillelagh on the floor of the cart just in case. Now alone, she felt vulnerable and intrigued in equal measure. Hawkers sold everything from pies to parakeets, and painted polls lolled from the doorways, greeting her with warm smiles and cold eyes. In the market she bought three Holland shirts, a silver dagger and some stout underwear. She ate a pasty and wolfed it down where she stood, for she had not eaten all day, and besides she could carry no more with her, except one more tiny item – she bought needle and thread from the haberdasher's, smiling secretly at the look of surprise on the stallholder's face that a brisk young fellow such as she should have need of such womanish things. Laden with purchases and the heavy uniform, she found the Red Lion in a crowded mews just as the sun was dipping down. The lion on the sign looked just like the one on Kavanagh's and Kit chose to see this as a good omen. She shoved her way through a crowd of drinkers to the bar and called to the barkeep. She could barely make herself heard above the hubbub but he had the measure of her at once. 'A bed for tonight? Sailing tomorrow?'

She nodded.

'Cheapest to sleep in with the other lads, six to a chamber. Halfpence for a hammock, penny for a mattress.'

This would not do – she needed privacy. 'I'll have a room to myself,' she shouted. 'If there is one.'

He shrugged. 'That'll be a shilling.'

She paid over the Queen Anne coin.

'Want to be knocked up at dawn? For the ship?'

She had not thought of this – of course she would need to be woken, she couldn't miss the tide and the chance to see Richard. Agreeing readily, she eyed the barkeep. 'I forgot,' she laughed, 'where are we bound?'

He smiled. 'Get over,' he said, and turned to serve another customer.

He'd thought she was joking, rightly assuming that only an idiot would join a ship without knowing its destination. She pushed her way through the noise. The drinkers were all new recruits, but she dare not talk to another soul until she'd made her preparations. The green young soldiers were busy drinking their brand-new guineas away, forging friendships and finding, in good company, some courage for the voyage ahead. There was no such comfort for Kit. Alone, she mounted the stairs. There was much to do.

Her room had a truckle bed, a jug and basin and a small looking glass. Kit lost no time in shedding Richard's clothes and trying on her uniform. The material was heavy and felted, here and there showing the moth's tooth. The bright red coat was missing two of the gaudy gold buttons and the once white facings were dirtied with a russet brown stain. *Blood*, she thought, with sudden misgiving. The shirt was threadbare and grubby about the collar. One of the scuffed brown boots was parting company with its sole, and the black tricorn was trimmed with faded lace. Kit wasted no time but got to work. She wiped the facings with a shred of damp cloth, brushed the hat, sewed the sole of the boot with stout thread, and moved two less visible buttons from below the collar to the stomacher of the coat. When she had done all she could she put everything on and examined her soldier-self in the glass.

She had had no great confidence in the uniform fitting well, but in this she did a disservice to the tailor, whose experienced eye had guessed her dimensions fairly accurately. One thing he had not guessed, though, was the form of her body beneath Richard's clothes. She could barely see the swell of her breasts under the brave buttons, nor the curve of her hips below the fall of the skirted coat, but she was not taking any further chances. She had fooled the cooper and the ensigns, but she could not risk discovery.

She took everything off again bar the shirt and settled down on the bed with her needle and thread. She made a long bandeau to tie tightly around her breasts like a bandage. She then quilted her waistcoat about the waist to thicken it slightly and further de-emphasise her bosom. Then there was the problem of her money. Besides the guinea from the army she had a full purse of silver from Kavanagh's. But as it was forbidden by the customs men to take more than five shillings from the country she had to think of a way to conceal the money – she had no notion of how much it might cost in drinks and bribes to find Richard and she was not going to risk penury. She hit upon the idea that she could solve two problems in one; she made a purse stitched on to a long broad hammock of fabric that she could hang between her legs. It was lamplight before she'd finished, and by the light of one poor candle she tried the entire uniform on again. She took the looking glass from the wall and perused her reflection from all angles, much satisfied with her new masculine outline. Her purse made a subtle swelling at her groin which, she hoped, would convince others that she had what she lacked. She walked to the window and looked out at the ships, a silver fleet in the dark blue night, a new moon making a shimmering path between herself and Kit, leading to the horizon. And beyond that? Where was she bound?

Suddenly afraid, Kit shed her new skin, and stood naked in the patch of moonlight, peeled and white and original. She ran her hands over her body, her woman's body, shivering slightly as she grazed her bone-white breasts and buttocks, caressing the curves that were henceforth to be covered. This is what she was beneath the ugly bulky clothes, the clothes that flattened her here and fattened her there. This is what she would always be. She would always be Kit underneath. Something crumpled below her foot like a leaf – it was her tally of the days without Richard. It stood at forty, forty days and forty nights. She crumpled the paper and set it on the nightstand. Enough of the wilderness. That Kit was gone – leave her there wandering among the thorns.

She washed from head to foot with the water from the basin – for who knew when she would wash again? She pulled on one of the new Holland shirts over her damp red hair, settled into bed and huffed the candle out. But before she settled herself she took her new dagger, silver in the moonlight, and, keeping her left hand clear of the coverlet, made a small cut across the back of her hand. For a blade that cuts you once can never harm you again.

As she lay down to sleep the words of 'Arthur McBride' came once again, unwanted and unbidden, to her mind. The sounds and bustle of the dock rumbled outside in counterpoint to the sharp sweet cries of the seagulls.

The rowdy recruits seemed in no hurry to be abed; she could hear singing from downstairs and shouts from the wharfside, and their carousing and the scampering words of the song kept her awake for the greater part of the night. Dead eyed and heavy limbed, she rose just before dawn to don her new persona, and before the landlord's knock Private Christian Walsh was ready to sail.

Chapter 4

Into the tide to rock and to roll . . .

'Arthur McBride' (trad.)

On a bitter and rain-lashed morning, Kit boarded the caravel that waited in Dublin harbour to take the new recruits to God-knew-where.

She had no knowledge whatever of vessels of the sea but could see that the ship was a good size and seemed sturdy. The ship's figurehead was a white-robed lady with golden hair rendered as if it were streaming back against the prow, holding aloft a burning torch in her white hand. The torch and the hair were painted in gilt, and the enamelling on her face had cracked from the elements so that her face looked older than the rest of her, like the wrong Mr Walsh. The same gold of torch and hair picked out the ship's name along the bulwark. Kit spelled out the words as she climbed the gangplank, her pack heavy on her back. *The Truth and Daylight*. It seemed an inauspicious name, when she remembered just how much she had to conceal.

Kit did not have the leisure to learn whether she was a good sailor or not, because the moment they were clear of the deeps of Dublin harbour and out in the open sea, they were caught in the eye of a storm. The storm offered a doleful choice between the soldiers' quarters, where the hammocks swung crazily and the floors were awash with piss and vomit, or the deck, where she was knocked from her feet by the stinging wash of seawater. She'd thought the deck preferable, but the wind rushed past her face so furiously that she could barely catch breath. She dodged the busy sailors, anxious not to get in their way, as they scuttled about, clinging to ropes and forecastle, performing their needful, incomprehensible tasks. Sails collapsed to the deck, the ship's wheel spun, and the crew shouted to each other in their secret language. Kit clung to the balustrade and gazed with horror at the looming dark and mountainous seas. These were dragon waters. No ship, however doughty, could survive such a swell. Kit felt a firm grip on her upper arm, and turned in time to see the wind snatch the tricorn of the wrong Mr Walsh. 'For God's sake, boy,' he bellowed, 'lash yourself to something or the sea will take you.' Dragging her to the bulwark, he tied her wrists firmly between two lines as if she were a loose cannon, putting his boot against the forecastle as he hitched the knots tight. 'Take heart,' he cried. 'Hold tight and we'll soon be through the worst. It's the channel winds. They blow straight from the devil's arsehole.'

Kit did not know how long she was lashed there, gazing at the heaving waves. It seemed that the ship was going down such a steep incline that she stared directly into the deeps. As the ship hit the deepest valley of the pewter ravine, the bows kicked up an almighty splash which almost drowned her, and as she coughed lungfuls of seawater back into the brine, she felt a great bubble of laughter rising up with the vomit. She laughed harder and harder as the ship lurched, poised on the crest of the wave and then tipping once again into its sickening drop. She was laughing at that one moment, more than a month ago – *Forty-three days without Richard* – when she'd stood in Kavanagh's bar on a quiet Friday and longed for adventure. 'Well, here it is!' she yelled at herself, at the elements. They were the first words that she'd spoken on the ship, and they were snatched and silenced by the screaming winds. 'Here's your adventure!' She knew she was being punished for that idle thought all those weeks ago, but surely God would not take down a whole ship to punish her for a momentary desire in an idle moment? She was a fool, for Richard was safe in some harbour, and she, by following him, had placed herself in more danger than he. For hours she was battered by the elements, watching the towering seas through streaming eyes. She knew she had been forgotten – of no more consequence than the single loose cannonball she watched rolling uselessly about the deck. She wished she were Finn McCool, the giant hero of one of Maura's tales, who could cross the Irish Sea in just a few leviathan strides, with little ships riding in his hair like thorny crowns.

But at nightfall she saw the wrong Mr Walsh again. 'It's worse,' he said. 'Get below, or you'll drown. Two seas meet here, and they're both angry.' He untied her raw wrists, grabbed the back of her soaking coat and all but threw her into the men's quarters. Standing braced in the door frame, lashed by rain, he shouted to all the green, gathered men. 'Make your vows and your prayers,' he bawled above the maelstrom. 'Confess your sins, make all right with your God, call upon your personal saints, for we may not see morning. Lamps out, for we don't need a fire as well.'

Kit curled in a corner, in the dark, crowded but alone, making herself as small as possible. Some of the men were praying aloud, barely to be heard above the screaming timbers, some hardy souls even tried to sing hymns, but most were mouthing silently into their clasped fists. Kit shut her eyes as the sea shunted her painfully between two timbers, bruising her shoulders even through the heavy felt of her coat. She tried to think of an appropriate saint who would get her through this storm. Her frightened brain scuttled through the candlelit side-chapels of her childhood and recalled those burly bearded men in golden halos and wind-whipped robes who held back mosaicked waves with one lift of a saintly hand. But would St Brendan the navigator or St Finian who'd sailed to England know what to do in these foreign waters? 'The Madonna della Fortuna,' shouted a Genovese sailor, as if in answer to her unasked question. 'She is the only lady with the power to help us. We must all pray to the Madonna – her shrine is at Genova where we're bound, and she'll bring us safe home.'

Slowly, stupidly, she realised what the landlord back in the Liberties had told her in that raucous bar. Not 'Get over'. *Genova.* They were sailing to Genova, wherever that was; and she'd found out where they were bound just as it seemed sure they would never reach it.

It seemed fitting, though, at her last hour, to pray to a woman; to Mary mother of all, to feel that sisterhood at her last. Genova's Madonna would do as well as any other incarnation at this pass. Kit closed her eyes tightly; she knew what she had to promise. 'Madonna della Fortuna,' she prayed, 'please let me live and find Richard, and I will never ask for adventure again. I will be a good wife and be happy, and contented, and make a home with him, and children, and I will never leave Kavanagh's again.' It was not likely that she would be overheard, but she was past caring – she just wanted to save her skin, whether it be male or female. Kit prayed for the rest of the night, making the same promise over and over again. The Madonna della Fortuna did not answer at once; perhaps she too could not hear her above the howling winds and screaming timbers. But slowly, slowly, over the next dark hours, the roll of the ship lessened; Kit's poor shoulders were buffeted less, and by the time the grey dawn seeped into the hold, the ship seemed to be holding level. Slowly, slowly, the grey-faced soldiers emerged into a grey world; the sea was a dun silver looking glass, the sky sullen and flat, but the storm had passed.

Kit found the boredom of a sea voyage almost as trying as the excitements of the storm. She had expected vaguely, from stories she'd heard of seagoing in Kavanagh's bar, to be swabbing decks and hoisting sails. But of course, the ship had a regular crew and the soldiers were merely cargo, three score and ten of them crammed into the keels like so many cattle. Now the wind had dropped there was nothing for them to do except collect their meals of salt pork, sour cabbage, ship's biscuits and beer from the quartermaster three times each day – the same victuals for each meal. When their first rations were handed out after three days of storm with no food or water, Kit was ravenous, and wondered why the other men were tapping their biscuits on the deck before tucking in. When she did likewise, her stomach growling, she saw a pair of weevils fall out upon the planks and calmly walk away. That first day she could have eaten them too.

Once she was sated, she waited eagerly for instructions, but they were given neither orders nor information. She saw the wrong Mr Walsh again, but he seemed too busy with the officers to pass the time of day with his counterfeit kin. When land was called nameless coastlines sailed past – she had a vague notion that they were rounding Spain, but there was nothing to divert the eye in the miles of arid beaches beyond the odd windmill.

And the calm brought the further problem of discovery. In the storm there was no risk of detection – the men were too concerned for their skins to notice her. But as soon as the storm had passed and Kit started to eat and drink again, a significant problem presented itself – one which she had never even considered when she'd blithely donned Richard's clothes and gone to enlist.

During the maelstrom sailors and soldiers had urinated where they stood, lashed to mast and bulwark; but now that normal sailing had resumed Kit wondered how she would be able to relieve herself in private. She was not in suspense for long, for their lieutenant, a cold fish by the name of Mr Gardiner, came down to quarters to enlighten them. 'Sanitation,' he declared, 'is very important to the English Army. We are not savages. We had a bad start, but now that the waters are calm, there will be no more easing yourselves in the quarters or the hold. Typhoid and fever carry off as many men at sea as storms do, so you will clean these berths thoroughly, and henceforth use only the "heads", which are the water closets at the beakhead of the ship. Anyone found guilty of unclean behaviour may expect a flogging. If any man is sick or has broken bones, he may request a covered bucket from the carpenter for his necessary occasions.' He left as if there was a bad smell under his nose, which, of course, there was.

Kit investigated the heads right away. She saw two round holes, surrounded by simple wooden seats on either side of the bowsprit right at the head of the ship. Peering though one of the holes, she looked down a vertiginous drop right into the pewter sea. Waste would land directly on the lion's head, a carved wooden visage of a lion, but the creature was cleaned at every moment as the waves, rising to the bowsprit as the vessel cut a course, naturally carried away the mess and waste. As she peered down, a biting wind and a shock of salty water dashed through the hold with each break of a wave. This necessary house would not be comfortable, but at least it would be private; only one seaman could use each room at once, for the timbers narrowed to a pair of tiny triangular chambers. She sat down, alone, with considerable relief.

Still, Kit did not feel entirely safe. Now that the seas were calm and there was nothing to occupy the men, her brothers in arms had the leisure to comment that she was young for a soldier as her cheek had not seen a razor, that she was skinny, that she was quiet – was she a Hottentot, could she not talk the Queen's English? Kit was, by nature, a sociable animal, and had taken to alehouse life readily after her years with a sullen mother who only spoke to her to bark peremptory orders in French. She was a chatterer, and according to Aunt Maura the gravedigger's donkey only had three legs because Kit had talked one of them off. She loved to talk and to laugh, but on shipboard she was afraid to do either, lest she give herself away. Instead she became a listener. She used the time to educate herself – not in shipcraft or even soldiery, but in the art of being a man.

She could not be discovered before she was reunited with Richard. So she watched and she listened, and she learned. She learned to plant her feet as if pounding the ground. She learned to shove her thumbs into her pockets or belt to prevent her from holding them delicately before her, as she used to. She abandoned kerchiefs and blew her nose on her sleeve as the others did till her red and gold cuffs were covered in snails' trails. She noted how men spoke loudly, even when – especially when – they did not have overmuch knowledge of what they said. They talked with their chins thrust forth, their feet apart, their shoulders square. They would punctuate their speech with a jabbing finger to make their point. In her only private moments, while relieving herself at the heads, she would talk to herself in a low gruff voice, trying to perfect her new male tones. But men, she noted, were not always brash. She noted, too, their gentler moments. They would pass the days playing dice or cards, and beneath the bluster and banter she would see little kindnesses – a man pulled his mate's rotten tooth and gave up his day's grog to dull the pain. A mountain called O'Connell, who did not look as if he had a note of music in him, had brought a fiddle in his kit and played sweet airs by the mainmast in the starlight. Kit crept among the crowd about him and sat, her knees humped under her chin, as he played those achingly familiar tunes – 'The Humours of Castlefin', 'John Dwyer's Jig', 'The Maids of Mitchelstown'; all the old favourites that the regulars played at Kavanagh's on their fiddles and squeeze-boxes. Songs that were as merry as Yuletide, but had the power to wring tears from Kit, tears she didn't dare let fall. She steeled herself to hear the inevitable 'Arthur McBride', but her father's ghost let her be for now.

At night, she rolled herself close into her hammock, and the canvas met over her nose. She would screw her eyes tight and try to stop her ears against the snores and sighs and the other noises too, noises both alien and familiar. Shufflings, and rhythmic rubbings and groans just like the groans that Richard sometimes let go when he and Kit were together. But these men were alone – they had no one to lie with. Kit could only imagine that they relived in their dreams the memories of their wives or sweethearts, and tried to curl the biscuit-flat bolster about her head to muffle the sounds.

During the long days on deck some of the fellows, seasoned soldiers on their second or third commission, spent their days honing their swordplay. She watched them at their fencing matches, noting the new styles of thrust and parry, and saw how they challenged themselves to find their balance as the ship lurched and rolled. She did not have the courage to join in, but watched on, and the next day she instituted a regime of her own. She ran back and forth on the foredeck throwing her sword from hand to hand, twirling around the foremast and turning and feinting and parrying with an invisible opponent. She would hang from the ropes and swing, supporting her whole weight, and balance on the stairs of the forecastle, one foot in front of the other, sometimes with eyes closed, sometimes open. Sometimes her acrobatics invited comment, but she merely smiled and carried on. Once two recruits, by the names of Harris and Stone, pushed her over as she balanced on the beakhead. She sprang up at once, resigned to a beating. But the Marquis de Pisare himself, all royal blue facings and gold tassels, emerged from his day cabin at that moment and rebuked the sniggering men. 'You two should learn a lesson from the boy,' he said, 'and practise your swordplay. For you'll not be picking strawberries in Genova.' The wrong Mr Walsh, who was at his commander's elbow, was more explicit. He slapped both men smartly about the face. 'If you want to knock someone about, save it for the French,' he said. 'We do not fight each other.' Kit paid little heed to the teasing or her rescue for she now had another nugget of information. They were to fight the French. None of it made any sense: France and

Spain were at war, that much she knew. Richard had been taken by the English Army, and shipped to Genova. It sounded like a parlour game.

She could not puzzle it out, so day by day she carried on doggedly with her exercises. She did not seriously think she would ever see combat; she was still convinced that as soon as she landed in Genova she would find Richard and somehow take him home. As far as she was concerned her exercises served purely to make her more male. She could already feel the changes in her body. Her soldier's coat began to strain over her shoulders – she thought that once on land she must pick the seams. Her arms were harder, less rounded, and her grip stronger.

Cleanliness was required aboard ship, and the soldiers bathed in freezing buckets of seawater on deck. Some stripped to the waist, and some hardy souls stripped entirely and poured the entire contents of the bucket over their gooseflesh. Luckily, there were many who elected to do what Kit must; to wash face and hands, and duck the head in the bucket. At such times Kit was to learn what a variety of shapes the male form could assume. Some were burly and muscled, some as skinny as she, some had run to fat. And their man's parts differed likewise. She had only seen Richard without clothes, and at the sight of her first naked soldier looked modestly away; but thereafter she forced herself to look. She needed to know how men were constructed – such sights had to become familiar to her, even commonplace. But how could she become used to a part of a man that seemed different on every sighting? Some were plumbed with a skinny long pipe, some had shorter, fatter appendages, some were generously proportioned. And the size of the members seemed to bear no relation to the size of the man himself; it was most confusing. Kit was struck by how immodest the men were, and how close was the relationship between a man and his member. They handled themselves, they handled each other, they twitted each other about their pricks, they stood naked with no trace of modesty. In the space of a fortnight she heard a man's appendage named as prick, cock, pouting stick, honey pipe, pretty rogue, and stiff and stout. She envied men this ease, remembering how, that last night in Dublin, she'd stood peeled and naked before the window. She had foreseen then, in that moment of premonition, that she would not be in that most natural and naked state for a long time.

Her clothes became her shell. She never removed them – she lived in them all day and slept in them all night. They were spattered with seawater and vomit and piss from the storm, and spilled rations of food and grog from the calm. Even in tranquil waters she had not yet acquired the skill to eat and drink at sea without spills. She had soaked the jerkin and shirt with the acid sweat of fear. They had become hardened and greasy and fitted to her body now like a skin. The uncomfortable, heavy woollen felting had moulded to her, she was used to the twin buttons digging into her back as she lay in her hammock, the lacings and facings and buttons and ties that prodded and poked and pressed their impressions into their flesh had become part of her. She had some company in her clothes, as head lice fed daily on her scalp and their cousins feasted upon her delicate flesh. She begged some tar oil from the carpenter and washed her hair in it, but the lice soon came back.

Her women's courses were to be another problem. She had bled just after Richard had gone, and now she was bleeding again. But because there was no privacy she must suffer the cramps and the discomfort in secret. Regretfully she tore one of her good Holland shirts into rags and stuffed them into her money belt to stem the flow. She wondered how to conceal the bloody hanks of rag, until she watched, once, the Dutchman's log being tossed overboard – the master cast a piece of wood into the waves from the bow and gauged the ship's speed by noting how long the stick took to pay out a reel of knotted thread over the keel. The process provided Kit with an easy solution – each day she dumped the bloody rags down the head and the rolling sea took them. She watched them rush to the bow and out of sight with relief. But at night the shrewd rats scampered below her hammock, tempted by the smell of her secret female blood. There was no possibility of laundering the uniform, and there were no spare shirts to be had nor undergarments to be bought. The regular crew wore short 'slop' trousers and could purchase spare slops from the purser; but there were no uniforms to be had and Kit must live in her own stains until Genova. But, however much the spicy, salty smell of her own body offended her, it was nothing to the general stench of three score men in the same state.

Of all the lessons Kit learned aboard *The Truth and Daylight* the most surprising was the whole new language she added to her lexicon – not Dutch nor French nor even Spanish: but the language of Filth.

The night when the regiment had descended on Kavanagh's was, she now realised, a taste of what was to come. The word 'fuck', which she had never heard uttered once before the regiment drank in her bar, punctuated every sentence that was spoken, by soldiers and crew alike. This useful word could be used to precede all other words, in an endless and imaginative stream of obscenity. The men called each other cunt-bitten crawdons, turdy-guts, shite-a-bed-scoundrels, lickerous gluttons, ruffian rogues, idle lusks, fondling fops, scurvy sneaksbies, gnat-snappers, gaping changelings, shitten shepherds, cozening foxes, codsheads, loobies and mangy rascals. And the words were not absolutes, but had a confusing usage; close friends spoke to each other in these dreadful terms, with something approaching affection, without giving a jot of offence. But now and again a fight would break out and the selfsame words would be used, but with spite and vitriol and intent to injure, and then the words lost their comic sense and assumed their full power. One Friday she saw a man flogged, the man who had started just such a fight, and heard, as the cat-o'-nine-tails bit into his shoulders, these same terrible curses leak from his mouth, some strange panacea for the pain.

Curse words, it seemed, always had a target; always to be thrown like poniards at someone or other. Women, she noted, came off badly; the men spoke of women as if they were afraid of them, not as if they loved them. Women were whores, damned abandoned jades, Jezebels. She once heard a soldier speak of his lover as a 'salt swol'n cunt'. The only creatures below women, she discovered, were the Rome-runners, buggers and Jesuits. These, she divined after much careful eavesdropping, were men who loved men. She had never heard of such a thing, and no wonder; this was a particularly foreign sin, which seemed to be a particular province of the popish Romans, and peculiarly connected with the Catholic Church. She was sure no one in Ireland, though sharing that religion, practised such a perversion – then she remembered the cooper on the cart, and his hand on her leg.

Now, at night, she repeated the words she'd learned like a prayer, a rosary of knobbly, guttural curses threaded on a string of obscenity – an unending, secular cycle keeping time with the rock of the hammock until she fell into a swinging sleep, to dreams soaked in swear words.

Kit's education ended abruptly when the lookout spotted landfall. The benevolent Madonna della Fortuna had led them safely into her haven. Kit crammed her belongings in her pack like the rest, and left her hellish hammock without a backward glance. Upon deck a thousand white gulls greeted them in the shallows, the fellow with the squeezebox played a merry shanty, and everyone was handed a jigger of rum. The recruits crammed eagerly to the larboard bulwark. Kit had half-expected to see a city afire, to hear a boom of cannon from the hillsides and the screams of women and children. Instead she saw a blue sea and a green hill, a sunny whitewashed town and a lofty lighthouse painted with a red cross. It was sixty-two days without Richard, and she was in Genova.

The wrong Mr Walsh sat on the bowsprit with his ever-present list, ticking the recruits off as their boots hit the jetty. When Kit landed she stumbled, suddenly sick. The wrong Mr Walsh jumped down, picked her up by the scruff of her neck and set her on her feet. 'It is the land,' he said. 'It will confound you with its stillness. You'll feel like a newborn foal for a few hours.'

She steadied herself. 'Are you coming with us?'

'No – back to Dublin for the next new hatchlings.'

She would be sorry to see him go, for he seemed her only ally. 'Then thank you, sir,' she said, low voiced, 'for your many kindnesses.'

He peered at her closely, and seemed to hesitate. 'You're not really from Kerry, are you?'

Kit met his gaze. 'No.'

He narrowed his eyes. 'Are you even called Walsh?'

'Yes,' she said fervently. 'Christian Walsh as I live and breathe.'

'Hmm.' He smiled half a smile. 'Well, Christian Walsh. Keep living and breathing for as long as you can.'

Chapter 5

And a soldier he always is decent and clean . . .

'Arthur McBride' (trad.)

They were a shambling, sorry set of soldiers that landed in Genova, with no formation or pride. Kit followed her fellows, her red back heating uncomfortably in the sun. The whitewashed buildings of the docks gave way to tall palaces and churches, so crammed together as to form shadowy alleys which the keen sun could not penetrate. Everything here seemed black or white; a pied city. The only stroke of colour seemed to be the slash of the red cross on the lighthouse. The marble was very white, the shadows very black; the plaster houses bright, their inhabitants dark as Romanies. Underfoot there were black and white chequered pavings, which gave Kit the uncomfortable feeling that she was a counter in a game of which she did not know the rules.

Within a furlong she saw more grand, lofty marble houses than she'd seen in the whole of Dublin, and they all seemed impossibly tall, with many storeys piled one on top of the other, with ornate pillars and decorative windows. The local Spaniards, a swarthy sort of people, jeered at them from the dark doorways and threw cabbage leaves. One offending leaf sat on Kit's shoulder for a few steps of the march like a malodorous epaulette. She brushed it off, perplexed. She'd understood that they were to be fighting the French, so the Spanish were presumably their allies. Why, then, were they not greeted as conquering heroes? Perhaps it was a consequence of their shabby appearance. The officers, at the front of the procession, gave better face – they at least had shining buckles and brushed hats, and their boots showed at least some acquaintance with polish. The Marquis de Pisare, who made the head of the snake, led his men to a great white house deep in the heart of the city – such a place must be the home of a mighty man indeed, some local grandee. The dwelling had great double doors with a tiny door set within. The marquis knocked imperiously at the eye of the needle and a wizened priest appeared. It was only when Kit followed the others inside to a hushed candlelit interior, heavy with incense, that she realised that the house was God's. The foot soldiers hung back while the marquis knelt at the shrine; a lifesize plaster figure crowded about with all manner of ex-voto objects – helmets and shields of days past, shredded banners, seashells, driftwood, planks from the clinkers of ships, a baby's rattle, even a set of wooden teeth.

The priest came down the line of shabby soldiers, dousing them with holy water shaken from an olive branch. After her personal rain shower Kit tugged at the black sleeve of the priest. She pointed to the shrine and shrugged expressively. He understood. '*La Madonna della Fortuna*,' he whispered.

Kit's dry lips parted. The Madonna della Fortuna. The Marquis de Pisare was clearly determined that they should thank their saviour, and so she was to meet, face to face, the heavenly lady who had saved her from the waves. Yes, the Madonna had saved all these others too, but Kit felt that it was *her* personal salvation. She shuffled forward in the velvet, scented dark, and at length it was her turn to kneel. Instead of looking down in penitent thanks she looked up into the figure's eyes, the orbs painted crudely in the black and white of the city. Kit could see, from this distance, that the Madonna was not a plaster saint. She was made of wood. She was a ship's figurehead.

Kit gazed up at the Madonna, a Madonna who had also been saved from the sea. She had been crowned with gold and clothed in a cerulean blue cape. She had been given a coral rose to hold in her pinched fingers, and handed a child that wasn't hers to hold in her crooked arms.

Kit felt comforted. This was not the Virgin. She was in disguise too. Kit felt a kinship with the wooden impostor and wondered what her story was. What had her ship been called? Who was she really? She might have been a Jezebel, a wooden whore.

It was a salutary lesson. She realised how different the male Kit she had created was from the female. As a woman, she had been confident, funny, talkative, brave, courageous. As a man she was a mouse. What she had to be was Kit, the essence of herself, but as a man; Kit as if she had been born a boy. She had to talk and laugh, and hold forth, and run down hills, just as she had as a woman. If she retreated into herself, the men would try to draw her forth. And once they started looking, they would most likely find her out. She could not risk discovery now, now that she walked on the same foreign soil as Richard.

As she straightened up from her kneeling position, the next fellow jostled her as she rose, impatient to take his place. 'Mary's tits,' he said, 'did you tell her your whole history? There's others a-waiting.'

Kit took him firmly by the arm and looked in his eyes – the first time she'd looked directly at anyone since she'd donned her disguise. 'Step back, sir,' she said, gruff and low. 'And mind your tongue. You are in God's house.' She saw the fellow take a pace backward to let her by, and as she walked down the aisle, she noted the Marquis de Pisare regarding her with approval for the second time in her short career.

They marched forth to a ruined marble palazzo near the cathedral where they were to be billeted for one night. Kit had never seen a place so grand, nor so shabby. The place presented its own problems; there were flea-bitten straw pallets strewn on the floor and the dragoons must sleep as close as maggots crowding cheese.

The necessary house was no more than a bucket in the corner which stank strongly of nightsoil.

Lieutenant Gardiner, in his peremptory tones, answered her unspoken questions. 'Tomorrow we march to meet Tichborne's regiment of foot. Your evening is your own, but we meet at dawn in the square before the cathedral in full uniform. No man shall be tardy nor jug-bitten.'

As the men scattered, cheering faintly, Kit stood rooted. A march to meet Tichborne – and Richard. Joy and fear fought in her breast – she would see him soon, but how long would the march be, and to where? She looked at the little necessary bucket in the corner, covered with a stained cloth. An idea had formed in her head on that long voyage, and now she must be a man for a little longer, the idea must become a reality.

While the others set out to drink their pay in the dockside taverns, Kit went her own way into the black and white town. As the citizens gabbled around her pointing at her clothes, she memorised her route back to the large square where the soldiers were billeted. She felt entirely alone in this odd place where churches looked like houses and houses looked like churches. Perhaps everything was in disguise. The cathedral, guarded at its steps by roaring stone lions, was rendered in black and white marble in crazy stripes. Kit did not enter, but walked into the tiny alleys behind the duomo; here, cheek by jowl with Genova's greatest church, she was sure she would find what she was looking for.

And she did indeed. She paused outside the door and looked up at the universal sign for a silversmith; three splayed silver arrows, just the same as the smiths on Dame Street in Dublin. Here, as there, there was a burly guard to watch the door – this one a hairless giant bristling with weapons. But he nodded benignly enough at Kit as she laid her hand on the door and went inside.

She was almost blinded by the glaring constellation that awaited her within. Everything was rendered in silver: goblets, coin chests, spoons, daggers, bracelets, even an arquebus with silver shot. Here too she looked into the countenance of the counterfeit Virgin; the Madonna della Fortuna was rendered over and over again, in miniature no bigger than a silver egg, on a huge canvas in an ornate silver frame that sprouted leaves and curlicues, in silver statuary; her face reflected a thousand times in the silver-backed looking glasses that hung about.

In all the glory Kit did not at once see that there was a living figure among the glory. A woman stepped forth.

'*Mi dica?*' she said.

Kit, remembering just in time, doffed her tricorn. She wondered, as she bowed, how she would possibly explain what she wanted to buy. 'Can you understand me?' she asked tentatively.

The woman shrugged. 'Certainly.' She spoke English with a strange accent, making a 'Sh' sound on the C.

'Are you English?'

'I am a Hollander. But I speak a little of most languages and more of a few. In trade one must be able to speak to all nations.' The woman had a pale face, tidy ash-blond hair and a fringe cut across her brows, not unlike Kit's own style. She held her hands before her, clasped not above a full skirt but over a leather apron. Her hands were her strangest feature, for they were as green as holly, stained by some nameless compound; fingers, palms and all.

'Is the silversmith within?' asked Kit.

'I am the silversmith,' said the lady, 'my name is Maria van Lommen.' She held out a green hand.

Kit took it. 'Christian Walsh. You made . . . all this?' Kit's gesture embraced the glory about her.

'Of course. This is my business. My father makes silver in Amsterdam. I make silver here.'

Kit was impressed that a woman owned all these riches, let

alone crafted them. A woman, moreover, who seemed not much older than herself. But for now, Maria's sex made Kit's task more difficult. It would be harder to explain what she wanted to a female.

'It is of a . . . personal and delicate nature. I need . . . an appendage resembling . . .' Kit mentally rejected all the shipboard vocabulary she had learned for the male member. 'A man's parts.'

Maria van Lommen nodded, her face impassive, as if Kit had asked for a silver spoon. 'Come into the back. Gennaro!' she called, and the giant stooped to enter the shop. '*Guarda qui.*'

The treasure guarded, Maria swiped back a heavy blood-velvet curtain with one green hand, and led Kit into a little atrium. 'Is this what you are looking for?'

Ranged around the wall were raked shelves, lined with the same crimson velvet, displaying the strangest objects and contraptions Kit had ever seen.

'You see anything you like? I got more in the drawers, different sizes, different attachments. You just say, I make bespoke.'

'May I?' Kit picked up one of the objects, astonished. As she turned the thing over in her hand seeing her face reflected crazily in its contours, she was flabbergasted. The thing was almost exactly what she'd imagined she needed. It was a long silver tube enclosed at one end and rounded like a male member. Below the tube hung two globes, and complicated soft leather straps were threaded through silver eyelets to attach the thing to the lower body. But surely she must be mistaken – no one could need what she had in mind. 'What is it?'

'Here they call it a Venetian finger.'

'A what?'

'A staff of love,' said Maria. 'A quillety, a faucetin, a dandilolly. It has many names for many nations. It straps on, so you can pleasure your man. That is what you meant, is it not? That is what you came for?'

'No. That is . . . No. That is *not* what I wanted at all.'

'See here,' said Maria van Lommen, pressing her green hands together as if in prayer. 'I am not your priest. I am not here to take your confession. You can dress as a soldier-boy and play your bed-games, whatever pleases you. I sell you anything, no judgement. It is good disguise, I grant you. But let us not waste time. I knew you for a woman as soon as you walked through my door.'

Kit smiled shakily at the silversmith. The discovery she most feared had come, and not at all from the quarter she'd imagined.

'Be at your ease,' said Maria. 'I am not going to give you away. Why would I? Come though to the workshop, and explain to me exactly what you need.'

The workshop was a well-lit room with a long workbench littered with alien tools and compounds in small copper dishes. Crucibles and limbecs suspended above the bench connected by crazy pipes, and half-finished lumps of silver twisted into miraculous shapes, as if they were being birthed from the metal. The whole room had an odd, tangy smell, despite the casements being thrust fully open in the warm evening.

Kit talked as Maria drew on some parchment with a piece of charcoal. 'I need an appendage that gives me the male appearance through my clothes, but I need to piss through it convincingly – as a foot soldier I will be on the road with three score men for a time, with no privacy whatsoever, and must not reveal myself. That is . . .' A thought stopped her tongue.

'That is . . .?' prompted Maria gently.

'That is if I have not revealed myself already.'

'How could you have?'

'Well, you knew me at once.'

Maria spread her strange hands. 'But I am a woman. Believe me, for most men, once a person's sex is established, that is the end of the matter. Generals of armies, admirals of navies, prime ministers and kings, priests and bishops they may be, but few of them are as perceptive as you might think. Most of them see the moon and call it a shilling.' She rooted in a little drawer and brought out a handful of silver beads, then turned back to Kit.

'None of my current models will fit your purpose,' mused Maria, a pinprick of unquiet, excited fire igniting her tranquil grey eyes for the first time. 'This will truly be a challenge. For unlike my pleasure pricks you will need a hollow member with a hole in the tip. The thing should have a pipe inside, so your urine can flow, and the pipe should turn up at the tip so that the piss arcs convincingly. But the whole apparatus must be as wide as the span of a hand, to catch your flow like a funnel.'

'Can you do it?'

'Yes,' said Maria without hesitation. 'Get undressed. There are certain measurements which must be taken. You permit me?'

Kit swallowed. 'Yes.'

She removed her breeches fully for the first time in two weeks, conscious of the spicy smell of body odour. But Maria seemed unconcerned as she measured the distance between the top of Kit's thighs and the distance from her buttocks to the front of her treasure pouch. 'In the normal way the fit is not important, for the woman wears a Venetian finger for the act itself, and then takes it off and lays it by until next time. But in your case you will be wearing it all day, every day. So it must be light and serviceable and comfortable, and must not dig your flesh nor tarnish.' Then Maria used her fingers, speaking more to herself than Kit. 'The stream comes from here at the front . . . Venus hole farther back . . . anus farther back still.' Kit, whose anatomy was largely a mystery to her, began to be acquainted with her own body. It seemed a woman had as many holes as a cheesecloth – three to contend with in this design alone.

Maria straightened and stood. 'Cover yourself,' she said. She rang a small silver bell and gave an incomprehensible command to the swarthy girl who appeared. The girl brought a jug of ale, which she handed to Kit, and a chamber pot which she placed on the floor by the legs of her chair. 'Drink,' said Maria. 'For we must test the design.'

Kit drank thirstily – for she had had no refreshment since shipboard – while Maria worked with sticky white plaster and silver wire, shaping and moulding with her discoloured fingers. The silversmith talked as she worked. 'We must consider how this will look in your clothes. We must consider the length and thrust of the thing – for men have two states as you must know.' Of all the information Maria had imparted this at least she did understand, for in the short sweet months of marriage to Richard she had come to understand both states. 'Obviously you cannot stand stiff as a poker. But there should be some protrusion in your breeches to make your disguise authentic.'

Maria made a model out of plaster, and Kit drunk quart after quart of ale to fill her bladder. Tipsy enough not to mind removing her breeches, she fitted the funnel between her thighs, and let go into a chamber pot Maria had placed for the purpose. After leaks and dribblings and alterations to the design, Maria had a model she was happy with. 'I will now cast the real one,' she said, lighting a blue flame and setting a crucible of silver beads upon it. In the growing dark the flame bleached Maria's hair to silver too. 'Can you wait?'

'The muster is tomorrow at dawn,' said Kit, watching, fascinated, as the silver beads became a bright puddle in the dun-grey crucible.

'That will be time enough,' said Maria to the crucible, not looking up. 'You can stay here the night.'

Kit looked unsure – 'We were directed to stay at the palace by the cathedral.'

Maria looked almost as if she could smile. 'Your fellows of the regiment will all be in the cathouses by the harbour for the night. I'll wager my whole shop that not one of them will stay in the palazzo. After a fortnight at sea they'll be as sharp set as a man in a desert. And that,' she said, looking up at Kit, 'is how you may be quiet in your mind that none of them knows you for a woman.'

'How may I be sure?'

'Did anyone touch you on the ship?'

'Two braggards pushed me over.' Then she understood. 'No.'

'Then they don't know. If they'd known, every one of them would have had you. You make such a pretty boy that I am surprised that they did not try you anyway.'

Kit was taken aback by such frankness, but saw an opportunity to further educate herself. 'Then men do lie together like man and wife?'

'Since time began. You know your own anatomy now; there is one hole we all share.' Kit considered this, horrified and fascinated, while Maria dropped some more silver beads in a crucible, hesitated, then added a couple more. 'Of course it happens. Confined space, long voyages, no women. And of course, for some men it is their preference.'

'They *prefer* that? Men to women?'

'Some do, yes. Just as some women prefer women.'

Kit looked sharply at Maria. The words seemed to have some weight, but the silversmith was concentrating on poking in a tiny drawer in her apothecary chest with one green finger. 'I will mix an alloy in with the silver. Else it will tarnish and your women's parts will turn as green as my fingers.'

And . . . she thought of her nights in the hammock, hearing those rhythmic rubbings and groans. 'Can a man do it . . . by himself?'

'Not the act, of course. A man is not made to twist like a serpent and reach his own hole, though some would if they could.

No; when there aren't any holes to be had, or a mouth, a clasped hand will do.'

Kit digested this. 'But if men lie with men, then why *wasn't* I . . . molested on board ship?'

'Because of the consequences. The English Navy has regulations against sodomy. If two men are found bedding together, they are lashed together and thrown overboard.'

Kit swallowed.

'Would you like a bath?' asked Maria, as if they'd just been talking of the weather. 'I'll get the servants to fill you a bath.'

Kit forgot the ways of men. 'You have a bath?'

Kit luxuriated upstairs in a small square chamber hung with green damask, and lit by a constellation of candles. She lowered herself into a large silver bathtub with animal's feet. It was full to the brim with warm milky water and floating with lavender heads. She scrubbed every inch of herself, removing two weeks of grime. She had never appreciated before the sheer simple pleasure of being clean. She washed her hair with the lavender, and soaked until she dozed. The bliss, the utter bliss of being immersed and caressed by the warm water, of being naked for the first time in two weeks, of being free from the prison of the greasy and besmattered uniform she'd come to detest. She must have stayed there for hours dozing and drifting, till the water was no more than tepid. When the door opened Kit instinctively covered her breasts, but it was only Maria bearing a covered jug – Maria, who had not only seen, but measured, her most intimate parts. She lowered her hands and smiled.

'It is done,' said the silversmith, 'but the metal must cool slowly so the alloy does not crack. Take your leisure.' Maria poured the contents of the jug into the bath and the hot water refreshed the bath once more. Then she knelt, took a linen cloth, dipped it in the bath and began to rub Kit's shoulders. The moon watched at the window. 'That is the same moon that bade me farewell in

Dublin.' Kit spoke almost to herself, dreamily, not expecting Maria to understand, too sleepy to explain. 'The moon watches over all women,' said Maria. 'She controls the tides and so the cycles of our own bleedings. And silver is the moon's metal,' she went on, washing Kit's shoulders rhythmically. 'The emblem of my house is the silver arrows, the arrows of Diana, the huntress. Silver is a woman's metal too. Mirrors, picture frames, arrows, daggers, jewellery. Reliquaries for the Virgin.' The cloth made soothing circles on Kit's flesh. 'These are female things. That is why we use silver for those love toys for women such as I showed you. I do not make mail or swords or helms; the steelmakers cast the rings for armour or the blades for battle. Silver understands us; our femininity, our vanity, our changeability, our dreams and desires.' Maria's voice, sing-song and sibilant and soft, was making Kit sleepy, and the motion of the cloth on her shoulders made her shiver with pleasure though the water was so warm. Dreamily, she watched the moon fracture and ripple on the surface of the water through half-closed eyes, but she knew she must break the spell and ask a dangerous question. 'When you spoke of women loving women, were you talking of yourself?'

The cloth stopped in its progress. Started again. 'Yes.'

Kit steeled herself. 'Just how much will this silver prick you are making cost me?'

Maria's lips pursed a little, and she almost, *almost* smiled. She wrung out the cloth with her discoloured hands and laid it neatly on the side of the bath. 'There is no price. Unlike most men I've no interest in seducing women who do not want to be seduced.'

Kit relaxed back against the curve of the silver bath.

Maria stood. 'I will leave you. Come and see me in the morning – your disguise should be cool enough to try.'

Kit was asleep as soon as her head touched the feather pillow of her bed, and slept the blank dreamless sleep of the truly exhausted.

In the morning she rose before the sun, at the gentle knock of a servant, but felt more refreshed than she'd done since Richard left. The silver prick lay on top of the folded clothes, and she tied it on first before donning her breeches. She would never have dreamed that something wrought of metal could be so comfortable – the thing was light and discreet, and its moulded seams sat smoothly against her tender parts with no chafing. But she almost cried when she had to don her uniform, stiff with sweat and seawater and greasy with stains. Now she must remove her treasure pouch from between her legs; instead she tied the heavy pad of coins around her waist, thickening it and giving her a cleaner male line from shoulder to hip.

She went downstairs to find Maria at breakfast, at a table set with silver platters and spoons, and lit with candles anticipating daylight.

'How is your prick?' asked Maria with no preamble.

'It feels like a part of me.'

Maria inclined her head, taking this strange statement as the compliment it was. 'Gennaro will guide you to the Piazza Reale.' She called for her giant, and he appeared with a noiselessness that belied his size. 'We don't open till sunup, so I don't need him till then.'

Kit felt for her purse. 'First I must pay the reckoning.'

Maria shook her head, and her pale hair flew about her face. 'I told you there would be no price. Your problem challenged me. If you are satisfied, then I am too.'

'I will always be in your debt.'

And slowly, deliberately, Kit placed her hands on the table among all the silver plate and the candles, bent down and kissed Maria van Lommen chastely, but firmly, on the lips.

Chapter 6

And we met Sergeant Knacker and Captain Vamp . . .

'Arthur McBride' (trad.)

The shady square before the pied cathedral was coloured with redcoats, ranked in approximate positions, under the haughty eye of the Marquis de Pisare. Kit hurried along the lines, noting the shadowed eyes, yawning mouths and rank breaths smoking in the foredawn, and knew Maria had been right – they had all of them spent the night at some tavern or molly house. At last she recognised some faces from *The Truth and Daylight* and pushed into the lines alongside them.

Of all people, the recruit she'd rebuked at the shrine joshed her as she fell in. 'Didn't see you at the tavern, you sly fox. Been a-burrowing in some trugging place?'

Kit smiled and winked broadly. 'I spent the night with a woman, yes.' She leant close to his greasy ear. 'As I do every night.'

He shouted with laughter and clapped Kit on the back between the shoulder blades. It was working.

Lieutenant Gardiner paced before them, as correct and chilly as ever. 'If I call your name, step forth.' Kit half-listened to the names, mostly good Irish names from Mayo, from Cork, from Waterford. Then she saw the marquis murmur in Gardiner's ear and point at her. 'Christian Walsh.'

She stepped forward, the blood thrumming in her ears. Had she been discovered? She looked about her; she was in company with a row of ten or more strong men, all of whom she recognised as the ones who had been practising manoeuvres on the ship.

'You dozen will report to Captain Ross at the lighthouse. You're to be enrolled in the dragoons.'

The lighthouse stood on a pretty rocky cape on a peninsula reaching out into the blue sea. The tower was constructed in two square portions, each one capped by a crenellated terrace crowned by a lantern. The lower prism was painted with a red cross on a white ground, and Kit recognised the symbol from the ship – the first sign she'd seen of Genova.

Kit followed the dozen down to the shingle, and saw ahead, standing on the promontory, a tall figure, entirely in shadow against the bright background. He had one foot on a rock, a hand on his knee, and was shielding his eyes to look out to sea. A tall ship grazed the horizon, and Kit wondered whether the figure watched *The Truth and Daylight*, forging a path home to Dublin. The sun sparkled on the water and as the small band approached the figure turned and stood at attention while the dozen formed a semicircle around him. He was clearly not the captain they sought, for he was no older than Richard; but while he waited for them to order themselves she had a little time to study him: this then, was a dragoon.

He was immaculate from crown to toe; an ideal soldier. His appearance put the shabby dozen to shame. *You may aspire to be me*, he seemed to say, *you may become like me in time, if you work hard*. He was at least a head taller than any of them; broad of shoulder and lean of hip. He had glossy black hair, brushed forward over his forehead and above his ears in the latest style, but his eyes were such a bright blue in contrast to the blackness of his hair that Kit thought at once that he must be Irish. His uniform fitted him like a skin and was pristine; he wore a red coat with a dozen buttons of sparkling gilt. His jacket had royal blue facings and the peeping cuffs and collars of his shirt were starched and bright. His breeches, tightly fitted, tucked into long black riding boots as polished as any dandy's and one arm cradled a beautifully brushed tricorn with white piping and the badge of the dragoons.

This vision looked them up and down with a sardonic twist of his handsome mouth. 'Dear God,' he said. 'You all stink like a Monday fish market.' Then, before Kit realised what was happening, he calmly went down the line and pushed them in turn off the promontory into the sea.

Despite the heat of the day the first cold douse was a shock, followed by a moment of sheer childish pleasure at being immersed in the water; but the heavy felting of the uniform and the pad of silver coins about her waist and the silver prick in her breeches dragged her down. Striking desperately for the surface, she could not rise an inch. Lungs bursting, she heard a swish and roar, saw a dark plunge and a forest of bubbles, and then was taken beneath the arms and heaved skywards. Her head broke the surface and she gulped a lungful of air. She was in the arms of the smart dragoon, who was now looking considerably less groomed, his black hair plastered to his forehead, his dark eyelashes splayed like starfish. The sardonic look had left him and his blue eyes were all concern. 'Gracious, lad, you sank like a stone!'

Kit was an able swimmer, and had swum in the stream on her father's farm since she could walk, but she had never attempted it while carrying her particular form of ballast. 'You . . . you . . . cunt-bitten crawdon! You turdy-gutted, shite-a-bed-scoundrel! You scurvy fucking rascal!' She spat the dreadful words at him with the seawater.

'Don't talk,' he gasped, laughter bubbling in his voice. 'And don't *cling*. Let me do the labour. You're quite safe.'

Still vomiting seawater and swear words, blinded by the stinging brine and the Spanish sun, Kit let herself be towed like a tug. The dragoon and the tide combined threw her on to the shingle.

Where she lay, gasping, facing seaward, cheek to the salty stones. She could see the other soldiers, most of them having shed their clothes, disporting themselves in the sparkling waves, and she envied them. Naked and carefree, they were splashing each other, swimming easily and slapping their sodden red coats on the water in play. Kit rolled on to her back, gasping like a landed fish, her soaked uniform clinging to her, the silver prick standing forth like a poker. She sat, hurriedly, to conceal it, wondering uncomfortably whether her saviour had felt it dig when she'd clung to him in the sea. She looked sideways at him with stinging eyes. The dragoon, breathing heavily from his exertions, watched the soldiers disporting themselves, flicking the sodden hair from his eyes. He glanced at her, then spoke to the playing soldiers. 'That's quite a vocabulary you have for one so young,' he said. 'But as you were under certain . . . duress, and as it was so early in our acquaintance, I feel it would not be the act of a gentleman to put you on a charge.' He had the clipped tones of a nobleman, a man born to command. He could not be farther from the Black Irish she'd taken him for. She was so filled with a mixture of curiosity and resentment that she did not at once register what he had said.

'A charge?'

'For swearing at your superior.' He shot her a direct blue gaze from beneath dripping slabs of hair. 'I am Captain Ross, the commanding officer of the Scots Grey Dragoons.'

'Oh.' She scrambled to her feet, dripping everywhere, face scarlet. 'I . . . beg your pardon, I'm sure.'

He squinted up at her.

'Let us say no more about it. Let us rather call it a strangely worded paean of gratitude for my saving your life.' He waited.

A sulky pause. 'Thank you for saving my life,' mustered Kit.

'There. Much better.'

Captain Ross stood, and such was his natural authority that

the eleven other men scrambled to the shore to form a semicircle around him.

'Now that you have . . . *bathed*, we are going to march in an orderly fashion to the Palazzo Reale, where you will be given your uniforms and your mounts.' There were delighted murmurings among the men. 'That is correct, I said mounts; for unlike your unluckier brethren from the good ship *Truth and Daylight*, you will be *riding* into the mountains while they *walk*.' Ross began to walk about them, weaving in and out, his wet boots squelching on the shingle. 'Your officers on board ship have seen something in you which has marked you out as sheep from goats, Jews from Samaritans, wheat from chaff. I myself have not yet perceived your qualities, but hope to learn of them soon. Mr . . .?' He spun quickly and turned on Kit.

'Walsh,' supplied Kit.

'Mr Walsh, perhaps you ride better than you swim.'

In this she was confident. 'Yes, sir.'

'Good. Fall in.'

There was to be no talking in the ranks as the dozen men returned to the city proper, but by the time they had gained the palace Captain Ross seemed to know the names of every one of them. Kit's thoughts pattered nervously, keeping step with her marching pace. She had told no lie – she had been riding since she was a babe, for there had always been horses on the farm. Richard had been no rider, he had ridden nothing but the drays from the brewery, so she would wager he had remained in Tichborne's company of foot. She had a better chance of catching up with him on horseback – but she must not make any more mistakes.

Ross led the company through a white arch into the courtyard of a great palace and dispatched them to a long room where bales of clothes waited. Once again Kit was given a uniform. The coat was yet again red but instead of the cheap felting of her old coat she noted the bright brave scarlet of the dye and a better class of fabric. It differed from her old suit of clothes in several particulars, and all of them an improvement; royal blue facings instead of white, denoting the royal status of the regiment following the late king's inspection. There were wide blue turned cuffs fastened with three gold buttons apiece. She noted with relief that, the coat being cut for riding, there was a wider, almost circular skirt to it, which would conceal her calls of nature even more effectively.

She saw with great relief that she must change only her over-clothes in the company of the other men, so she donned her smart new coat first, removing her damp breeches under the cover of the long flared skirt of the coat. Her fresh attire pleased her. The new cross-belts helped to flatten her bound breasts. The breeches were snug as they were made for riding, but, as they were cut for a man, made enough room for her new appendage. The boots were long and supple with an ample handspan of turned-over leather at the top, to protect the calves when riding. She crammed the new tricorn on her red locks and went to line up in the courtyard with the others.

Ross was there, impatiently tapping a riding crop on his boots. 'Much better. Now you look like dragoons. But can you ride like them? There is only a handful of you, and with good reason – you'll be joining the elite of the queen's cavalry. It is true that we are in somewhat of a hurry. Events are marching forth in the mountains. But as we will travel faster than the general regiment of foot I am going to beg one week of your time to train you in the very basics of our craft. For no man of mine will go into battle without training.'

A week! Another seven days without Richard seemed a cruel delay. That would take her to seventy days without him. Kit could almost wish herself back among the foot soldiers; at least they would march right away. She stood impatiently, shifting her weight from foot to foot, while an ostler walked out half a dozen grey horses and led them round the courtyard. The mounts stood reluctantly, dipping and tossing their heads in turn.

'These are all quarter horses,' announced Ross, 'donated to our cause from our friends at the Dutch Horse Guards.' Kit could not divine, from Ross's sardonic tone, whether the Hollanders were allies and had given this fine horseflesh as friends, or whether the English had stolen them from their enemies. Ross walked to the horses and looked from them to the men, as if mentally pairing them like tricks at the whist table. 'Shadow to Mr Locke. Ghost to Mr Southcott. Pewter to Mr Book . . .' He rolled off every name until at last he said, '. . . and the mare, Flint, for Mr Walsh, as he is a slight fellow.'

Kit walked over to take the head collar and ran a practised eye over her mount, doubtfully. Handsome the dozen greys certainly were, and finely matched, but were they warhorses? Her mare had strong slim legs, but seemed full of nervous energy, skittish and highly bred from velvety nose to quivering fetlock. Kit eyed the mare, and the mare eyed her back, rolling the whites of her eyes in warning. *Flint indeed*, thought Kit. *One spark and there'll be trouble.*

Once the new dragoons were mounted, Ross had them canter in a circle, and rode around correcting their seats. Kit kept her eyes on the grey mane before her, short as a bottlebrush, cropped to avoid catching in the swipe of a sword, listening to Ross criticising the others, hoping she would not come to his notice.

'You're riding like a laundress, man. Sit up, sit up.'

'Heels down, lad. You're not dancing a morris.'

'Back straight. You are made of bones not macaroni.'

She rode self-consciously, attempting to relax in the saddle, not trying too hard, letting her muscles remember riding every nag and shire and unbroken foal on the farm. Flint skipped around, napping at the bit, skittering sideways, her hooves striking sparks on the pavings. But Kit knew these tricks of old and pulled the mare up sharply. Back on the farm she'd spoken softly to the difficult horses, whispering in their twitching ears. She leaned forward now to put her lips to the feathery grey ear. As soon as she heard Kit's voice so close Flint brought up her head smartly, hitting Kit in the nose, causing a stinging pain and a gush of blood.

Tears sprang involuntarily to her eyes, but she swallowed them down, concentrating on wiping the blood away with her fingers, reminding herself that a man would barely even notice such a trifling injury.

Ross tossed her a kerchief from horseback. 'Don't bleed on your coat, Walsh,' he said, not unkindly, 'that is only permitted in battle.' She caught the neckerchief and mopped her swelling nose. Furious, she dismounted, walked round to Flint's head and held the horse's bony velvet cheeks firmly in her hands, making sure she had the mare's attention. Then she drew back her right fist and punched the horse as hard as she could on the nose. Flint stood stock still, stunned, shaking her head as if trying to shift a bothersome fly, not at all sure what had just happened to her.

'Aye, now you'll listen,' said Kit softly and dangerously, her accent suddenly very Dublin. 'Don't try any more shenanigans, miss. I know them all.'

Then she gathered the reins and mounted; the horse stayed meekly still. She pushed Flint into a canter to rejoin the exercise. The horse obeyed without demur. Ross caught her up.

'Where did you learn that trick?'

'I was raised on a farm, sir.' Kit spoke the words defiantly, for she knew how lowly this must sound to a man of his quality. But he merely nodded without comment, and later, when he rode around to watch her exercises, he said, 'Far from bad, Mr Walsh, you have a good seat,' and somewhere under her gilt buttons her heart swelled with pride.

For a week they trained and Kit and Flint both champed at the bit. Kit was careful to conceal her impatience, and had to concede that she had much to learn. She learned to ride her grey without the reins, directing the mare with only the slightest pressure of her knees. Then she learned to use the reins only, taking her feet from the stirrups. She learned to use her horse as a shield, swinging one leg over the cantle to ride in the lee of her mount, before swinging herself back into the saddle and riding on. She learned to give Flint a signal to rear on to her hind legs, hooves flailing, while she rained blows from her father's sword upon an invisible enemy. She even learned to ride blindfold, as the dragoons were trained to ride their horses hard at the palace wall and check and turn before impact. She learned, in this heart-stopping exercise, to read Flint, to feel through her legs and seat the horse's fear, to feel the stutter of the hooves as the wall approached, and to yank the reins at the last moment. She began to trust the mare, and Flint learned to trust her.

Each morning, as Kit rose from her straw pallet, every muscle ached. Her legs and seat, arms, shoulders and back throbbed as if she had been flogged, and her sinews screamed as she tried to walk. There was to be some respite from riding, though. On the fourth day, in the cool shady arches of the loggia, Ross was joined by his deputy, an English sergeant called Taylor, a red-headed, stocky bulldog of a man. Taylor's function seemed to be to save Ross the trouble of shouting, for all he did was to repeat his captain's instructions at a bellow, the exertion of which made his face as red as his hair. Ross directed Sergeant Taylor to hand out an armful of long-muzzled guns. 'This is a matchlock musket,' the captain announced. 'This fellow will be your dearest friend. If you look to the right of you, and to the left, one or both of these men may not be riding with you at the war's end. But your musket should be your constant companion.'

Kit soon realised they were to take the captain at his word –

they were to keep their muskets with them at all times, even at night, when they must cradle them like sweethearts – wood and metal in place of flesh and blood. Each dragoon marked his initials on his own, and more; little carvings appeared to reflect the manner of the man that carried the gun. A heart for a romantic soul called Hall, cleft with an arrow and carved with the initials of him and his lady, as if the musket grew in the greenwood. A cock and balls for Taylor. Kit looked at the broad, smooth stock and knew straight away what to carve – she made sixty-four neat marks in a long book-keeper's tally – one notch for every day she'd been without Richard.

The next several days were devoted to musket training. Kit rested the heavy gun on her collarbone as she was shown. She learned to lift the thing to her shoulder, lay her chin along the cool barrel, suck in her cheek to protect her side teeth, close her right eye. She learned to know the tinder-strike of the spark, to recoil from the punch of the discharge, not to cough from the tiny cloud of acrid smoke that rose from the lock. She learned to load, fire and reload at tethered scarecrow dummies which were shot repeatedly until they lolled at their stakes and spilled their straw entrails over the palace paving. The killing done, she would blow the grit of gunpowder from her nose, and beat at the lines of grey dust that mapped her palms. The dragoons were directed to dismantle and clean the guns, then reassemble them, firing once more to check their workmanship. Kit could not get the trick of it and was made to stay at the loggia until her task was complete, under the impatient eye of Sergeant Taylor, the most disagreeable man she had yet met. She was still there when the moon that had been stalking her since Dublin rose to mock her. Ross watched her for a time, sighing periodically, until at length he took his leave. 'You'll excuse me,' he said, mock-courteous, 'but I have a dinner to attend.' And he strode off across the courtyard, leaving her to the tender care of Sergeant Taylor.

She watched him walk across the courtyard, and enter a door to the family quarters of the palace. She struggled on with the gun in her lap, her fingers sore and sweaty with effort, while from inside the palace she heard the clash of crystal and the tinkle of laughter. She imagined Ross charming the ladies with his short vowels and his tall stories. She imagined them lowering their fans, rapt, to show painted faces and wine-sparkled eyes. So she was not allowed to swear at him? She cursed instead the stubborn mechanism of the musket. 'You piss-burned shitsack,' she told the gun. 'You turd-eating cunt-bitten dandy.' For a moment her fingers slackened on the gun as she imagined herself out of the heavy uniform and clothed in cool beaded silk, her copper hair grown again and scented and piled high with jewelled combs. She'd wear a little rouge high on her cheeks, and a patch and a little coral salve to redden her lips. She'd walk into the room and stand under that chandelier, the brilliants of which she could just see from the loggia. She'd just stand there and stand there and the room would go quiet and then he'd turn and she'd dazzle Mr high and mighty Captain Ross, so he couldn't even see those simpering Spanish misses any more . . . Mary and Joseph, she'd knock his eyes out of his head! Perhaps a green satin gown . . . she'd always worn green for Holy Days . . . yes, a green Rockingham mantua costing thousands of golden guineas . . . She would—

A stinging cuff around the head sent her ears ringing. Suddenly Sergeant Taylor was behind her. 'Stop daydreaming and start polishing,' he said. 'You think I got nowhere to go? I want that barrel shining like a shit-barn door.' Kit bit her tongue, and got her head down.

She had better luck the next day with swordplay; for though she was not the strongest of the company, she was quick and agile, and had had a good tutor in her father. As she practised with wooden swords and then sharpened weapons, her body recalled how to turn and parry and strike. Ross, leaning on his pikestaff to watch them, was more than usually testy that day, and there were betraying violet shadows beneath his eyes. *Too much merrymaking*, thought Kit sourly. Tired the captain may have been, but he certainly would not let his dragoons rest; he had them fighting on barrels and beams in the palace courtyard, from above and below, to become used, he said, to fighting on uneven terrain and mountainous inclines. The dragoons were also introduced to the partisan, a long pike with a tip of Spanish steel, and punctured the poor dummies over and again. Ross gave the dummies Spanish names, and as the dragoons made a mess of Felipe and Alfonso and Miguel, it seemed odd to Kit that having supped with the Spanish, Ross would now turn their own steel against them. The captain made them fight blindfold too, practising with plain staves until they were black and blue with blows, so that they might use all their senses in combat. 'What you hear and feel is almost as important as what you see,' Ross said. The dragoons learned the meaning of every call of the trumpet, every beat of the drum, every fire of the gun battery. 'Listen to your own person too,' urged Ross. 'The pricking of your thumbs, the hairs rising on the neck – these are tools. Use them. If you feel that a blow is about to fall, the chances are it may.'

Ross made them learn their regimental motto by heart – *Nemo me impune lacessit*; No one cuts me with impunity. Kit did not understand the English any more than she did the Latin, but she learned the tag obediently. Ross would pace about them like an attorney, catechising them about their new regiment.

'Who are we?'

'The Scots Grey Dragoons.'

'For whom do we fight?'

'For queen and country.'

'What is our role?'

'Reconnaissance and security.'

'And what is our motto?'
'*Nemo me impune lacessit.*'
'Very good. Again.'

Now and then, she would see at the windows and balconies of the palace shining characters who overlooked their manoeuvres. These, she supposed, must be the Spanish grandees, or even the family of the Doge himself, the Duke of Genova to whom the house belonged. As she rode about the courtyard in the strong autumn sunshine, she looked up through beads of stinging sweat and imagined what it would be like to be rich enough to call this place home.

Gazing through the glazed windows she would see the hanging brilliants of a chandelier, or the corner of a fresco depicting green and rolling hills. When she saw the ladies in their satins gathering on the delicate balconies, she imagined what it would be like to be a Spanish princess. *The King of Spain's daughter*, she thought. Oh, to wear cooling satin, and cold dewdrop diamonds at your ears and throat and to waft your face with a fan, and if the day grew hot to retire inside into the costly shadows and drink iced sherbet. Yet she knew, given the choice, she would lay by the satin and unhook the diamonds, fold up the fan and set down the sherbet, for a chance to wear a red coat and find her husband again.

She was impatient to ride to the mountains, to find Richard before winter set in. Each day they were joined by more recruits, chosen ones pruned from the shiploads of soldiers arriving from England, from Scotland, from Ireland. At night they slept in the ruined palace, in conditions that became more and more cramped. Kit jostled for her bed space with the rest, learning that nothing ill came from standing her ground. She was glad of her silver prick, for there was only the covered bucket in the corner for their functions, emptied once a day, so she and all the others pissed in the gutters, as did all the citizens of Genova; white piss and black shit to match the pied streets. The dragoons seemed altogether a better class – as if being elevated by their horses lifted them to other heights. They cursed less and quarrelled less, and although there was still language enough to make her blush, she felt comfortable in the company of the dragoons by day.

But by night the education Maria van Lommen had given her had birthed a new fear, and in her flea-bitten cot she curled in upon herself like a spiny urchin, both hands crammed between her legs, clasping her silver prick, ready for the touch of a hand or worse upon her rump. But she spent every night unmolested, and began, little by little, to trust; to learn names and make friends. She became acquainted with Southcott, a bearded fellow as merry as Falstaff; Hall, a blond, blue-eyed cherub as young as she; Book, who looked like a wrestler and had never, he claimed, read a word; and O'Connell, the big black Irishman who had played the fiddle on board *The Truth and Daylight*. She befriended, too, fellows by the name of Wareham, Swinney, Rolf, Noyes, Crook, Page and Dallenger. She passed the time of day with Kennedy, Lancaster and Farrant, and took a drink with Gibson, Laverack and Morgan, the one Welshman in their company. But one name she never learned was the Christian name of Captain Ross; he never owned it, nor did anyone seem to know it. He was Ross to all his men, or just 'the captain', and as all the men seemed to love and respect him, she kept her opinions to herself.

Instead she listened eagerly to those who had been in battle before, in the Low Countries, where the Hollanders lived, and listened fascinated to stories of boggy wetlands where the water lay in vast planes like dropped mirrors, and foot soldiers trekked from Schellenberg to Maastricht to Bruges without ever engaging with the enemy or knowing the comfort of dry feet. 'My boots were waterlogged,' said Southcott, 'from one year's end to the next.'

'And what was the purpose of the campaign?' asked Kit. 'Who was fighting?'

But no one seemed to know, any more than they knew where they were going now, just that there was some great coil involving France and Spain, in which England had somehow become entangled. Kit was not alone in her ignorance.

Although the year was well into autumn and it was cold in the morning and at night, the sun shone relentlessly down upon the dragoons drilling in the courtyard of the Palazzo Reale for every day of their training, and by the end of each one Kit was sick of the sight of Captain Ross. She hated his constant instruction, his incessant cool corrections. He had them ride up and down the court until they ached. Kit's tailbone pained her, her teeth rattled in her head from the rising trot and she boiled in her uniform like a kipper in a kettle. Her calloused fingers, wrapped about the reins for hours on end, seemed set into claws. The silver prick, which had once seemed so cool and comfortable against her skin, heated to a hot poker and, when in the saddle, dug into her from all sides. Her head ached from the blinding sun on the marble pavings and her mouth was as dry as a hay barn.

But despite all these discomforts Captain Ross was a stickler for a smart appearance; they rode all day in the burning sun, but sweat stains were unacceptable. They rode on a clay gravel, and yet dusty boots could not be seen. Every button must be polished, and as she spat on hers every night and worked them with a scrap of leather she imagined she was spitting at Ross, right in his handsome face. At night when she punched her flea-ridden tick mattress and bolster she pictured herself pummelling his lean body. She hated Ross, *hated* him. And once the lamps were blown, and she was alone with the dark and her thoughts, she was glad to hate him, for then she did not have to entertain her most disloyal and secret of thoughts: that he was the best-made man she had seen in her life. She screwed her eyes tight shut and tried to conjure up the green eyes and brown hair of Richard Walsh, instead of the black hair and blue eyes of Captain Ross.

The only man in the company – besides Ross – whom she really disliked was Sergeant Taylor, who had begun their acquaintance by cuffing her over a musket barrel, and seemed disinclined to make amends as the days marched on. Taylor was a brutal, broken-nosed man; fate had knocked him in at the edges like a cheap kettle. Everything about him was blunt – his features, his teeth, his manner. His repeated boast was that he was once the Duke of Marlborough's footman – Kit could only think that the duke had promoted him, not upon his merits, but to get him out of his household. Taylor was a stickler, he never smiled, he cuffed the men about the head and face, and Kit became used to his blows if she rested her musket on the wrong shoulder or turned her mare's head the wrong way. Taylor seemed to have chosen Kit as his particular target, perhaps because she was the youngest of the recruits. Or perhaps because, alone among the men, she shared the same striking red hair as Taylor; but where Kit was slim and lithe, Taylor was a barrel of a man, square and ugly in appearance and manner. Kit soon learned to avoid – as much as she could – his evil little eye.

Ross worked hard to ensure that each man caught up with the lessons that had gone before, until they were a perfectly drilled troop numbering over a hundred. The muscles Kit had discovered aboard ship grew and hardened, and she was glad of the new, more generous coat. She had always been good with a sword, and now she was a decent shot and had learned the little ways of her gun – that it kicked like a mule, that the hammer always stuck after reload, that the shot veered to the left, that she must ram four times not three – and if she could remember all these things she might just stay alive. By the day they were ready to ride, she was ready to fight.

On the dawn of their seventh day Ross addressed them all in

the courtyard. 'No man of mine shall be ignorant of his orders,' he declared. They were to ride to a place in the mountains called Rovereto, many leagues away, to join Captain Tichborne's company of foot and the other English forces, and begin their campaign. Kit's heart beat painfully beneath her blue facings. Richard was with Tichborne's company. *Day seventy without you – I'm coming, my love.*

Sun up and orders given, Ross instructed them to see the quartermaster for their rations. Kit staggered under the weight of the panniers she was given, stuffed with pemmican and biscuits and tobacco, and could barely lift them to drape them across the now obedient Flint's neck. On the command the troop rode forth on the grey horses that gave the regiment its name.

Chapter 7

I neither will take it from spalpeen or brat . . .

'Arthur McBride' (trad.)

Over the next days and weeks Kit snatched tantalising glances of the country she'd come to save. As she carved each notch on her musket stock, *seventy-two days without Richard, seventy-three*, she felt as if she had ridden right into that green and insubstantial fresco she had glimpsed on the palace wall. Here was some rural fantasy, which lived only in the mind of a long-dead painter, all lands and none.

She would hear distant bells and turn to see, over the tops of plane trees, the gilded domes of infidel cathedrals. Down a sunlit lane she would see the golden pediments of huge stone villas, and between two hills she would see the silvered slice of a many-towered monastery. She was always on the outside, and knew in her heart that some great beauty was being hidden from her. All these citadels seemed impossibly far away, like the places she'd heard about in Maura's tales; Mag Mell or Tir nan Og. Kingdoms whose doors were closed to the common traveller, whose golden keys were to be sought for years or bartered for with all you had. And the peaks she could see on the horizon, rocky teeth that held, somewhere in their stony maw, Richard, trapped like Jonah, were the faraway mountains from the stories, mountains that couldn't be reached however long you journeyed, always on the other side of forests stuffed full of enchantments, or boiling rivers that could not be forded but must be gone around.

It seemed that Captain Ross was acquainted with these rules of folklore, for the dragoons' route was always circuitous, and their progress as discreet as a hundred horse could be. Cities and towns were avoided and Kit began to understand that they might not be welcome here in this country they had come to liberate. They were never billeted on any of the towns or hamlets, but camped in the countryside, in bosky dells or woodland caves. She would hear foreign names passed down from her commanders, as the days and nights strung together along their path, collecting a string of cities: Parma, Guastalla, Mantova. All seemed peaceful, green and tranquil, the sun always shone, there was no boom of cannon or cries of combat. Kit was reminded of the soldiers' tales of trooping up and down the sodden Low Countries without ever engaging with the enemy. She found it hard to believe in the war, hard to be afraid.

She began to believe in the place called Mantova. The dragoons had been told that they could expect a bed that night for they would be welcomed through the gates, at last, of that great city, and indeed, they emerged from a dark and twisted forest to see a calm jade lake, with a distant palace set upon it like a diadem. But there was something amiss – black smoke rose from the towers in plumes. Captain Ross raised one gloved hand to halt them. 'Back,' he hissed, 'back under tree cover.' He wheeled his horse around; his mare reared and turned. 'The French have beaten us here.'

There was nothing to do but wait for dark. The dragoons dismounted, tethered their horses and settled in the wildwood. There was to be no talking so many slept; but Kit sat, heart thudding, under twisted black branches as the light died and the mosquitoes came out to feast. What was happening in the city? Across the lake and by some trick of the water she could hear muffled cries, the crackle of a blaze and the screams of falling timber. From the blasted windows of the castle she could see fiery figures falling, to break the surface of the lake. Flint, who had become fond of her mistress, nibbled her shoulder consolingly, but Kit stared fixedly ahead. The French had forced entry to Mantova, had rammed and battered and blown the gates in.

At nightfall, when the sky above Mantova had become a saffron glow, and the castle watched them with fiery eyes, Ross and his deputies quietly gave the orders to mount. Silently the horsemen filed from the undergrowth. Kit's moon was there again, shining as if nothing was amiss, and as they walked the greys around the frill of the lake Kit looked down to the water and caught what she thought was a reflection in the corner of her eye, a brave red coat and a white blob for a face. She turned her head and looked more closely. What she saw there made her throw her leg over the pommel and slide to the ground. She waded into the shallows and dragged at the body, impossibly heavy and waterlogged. The effort made her fall back and sit heavily on the shingle. A tall shadow fell over them, and Ross's voice spoke above her. 'Mount your horse, Walsh,' he said, not unkindly. 'He's long gone.' For a moment she could not move. She sat on the hard, wet stones of the foreshore, breathing heavily, looking at the white, water-softened flesh, the open eyes translucent as the pebbles, the sodden uniform so like her own. 'Walsh,' said Ross, with an edge to his voice. 'I order you. Would you endanger us all?'

As they rode on, Kit saw many more bodies – some half in, half out of the water, some in a grisly swirl of blood, some missing limbs or eyes. She forced herself to turn away, to breathe in the night, and to look towards Richard's mountains and the jagged line of moonlit silver dawn that described their peaks.

She thought about those bodies all night, and the first man, the man she'd held. She'd recognised him. They'd been on *The Truth and Daylight* together, vomited from the storm, pissed down the heads, eaten the same maggoty biscuits. And because he'd not caught the eye of the Marshal de Pisare, because he'd marched a week ahead, he'd met the French and his death. He was chaff, as she was wheat. Kit thanked the Virgin – not Mary mother of God, but the wooden Virgin of Genova – that Richard was farther in and farther up and in the mountains.

As they progressed into the lakes and then to the mountains, the fairytale landscape took on the dark hellish shadows of conflict. Now the ugly face of war leered at her from all sides. As they rode, Kit saw burning villages, homeless, grubby families wandering the roads, who, upon meeting the dragoons, would bleat 'pane, pane' in unison like so many goats. They would stare with eyes blank with hunger, and hold out their hands in pleading supplication. Kit did not understand this word she heard so often, until Ross ordered the bannermen to give out the crusts from the bread wagons. These crusts, so hard they would break teeth, were devoured at once; and members of the same family would fight each other for the privilege of eating them. Again, Kit learned to turn her eyes away.

At sundown they reached the town of Villafranca. 'City of the French,' translated Ross grimly. 'I hope we beat them here.' But the first coats they glimpsed in the town were red. The better part of Gardiner's company of foot from The Truth and Daylight had scattered themselves about the little town under the lengthening shadow of a crenellated red castle. As the dragoons rode up the main thoroughfare, they saw the windows and doors of the houses pushed open, with painted women lolling from the casements. One foot soldier stood against a wall with his whore, locked in an embrace like mating curs. Another openly fondled a woman's naked breasts. Kit glanced at her commander but Captain Ross held his tongue, the muscles of his jaw quilting with the effort of silence. Gardiner's men were carousing as if the day had been won; but their celebrations seemed curiously joyless. Ross kept his peace until they happened upon several foot soldiers drunk and wearing half a uniform. Ross stopped three of them in the street by merely holding up his hand; his pristine presence, together with the hundred horse at his back, sobered them abruptly. 'Where's your hat, soldier? And your friend's coat? And this third fellow seems to be missing the full complement of boots. Taylor.' The red-headed sergeant was at his elbow at once. 'Put these men on a charge. You. Where is Lieutenant Gardiner?'

The hatless man, who seemed less jug-bitten than the others, said meekly, 'Directing operations from the castle, Captain.'

Captain Ross nodded curtly. 'Taylor, with me. Also Walsh, Ingoldsby, Irwin.'

Night was falling fast, and the advance party rode swiftly to the castle, skirting the disused moat. A horse stood at the brink of the trench, its lip curled back above yellow teeth, while a dame held it by the head collar, her apron thrown over her head, as if there was something she did not wish to see. A redcoat stood on the high bank, breeches by his ankles, his face working with pleasure, his hands holding the horse's wiry tail high, his loins thrusting at the glossy hindparts.

Ross acted at once. He dismounted and clubbed the man on the back of his head with the stock of his musket, dropping him to the ground. 'Taylor,' he said over his shoulder, 'when this man awakens he should find himself in irons.' Then, without hesitation, he shot the horse through the temple, took a purse from his belt and handed the money to the dame under the apron. Kit had to use all her skill to stop Flint from bolting at the noise and the sight of the mountain of horseflesh collapsing to the pavings. Ross spurred his mare to the drawbridge and she followed, sick at heart. Maria van Lommen had left this most detestable sin out of her roll call of sexual peccadilloes, and Kit wondered to what hell she had descended.

In the red courts of the castle Ross found Mr Gardiner. The ensign was sprawled drunk at the base of a fountain, his coat open at the throat and one sleeve in the water. When he saw Captain Ross he lifted his hand out of the water and fluttered it at him, in a half-wave, raining droplets on his breeches. 'We met the French at Mantova,' he slurred. 'They've taken the city. Made . . . made a mess of us.'

This was perhaps more of a shock to Kit than anything she'd seen – chilly, correct Mr Gardiner, who had been so insistent about decorum and cleanliness the day after the storm, could hardly stand. Kit formed, in that moment, a grudging respect for Captain Ross, standing tall and scornful, buttoned and buckled, eyes blazing, mouth hard. 'Where is the marquis?' Ross demanded.

'Within.' Gardiner waved towards the castle keep. 'He is writing letters to command – to get us out of this. We are riding to the grave.'

Ross cast a quick look at the trinity of dragoons behind him. 'Silence,' he hissed. 'Where is Tichborne stationed?'

'Above Rovereto.'

'Then we shall ride ahead. We do not care to share your billet.'

'Drink to the regiment before you go?' Gardiner raised his other hand, which held a bottle, and shook it enticingly at Ross in the manner of a nurse showing a babe its milk.

Kit could see that Ross would rather choke – but since his regiment's name had been invoked he could not demur; he barely touched the flask to his lips before handing it back. 'The queen,' he said.

Gardiner doubled up with laughter. 'The queen!' He laughed harder, as if it was the best jape he had ever heard. 'The queen!' and he collapsed backwards, completely immersing himself in the fountain, still laughing. Kit wheeled her horse and followed Ross through the gatehouse, wondering what Gardiner could have seen in the space of a fortnight that changed him so.

Ross emerged with a face of stone from a very short conference with the marquis, and led his hundred horse right out of the town without a word. Kit took pride that the Scots Greys were a breed apart; that they would not share a billet with Gardiner's disgraced men; that they were a cut above. Her one regret was the fare they might have enjoyed in Villafranca; the food in camp was no better than shipboard fare, and all of it dried for being on the road. There was no leisure to hunt and kill and cook, and Kit's stomach grumbled for fresh meat. Oh, for a tender haunch, roasting and dripping and crackling! The venison mess in Maria's house seemed very far away.

And so the Scots Greys rode on, day after day, and at some point in those weeks on the road Kit became one with her horse. She merely had to turn her shoulders in the direction she wanted to go for this will to be directed to Flint. The mare would stand still for mount and dismount, flick her ears backward when Kit talked to her on the road, and nuzzle the buttons of Kit's coat, huffing and blowing and whickering with friendship. And Flint was no longer her only friend; the dragoons now knew her well enough to tease her – and she felt the balm of their teasing, for she knew it was a hand of friendship. Mr Morgan, the Welshman, was teased about his accent; Mr O'Connell, who was missing a tooth and made a whistling sound when he spoke, was called Whistler. Kit, who was ever twitted for her whiskerless cheeks and full lips, was called 'the pretty dragoon'. It meant she belonged. Pretty she could leave aside; what she loved was that she was called a dragoon. But she took warning, too, in the name; and determined there and then that she should conceal her true age – as a girl she might look twenty, but as a boy with no whiskers on his cheek she elected that she would lose four years and claimed thereafter to be sixteen.

Growing up, she had felt a pride in being called pretty; but now she had new pleasures. She loved the long lean muscles in her legs and arms, she loved the calluses on her hands where she grasped the reins, she loved that her formerly soft white thighs were now as firm as marble and that her legs and seat no longer ached after a day's ride. She had not seen her reflection since the silversmith's house, but she knew she was certainly changing. She knew her hair was growing for her fringe fell in her eyes – there was nothing she could do about it on the road, but she pushed the heavy red locks to the side, and crammed them under her tricorn to keep them out of her eyes. Her back hair she sheared off, now and again, with her bayonet. She didn't care if it curled unevenly, she just couldn't afford for her creeping locks to steal down her collar and give her away. Even when trimmed, she wore the lengths in a pigtail down her back, greased with wax to darken the colour, and tied with twine into a neat queue. Ross, whose dark hair had also grown in a month on the road, did likewise, but with a velvet ribbon as his one remaining concession to vanity.

After many days' ride, Kit noticed that the ground began to rise and the terrain about her changed. The flat lands had boiled and risen into looming peaks which looked fit to topple and crush them all. Vertiginous valleys cleft through the rock, and clustered villages and little onion-spired churches clung to the lofty summits. The slopes were hard on the horses and the dragoons made less and less progress every day.

One morning, just after dawn, they made their way through a deep gorge. All was silent as the new sun peeped over the high crags, and Kit felt a prickle on the back of her neck, a heightened awareness and an unshakeable feeling that they were being watched. She gazed up at the heights with awe and dread and fear suddenly throttled her. If the enemy was waiting and watching to fall upon them they were lobsters in a pot, for there was only one entrance to the gorge and no possibility of escape up the steep verges. The valley was too quiet, the sun stealing down the scree until their stony path was illuminated. But no birds sang, no creatures were warmed awake to scuttle underfoot. Ross looked about him constantly, alert and watchful. The gentle chatter of the men seemed too loud in this eerie place and Ross called for quiet. Kit looked up sharply as the Scots Greys fell silent. Ross pressed his grey onwards in haste to be gone from this place. Kit kept her eyes fixed on her commander – no matter how much she disliked Ross's arrogance, she trusted his instincts.

But Flint was of a different mind; the mare reared suddenly and without warning, nearly knocking Kit from the saddle. Kit slapped her smartly with the folded reins, but the mare reared again and turned in a circle, blocking the mounts behind her. Kit pulled savagely on the reins, then realised that the mare was genuinely unsettled. Ross turned back, exasperated. 'If you're having trouble with your nag, Walsh, dismount and lead her. I've no wish to linger here.'

Kit slid from the saddle, gentling the mare with a hand to the velvet neck. The nap of Flint's coat was on end, prickling with fear. Kit slipped the reins over the mare's head and led her forward; but when the horse reached a certain thorny bush she would move no further.

'Come *on*,' barked Sergeant Taylor, from the vanguard; but Kit had seen something in the bush. She dropped Flint's reins, went to the bush and parted the thorns, dreading what she might see. She could never have predicted what nestled there.

It was a baby, so small as to be almost newborn, and curled up asleep in the branches. 'Mother Mary,' she breathed.

Ross rode back. 'What's amiss?'

She leaned in and regarded the child; so small and sweet and soft. It seemed a pity to disturb such a peaceful sleep but the child was not swaddled and the dawn had the nip of approaching autumn. She had seen a church at the head of the valley – perhaps a priest could take the foundling. She poked the babe gently with one finger.

It was cold. With a rush of chill horror, she drew the child out. A grisly cord clung to its distended little stomach, and its back was covered in scratches from the thorns of the bush. It was quite, quite dead. Unable to speak, she held the child aloft. Ross stopped in his tracks; some of the men crossed themselves. Before the captain could gather himself to speak there was a shout from the van and the rear almost simultaneously. 'Captain Ross, there's another one here.'

'And here.'

The second child was halfway up the scree – too high, it seemed, to have bothered the passing horses. The other was ahead of them, right in the middle of the path.

Ross shortened his reins. 'Dismount,' he ordered grimly. 'Fan out, and search the valley top to bottom.'

They found five in the end, two girls and three boys; all newborns, all naked. They had not lived long enough to be dressed. No one had cared enough to swaddle them, or to push little limbs into fondly knitted sleeves. The dragoons laid them tenderly in a little sorry row. Some, like the child in the bush, seemed untouched – two were battered and bruised and one had his little head stove in.

'Dropped from above,' said Taylor, and Ross nodded curtly. Kit looked up to the crags, to the little onion church. Who would cast a child from a mountain? And why? She looked at Ross, but he said, 'Dig five graves, deep enough to be safe from animals, away from the path where they may rest in peace.'

Taylor spoke, not noticeably diffident or respectful. 'Sir, we should rather go. We may be overlooked from the peaks, and they're only babes.'

Ross rounded on him, his eyes very blue in a ghost-white face. 'Bury them. And that is an order.'

The bells of the onion church had tolled eight times before the babes had been committed to the ground. Captain Ross dismounted and sat on a nearby outcrop, knife in hand, savagely whittling sticks. Kit laid the child she had found in its grave herself.

She ran her finger tenderly down the tiny nose. Then she covered it up gently in a dark blanket of earth, as if she was tucking it into its cradle. She felt numb. Nothing in her training had prepared her for this. She knew that she might be called upon to fight, and would do it too, in order to reach Richard. She would scythe down grown men like grasses if need be, grown men with beards on their faces and the free will to enlist. But could the French really be making war on children? *The Gravediggers*, she thought, the common name for Kavanagh's pub. Now she had turned gravedigger too.

As the last sod of the five graves was in place, Ross stood and buttoned his jacket. 'Fall in,' he commanded. 'Stand to attention. Coats on, hats in hand.'

The Scots Greys obeyed, and watched as Ross placed the five little crosses he'd been whittling into the mounds. Taylor tutted under his breath. Ross stood, his face unreadable.

'*Behold, children are a gift of the Lord,*' he intoned, his voice ringing about the valley. '*The fruit of the womb is a reward. Like arrows in the hand of a warrior, so are the children of one's youth. How blessed is the man whose quiver is full of them; they will not be ashamed when they speak with their enemies in the gate. Amen.*'

All but Taylor said the Amen, and mounted upon Ross's order. No one, now, needed to be told to be silent. Ross rode ahead, still white as paper, his dark brows drawn together, his lips pinched to a tight line. No man dared speak to him until the valley of the foundlings was many leagues behind them.

Kit was shaken by the grisly discovery. The babies haunted her, and in the night, when she was dropping, half asleep in the saddle, their little forms, insubstantial and glowing, seemed to follow her. They would circle her drooping head, plump and bewinged like church-wall cherubs. By day, the babes were gone, and Kit straightened up. If she could be a man in her heart like the others, then she could ride on and leave the babies behind. If she could be a man in her mind, she would not mourn for the last breath of another fellow's child. It would not trouble her that the mountain blackthorns had pierced the infant flesh, like Christ's thorns, Crucifixion and Nativity cruelly compressed.

She could tell herself such things, but Ross gave them the lie. This perfect soldier, the kind of fellow they sang about in ballads, *cap-a-pie* in his appearance as if he'd stepped from the page of the chapbooks they sold on street corners, was more affected by the valley of the foundlings than anyone else. For days he seemed dazed with shock, his blue eyes glazed, his manner irritable.

Ross had barely blinked when they'd found a lake full of soldiers in Mantova, but for those tiny unshriven souls he had risked a hundred lives, tarried in a place of danger and spent a brace of hours making sure the children had their proper respects. Ross, single-handedly, had taught her that emotions, deep and searing, did not just live in the female heart, but were a male province too. Kit began to watch him, and once she had started, she could not stop.

Chapter 8

And a crown in the bargain for to kick up the dust . . .

'Arthur McBride' (trad.)

Under Captain Ross's command the dragoons wanted to be better soldiers. In his company they stood a little straighter, spoke a little louder, rode a little harder. Ross himself never raised his voice but expected his orders to be followed without question. Every day they heard his common phrase – 'No man of mine'. 'No man of mine rides without a hat.' 'No man of mine is ignorant of how to light a fire.' And once, when Kit forgot to doff her hat to a passing goodwife, 'No man of mine neglects to salute a lady.'

No one minded these corrections, or that they were couched in terms of ownership. The dragoons were Ross's men, and proud to be so – to be numbered among the Scots Greys was a badge of honour. He would speak of the red coat reverently, as if it was a mantle of office as worthy as a judge's robes or a bishop's cope. When in uniform they must act at all times in a manner that did honour to their coat. That humble red felt was the queen's cloth, and it bound them to each other, close as brothers. Ross's devotion to his men was clear; they were his charges and his family and he loved them. Kit could see, now that she chose to see, that they loved him back. She admitted too what she had always known since he had pushed them into the brine, that he was amusing – he did not enjoy vulgarity but would take pleasure in japes and sallies, and his own taste in wit ran to clever wordplay or the ridiculousness of the human condition. She never once heard Captain Ross swear; 'I leave,' he would say, 'Billingsgate language to women and cowards.' Kit did not know where Billingsgate was, but she certainly knew the sort of language to which he referred, and was embarrassed to think that she had begun their acquaintance by spitting such words in his face. Ross managed to convey, without expressing it in so many words, that such language was good enough for the company of foot, but not quite the thing for the dragoons. And so Kit's language, which had plunged to the very depths since her education at sea, began to elevate itself once more. She still swore, but less frequently and violently, and certainly not in her captain's hearing.

Now that she could see Ross in a different light – not as a lofty, entitled English gentleman but as a man to admire – he seemed to warm to her too. He sought her company as they rode – he on his favourite grey Phantom, and she on Flint – and it became a habit with them to ride together. Kit recognised that he was taking the trouble to educate his greenest, youngest recruit. And it was working. As the days passed, and the calendar of notches on her musket stock grew longer, his speech no longer seemed so clipped and gentlemanly to her, and she knew her own speech had become more like his. Her Dublin brogue was softening and she began enunciating more clearly, finding her vowels shortening, her consonants hardening. Sometimes she caught herself pronouncing something in the English way, and wondered what Richard would say when he saw her again. At nights along the road she would bed down later and later, preferring to stay at the fireside until there were only one or two hardy souls awake with Ross and her, and sometimes, on rare occasions, she would be alone with her captain. At those times it occurred to her, fleetingly, that she would miss his friendship when she was reunited with Richard – she rehearsed the notion of the two men, husband and captain, becoming acquainted; Ross striding into the snug at

Kavanagh's and ordering a jorum of port. But she dismissed the fantasy almost at once; the two men would have nothing whatever to say to one another.

Once Ross asked her about the marks on her gun. The stock was now stippled with notches, tallied with four and one across, like miniature versions of the gates on her father's farm. Kit thought for a moment. 'They mark how many days since I began my journey,' she replied with perfect truth. And indeed, her life without Richard was quite a different path to the one she had trodden before. She journeyed with Ross through entirely unfamiliar terrain. She acknowledged that Ross could tell her things that Richard could not. She enjoyed the captain's society, not just for the balm of friendship, but also for the fact that he was a man of information. Ross was a man of possibilities, he had travelled widely for one so young, and been promoted far beyond his years. He was a man who could be described in that one tantalising word that she'd always loved; that wonderful, troublesome word that had brought her here. He was a man of Adventure.

It was Ross who enlightened her on the whole business of the war. They were sitting by the fireside, their seventh night in the mountains, a week since they'd found the children. She and Ross sat awake the longest, long after the other dragoons had wrapped themselves in their blankets, watching the dying of the fire. Ross did not, for once, seem inclined to talk, but Kit was anxious for news. They had climbed a steep gradient all week, ever since the valley of the foundlings, and she knew that the higher she climbed the nearer she came to Richard. 'Are we near to Rovereto, where Captain Tichborne awaits?'

He raised his eyes as if it were an effort. 'We should reach there tomorrow, or the next day, perhaps – we are very near the Imperial borders.' He sounded tired, but Kit would not be discouraged. 'Have you fought in many lands, sir?'

'Too many,' said he. 'And after a time they begin to resemble one another. But I learned very quickly that everywhere has a horizon – ride towards that before the enemy gets you, and you'll be all right.'

She digested this. 'You said we approached the boundaries of an empire. Do we then leave Spain for Imperial lands?'

He sat up straight, his brows drawn together. 'Spain? What do you mean?'

'Well – if we are reaching a mountain border, have Tichborne's regiment already left Spain?'

Ross clasped his hands together. 'Let me properly understand you. You are asking me if we are about to leave Spain?'

Kit's voice was small. 'Yes.'

He laughed, throwing back his head, and the dragoon nearest him grunted and shifted in sleep. She felt a little uneasy and foolish, but was glad to see him laugh, for he had not even smiled since they found the babes. He wiped his eyes and shook his head. 'Christ, boy, you think we've been in Spain all this time? Since Genova? You think those great cities, Genova, Mantova, Villafranca, that they are in Spain?'

She shrugged unhappily. 'Is not Parma in Spain? I could've sworn . . . someone said the name in an alehouse once . . .'

'Well, you've bested me there, Mr Walsh. Palma is in Spain. Parma is in Lombardy.' Kit, who didn't know the difference, held her tongue. A pox on all educated gentlemen.

'And since we are at war with Spain, they would have trussed us like chickens and snapped our necks had we landed at Palma.'

'Wait.' Kit was confused. 'That is . . . I thought . . . the French . . . do we not fight the French?'

'Aye, them too.'

She ceased to enjoy his mirth, and grew sulky.

'Forgive me, Walsh.' Ross sobered with an effort, straightening his face. He shuffled forward on his log. 'See here – what's your given name?'

'Christian, sir, but most folk call me Kit.'

'See here, Kit. A young fellow like you should have *some* grasp of the rudiments of geography. Didn't you have any schooling?'

Kit thought of Aunt Maura, kindly, laboriously teaching her her letters, telling her stories, doing her best. For a girl who thought she would never leave Dublin, it had seemed more than adequate. Now she realised that she knew more of mythical kingdoms than real ones. Tir Nan Og disappeared, abruptly, into golden dust. 'Not enough.'

'Well, I had too much. And no man of mine shall enter into battle without knowing why he fights, or *where* he fights.

'Look . . .' He threw back his blanket and cast about for a stick, his face animated, a different man to the one he had been. He kicked stones and clods away, clearing an area of smooth mud, and began to draw with the point of the stick. He drew, first, an outline that looked for all the world like one of her own boots. 'Here,' he said, 'is a collection of states that shares a common language. At the top, here' – he drew a cross at the top left of the boot – 'is Genova, which is in Liguria. Then we crossed to Lombardy, skirting the city of Milan, for the Duchy of Milan is now controlled by the Spanish, and Mantova, as you saw, has been taken by the French. Then we crossed the Veneto, where we met Gardiner's company in Villafranca, and we are now in Savoy, heading to Rovereto in the Tirol.' He drew smaller blobs moving up the boot. 'This,' he drew a larger block at the top of the boot, 'is the Habsburg Empire, whose frontiers we now approach. Here is France,' he drew a star-shaped nation, 'and her neighbour, and ally, Spain.'

Kit concentrated on the map, trying to memorise the borders, appreciating now just how wrong she had been.

'Well. Earlier this year, King Carlos of Spain, the second of his name, died. He was so deformed that he was known as "The Bewitched" and the particular deformities of his body, coupled with his dreadful appearance, prevented him from providing Spain with an heir. Crucially, he was the last Habsburg king of Spain. The Habsburgs are . . .'

'. . . The family of the Emperor,' broke in Kit, anxious to redeem herself.

'Precisely.' Ross paced around his map with his stick under his arm. 'So: Carlos, a Habsburg, dies without an heir. Leopold I, Holy Roman Emperor, naturally supposes that he, a Habsburg, will inherit the kingdom.'

Kit nodded. 'Seems fair.'

'Yes – except that before his death Carlos willed the crown of Spain to Philip of Anjou, grandson of Louis XIV, the King of France.' On the mud map he scrubbed out the border between Spain and France with the toe of his boot. 'This would effectively unite the kingdoms of France and Spain under a single crown. Now.' He began to draw again, a map apart, an island across a sea, floating alone, with just a narrow channel of water separating it from the continent. This shape seemed familiar to Kit. 'This is England,' said Ross, 'Wales, Scotland, and,' he glanced at her, 'Ireland.'

She stared at the little clump of mud that was Ireland till her eyes smarted. 'Please,' she said huskily, 'where is Dublin?'

He pressed into the mud with the point of his stick. 'Here.' Kit looked at the little depression – in that muddy little hole lived Kavanagh's, Glasnevin cemetery, the Customs House, the harbour, Patrick's church, the Wicklow mountains, Killcommadan Hill and everything she'd ever known. How small it was, that old world of hers. How insignificant. How important. Her eyes blurred in the firelight and flashed with gold.

Ross continued, unawares. 'Queen Anne of England was unable to tolerate such an outcome. Why?'

Kit tore her gaze away from that dear muddy little hole.

'Why would our queen not wish the throne of Spain to fall to the grandson of the French king?' he pressed.

'Because,' said Kit slowly, 'the nations would be effectively unified. France would have too much power.'

'Exactly. So the queen declared war on France, in support of the pretender Leopold. England has now formed a "Grand Alliance" with the Holy Roman Empire,' he pointed to the great mass right in the middle of the map, 'and Holland . . .' He pointed again, to a smaller coastal country just above it. She looked at Holland with interest – home of Maria van Lommen, site of so many hopeless campaigns. The country clung to the edge of the sea, which perhaps explained why it was waterlogged. 'The wet lands,' she said, anxious to display her single piece of geographical knowledge.

'Indeed,' he said. 'I have damped my own boots there these two years past. So, to recap: the Grand Alliance have pitted their forces against the army of the "Two Crowns", and here we are.'

'So . . .' Kit said carefully: 'France and Spain are fighting with England and the Empire.'

'Yes.'

'But . . .' She frowned, finding her way. 'For the last several weeks, we have seen fighting in lands which belong to neither Spain, nor France, nor the Empire. Why is this boot-shaped region caught up in this coil?'

He pointed the stick at her like a schoolmaster. 'An excellent question. Because,' he sat beside her and pointed at the mud map, 'this region is a crucial counter in the game. Our job is to defend this boot. It is a makeweight. He who takes the peninsula takes the crown. If Louis holds it, he has a buffer between the Empire and France. If England holds it, we can march right through France's back door.'

Kit nodded, slowly. She could see the significance of that oddly shaped piece of land.

'Defend it we will; and to that end the queen herself has sent her finest weapon, John Churchill, 2nd Duke of Marlborough, to lead us.' He spoke the name as if he spoke of Christ himself, with something approaching reverence, and he made a little cross on the map at the edge of the empire of mud. 'We are to meet him here, at Rovereto, and unite our forces.'

'Tichborne too?'

'Us, Tichborne, Gardiner – if he can surface from his fountain. With Savoy's troops too, this will be the biggest defensive force ever deployed.'

'Savoy?'

'Eugene of Savoy, prince of this region, and nephew to Leopold, the Holy Roman Emperor. He has a fearsome army.'

'And now,' she said, 'we are in friendly territory.'

'Yeees,' he said, stretching the syllable out. 'There are pockets of rebels who are against Savoy, and think the prince is trying to make incursions into the other regions of the peninsula. So there may not be friends everywhere. Mantova, as you witnessed, is under French control. Every day we must be on our guard. Our friends may not make themselves known, but our enemies doubtless will.' He crouched before her and took her by the shoulders, giving her a little shake as if she slept. 'We are riding to make history, Kit.' Her eyes met his, and she could see tiny campfires burning in them; sparks of excitement.

He stood abruptly. 'Now, to bed, we must be rested and ready.'

'Sir?'

He turned. 'Yes, Kit?'

'One more question.'

'Yes?' He looked so animated that she was reluctant to raise the issue. But she had to know.

'The babes – were they part of the war?'

She saw it at once, the veil descended on his face. 'In a sense.'

'Forgive me . . . in what sense? Where did they come from?'

Ross sighed, sat. He looked at her with something approaching affection. 'You are really just a boy, aren't you? How old?'

Kit remembered. 'Sixteen, sir.'

He nodded. 'No father to tell you such things?'

'He died, sir. In the Williamite war. This is his sword I wear.' She shifted to show the handle, and he touched it with one fingertip. 'Wear it with pride.'

'Oh, I do.'

He clasped his hands together on his knees and looked into the fire. 'Those babes were sons and daughters of soldiers too. But not true born. They are the bastards of the regiment.'

'But . . . We've only just arrived.'

'*We* have. But there's been trouble here on the border with the Empire for years. Eugene of Savoy's troops are all but stationed here. When they don't fight, they are bored. The women are . . . raped by the soldiers, and they cannot keep the children.'

'Why?'

Ross seemed discomfited. '*I* don't know, Kit. They are married, or they cannot afford their keep, or the child would show them to be impure, and prevent them finding a husband. Many reasons.'

Kit digested this in silence. Ross, settling by the fire once more, was clearly unwilling to discuss the subject further. She answered his distant goodnight, and rolled herself in the horse blanket, which smelled comfortingly of Flint.

She settled down and watched the fire through half-closed eyes. She heard again Ross's voice softly talking. A deformed king, an empty throne, seven kingdoms at swords drawn. It sounded like one of Maura's stories, but this tale was true. She saw in the flames the map of Europe, rendered in gold, on fire; the flames spreading to each region until the continent was a raging conflagration; and the babes and she and Richard and Ross were all in the middle of it.

Chapter 9

Where we would be shot without warning . . .

'Arthur McBride' (trad.)

As the dragoons travelled ever upwards, the cold and ice descended like a bride's veil.

'We've ridden into winter,' Kit remarked to the dragoon beside her, a gloomy young man called Ingoldsby.

Ingoldsby shrugged his head right down into his shoulders, tucking down his chin. 'It's always winter in the mountains.' Frost laced the tough mountain grass, snow eagles circled above. 'Waiting for someone to die,' said Mr Ingoldsby. The cold wreathed their lungs, pinched their cheeks, froze their extremities. Kit's fingers and toes seemed strange to her – as if they belonged to someone else. Each inhalation was raw; her lips were thick and slow and dumb, her ears a burning numbness, her fingers smarting. Her breath smoked like clouds of incense.

Captain Ross explained as they rode that it was Eugene of Savoy who had commanded that the Alliance forces gather covertly using obscure mountain passes. And so they were climbing in the hurting cold, and winter, as if to mitigate her harshness, showed off her great beauty. Even the constant aching discomfort of the cold could not blind Kit to pine trees rimed with crystals and impossibly high white cataracts frozen into folds like candle grease. The dragoons climbed the steep valley, not by a rocky pass or goat road, but a miraculous stone staircase cut into the mountain and known as the Six Hundred Steps. There was a monastery at the head of it with a welcoming cross set upon its finial, a monastery which they had to reach by nightfall or freeze. They would billet themselves on the good monks for the night, whether they were welcome or no. The steps were broad enough, barely, for four feet of a horse to stand upon, but their breadth and gradient made the climb arduous for the greys, and anxious for the riders, for a mere stumble could pitch both horse and dragoon to the foot of the ravine. Kit kept her eyes on the stairs, lengthening and shortening Flint's stride to fit each step, but now and again flicked her gaze to the monastery above, a miraculous structure which seemed to be cut out of one piece into the very rock of the mountain itself. The lowering sun turned the humble hermitage into a place of gold, and cut deep black shadows beneath the staircase. Weary and freezing, Kit counted fifty steps, before losing count. For every step thereafter she cursed instead, with her precious new vocabulary, the unknown prince of Savoy.

Ross caught her up on the stone stairs. The ground was now too hard for Ross to draw his maps for Kit, but he still took pains to explain matters to her. 'The prince of Savoy is a master strategist,' he said, as they rode side by side up the steps. 'He is making evident plans to descend on the French via Brescia and the Adige. But in reality, his and Marlborough's forces are amassing covertly at Rovereto, using obscure passes like this one. Some of these ways have not been used for centuries – this one has not been used since Charles V was Emperor.' Kit did not know when this was, but the way Ross said the name it sounded like a long time ago. 'Of course, this means we must be alert to French outriders and spies.'

Kit nodded and tucked her chin into the flimsy comforter which covered the lower part of her face. Her heavy felted uniform felt as thin as onion paper. Outriders and spies seemed as nothing to the creeping cold, a shapeshifting and insubstantial enemy: a stalking horse whose ribs you could number, a skinny grey she-wolf watching from the ravine with bleak and ravenous eyes, the white raptors wheeling watchfully above, the grey creeping spectre of a hermit collecting wood with white hands like jointed spiders. The cold was all these things; it was everywhere, watching behind every tree and in the very air, rolling over every ridge, an ever-present and, it seemed, much more tangible threat than the French. But she was so numb she could not seem to care; her crystallised lashes closed in such a welcome sleep that when the shooting started she was almost too stupid with cold to know what was happening.

Her mind, snail-slow, told her that it was the crack of a whip; that one of the dragoons had had to lash his mount up the steep pass. The whipcrack rang out, the sound bouncing from both sides of the valley. Flint knew something was amiss before she; the mare reared and Kit had to cling to her saddle – but her efforts were wasted because as soon as she had settled the mare Ross pulled her roughly from the saddle.

Ingoldsby began to panic as the rest of the dragoons hit the frozen stone. He ran back down the stairs, jinking and checking like a coney, but the next blast lifted him clear off his feet. Kit could see he was hit, and he dropped and lay twitching like game. She crawled to him on her elbows and raised his head for him, for he could not. It was an easy task, for the back half of it was gone. Still he tried to say something; but when he opened his mouth he spoke only blood. It poured down his front; carmined his jacket and turned his buttons to rubies. Kit felt herself being pulled away, the hot jellied mess of brains on her hands steaming in the cold. All she could think was that her hands were warm for the first time that day.

More shots rang out from above. They seemed to be coming from the monastery. She was now deaf to the musket shots but could still hear them in her ribs. Her bones seemed to have turned to rope, but she stumbled up the stairs with the rest, leading their horses, panting noiselessly like seeker hounds.

Silence fell, as threatening as the barrage before.

Ross, ducking under his horse's belly, grabbed Sergeant Taylor by the shoulder. 'Do we sound the retreat, sir?' hissed Taylor through his broken teeth.

'There's nowhere to go,' Ross whispered back. 'We're wide open, they'll make marchpane of us. We must storm the monastery. Command the trumpeter.'

Taylor, his disdain for this idea written on his blunt features, forgot to salute and ran down the stair to the trumpeter. The bittersweet song sounded the attack, the blaring notes bouncing off the rocks. But through the melee the training of the Scots Greys showed through – all the dragoons stalked behind their horses, using the meaty flanks to protect them. The batteries began to play the 29th, and every tenth man took charge of ten horses and the remaining dragoons streamed up the stone stairs.

Kit, numb with shock as well as cold, was one of the first to the gatehouse and one of the first to apply her partisan to the studded door; carried forth on a wave, not knowing what she did. From the sheer weight of the battering soldiers and clamouring muskets the door gave way and Kit found herself in an inner courtyard. Cowled figures ran about everywhere, hay swirled in the air like snow, and chickens rose to the skies to be felled by nervy muskets. Kit was shoved bodily behind a tower of barrels, and she breathed hard as she raised her musket. Cheek along barrel; aim. Pull back matchlock; click. Lift cheek, fire. She felled, with her first shot, a musket-wielding monk, and was as surprised as he was. Strip, lower, reload, ram. A cowled monk ran towards her, holding an axe high like an executioner. But her matchlock had jammed from the cold. She spat and rubbed, the monk grew bigger, loomed. Then a sword protruded from his chest and the axe dropped, useless, to the ground.

'Use your blade, Kit,' Ross bellowed, dragging his sword from the monk. 'You may trust that, at least.' She dropped the musket and drew her father's sword. The next few moments – hours –

were a blur. She fought, hand to hand, not knowing how many she felled, until she began to tire and slip and stumble. A blade bit her shoulder. Time collapsed, for the bell of the little tower above bawled out, giving clamour to the mountains, ringing out through the icy air. Even in the melee, its insistent chime rang in Kit's head, and after ten, twenty, fifty strokes, she understood its meaning. A bell always rang for a reason. A soul has passed. There is someone at the door. Time at the bar. Come to mass.

Help us.

She grabbed a bunch of Ross's uniform at the shoulder. 'Sir,' she bellowed. 'We should silence that bell. It is a call for help. There may be more of them in the hills.'

He nodded curtly. 'Do it,' he ordered.

Kit stumbled into the dark stairwell of the bell tower. She leant for one blessed moment of reprieve on the cold stone wall, before she could bring herself to move. As she climbed, she imagined cowled monks streaming from the crags to reinforce their brothers. In the belfry, straw-scattered and blindingly bright, she came upon a monk energetically pulling on the bell rope, the recoil of the cord almost yanking him from his feet. Standing there, unseen and unheard, reeling from the close cacophony, Kit could not stab a monk in the back for ringing a bell. She drew her father's sword and sliced the rope through; the bell fell with a clang on the wooden belfry board. The monk turned, a knife in his hand, dropped the redundant bell rope and swiped at her, slicing her sleeve. After that it was easy. She ran him through, and watched him fall across his bell. She gulped a breath and leaned out of one of the four windows, open to the four winds. Down below, tiny dragoons and monks darted about frantically. She could stay here; hide until it was over. And then she saw Captain Ross. She sheathed her bloody sword, and, mindful of the directive to collect booty, picked up the heavy bell with an effort and staggered back down the stair. At the foot Sergeant Taylor was waiting and wrenched the bell from her arms. 'I'll take that,' he said. 'Worth summat, bell-metal.' The bell made a faint sound as it met the buttons of his coat. Kit opened her mouth to protest, closed it again and ducked past him to re-enter the fray.

But it was all over. Dragoons were dragging the monks into the courtyard, accounting for all bodies. Ross was stripping the cowls from the fallen monks. 'No tonsure,' he said.

'French?' asked Taylor briefly.

'For certain,' said Ross. 'Blue coats.'

'Then what happened to the monks?' asked Kit. No one answered; no one needed to. The ravines were deep; there would have been no need to kill them first.

Only two of the Scots Greys had been killed, as well as poor Ingoldsby at the door. Ross took their names and personal effects, but had their bodies cast down the mountain after the monks. In death, all men were equal.

Taylor, his bell under his arm like a helm, was charged with building a fire. He started the flames with a handful of manuscripts, priceless, beautiful inscriptions, scripture turned to kindling. A cohort of dragoons followed him, with armfuls of scrolls and books. Sickened, she turned away.

Charged with the rest of the dragoons with searching the monastery for firewood, Kit, bloodied and disoriented, found herself alone in a little chapel. From exhaustion more than devotion, she sank to her knees.

Above the little altar was a fresco of a saint, holding up one hand, like St Barnabas holding back the tide; but it was a dragon not an ocean that shrunk under his hand. The creature's smoky breath was subdued, not rising like a cloud but rolling to the ground like morning mist. Bluff, bearded and friendly of face, the saint was benignly plucking a naked child from the dragon's mouth by the ankle. Other babes shrunk behind his robes, a queue of little figures, saved from the painted dragon. The scene took place in a deep green ravine with a blue river at the bottom, and in the jagged mountains above perched a little monastery with a tower and a bell. 'St Columbano' read the golden legend wreathed about the saint's head.

Kit's chapped lips parted. The miracle of the saint and the dragon had happened *here*. Not just on this peninsula, but in this very valley, and the monastery had been founded in the saint's name. Why, then, she wondered, had that saint not saved the babe that she found in the thorn bush, in that very same green valley below? Had St Columbano been sleeping that day? Perhaps he'd been driven away by the French – maybe his spirit had left this place with the monks.

The fresco was not the only treasure in the place, for below the saint stood a chalice on the tabernacle. It was silver and round with a wide cup, and studded with jewels about the brim. It looked as she had always imagined the grail to look in the legends told to her by her father, by Maura. She reached out a finger and flicked the rim with her fingertip. To Kit, the cup sounded an ironic note. The grail was the end of a quest. Her quest to find Richard had barely begun.

'Take it,' said a voice behind her.

She spun, and Ross was in the doorway, Sergeant Taylor at his shoulder like a malign shadow.

'Take it in your hands,' Ross urged. 'It's yours.'

'Christ, you can't give him that!' spluttered Taylor.

'Booty,' said Ross briefly. 'Quite legitimate.'

'But . . . his rank!'

'Irrelevant,' replied Ross. 'We are all equal in rights of plunder. He found it. He keeps it. After all,' he said pointedly, 'you *found* that bell you carry.' The captain's voice hardened to command. 'Fall the men in to the dormitories. We must make camp – we'll reach Rovereto tomorrow.'

Alone again, Kit stood, back to the altar, clutching the chalice.

She felt something rising in her throat that had been begging for expulsion since she had lifted Ingoldsby's broken head. She vomited into the silver grail in a warm gush, then set the thing carefully down, lying down flat on her back on the floor, wiping her mouth, eyes streaming into her ears. She looked at the painted saint above her until her innards had settled, her rancid breath smoking like that of the subdued dragon. Her battle-addled brain could not make sense of the strangeness of the day, of her first battle. Ever since she had buttoned herself into her uniform, she had pictured a grand, sweeping, emerald-green battlefield, with immaculate ranks of soldiers and cavalry clad in chain mail and lined up precisely on the sward. They would to run towards each other at the sound of a trumpet as if in some medieval joust, fighting hand to hand with honour towards a clean bloodless outcome. Instead, her first battle had been a messy scrap bottled up in a stone jar, with musket shot ringing from the walls, monks who were not monks, and the loss of three of their number. Kit got slowly to her feet. She emptied the chalice from the window, through the smashed stained glass, and wiped it out with the tail of her coat. Then she set it back on the tabernacle, where it belonged, and went to join the others, averting her eyes from the burning pyre in the courtyard.

Night had fallen, and the moon shone above them, promising a night frost. The tenth men had led the horses into the church for warmth and shelter, while in the dormitories the Scots Greys took the little truckle beds or the floor. But the dormer windows had been smashed by musket balls and the cold sneaked in. Fingers and toes froze, noses pinched, ears stung; impossible, unbearable to sleep like that. One by one the dragoons dragged their tick mattresses from the cots and crept to the courtyard, to settle down by the fire of priceless manuscripts. Kit curled up in the guilty heat with the rest, and watched the flames lick around the illuminated letters; the gilt shimmering and blackening, a perverse alchemy turning gold to ash.

Chapter 10

And left them for dead in the morning . . .

'Arthur McBride' (trad.)

And the cold did return.

Overnight the first snows had come, and doused the fire to twisted blackened ash. It blanketed the courtyard, and the sleeping dragoons too. The Scots Greys woke in the white dawn, dead eyed and shivering, their uniforms heavy and freezing with snow-fall. Miserable with discomfort, they mounted and began to ride again, ever upwards.

Kit discovered, on that climb, just how many kinds of snow there were. Flint's hooves slipped on packed ice black and hard as iron, crunched into compact crystals of slush, or sank and floundered in insubstantial powder, finer than potato flour.

They climbed until all landmarks were a memory; Kit longed for the clustered villages and the churches with their alpine onion spires. Nature herself was unrecognisable; rocks and trees alike were white formless tumours on the mountainside. As a child she had learned to fear the dark, and the nameless terrors that lurked in the night-time farmyard when she was sent by her mother for a lump of peat or a pail of water. Now she knew that light was far more dreadful. Everywhere was such a blinding, dazzling white that it was painful; once the milky, cold sun was high in the sky she had to pull her tricorn over her streaming eyes. When the men stopped for a piss they would clasp them-selves in two hands, practically urinating through their fingers lest the frost nipped at their most tender parts. Kit had a different problem – her silver prick, hot as a poker in the Genovese sun, now burned her flesh with cold, and her fingers, beneath the skirts of her coat, all but stuck to the frosted metal.

The dragoons rode for hours, hardly speaking, until they had left the monastery of St Columbano far behind. The sun was already high when Ross stopped and took a map from his coat, consulting the truculent Taylor on the whereabouts of the narrow mountain pass down to Rovereto. While the officers consulted, a dark head and a red one bobbing together over the fluttering paper, a shot snapped out, impossible to say from which direction. The company rode hard for a little coppice of white trees and shelter. Southcott had been shot clean through his hand. Safely in the undergrowth he showed Kit the wound in his palm, proud as the Christ. 'C'n see the sun right through it,' he said, as he held the hand high. Sure enough, Kit could see a prick of light through the hole. 'It's hardly bled at all,' she said, comforting.

'Too damn cold,' said Southcott.

'And a good thing too, for we've no surgeon with us,' said Ross. 'He awaits us at Rovereto, for we were not yet to engage. Walsh, tie it up.'

Kit tore the stock from her neck and bandaged the palm. Ross, who was the only one of the company issued with gloves, passed one of them to the injured man and Southcott put it on over the wound.

Ross and Taylor gathered together for another conference, and Kit was near enough to hear the whispered exchange. 'The French are between us and the pass,' Ross murmured to Taylor, beneath his breath. 'There is nowhere to go but up. We must find another way to descend into Rovereto tomorrow, else face another fight.'

Taylor squinted at the lowering sun with his pale little eyes. 'Might mean another night in the cold.'

Ross pursed his lips. 'Then we collect firewood while it is still light. It is as it is.'

That night, round the pale and heatless flames, no songs were sung. O'Connell left his fiddle in his pack, lest it ended up on the fire. When the ashes were cold, the dragoons slept together like a litter of puppies, a tangle of limbs, wary of an exposed foot or hand that might be lost to the frost in the morning.

In the coldest part of the night Ross's arm crept around Kit, and, half asleep, she nestled gratefully into his shoulder, burying her face in his dark fall of hair. Warm at last, she slept through the small hours as if she was in a feather bed.

She came to at dawn a little apart from the pile, cold again, innards twisting with a nameless shame. In those half-lands between sleep and waking she had dreamed of sleeping in Ross's arms. As she woke she plucked a hair from her mouth. It slid between her teeth, oddly intimate, twined about her tongue. She held it before her face, threaded with diamonds of saliva. It was long and dark; his hair. It was as if they had kissed.

The others were yawning and stretching, counting their fingers and toes. No one made comment – no one thought it strange that they had all slept so close – it was life and death, it was necessity. It was the army. But her cheeks burned with cold and shame. The captain too seemed busy himself, making plans for their descent, and she thought he avoided her gaze.

They rode on, trying to forget what had passed in the night. But much later, as they rode down the pass, Ross said, out of the blue, 'You said something, last night, and aroused my . . . curiosity.'

Her pulse in her ears, Kit stared at her chapped hands, clasping Flint's reins. This was it – she was unmasked. In his arms she had whispered something that had given her away.

'That is,' he said hurriedly, 'my *intellectual* curiosity. Forgive me: what is *Virtus Ipsa Suis Firmissima*?'

Kit looked at him, relieved but jolted. She had never heard the words spoken aloud before, yet they transported her instantly home. *Virtus Ipsa Suis Firmissima*: the Latin tag inscribed below the family arms on the sign of Kavanagh's Inn 'It is a motto, a family motto.'

Ross looked at her, his eyes very blue. 'You uttered it in your sleep.' She dropped her eyes.

'Do you know what it means?'

'No. I never learned.' It was true. No one in the alehouse could read Latin, and the meaning, if it was ever known, had been long forgotten.

'It means "Truth relies on its own arms". A good raison for a soldier.' And then he rode on ahead.

Kit, breathing out a smoky breath of relief, fixed her eyes on the view – far away a blue smear of a lake sat in a green valley. And beyond that, over the seas somewhere, a little alehouse where a sign swung in an autumn breeze, the benign cousin of this keen icy wind. A sign that said 'Truth relies on its own arms'. She was glad to know the meaning of her motto, but now the homesickness clasped her heart, colder than the ice mountain. She wanted Richard. She wanted to go home.

But Richard and home were farther away than ever. They marched another day through the white alpine desert, searching hopelessly for the pass, hardly knowing which way was up, which down. Maps were now irrelevant, for the snow had erased all borders. Ross did not know any better than they where, fathoms below their frozen feet, those broken cartographer's lines demarcated Savoy from the Empire. They rode on, wasting the rest of the hours of daylight, and by sunset found themselves back in the coppice where they had looked at Southcott's hand. They made camp as best they could. 'Picket the horses to the trees so they stay on their feet,' Ross commanded. 'For if they lie down they'll freeze.'

His chin was still high, his tones still commanding, but Kit heard a new timbre in them, like the metallic clamour of the bell of the monastery, calling for help. He was lost. His happy youthful confidence, his surefootedness, his unquestioning aura of being born to command, had carried them all forth on this fool's errand – they had followed him in a circle, all day, and now they were at the mercy of the mountain for another killing night. His confidence had got them lost, and the very thing that drew her to him, drew them all to him, and made them follow him unquestioningly through fire and ice and this valley of death, had doomed them to freeze. Too heartily, around their meagre fire, Ross told them of a unit called the Salvatores. 'Eugene of Savoy has instituted a troop of outriders who patrol the mountains looking for approaching regiments and assessing whether they be friend or foe. They will find us and guide us to the muster. Be of good cheer.' She could see him trying to believe it, determined to believe it, as if his confidence and his will alone could conjure an outrider from the drifting smoke.

In her frozen-headed fantasy Kit imagined Richard being just such a one, dressed not in uniform but in the robes of St Columbano, riding to them cheery cheeked and warm of blood, folding her frozen hands in his warm ones, embracing her in the circle of his arms.

Huddled around the pale flames, the dragoons all said the same thing to each other, like a catechism. Kit saw, with a mixture of pride and despair, that they still relied upon Ross; the captain's word was their gospel.

'The Salvatores.'

'Yes, the Salvatores.'

'They will see the fire.'

'They will come tonight.'

'They will come tomorrow.'

'Of *course* they will come.'

One by one they slept, bundled together once more; but Kit, afraid of her sleeping self, stayed awake. The fire died and her head dropped – until, through her half-closed eyes, a flame ignited once again, far below, drew closer, flaring and flickering. A horseman on the path below, the torch he carried lighting him like a link-boy. He wore a red coat.

Kit woke the captain first, and he and all the others stumbled to their feet. 'Muskets to shoulder,' commanded Ross.

Kit, heart thudding, drew behind the tall captain, and took aim at the approaching horsemen with the rest. She was so sure that this was going to be Richard that she began to panic that one of the dragoons would loose a careless musket ball, and kill her husband. But as the outrider came closer, the dragoons lowered their muskets at a word. It was not Richard.

But, curiously, it was someone she recognised. Sure now that she was still dreaming, she waited calmly for the rider to say the name that she knew.

The horseman reined his mount, the horse rearing a little and dancing on the icy path. 'Captain Ross?' he said. 'I am Captain Kavanagh. I am charged to bring you to Captain Tichborne.'

It was Padraic Kavanagh – the cousin she had known as a tow-haired lad who visited the farm, and followed her uniformed father around with dog-eyed admiration, and who, as soon as he was old enough, enlisted for the army. As she mounted Flint and fell in behind Ross, listening to him recount their adventures, with all the wonderful, dangerous confidence back in his voice, she wrestled with a dilemma. Should she reveal herself to Paddy; invoke their childhood friendship and beg his help to find Richard? Or by revealing herself, would she sabotage her own search, having come so far? The choice was taken from her, for Ross's tale had reached the events at the monastery. With the same dread and excitement with which she had watched the approaching rider, she heard him say, '. . . and then Mr Walsh here cut the bell.' She felt Kavanagh's gaze settle upon her, in the light of his torch, and raised her eyes to his face. But the blond captain turned back at once to Ross without a flicker of recognition. 'Well, your Mr Walsh acted wisely, for the dastardly French are stationing many of these clandestine pockets of men in the mountains.'

Kit heard no more. Her cousin had seen her face, and did not know her. She was now truly a different person, not because of her changed clothes, but because of what she had seen on the mountain.

Chapter 11

And now says the sergeant, I'll have no such chat . . .
              'Arthur McBride' (trad.)

As the Scots Grey Dragoons rode into Rovereto, Kit barely noticed the pretty church, or the painted houses with their flowered window boxes. A huge crowd had gathered in the principal square and were baying like a pack of curs.

Ross halted the company while Captain Kavanagh went to seek Captain Tichborne, and Kit scrutinised the hungry, rapacious faces, made ugly and pinched with cold. Some sort of punishment seemed to be taking place.

Beside her, Mr Van-Dedan, a trumpeter who had a smattering of Savoyard, leant from his saddle to converse with a local burgher. He straightened up to tell Kit his findings. 'Vell, Mr Valsh,' he lisped in his Hollander accent. 'It seems that a local lady has committed adultery with a neighbour. She is to be put into a turning stool.'

In the middle of the square a strange contraption sat like a monstrous spinning top. Wrought of wood, the machine looked well used. Before it, like savages dancing before their God, a motley collection of players was gathered and two of their number mimed a variety of the copulatory acts.

At the height of their drama a woman was led from the crowd; she was an ordinary lady of middle years, not notably handsome or voluptuous. She did not look like a strumpet, nor did she look like a dangerous felon, yet she was bound hand and foot and obliged to shuffle forth to her penance. At her appearance the crowd bayed louder, rattling the cookpots and pans they had brought with them. Some struck their vessels with wooden spoons in a deafening kitchen cacophony that would almost have rivalled the battery of the dragoons.

Now a little gate was opened in the railings of the machine, and the lady was pushed inside and forced to sit on a stool. Two burly townsmen began to tug on two heavy hempen ropes, and the round cage began to spin like a child's top. The unfortunate woman gripped the seat of her wooden stool as the heavy grey sky began to snow, tiny flakes falling like ash. She cried out as the contraption began to spin faster and faster, her face thrown against the wooden railings from the force of each turn, her skirts bellying and snapping like sails. She groaned as she emptied her stomach; her vomit spraying about her like a Catherine wheel as the crowd squealed and sprung back in delight. By now the woman had fallen, collapsed between the stool and the railings. Her flesh had a greenish tinge, her skirt was rucked up to show her small-clothes and a shadow of dark hair. One breast had fallen from her bodice. Still she turned, her humiliation complete.

Despite all she had seen in the last several days, Kit almost had to look away. She relived again the night she had spent in Ross's arms; oh yes – it had been innocent and chaste; how could it be otherwise? She had been as close on her left side to another fellow as she had been to Ross on her right, Ross thought she was a boy; and yet, and yet. She, a married woman, had spent the night in another man's embrace, just like this adulteress. Chastened, she swore that she would dedicate her every moment to finding Richard. Eighty days since she last laid eyes on him. It was enough.

Kit turned to Van-Dedan.

'Which is her seducer?'

The trumpeter pointed. 'There he sits.'

The man was a scrawny specimen with thinning hair, who sat

a little distance away, unable to watch, his feet in a pair of stocks and his head in his hands.

Kit snorted. 'He comes off easy.'

She watched as the adulteress was released from the machine, to collapse immediately to the floor. She was gathered up by a group of women from the crowd, who were pelted with rotten vegetables for their pains. Kit refrained from any further comment, for she could see that most of the dragoons considered this good sport.

'Hmmm,' said Van-Dedan, watching the sorry stumbling figure. 'She will not find a husband now.'

'Wait – she is unmarried?'

'Yes. He is the one who is wed.'

'And yet *she* is the adulteress?'

The trumpeter shrugged, his attention elsewhere; Ross was back in the square with Captain Kavanagh and another captain in tow. Kit fixed her eyes on the little man walking in Ross's wake – this must be Captain Tichborne, Richard's commander. Richard was here in Rovereto!

The dragoons rode in a swirl of snow to an ancient covered market with a timbered roof. Ross rode ahead with the officers, and Kit sensed, with a plunging heart, that she had been merely a distraction along the road, in preference to the crude society of Sergeant Taylor. Now better company was at hand. Ross was to dine and sleep with Tichborne, Kavanagh, the errant Gardiner, who, despite his transgressions in Villafranca, had beaten them there, and a new addition to their company.

A field surgeon by the name of Atticus Lambe, lately come from London in the company of the legendary Marlborough himself, stood a little apart – he was a chilly fellow with a young face but silvering hair, a tailcoat of greenish black Shadwell, and pince-nez set upon his nose. Mr Lambe gravitated at once towards Captain Ross and the two were soon deep in conversation. *Another educated man*, thought Kit with a curl of her lip; and wondered how long the surgeon would have lasted on the mountain. Then she scolded herself – she did not need Ross's friendship any more; for she now had a task in hand. Having secured her tick and bolster in the old covered market, collected her rations from the quartermaster, and her pay from Tichborne's ensign, she had a full belly, her pay in her pocket and was ready for the evening. This time she *would* go out on the town like the others. Most certainly. But she would be going to find Richard.

Rovereto was a very pretty mountain town, and in the benign evening it was hard to believe that they had had such an ugly introduction to the place. Though it was bitterly cold, candlelight streamed welcomingly from windows, and music could be heard leaking from the shutters of the taverns and eating-houses as the soldiers rid themselves of their pay. At every corner and in every red coat she passed, Kit expected to see Richard's sweet and shining face, and she trembled with cold and anticipation, but as the night wore on her hopes began to fade. Rovereto was a labyrinth of streets, and Kit found herself wandering aimlessly, afraid to take the plunge into the noise and light of the taverns. But as the bells reproachfully chimed the quarters, chiding her, she took a breath and opened the studded doors of a tavern called the San Maurizio.

Through the candle smoke and the red coats of the company of foot, Kit spotted two fellow dragoons. Mr O'Connell and Mr Southcott were a couple of jorums ahead of her, and were happy to toast their 'pretty dragoon'. She took it well enough, and stood the two gentlemen another round, but took her tankard to a neighbouring table, where some of Tichborne's men were drinking. Kit toasted the company of foot, then asked whether anyone had seen or heard of her brother.

'Richard Walsh,' said one, downing his tot. 'I think I remember him.' Kit's heart beat slow and painfully. ''Nother jigger might jog me memory.'

Kit raised her hand for another bottle and poured it round. 'Yes,' said the fellow, licking his lips. 'Blond fellow. Short. Lazy eye.'

Kit, sighing, got up and moved to the next table. There she heard that although no one knew of a Private Richard Walsh, there was a gang of Irish boys who had formed their own little unit. 'Regular band of brothers,' said one. 'Good little sappers. Tichborne left them at Cremona to dig a tunnel under the barbican.'

Kit's spirits plummeted. 'Where is Cremona?' she asked.

'Good bit down the river,' said the first fellow. 'Two days' march.' Kit gulped down her drink. How was she to find Richard if he'd broken from the main company? She could not tramp around the countryside as she pleased, and to desert would expose her to dreadful punishments.

'You're wrong,' said the second redcoat. 'Tichborne took the Irish up the castle above the town.' This sounded more hopeful, but the foot soldiers did not seem certain and began to argue among themselves, about Cremona, the castle, Marlborough, and a jumble of other unfamiliar names.

Kit emptied her tankard, and rose unsteadily, for she'd had to drink a skinful in the course of enquiry. She walked unsteadily to the door and had just laid her hand on the latch when she felt a tap on her epaulette. 'I say, horseman.' She turned to see the small rat-faced foot soldier she'd seen at the first table. 'Try the Gasthof by the church. Lots of the Irish lads drink there. Turn left out the door, and up the hill.'

She thanked him, opened the door into the night, breathed in the sobering cold, turned left into a narrow alley and was met by a disturbing sight. A man and a maid struggled together in the dark shadow. At first Kit thought to pass by, but she realised that this was no willing coupling.

The girl was defending herself but she was no match for the

brutal bulk of the man. In the scuffle the girl's lace cap had fallen to the gutter, and her dark hair tumbled down almost to the pavings. There was a ripping sound as the man rent her clothes to reveal a white crescent of her back like a sliver of moon. Now he had her turned around and folded over like a page as he bunched her skirts around her waist and fumbled with his own breeches.

As Kit hurried closer she realised that the aggressor was a dragoon. She remembered Maria van Lommen's words: *I would never seduce a woman who does not want me – which is more than I can say for men.*

Kit reached for the scruff of the cur's neck. She pulled him off the girl with a strength she did not know she possessed, and threw him against the wall of the alley. It was only then that she recognised the bullish features of Sergeant Taylor, and by that time it was too late.

'Look away, Walsh,' he spat. 'This is not your quarrel.'

Kit gathered his uniform in a bunch at his throat. 'I see no quarrel, for that word has too much honour in it for what plays out here. I see a boorish man insulting a lady.'

'She's a dago slut, a *macaroni*. What do you care?'

What to say? That she could not bear to see another woman hurt today? Kit cast about for her riposte, and found it in the uniform they both wore.

'It was Captain Ross himself who said that if you dishonour the dragoons' coat then your actions are the quarrel of every man in this regiment. If I'm to be included in this insult, then I'm damned sure I'm worthy enough to chastise you for it.'

Now Taylor took her by the stock and pushed her to the opposite wall. 'You little fucking prick. You prodigal, shit-mouthed cunt.' Taylor's broken-nosed brutal bulk was considerable; he was a barrel of a man and she could feel the strength in the fist under her chin all but lifting her slight frame from the ground. His victim had picked herself up and was retreating into the shadows. From the other direction the door of the tavern opened, light streamed into the alley, and Southcott and O'Connell stumbled out. Kit heard their piss slap on to the stones and saw the steam rise. She punched Taylor's hand away.

'I leave,' said Kit, quoting Captain Ross again, 'Billingsgate language to women and cowards. I have no wish to tongue-battle with you, Sergeant Taylor, but if you wish to use swords in place of words, I am your man.'

Taylor raised his fist, flicked a look to the dragoons by the alehouse door, and turned the fist into a finger, pointing, threatening. 'You invoked the regiment, boy, but you've no idea of what you're yapping about. If you did, you'd know that you may not challenge one of my rank. You like fancy fucking officer language? Very well, you have already *transgressed* by *striking* a *superior*.'

Kit, heart beating wildly, had no idea where her words were coming from. She spoke to Taylor, to the cooper on the cart, to every man who thought they could take a woman's most precious possession.

'Superior in rank perhaps,' she retorted, 'but in no other regard. I might venture to say that the Duke of Marlborough had too good an opinion of you when he took his livery off your back and gave you the queen's.' Kit knew Taylor had been footman to Marlborough, for he never ceased to talk of it, and she could see this last stung him to the quick. Southcott and O'Connell, who had relieved themselves and were now standing easy in the doorway listening, sucked in their collective breath. Taylor's face grew red as boiled ham. 'By God, I'll have you on jankers for the rest of your days,' he spat. 'Expect your arrest at dawn. These men are my witnesses,' He swung his arm drunkenly towards Southcott and O'Connell, where they lolled in the doorway looking on.

Kit looked to them in appeal; they were not long friends, but had been through much together in a short time. Taylor was unpopular, pursuing his paltry feuds and exacting petty punishments, and the dragoons had a code of loyalty to each other. Kit had fought well at the monastery of San Columbano, she had run towards Ingoldsby when everyone else had run away, and she had bandaged Southcott's hand with her own stock. She could only pray they remembered her good offices now. Southcott and O'Connell looked at each other and then at Taylor, wide eyed. 'I didn't see anything. Did you, Mr O'Connell?'

'No, Mr Southcott, not a thing. Truly, the streets are very dark after the bright lights of the tavern.'

Taylor looked from one to the other. Southcott's merry face was serious for once, and O'Connell, the towering Irishman, stood with arms folded across his massive chest. Taylor looked back at Kit, his bluster gone, his malice redoubled. 'I'll cool your courage soon enough, boy.' Then he spat at Kit's feet, and stumbled away down the little alley.

Kit slumped with relief. '*Thank* you,' she said to her fellows, heartfelt.

'He'll be on your back now, Walsh,' said Southcott, patting her shoulder.

'And ours,' said O'Connell.

'When isn't he?' rejoined Southcott. 'Come on, you great mountain; let us have another drink, and Walsh can pursue his amours in peace.' He nodded to the shadows, where Kit could see the girl in white still cowering. Taking his fellow by the arm, Southcott turned O'Connell round and back through the door into the welcoming light.

Kit walked hesitantly to the girl in the shadows, hands held out before her to show that she was no threat. The girl had covered herself up as best she could, and now looked up at Kit with trusting eyes. Kit stooped to rescue the sorry lace cap where it lay in the gutter, but it was ruined and she let it be. She turned to the girl and performed a little pantomime of pointing and shrugging, saying slowly; 'Where do you live?'

'I understand you perfectly,' said the girl in a pretty accent. 'I am schooled in a little English, and your regiments have been in our region for years.'

'Then tell me where you live and I can escort you home.'

'No,' she said quickly. 'You must not tell my father. If it becomes known that that man even laid his hands on me I would be forever tarnished.'

'But you were entirely innocent in the case! I can explain the particulars . . .'

'Explain what?' said the girl with some heat. 'That I was passing by a tavern late at night? That I stopped to speak to a soldier? Even such small sins are enough to damage my reputation. One day, I want to be well wed.'

Kit shook her head. 'Very well. But let me at least escort you home. And for God's sake take my jacket.' Kit unbuttoned her coat and wrapped it like a cape about the girl's naked shoulders.

She shrank from the heavy felt as if it burned. 'What kind of figure will I cut in such a coat? I would look for all the world like a soldier's doxy.'

Kit buttoned on her coat once more, and they walked through the little streets garlanded with flower boxes. It was hard to believe that Taylor's brutal attack could have taken take place somewhere like this.

'What is your name?' Kit asked.

'I am Bianca Castellano. And you?'

'I am Christian Kavanagh. Kit.'

'And you are not English, are you, Kit? You do not sound like the rest of them.'

'I am Irish.' There was pride in Kit's reply. A thought struck her: if this girl could detect her accent, would she know whether other Irish had been billeted on the town? She postponed the question for a better season. They walked on until they reached a grand house; the best on the street, perhaps in the town. Candelabras lit the windows and a hurricane lamp burned in the doorway, swinging like a pendulum from left to right, scanning the street. 'My father,' said Bianca.

Kit straightened. 'Leave this in my charge.'

A tall white figure held the lamp, a man who wore a nightcap like a candle snuffer and a nightgown down to his feet.

Kit doffed her tricorn. 'Sir,' she said, 'I have the honour to restore your daughter to you. She stumbled in the street and became a little disarranged, but was not much hurt.'

The man lifted his lamp to look in Kit's face. Beside her, Bianca was holding her breath. Kit kept her gaze straight and felt a gradual lessening of tension. At last the lamp was lowered, the nightcap nodded, and Bianca released her breath in a low rush. 'I thank you, sir,' said a gravelly, heavily accented voice, 'for bringing my daughter home. I bid you goodnight.'

Bianca was bundled in the door, the lights were extinguished one by one, and Kit went back to the silk market. The Gasthof would be closed by now, and she was too tired for further excitement.

Chapter 12

Out for recreation we went on a tramp . . .
                                        'Arthur McBride' (trad.)

Nothing happened.

The one requirement placed upon the dragoons was that they collect their rations each day from the quartermaster at the silk market. They were paid and victualled properly for the first time; five farthings a day for tobacco, a pound of bread, a pint of wine, and clean bedstraw each night. Kit tried to smoke as she thought the habit would add to her male credentials, but found it unbearably bitter. The soldiers wanted for nothing but occupation; they kicked their heels about the little mountain town, and of course, there was little to do but drink.

Kit did not see Ross, as he was closeted with the captains at the castle above the town. Nor did she see Taylor, and for this she was grateful, for in the cold light of day she regretted the events of that first night – not her actions, but the words she had chosen, words that seemed calculated to inflame Taylor and make him her implacable enemy. Happily, Taylor was also kept busy with some business at the castle, business of which he boasted often but simultaneously insisted was deadly secret.

Orders were handed down from Tichborne's ensign, and those orders were always the same, day after day. Wait. Just wait. *Eighty-three days without Richard. Eighty-four.* Kit, twitching with impatience, continued her search about the town, and heading off on goat tracks in the direction of Cremona, but each time returning by nightfall without reaching it. She had tried walking up the hill towards the imposing castle, but she had been turned back on the path by guards wearing a uniform she did not recognise.

Although Kit had friends among the dragoons, Southcott and O'Connell and the others were happy to pass the time in the taverns with their backgammon and tobacco. On the third day, a mizzling, freezing rain set in and Kit, sick of taverns and mountain walks, decided to visit Bianca Castellano and see how she did.

She ran splashing through the streets, the rain filling up her tricorn, till she came to the street where she'd left Bianca three nights past. She knocked on the door of the painted house, and a neat maid answered it.

Kit doffed her hat. 'Signorina Castellano?'

The maid shook her tidy head. '*No soldato.*'

Kit frowned.

The maid said, brokenly, 'No soldier. Lady say. Father say.'

A tall shadow loomed behind the little maid, and barked something at her. She stood aside and an imposing man filled the door. Wealth was powdered into his hair and embroidered into his waistcoat. Kit recognised the man she'd met three nights before, a more impressive figure without his nightcap and gown. He looked Kit up and down. 'How may I help you?' he said in accented English, with a courtesy that belied his hard tone.

Kit cleared her throat nervously. 'Sir, forgive me. I am the dragoon who had the honour of assisting your daughter three nights past. I came to see how she does.'

'She does very well,' he said shortly. 'I thank you now, as I did then, for your assistance. That should be enough.'

'Is she . . . may I see her?'

The chilly features thawed slightly. The man stood aside and gave a short order to the maid, who led Kit into a little parlour.

The silken walls were hung with portraits; too many portraits of people with long expensive faces. The light was multiplied by faceted mirrors, and fine carpets softened her tread. There was so much to look at that Kit did not, at first, see anyone else in the room. But Bianca was there, a circle of embroidery on her lap, looking from an expensively glazed window on a peerless mountain vista smeared and spoiled by rain. She turned her lovely head and jumped up with a little cry.

'I have been hoping you would come! I have been wanting to thank you.'

The maid settled herself discreetly in the corner, pulled out some lace tatting from her pocket and began to work with great concentration on a little snowy cap.

Kit was the cheapest thing in the room, in her coarse woollens and brassy buttons and faded lace. She sat as she had seen Ross sit – even in nature, even on a fallen stump, he sat with one foot forward and one crooked to the knee with his forearm resting upon it, easy and elegant.

'I have been walking abroad with my maid to find you,' announced Bianca.

A recklessness had replaced the timidity with which she had crept home at Kit's side.

'That I would not advise,' replied Kit. 'And I am not surprised at your lack of success, for I think it reasonable to say that any place the regiment might be, a respectable woman would not.'

'So my father says. But I wanted to find you.'

Kit frowned. 'Your maid,' she lowered her voice, glancing at the servant in the corner, 'she said no soldiers.'

'Yes.' Bianca looked down at her abandoned embroidery. 'My father is inclined to protect me.'

'Of course. But it was the maid told me: "*Lady say.*"'

There was a silence. Bianca looked down at her lap. 'There *is* one particular red coat I wish to keep from my door.'

Kit breathed out. 'Sergeant Taylor.'

'Yes. He has been . . . visiting. He offers me marriage.'

Kit sat forward, all her attempts at elegance abandoned, her hands clasped before her on her knees. 'You mean . . . he has been paying his addresses to you? After how he treated you three nights past?'

'Yes.'

'And you cannot tell your father—'

'Oh, my father would kill him,' Bianca interrupted, sharp as a knife. 'My father was a butcher. He acts the fine gentleman, but we are trade. Everything you see in this room has been bought, not inherited.' She stood and wandered the room as if taking an inventory. 'These portraits are not of my blood. This chandelier is newly shipped from Venice, these mirrors too, for two beef steers. These silk drapes come from Bergamo, swapped for six sides of mutton, carpets from Turkey exchanged for forty hams. My English lessons were salaried in sausage. It is all paid for with flesh and blood, for we have no lineage. Our family tree is populated by pigs and cows and sheep.'

She sat down again. 'My father grew up with knives. He grew up as a peasant, slitting pigs on the hillside. He has forty butchers working for him day and night; but he would do Sergeant Taylor himself. He'd be split and trussed in a quarter of the bells.' There was relish in Bianca's voice; the butcher's daughter.

'And you *don't* want that?'

'Oh, I do. I would love to see his blood run for what he did to me. But his disgrace goes hand in hand with mine. My father cannot know what passed between us in the alley.'

'Is that why he caused your maid to sit with us?'

'Concetta? She is here for me. *I* ask for her to be with me always. My reputation must be beyond reproach.'

Kit sat back, tingling. When she wed Richard, she'd been an heiress too; but Maura's easily quashed objections had been nothing to the rules that governed this Trentino miss. The

Castellanos were trying to build a bloodline from nothing, from this one piece of luck in their heritage, this freakishly beautiful girl. Their line was not even so established as Kit's; the Kavanaghs could boast the earls of Leinster in their family, but Bianca's father was a cut-throat turned count. 'So, you could not be a soldier's wife.'

'It is not in my stars, for my father will arrange something to my family's greater advantage. He would never settle for a sergeant, but an officer of very high rank would not settle for me.' She looked up coquettishly with her strange and beautiful purple eyes.

There was a short intense silence that Kit could not quite define. Then Bianca spoke again. 'And you? What do you wish for?'

Kit considered for a moment. It was so much of her habit to dissemble that the truth came hard. 'I am looking for someone.'

'Who?'

Habit returned. 'My brother.'

'He is here also?'

'Yes. I have followed him all the way from Ireland. He had a month's start on me. But the company has divided all over this region; my brother may be anywhere. It seems a hopeless quest at present.'

A door opened somewhere along the passage. With a glance at her maid, Bianca said hurriedly, 'My father comes. But visit me again tomorrow; in the morning he is from home at his bloody business.'

Kit stood. 'For what purpose?'

'My father supplies the army with their rations of meat. Your regiment will be marching on his blood pudding, his white sausage, his *capriolo*. He knows where all the men are placed, for he feeds them all. He comes!'

The gilded handle turned, the door opened. Signor Castellano seemed to fill the spacious room. 'Sir. For the service you rendered my daughter I thank you and will always be grateful. But I believe now it is time for you to go.' Kit bowed to him, and to his daughter. Bianca took her hand briefly, pressed it. *Come again*, the pressure said.

Kit walked home clasping her arms against the rain, warm with friendship and hope. She had missed the society of women. Her mother she had never mourned since she left the farm without looking back, but she often missed Maura's wisdom and regard, and had enjoyed, today, the balm of female company.

The next day she returned to the house, and the next, and the next. Each day Bianca thought of a new way to bring her back – a promised map of the hills which she would get drawn tomorrow – she would talk to her father's carter tomorrow – Kit could reach Cremona on the meat truck and be back by the dragoons' curfew. Tomorrow; always tomorrow. *Eighty-six days without Richard. Eighty-seven.* One day she had to refuse to return the next day; the dragoons had been told that they would at last meet the fabled duke at the castle above Rovereto. 'I know,' said Bianca calmly, 'my father has already sent his best cuts to the castle. All the regiments will muster there.'

There was a silence. Kit looked from the casement at the mountains, beautiful and peaceful for now. 'Signorina Bianca. What do you think of the war?'

'I don't know.' Bianca smiled a little. 'My father says that war is not the concern of women.'

Now Kit smiled. 'Sometimes it can be.' Then she urged, 'Think. Use your mind. Your opinion matters. You, and all the citizens of Rovereto, have to live with the war. You are now a garrison town, and must expect battle daily.'

Bianca shook her head, at a loss. 'I suppose . . . I place my trust in our Prince Eugene. I know that he will protect us – that you will all protect us.' She stood to take her leave of Kit. 'Not tomorrow, then. But perhaps the day after?'

Kit felt a pang of envy this time as she left. Just for a fleeting moment, just as she had once stood in Kavanagh's bar and longed for adventure, she considered how comfortable it must be not to worry about such things, war and borders and living and dying and the crushing responsibility of keeping safe the daughters of butchers and bakers and chandlers. What ease to hide behind pearls and curls and corsets and petticoats, safe and protected by men . . .

Chapter 13

Now mark what followed and what did betide . . .

'Arthur McBride' (trad.)

Immaculate in his uniform, Captain Ross was king of the market square.

Kit was jolted by his appearance. His hair had been trimmed and tamed, his uniform dressed and his boots polished – he was magnificent. But it was only right that they were distanced, she told herself – she might this very day be reunited with her husband, and the insuperable chasm of rank made it easier to be parted from her captain.

Besides, Ross had with him a constant companion. The field surgeon Atticus Lambe was even now at his elbow – he wore the colour sash of the dragoons but his suit of clothes was charcoal grey; he was armed but lightly, and the weak sun burnished his hay-coloured hair, for he wore no hat. Lambe talked in an undertone to Ross, smiling rarely, the small pince-nez on his nose flashing two bright circles as he became animated. But the sun shone on the rest of them too, and Kit was glad to be with her regiment once again, lined up and pristine and primed for action. Her heart gladdened to see Flint, who had been at livery in the town for the last week. Southcott, O'Connell, Hall and the rest, who had spent the week in jug-bitten, dishevelled mayhem, had become smart, erect and dangerous cavalrymen again. She'd even missed the odious Taylor, shouting at them with spittle-flecked fury about their buckles and lacings, with his familiar refrain – 'We wouldn't have stood for it in the Duke of Marlborough's household.' She blocked her ears and fixed her eyes on the castle, solid and crenellated and packed with promise. Far above loomed the snow-capped peaks, mountain eagles wheeling blackly above their tops. Kit breathed in the cool sharp air and thought how good it was to be a dragoon. For today she would see Richard again. Ninety days. Three whole months. 'All the regiments will muster,' Bianca had said. *All*.

It was a pleasant ride from the marketplace to the castle, up a vertiginous, well-paved hill and over a high bridge with the sluggish winter waters of the River Leno rolling below.

Under the gatehouse, an ensign checked Ross and his number against a list. And they were through to the vast courtyard, with four crenellated bastions at each corner and a great round barbican at the river drop. The place was crammed with perhaps a thousand company of foot in their brave red coats, and hundreds of cavalry. The place smelled of men and horse and buzzed with anticipation.

Kit lined up with the rest, positioning herself carefully behind Southcott's bulk, and out of Taylor's eye, but with a good vantage to watch what was to pass. She searched the white-blobbed faces of the company of foot – looking for Richard's features, heart beating fast. She would know him at once; but would he recognise her? She could not, for the moment, see him, so she turned her attention to a cohort of Imperial soldiers lining before the doorway of the castle, the black Habsburg eagle on their standard. They wore polished black breastplates and black helmets with bronze facings, and stood in neat ranks, facing front, with their halberds perfectly in line, eyes glittering beneath their helmets.

Kit was so taken by their appearance that she did not at once register the man in their very centre. He sat on a white horse with grey points, as still as a statue. Swamped by a tightly curled grey wig which fell to the saddle, he wore a bronze velvet coat worked delicately with gold filigree at the collar and skirt, and a polished black breastplate chased with bronze curlicues and clasps. A sword, worked with gold at the haft, hung at his scabbard. His eyes were deep set and pleasing but he had what Aunt Maura would call a nose that would spoil a face. His appearance was not unattractive but he seemed rather weak and timid, and his two protruding front teeth put Kit in mind of the coneys she used to snare for the pot. He looked like a man more likely to turn and run than stay and fight. Yet this must be the famed general Prince Eugene of Savoy, victor of untold campaigns. The man who had ordered his forces to gather in the mountain, the man who had given her frostbite, and had driven her into Ross's arms for warmth. She looked away and again began to scrutinise every white face above every red coat, looking for the much-loved features of Private Richard Walsh.

The wait for Marlborough seemed interminable. The snow began to fall, fine as gossamer, as if even the clouds grew impatient. The greys shifted their weight patiently, and the dragoons began to murmur among themselves.

'He was once a lowly page for the Duke of York.'

'He's the richest man in England.'

'He shared the old king's mistress.'

'Had to jump out of the window once with his cock in his hand.'

'Frog king Louis himself commended his courage.'

'Spent a month in the Tower for treason.'

'And set a crown on William's head.'

Then, a fanfare cracked the freezing air, and a harbinger rode through the gates and stopped right in the middle of the courtyard. He blew his horn once more and cried, 'Stand to attention for the Prince of Mindelheim, Prince of Mellenburg, Master-General of the Ordnance and Commander-in-Chief of Her Majesty's Forces – John Churchill, First Duke of Marlborough.'

The company of foot stood straight as spears. Ross swept his blue eye over his dragoons. This was *their* commander who came, and they would show him and these foreigners British quality.

Into the courtyard galloped a figure on an ink-black mare. He turned the horse in a circle, and rode her about the front lines of the regiments, clasping hands, chucking cheeks, straightening partisans and hats that he had knocked askew. Despite their orders to be at attention, the troops broke rank and clustered about him, and their sergeants said not a word in protest. One fellow shouted for three cheers for the Duke of Marlborough, and the noise was deafening – a thousand tricorns met the snow in the air and fell back down with it, and there in the centre of it all was the duke. He too was of middle years but could not have presented a greater contrast to the rabbit prince. His face was florid and handsome, his shoulder-length grey wig as bouncy and buoyant as he. He was beaming, and it was as if the sun had come out.

Kit flung her hat in the air with the rest and cheered until her voice was hoarse. She was carried away with pride, pride that he was their commander, pride at the figure he cut next to Savoy. She felt trust, too. Here was a man who would take them into battle but get them out alive and victorious. His titles were like music to her, as were those other, unspoken titles that followed those heralded like the ripples of a stone in a pool. Philanderer. Traitor. Kingmaker. They only added to Marlborough's overwhelming glamour.

Kit looked across to the Prince of Savoy. His rabbity face was impassive, and his troops did not move a single muscle between them. He dug his spurred heels almost imperceptibly into his horse's flanks, the statue came alive and he walked his horse to Marlborough's, until the grey and the black mare were nose to nose. Marlborough, as though he were at his club, thrust out his hand, smiling. 'John.'

Eugene of Savoy raised one pale plucked eyebrow. 'Principe

Eugenio di Savoia-Carignano.' The prince put out a limp hand, and shook Marlborough's lion's paw with the tips of his fingers. 'I am delighted to make your acquaintance at last.' The prince's voice was thin and reedy and his protruding teeth gave him a slight lisp. To Kit's surprise he spoke English with a French accent. He sounded just like her mother. It made her, instantly, wary of him.

'Charmed, charmed,' boomed Marlborough.

'I congratulate you wholeheartedly on your expedient strategy against the Hollanders.' Prince Eugene inclined his head a fraction.

'And I hear you buggered the Turks,' said Marlborough, clapping him on the shoulder. 'Now let's deal with these Frogs. After you.'

Marlborough waited for Savoy to dismount first, then the two commanders walked into the castle together. A gilded Imperial marshal rode smoothly over to Ross. 'His Grace commands that you attend upon him to represent the king's dragoons. Bring a second and follow me.'

Taylor preened, sure he would be chosen for an audience with his old master. But Ross's blue gaze swept over him and settled on Kit. 'Mr Walsh,' he said, 'your education continues.'

Taylor's colour mounted furiously, his lips disappeared in a pinched white line. The dragoons held their collective breath, and even Mr Lambe shook his head. His pince-nez slipped from his nose to the ground. Kit dismounted, retrieved the glasses and returned them to their owner with a bow. The surgeon took them; his white hands, long fingers jointed like a spider, were cold. 'I thank you,' he said, his tones as chill as his flesh. Kit bobbed her head and followed Ross.

They entered the warmth of a great hall, with a roaring fire at one end and a minstrel's gallery at the other stuffed with heralds jostling for position.

There was a great banqueting table in the middle of the hall, loaded with meats and wine – flesh and blood for the officers, the finest cuts that Signor Castellano the master butcher could offer, the very meats which had bought Bianca's lineage and education.

'Bring my maps.' The duke clicked his fingers impatiently and a man rushed to his elbow with an armful of scrolls. Marlborough swept the plates from the table, the lace of his sleeve catching the goblets and sending them crashing to the floor. He rolled the map across the great board, and secured its stubborn corners with four heavy dishes.

'Chess set!' he ordered. A page stepped forward with a walnut box; Marlborough banged it down on the table, flipped open the lid and picked through the pieces. He brought out the white queen, showed her to the company like a conjuror, and set her down on the outline of England. Kit looked at Ross and he smiled with his eyes while his face stayed entirely immobile. 'Anne of England, God save her,' said the duke reverently. Then he selected the white king, and held it before Savoy's face. 'His Excellency the Emperor Leopold,' he said, 'your monarch.' He placed the piece on the vast swathes of the Empire. Then he sorted through the pieces once more and picked out the black king. 'Our belligerent, Louis of France.' The little dark figure was set in the centre of France, and then Marlborough rapped a beringed forefinger on a twisting border. 'Here we are,' he declared, 'between the Empire and the Republic of Venice. The French,' he went on, 'have Mantova.' Marlborough moved the black king and placed him on the little dukedom. The ebony skirts of the piece all but covered the entire duchy. 'Now,' Marlborough moved the king again, 'they have occupied Cremona. The Duc de Villeroi, their commander, sits there laughing at us.'

A cold sweat doused Kit – Cremona, where Tichborne had sent his Irish cohort. If Richard was not here today, he must be there.

And now that little ebony king sat upon that city like an ugly ink blot, a long shadow over the surrounding lands. Too close to where they were, too close to Richard.

'As I understand the position, our objective must be to stop the French making further incursions into the peninsula.' Marlborough indicated the boot-shaped lands Ross had pointed out to Kit. 'If this land is claimed the fight is done and the Two Crowns are victorious. Now, a large swathe of Alliance troops are now on Imperial land stationed here at Rovereto, Chiari, Luzzara and Carpi. I suggest a massed offensive – we descend from the hills and obliterate the French.'

'No.'

Marlborough was stopped in his tracks. Eugene of Savoy had not spoken at all since they'd gained the great hall, but his single syllable, low and quiet, stilled the room.

'It's a nice set.' Eugene of Savoy indicated the walnut box. 'Spanish?'

'Yes. From Salamanca,' Marlborough growled sulkily.

Savoy smiled a little. 'Where all this coil began. You play often?'

'Yes.'

'Well?'

'Tolerably.' Modesty sat awkwardly on the duke.

'Tell me,' said Savoy, walking to the box. 'When you play, do you send all your pawns out in a line and expose your king? Or do you move just so many as to send forth your flanking pieces to infiltrate your enemy lines; a bishop perhaps, or a knight?' He picked a piece out with his little fingers – a white knight. Kit suddenly felt a chill of premonition. The little ivory horsehead gleamed in the firelight. 'My dear Marlborough. I thank you and your excellent queen for coming to our aid. But this is an Imperial manoeuvre.'

Marlborough crashed his fist on the map. '*You* asked for us to come – your master the Emperor *begged* our queen for alliance. And now we are all amassed, surely you have a plan to use us?'

'Certainly. I am merely concerned with logistics – logistics can have an army on their knees quicker than the fiercest enemy.'

'I am well aware of that,' countered Marlborough testily. 'At Venlo, at Roermond, at Stevensweert . . .'

'I too,' cut in Savoy. 'Remember I – how did you put it? – "buggered the Turks". All your campaigns have been on flatlands. You are in the mountains now.'

'Then why the devil bring us here?' exploded Marlborough.

'My dear duke,' said Savoy quietly, 'they have no idea how many we are. They will not venture here; the ways are too hard. We are a vast force, we have sneaked round to their rearguard, and we are hidden. But your advantage is *me*. I know these hills, this is *my* country.'

Marlborough snorted. 'You were raised in Versailles at the queen's tit.'

'Indeed,' said Eugene of Savoy calmly. 'So I know Louis very well. We were once as brothers. He will not make his move yet.'

'Why not?'

'Because winter is here. Cremona is a citadel, just like Mantova. They will sit there all winter, safe and warm, and we may besiege them all we may. They will blow the bridges, pull up the draw-bridges.'

'Then why did you bring us here? Why now?'

'Because they will not expect it. And I like to do the unexpected.' Savoy walked to the map. 'If we show our hand in an all-out assault, we may be driven back to the mountains. And if we have to winter in the mountains we will all starve by Candlemas. Our horses will be eating leaves, our men will be eating horses. We will retake the lowlands in time, but we need to weaken the French *first*.' The prince delicately placed the white knight on the map next to the black king at Cremona. 'I would suggest that we leave the lion's share of the troops here. We send the cavalry, your dragoons and mine, down to Cremona. We will enter the city by stealth, through the aqueduct. I already have some of your sappers working there.' Kit held her breath. Was Richard among them? 'We surprise the French in their beds. We take Villeroi prisoner.' Savoy knocked over the black king. 'Without their commander, all will be confusion. Then we mobilise. Lorraine-Vaudémont can bring my company of foot through the Po gate, and you cut off the retreating French force at Luzzara. Then you may fire all the cannon, drum all the drums and draw all the swords that you want.'

The two eyed each other. Then Marlborough began to smile. He banged the Prince of Savoy between his shoulder blades. 'It might just work. Damn me, you little Frog. It might just.'

The two generals talked long into the night, until Kit's eyes began to droop. Ross, as the commander of the dragoons, was ever at the duke's elbow. She did not understand a half, even one quarter, of what was said. But she understood one thing – she had under-estimated the Prince of Savoy. He was a formidable strategist. But she was also sensible of what his proposals meant. As the hours passed, the spilt red wine slowly soaked through the map, obliterating Cremona with an ugly red stain.

Chapter 14

And bade them take that as fair warning . . .

'Arthur McBride' (trad.)

The morning after the muster at the castle, Kit went to see Bianca for the last time.

The maid showed her though to the salon, but left at once and closed the door behind her. Even then Kit did not take warning and, instead of receiving a heartfelt goodbye, she found herself receiving a proposal of marriage.

Kit looked down at the beautiful girl, in her expensive clothes and her expensive salon, and cursed the impulse that had led to her visit this house a week ago. A woman loved a man dressed in women's clothes. It would have been a ludicrous enough plot in a play.

She took Bianca's smooth white hands in her rough ones. 'I thank you for the honour you do me,' she said carefully. 'But I cannot raise your hopes, for there are certain . . . obstacles which would make our match impossible.'

'Surely love can surmount them?'

'And what of your father?' Kit said. 'I could not expect a rich butcher to give your hand to a foot soldier; you spoke once, yourself, of the objections to such an alliance.'

Bianca freed her hands, only to clasp Kit's more ardently. 'Then we will run together.'

Kit shook her head. 'How could I deprive your father of his daughter, and deprive you of a fortune? Think, Bianca. You would be stripped of all the comforts of life, exposed to hardships, and

gain in return only the reputation of a woman who follows camp.'
Kit's mother had been just such a creature – had left her country
and her family to follow Sean Kavanagh – yes, she had loved him,
but she had twined around him like a vine around an oak, and
when he had been felled, could not stand up without him. She
had rued the life she had chosen, and longed for the one she had
left behind in Poitiers, as the daughter of a French enameller,
with the finest house in town, a queue of suitors and every comfort
a wealthy young heiress could enjoy. Comfits and puppies and
golden harpsichords were things she could happily eschew for a
living lover, but things to be mourned and lacked for a dead
husband. Yes, Kit could have waxed quite lyrical on the subject.

'Such a reputation would mean nothing to me,' insisted Bianca.
'Let them call me a camp-follower and worse. Words cannot
injure me.'

'Yet last week you would not even wear my coat, for fear of
what people might say. Are you saying now that words are nothing?'

'All such things could be borne, so long as I am with you.'

'No.' Kit took the girl by the shoulders. 'If a likely fellow presents
himself, and there is love in the case, pledge yourself to another
with my blessing. I must take my leave – we are to muster at the
market for your prince.' At least this was the truth. Kit bowed to
Bianca, who cast herself on a sofa, weeping, and let herself out
of the parlour door.

Signor Castellano was waiting in the atrium. Kit bowed respect-
fully and made for the front door, but Bianca's father beckoned
her. The fingers were chubby for a slim man, the flesh stretched
and mottled – they resembled raw sausages.

Signor Castellano's own room was as male as Bianca's was
female – crammed like a cabinet of curiosities with many objects
– knives of all kinds, stuffed animals, wooden globes and books
crammed into shelves. Some of them were upside down – Signor
Castellano was no reader whatever his collection claimed. He

crossed the room and took a bottle and two crystal glasses, pouring a slick of amber liquid into each. He handed a glass to Kit. 'I give you the Prince of Savoy.'

Kit raised her own. 'The Duke of Marlborough.'

'So.' Signor Castellano walked to his window to look at his mountains. 'Off to Cremona, eh?'

'That's it, sir.'

'I imagine I will not be seeing you at my door again.'

Kit looked up sharply, but Signor Castellano still faced the window, and his powdered pigtail told her nothing. 'No, sir.'

'You know,' said Bianca's father, still addressing the view, 'there are pigs in those mountains. You can't see them from here, but they are there. They go high, oh, thousands of feet up. They can climb anything. People hunt them, have for centuries. And it's worth it. They're very tasty. Not fat, quite lean, but the meat . . . well, you've never had anything like it.'

He turned. 'You've got to follow them for days sometimes to get hold of them; but you always find them in the end if you know how to track them. And I do know how to track them.' He crossed the room and took hold of the upper part of Kit's arm in a butcher's pinch. 'Not much meat on you, signor, but by God, I'd find some.'

Kit shook her head slightly. 'Sir, I assure you, in respect of your good daughter, you have . . .'

'Shhh.' He raised one of the sausage fingers. 'I find specifics vulgar. I'm sure you take my meaning.'

Kit set down her glass carefully. 'I do, sir.'

'Then I drink your very good health.' Signor Castellano drained his glass, his eye bright with murder.

'And yours, sir.' Kit did not touch her glass. Signor Castellano turned back to the mountains where the pigs lived and Kit stole from the house, dismissed.

She was so upset by the little interview that she did not see Sergeant Taylor in the street, lurking beyond the frescoed corner.

Chapter 15

And we scarce gave them time for to draw their own blades . . .
                                        'Arthur McBride' (trad.)

Padre Alessandro Mattei was expecting the knock on his door that evening.

His benefice, a few miles distant from the city of Cremona, afforded him an unusual stipend – an old palazzo, dating from the time of Dante. But the palazzo itself was commonplace compared to what was beneath it. For the wine cellars, damp, cross-ribbed vaults which flooded year round with a foot of jade-green water, led to one end of a subterranean Roman aqueduct.

The dragoons had been riding for three days to find this place, in the company of Eugene of Savoy, and an English colonel wide of girth and loud of voice named Gossedge, whose primary function in the absence of Marlborough was to agree with every word the Prince of Savoy uttered.

The Scots Greys arrived at the palazzo some time after sunset. There was a large orchard in which to tie the horses, and as Kit left Flint munching windfalls, she could see Cremona in the distance. Walls, spires and crenellations – it looked impregnable, and yet, according to their new commander, there was a way in.

Prince Eugene of Savoy knocked at the padre's door himself with the handle of his Imperial sword, and murmured the password. The oak door opened, and the dragoons, shrouded in black hooded cloaks, streamed through. The cloaks were voluminous enough to conceal some strange weapons – not swords and muskets, but axes and picks. The priest conducted them silently down a spiral stone stair to his vault. They sloshed through the ankle-deep water, past the vast oak barrels and to an old stone archway, much older than the house. Each man took a firebrand, dipped it in a pitch barrel and lit it from the man before. Kit took a light from O'Connell and followed the Prince of Savoy into the dark.

The pitch made a bitter black smoke and the torches threw saffron lights on to the ancient stone. As the dragoons sloshed through the shallow water, Kit remembered Ross's tales of the Netherlands: 'our boots were never dry'. This expedition was different. This time they were heading into battle – not a skirmish with a handful of counterfeit monks, but a planned, expected strategy, the siege of a city. And so they had Atticus Lambe with them, black clad as was fitting for a harbinger of injury and death. There were other surgeons in their company – Mr Wilson, Mr Laurence, Mr Sea – but it was Mr Lambe who had been given the care of the Scots Greys and Mr Lambe who claimed Ross's company at every moment along the road.

Lambe and Ross had much in common – they had been at the same school, they had been up at Oxford, and then their lives had diverged to take in military and medical training. So they had much to say to one another and none of it included Kit. She kept company instead with Southcott, Hall, O'Connell and the others. She had not seen Ross since Rovereto Castle, and to be with him now, in such a confined space, put her out of countenance.

'The sappers have cleared the way ahead,' he whispered to her, 'and reconnoitred the exit. The aqueduct comes out at the western gate of Cremona; little used and lightly guarded. It is walled up, so we must break through. The sappers have helped there too.'

'Who were the sappers?' Kit asked.

'A road gang from Ireland,' he replied, 'some of Tichborne's men.'

Kit's heart thudded painfully. 'And where are they now?'

'Posted inside the city, posing as townsfolk. They've been going inside for days, in ones and twos, dressed as priests or peasants; so there will be certain of our men inside, but to take a regiment through that way would have taken a month . . . Wait.' He held up a gloved hand. A whisper came down from command, the dragoons stopped. Silent, they listened; far above and far away a great bell tolled. 'Eleven of the clock,' said Ross, low voiced. 'We have an hour to breach the wall.'

The dragoons picked up their pace, and at length the tunnel came out into the dark blue night, the stars. Another command came down; the torches were to be doused, and Kit duly extinguished hers in the icy foot of water, with a reptilian hiss.

They trod the ancient Roman arches, the aqueduct stretching out before them like a ribbon of silver, Roman constellations above. The swan, the lyre, the horse, the giant; stars her father had taught her to read, stars Roman fathers had named for their own children. Before and behind her hundreds of men marched, their breath rising to the stars. The bells rang once, again, a third time. The city loomed black out of the blue night, sleeping, but with a few pinpricks of light here and there, a dragon with his eyes half open.

Ahead she could see Eugene of Savoy, striding ahead, his shorn scalp in the moonlight – he had left off his wig tonight, and his hood. Not for him the comfort of a fireside; he was to be the first in attack, and he waded through the icy water like the rest of them. He too must be feeling that his toes were not his, that his calves burned. She forgave him, almost, for the chilblains of the mountain.

At the walls Savoy made a flapping motion with his hand, sank into the icy water, as low as he could, and held up two white fingers. Two guards were on the gate – just two. He nodded at Ross, who stepped forward silently with O'Connell. He raised his axe and cut down one French guard, splitting his head like a turnip, while O'Connell dispatched the other. Kit looked away. University man. Killer.

Ross gave a long low whistle and the dragoons emerged, dripping, their cloaks shining black, to mass by the wall. As Kit reached him Ross took a case knife from the Frenchman's body, drew it over the back of his hand, till a thin black line sprang forth, folded the knife and put it in his breeches. 'Why did you do that?'

'An old army saying. A blade that cuts you once can never harm you again.'

She was shaken, hearing her father's words like that, but there was no time to think; one man struck a tinder and Savoy examined the wall. Kit craned to see; the taper moved around the great bricks under a paler stone arch. Below the keystone was chalked a crude double-headed eagle, the cognisance of the Empire. It was a sign.

Axes and picks were lifted from dripping cloaks and cowls and sleeves. Eugene of Savoy held a hand high: *Wait*. And then the bells chimed again and the vanguard applied their peasant's weapons to the edges of the block, precisely, on each bell stroke. By the twelfth chime the block was punched though to the other side of the wall, leaving a hole the size of a man.

Savoy held two fingers high again, and Ross – must he always be first? thought Kit – clambered through with O'Connell hard on his heels. Kit held her breath, but Ross's beckoning arm appeared though the cavity. 'Clear.'

One by one the dragoons clambered through the hole left by the stone. At her turn Kit straightened up to find herself in a small deserted square with a well in the middle. Dawn was breaking and the sky turned a pearl grey – she could see the streets blurred with mist, a single black dog trotting from right to left. She followed Ross's beckoning hand. Savoy spoke in an undertone and Ross relayed his orders: 'Spread out in ones and twos – we are to disappear about the town. When you hear the trumpet' – Mr Van

Dedan flashed the gold bell of his instrument from underneath his cloak – 'we gather and form by the cathedral – you can see the tower yonder.'

Kit slipped like a shadow round the corner into a pretty market-place. Stallholders were already abroad, and Kit loitered by the well with Ross and O'Connell, instinctively staying by her captain. She watched the market produce arrive in box and barrel and cart, tomatoes and fish and bottles of wine being ranked on wooden trestles. Above the sea of chatter, one voice stood out.

The speaker was huge and broad, with a bald head, beefy fore-arms and pink flesh mottled and shiny like brawn. He was pointing out purchases from the stalls, picking up fruits and vegetables and turning them over, sniffing and squeezing them. There was a fellow with him in a blue uniform, with a sabre swinging from his belt, and carrying a basket of wicker. The big bald fellow handed the produce to his man, who stowed it in the basket. No money changed hands, and the stallholders handed over their wares resentfully. But the bald man did not notice. He was looking at the cloaked men dotted about the square in twos and threes and fours. Kit followed his gaze: they looked wrong; their stance overly casual, their conversations counterfeit, their demeanour watchful. Kit stole closer to the bald man, and strained to hear what he was saying. 'French,' breathed Ross in her ear. 'I can make out some, but not all.'

Kit listened hard, and heard the patois of the Haute-Vienne, her mother's region. 'He's the cook of one Lieutenant-General Crenan,' she whispered. 'He has seen the men gathered about the square. He goes to warn his master, and he is dispatching his guard to warn the Maréchal Villeroi.'

'O'Connell,' Ross ordered. 'Follow the cook. He does not reach his master, do you understand me?' O'Connell nodded and set off after the cook. 'Kit, with me.'

Kit followed Ross as they threaded though the stalls in the wake of the hurrying French private. She tugged at Ross's sleeve. 'Let us take him down now, before he gives us the slip.'

'No,' he hissed. 'He will lead us to Villeroi.'

The Frenchman's blue coat disappeared round a corner into a stone alley. The private was running now, scattering his produce as he went. A fish, an orange, a loaf. Kit and Ross followed on silent feet till they came to a small square with a large civic building with decorative windows. The blue coat disappeared through the grand doors, and Ross thrust out an arm. 'Wait,' he said, and pulled Kit into the deep shadow of the arch. 'It won't be long.' And he was right – the same man came out of the door, followed by a tall gentleman in a velvet coat. The coat was disarranged, the gentleman's hair was unpowdered, his sword unbuckled. He was fumbling with the gilt buttons on his coat with one hand and his other hand held, foolishly, a quill, the tip of the thing slick with ink and the fingers stained with black.

'Villeroi,' breathed Ross.

Kit watched the French commander hurry past. 'Shall we fetch the others?'

Ross considered. Commander and aide-de-camp hurried across a square. The captain waited until they reached the alley before he replied. 'No,' said Ross. 'It's two against two. Let's go.'

He took out his case knife, sprinted forth and in a moment had his blade at the maréchal's neck, while Kit held her dagger at the throat of the private. Man and master were forced to the paving, in the chill shadow of the alley, their knees cracking on the cold stone, stone the rising sun had not yet reached.

Maréchal Villeroi held his hands high in surrender. He noted the flash of red wool beneath Ross's cloak. 'Imperial forces.' He sighed. 'Very well.' He turned his head, the silver blade pressing into the loose folds of his neck, screwing his eyes around to Ross. 'English? German?'

'The former. And proud of it.'

'Then you have no loyalty to the Emperor.'

'On the contrary. My queen is his ally; that is enough to assure my loyalty.'

'I am the Maréchal de Villeroi.'

'That I know, monsieur. And that is why you are under arrest.'

'*Ecoutez.*' The maréchal's voice was reasonable. 'There is no one in this alley but you and your man and me and mine. What harm can there be in letting me go? You are a likely officer, I dare say – what would you say to a thousand pistoles, and a regiment, and the finest recompenses King Louis of France can offer?'

Kit looked at Ross over the blond head of the aide-de-camp, one hand across the man's body, the other clamped around his throat. His hair smelled of candle grease. She watched Ross. Ten thousand pistoles was a lot of money.

'I would say that your timing is unfortunate,' said the captain coolly. 'I have not served the Emperor for a sevennight yet, so it feels a little early to be betraying him.' The knife bit deeper into Villeroi's throat and the skin puckered like gooseflesh. 'Now, I'll trouble you to be on your feet – I must take you to the Prince of Savoy.'

The maréchal staggered upright. 'You and I are not done,' he said to Ross. 'There will be a reckoning.'

Ross, arrogant with triumph, laughed and put his knee to the maréchal's back. Kit followed with her captive and they hurried through the narrow way in the direction of the market. At the mouth of the alley Ross stopped abruptly, pulling the maréchal back. Ahead of them was a regiment of French troops, drawn up in their blue battle array. 'Not a word,' hissed Ross in Villeroi's ear, but the maréchal, spying one of his officers on parade, shouted, 'D'Entragues! *Attention!*' Ross bundled him down the alley, almost lifting the maréchal so his feet scrabbled impotently on the ground. He swung left to the cathedral, to meet, waiting on the stone stairs, the Prince of Savoy and his guard of Imperial troops. 'Sire, the French are readying themselves!' Ross's words tumbled out. 'We are pursued by a regiment of French troops we surprised on parade. We must sound the muster.'

Savoy nodded to Van Dedan, who raised his instrument to his lips. The prince then bundled Villeroi into the cathedral, calling to Kit over his shoulder. 'You,' he commanded, 'bring the maréchal's man.' Having no option, she followed Savoy into the dark. The trumpeter blasted the muster and from all corners the dragoons came running, gathering on the square like crows, drawing their swords and axes as they came. The French came running too, and as the heavy door closed on Kit she saw blue meet red with a clash of steel.

She climbed the great tower to the sounds of battle outside. There was no artillery, and the men fought sword to sword. At the head of the wooden stair she pushed her prisoner ahead of her into the blinding daylight. From the dizzying height of the tower she could look down past the gargoyles' stone features to see a fight in every street. She strained to see Ross but could not make him out – she spotted Sergeant Taylor, though, for he had lost his hat, and his hair, as red as her own, caught the sun. She watched him dispatch one French soldier after another – his fighting style as blunt as his manner – and had to admit that he was a fierce fighter. And from this height she could see too that, although the dragoons had breached the walls of Cremona, they had not reached inside the citadel – across the wide span of a bridge was a further city within a city, a close-walled barbican of a castle with sturdy sloping talus walls.

She expected the battle to be short and sharp, but it seemed as if they were holed up for hours, this strange little quartet, on the parapet. A prince, a maréchal, an aide-de-camp and a soldier who was a maid in man's attire. After a time Villeroi and Savoy began to talk, in the careful courteous French of Paris, the birth-place of both. Kit, loosening her grip on the aide-de-camp, marvelled. Here were two men having a civilised conversation, while their respective forces battled in the square below. Kit knew that Savoy would say nothing about his deputy De Vaudémont and his forces at the Po gate, and she wondered what Villeroi had to conceal in his turn.

'Your defence is so obstinate that you will give the whole town time to wake,' said Savoy dryly.

'That, Prince, is the idea,' countered Villeroi. The *maréchal* seemed as comfortable as if he was in a Paris salon, but Savoy's urbane mask had begun to slip and Kit could hear him rage, under his breath. 'Where is he, where is he?' And Kit knew it was De Vaudémont he meant.

Just then there was an enormous explosion that rent the air and shivered the bell tower. Savoy rushed to the parapet, but Villeroi stayed where he was, his back to the leads. 'We have blown the bridge,' he said. 'Your forces cannot now reach the citadel.'

A cloud of stone dust and gunpowder rose to the south – where there had once been a bridge there were a few crumbled piles in the blue-grey river. The barbican was cut off from the rest of the town.

Savoy beat his fist on the balustrade. 'The action of a coward!'

Villeroi folded his arms. 'Is it more cowardly than creeping into a town to murder soldiers in their beds?'

Savoy paced, pounding one fist into his other hand. '*Sang du Christe*,' he said. 'I can hear Marlborough laughing from here.'

Footsteps sounded on the stair, and the four of them fell silent. What colour of soldier could be coming – blue to liberate Villeroi, or red to imprison him? It was red. It was Ross. 'Highness,' he said, breathing heavily, 'the French have blown the bridge. What are your orders?'

Savoy held his lower lip in his rabbit teeth for an instant. Then, low voiced, hardly audible, he growled, 'Retreat.'

Then, before she could react, he grabbed Kit's prisoner and threw him from the tower. 'No!' Kit cried, and ran to the balustrade. Down below the aide-de-camp was splayed out like a spider, his blond crown broken, the battle raging around him regardless. As she watched, a figure in a red coat stepped over the body and entered the fray. He fought fiercely, but with no elegance, his sword held out to the full extent of his reach, turning from side to side at the waist, almost as if he were scything a field of hay. Such a strategy could be suicide but no one could get near him. His brown curls were the same, his shoulders like a pair of barn doors in the plain red coat of a foot soldier.

Richard.

Heedless of protocol, Kit dashed to the little doorway and clattered down the stairs, her sword striking sparks from the stones, the musket which had a hundred marks upon its stock knocking against her collarbone. Her footsteps boomed as she ran across the marble pavings of the cathedral.

Outside all was confusion. Both the French and the English sounded the retreat; the forces had parted and scattered. At least, she thought in her mad dash, Richard would not die before she found him; both forces were focused on their flight. She ran to the spot where she had seen him, but he was gone. She saw red uniforms scattered in all directions, but headed for the river – did he have sapper mates to rejoin? She ran until the dust road ran out. A jagged edge jutted over the riverbank and led nowhere – she was at the fallen bridge. A hand caught the scruff of her neck. It was O'Connell, bleeding from a cut in his black brows. 'There's nowhere to go, Walsh,' he said. 'We're ordered back to the aqueduct.'

There was nothing to do but run – the cathedral, the parade ground, the marketplace, all flashed past, until they reached the little square with the well. The dragoons ran for their bolthole in the west wall, only to find it blocked. Colonel Gossedge's gouty girth had trapped him as he attempted to climb through. He was unconscious, his cocked hat knocked to the paving, blood leaking from his eyes and ears. 'Back,' shouted Hall. 'He's bunged like a cork in a bottle.'

More dragoons crowded behind 'The way is blocked,' said Southcott. 'Push him through.' Two men applied themselves to the task, but the corpulent colonel would not budge. Kit looked up at the pocked wall and the crenellations high above. 'Give me a leg up,' she said. Hall cupped his hands, and she placed her foot in them, clinging to the old stones, climbing until she reached the stones set in the top of the wall. Pulling herself up on to the top of the wall, she slid and scrambled down the other side, and found herself outside the city once more. She pulled at the colonel's shiny boots till he came out of the breach, and the dragoons streamed through – led by Captain Ross. Just as she was about to follow, something made her turn to look at the colonel, in his once-white breeches and his once-red coat. Without his hat and his eyeglass he was just a man, a fat man of middle years. And he still breathed.

Cursing, she turned back and dragged him to the aqueduct. Once she'd launched him on the water like a great barge, she turned him on his back so he could breathe. The ground shook with a thousand footsteps and Kit's heart sank; but the column who now swarmed round the aqueduct were red not blue; De Vaudémont's men. A scout ran to her side. 'It's Colonel Gossedge,' she shouted. His commander came at a run – a noble-looking fellow with a hooked nose: De Vaudémont, Savoy's deputy; a man denied entry to the city, trapped on the wrong side of a broken bridge, and forced to walk around the walls. 'Rejoin your regiment, boy,' he said, 'we have him now.' He laid a hand on Kit's shoulder. 'Well done.'

She ran down the aqueduct, keeping as low as she could, feet frozen blocks of ice in her boots, gasping and retching with fear.

Behind her the artillery had begun – cannon booming and muskets cracking from the walls of Cremona. For the first time since she had left Ireland she felt alone, and being alone made her afraid. She could have cried. Now she had no one, not her father, not Maura, not Richard. No Captain Ross, no Southcott or Hall or O'Connell. She would die here, in this freezing ribbon of silver, on these Roman arches. 'I never did find Richard,' she said to herself, and tears of pity fell and froze on her cheeks.

Then, ahead of her, she saw a red figure, hatless, with a poll of dark hair. His hand was at his brow, shielding eyes that she knew to be blue. A musket shot rent the air and she dropped to the ground, face in the freezing mud, grit and dirt in her teeth. She stayed down until the volley of musket fire had passed, and when she stood, he was gone. He had not waited. No one had.

On she ran, racing to reach the priest's house and the horses picketed in the orchard. She wanted to smell the apples underfoot, to feel Flint's velvety muzzle tickling her palm, to put her arms about the mare and lay her cheek on the warm velvet neck, and close her eyes.

She tripped over something soft and solid, and fell. Captain Ross lay half in, half out of the aqueduct. The musket ball that had missed her had hit him.

With all her strength, she rolled him over the low balustrade and down the short drop to the grass beneath, and jumped down after him. She dragged him over the tussocks under the shelter of one of the old arches. Kit cradled Ross, crushing his dear dark head to her breast. When she looked at him next his eyes were open, but her delight was tempered by the sound of marching feet growing closer. In another moment the feet marched overhead along the aqueduct, and the water that they displaced fell like rain. She raised a finger to her lips, afraid that Ross would begin raving, but he closed his eyes and opened them again in a sign that he understood. She had been right to hide, for the marching men were French, but, singing at the top of their voices. the enemy column would not have heard a trumpet blast.

'What are they singing?' Ross's voice was breathless.

She strained to hear above the boots and the splashes.

> *Par la faveur de Bellone,*
> *et par un bonheur sans égal,*
> *Nous avons conservé Crémone*
> *– et perdu notre général.*

She put her mouth to his ear. 'By the favour of Bellona, and a happiness without equal, we preserved Cremona, and lost our general.'

He smiled faintly and strained to say something.

'Hush – don't talk,' she said. When she opened his coat, his shirt was as red as his jacket.

'Can *you* sing, Kit?'

She looked at him, hopelessly, and nodded gently, so as not to spill the tears that had gathered in her eyes.

'Do it, then.'

She could think of no other song but one and she was afraid of her sweet high voice giving her away, but when she looked at him, and saw the colour of his face, so sickly green and white it did not look as if it belonged to the rest of him, she knew there would be no harm in it, for he would not be telling anyone anything any more.

> *Oh, me and my cousin, one Arthur McBride,*
> *As we went a-walkin' down by the seaside,*
> *Mark now what followed and what did betide,*
> *For it bein' on Christmas mornin' . . .*

He did not watch her but looked at the sky above. She choked and stuttered to a stop. His eyes were closed anyway, perhaps he hadn't heard. But the blue eyes fluttered open and he looked at her at last. 'You have a sweet voice, Kit.' Then his eyes closed again.

She held him there, as the sun rose higher; she closed her eyes too and, worn out with battle and sorrow, slept for the second time in his embrace. It was thus that Atticus Lambe, field surgeon to Her Majesty's Dragoons, found them.

Chapter 16

Good morning, good morning the sergeant did cry . . .

'Arthur McBride' (trad.)

Kit had reached the lake at last, the lake she had seen in a glimpse from the mountains when she rode with Ross. But now as she rode along the foreshore she could think of nothing but Ross's eyes the second before they closed. She had become closer to him then than she had ever been to anyone save Richard, save her father. She did not know whether she thought of her captain as a father or a lover, but she could not but think of him – and she could not rejoice at Richard being alive if Ross was dead. She turned her eyes away from the blue lake, to think of Richard, but she could not. She tried to count the hundred days she had been without her husband, but could get no farther than one. A hundred days without Richard. One day without Ross.

She had heard nothing of the captain since Lambe had taken him away. The Scots Greys, under the temporary command of Sergeant Taylor, were stationed in the mountain town of Arco, safe again in the embrace of Imperial lands, but the surgeon and his cart were nowhere to be seen. All divisions which had retreated from Cremona were to be billeted at Arco, and were even now snaking through the mountains, but Kit was torn between her desperate need to find Richard, and her anxiety for news of Ross.

On her first morning in Arco she had just set out from her lodgings to see whether she could discover the captain's where-abouts, when she was hailed by one of Marlborough's runners.

'I am to escort you to the Palazzo Marchetti,' he said. Kit, bemused, followed the ensign to a large, low, timbered house, the residence of the town mayor. Marlborough was seated at a desk in a painted chamber. To her surprise he stood and came around the desk to greet Kit.

'Ah, the Pretty Dragoon,' he said heartily. 'Good and bad at Cremona, eh? We made some inroads but they are still clinging on. At Luzzara, we'll be doing things my way, and you shall see a difference, eh? Good, plain British attack, and no skulking around. You'll be at the forefront, I'll wager? I've heard much that is good of your conduct at Cremona.'

Kit did not reply; there was little chance to speak in Marlborough's presence. Marlborough, accustomed to young cadets being cowed to silence, carried on regardless. 'I hear you carried a man to safety. Brave boy, skinny thing like you. He was no feather that one. Pity he died; he was a good man.'

The room darkened, Kit's knees weakened, she felt she might fall. Ross was dead. Somewhere, Marlborough was still speaking.

'And for this service to Her Majesty and myself, I reward you with five pistoles.' Marlborough dangled a purse in his fingers. Kit stared at the purse, swinging like a pendulum. The little bag began to blur.

'Sir . . . My lord . . . Your Grace . . . where is he buried?'

'By the river, I think. We sent his medals to Lady Gossedge.' The duke turned to his ensign. 'We did that, didn't we?'

Kit could barely speak. 'No . . . no, sir, not Colonel Gossedge, Ross. Captain Ross. Where is Captain Ross buried?'

Marlborough gave a little shout of laughter. 'Well, we thought it best not to bury him, for he is not dead.'

'Not dead?' A wave of relief flooded over Kit.

'He's in the field hospital. They've put it in the church, I think. He'll be back to berate you soon enough. I'm told you had something to do with his rescue too. So you shall have . . .' he turned to his ensign, 'what is the name of the castle above us?'

'Castello Arco, sir.'

'That's it. I give you leave to search the castle before the divisions come. Here, take this.' He scribbled a dispensation and sealed it with his ring. 'Sole rights of plunder.'

She took the paper and tucked it in the purse. 'Thank you, sir.'

'Well, well.' The great duke seemed discomfited by simple gratitude. 'Off you go.'

Outside in the bright morning, Kit clasped her purse and took a lungful of freezing air. Ross was alive, she had five pistoles, and a castle to plunder too – her life with Richard could begin again in comfort and prosperity. But before she climbed the hill to claim her prize there was a visit she must make.

She went straight to the little white church and was stopped at the door by Atticus Lambe, wearing a butcher's apron spattered with blood. Her heart sank. 'Please, Doctor . . .' She was not sure how to address a surgeon.

'You may call me Mr Lambe.'

'May I see Captain Ross?'

'You may not. He is resting.'

'Just for a moment?'

'On no account.'

'Is he recovered?'

'He is much improved; I have removed the musket ball from his side. But he is still an invalid for all that and as such may not be visited. The Lord only knows what evil miasmas you carry on your person.'

He looked at her with a disapproving gaze.

'Will you tell him that I sent him good wishes?'

'Certainly not. I am not a post horse.'

Kit shrugged and turned away. Nothing could dent her feelings:

the sun was shining, there was a breath of spring and the mountains were beautiful. As she climbed to the castle, heavy key in hand, she scattered the cabbage butterflies, sniffed the rock roses and picked late brambles from the hedgerows. She was cock-a-hoop. She was a soldier, she had acquitted herself bravely, and she had been rewarded by her commander. She had been given the key to the castle. She could ask for nothing more in the world. Her captain was alive, and Richard would soon be here.

The castle stood at the top of the hill. She had expected it to resemble the great barbican of Rovereto, but long-ruined towers reached into the sky like a jaw of broken teeth. Kit had thought to stuff her pockets with the coins and treasure that would doubtless be scattered on the floor, but in fact a wrecked wagon had been upended in the broken doorway and secured by a chain. She unlocked the chain and drew it through the wagon wheels with a rhythmic clinking clatter, rolled the cart aside and entered the castle that was hers for the day.

It was a broken place. Ruined stairs led to nowhere, two shattered towers reached into the sky like surrendering hands, and windows were open to frame blue skies and mountains. She wandered from chamber to chamber, wondering what these rooms once housed; one had a huge stone fireplace, still blackened with the smoke of ancient feasts. Kit's buoyant mood sank into a nameless foreboding. The French had gutted the place and left their detritus behind; powder packets, ramrods, an old saddle, a broken stool. The remnants of a fire, a privy smell in the dark corners. She made her way back to the roofless great hall and then stopped as she heard a scrabbling sound. She froze, her hand flying instinctively to where her sword should have been. She picked up the broken stool and retreated into the shadow of a fractured doorway.

A pig came trotting into the middle of the cavernous room, as if it entered a forest clearing. Kit remembered Signor Castellano and his parable of the pigs in the mountains. All at once she was consumed with a hunter's instinct. She would have this pig, and she would take it back to her fellows and they would roast it and perhaps, perhaps, Richard would come marching up the hill in time to sup with them. If this was the only booty here, very well: it was hers.

It was an epic chase, around and about the broken walls, up and down stairs, into the ancient earthworks that lay beneath the broken floors. Once she had the pig at bay in a dungeon, but he dashed through her legs and out into the light again.

A freezing rain began to fall, turning the hall to mud so that Kit's boots slid around. At last she cornered the pig in the blackened fireplace. She threw a stool at his head and he dropped and lay there stunned, a gout of blood like a blackberry behind his ear. She wound her stock about his neck and tied the loose end to a stake, and sat in the oozing mud, elbows on knees, exhausted.

She felt a prickling at her back. Sergeant Taylor was sitting on a spiral stair that led nowhere, watching her. 'I'm the King of the Castle,' he sang. 'And you're the Dirty Rascal.' He laughed drunkenly.

She stood slowly, backing away, shielding the pig. Taylor took a pull from a clay bottle, his eyes never leaving her face. 'Marlborough himself gave me sole plunder of this place,' she said. Taylor flinched at Marlborough's name. 'If you challenge me you must answer to your master.'

'Plunder?' spat Taylor. 'You fled up the bell tower like a rat up a rope while the rest of us were fighting. And then, when it was all over, you pulled a fat old colonel from a wall like a cork from a bottle. That pig should be mine. I got my hands good and dirty in Cremona.'

'No,' she said. 'Not again.' He'd taken her bell at the monastery of San Columbano, he would not take her pig.

'Thank you for the bell, by the way. I sold it by the lump to a Jew. Got a pretty price. And now you've caught this pig for me. Didn't look easy. Better than the shuttlecock, watching you chase him like that.'

He stood, tossed his clay bottle down, and started towards her down the steps. Kit's skin started to prickle. He had a wicked little dagger in his hand, and she was unarmed. Out of the corner of her eye, she could see the pig waking, staggering to his trotters and testing the extent of his tether.

Taylor came at her. She grabbed the dagger instinctively, and it nearly sliced her little finger through. Shifting her grip, her hands slippery with rain and blood, she fought furiously over the blade. Blood poured from her finger and down her sleeve, and her arms buckled, black spots mingling with the rain before her eyes. She could feel Taylor's sour breath on her cheek as they grappled. Blind rage took her. She was not going to let this man destroy her life. Ross was alive and she was about to see Richard again. She screamed in his face: 'The pig is mine! Mine!' Taylor blinked in surprise and she realised she could use her rage as a weapon to overpower him. Slowly, slowly the wicked silver blade turned and with every muscle straining she forced the needle-sharp point towards Taylor's eye. His gaze flickered in horror as she pushed with the last of her strength and felt a pop and a rush. Taylor fell back, his body slack, and she almost fell on top of him as he dropped to the ground, screaming, clutching the dagger that had pierced his eye. The pig began to scream too; the animal squeals mixing with Taylor's until it was impossible to tell them apart. At last Taylor, writhing in the mud, found some words.

'My fucking eye! You're finished, Walsh!'

Kit untethered the pig and turned to go. 'As you said, no witnesses.'

Chapter 17

And sup on thin gruel in the morning . . .

                                  'Arthur McBride' (trad.)

Back at the camp, Kit handed the pig to Mr Morgan, a solid Welsh dragoon with a ready smile. He spotted her hand. 'Buggering Christ, Walsh, you got too many fingers or something? Get away to see Lambe, before you bleed out.'

Kit looked down at the rag scrunched in her hand. It was red. 'Give the pig to Hall,' she said, 'he's a rare cook. Save some for me.'

Cradling her hand, she hurried to the white church and banged at the carved door with her elbow. Lambe came to the door.

'What is the matter?'

She held out her hand to him. The gash was so deep it looked as if her finger was barely hanging on. The surgeon's lip curled with scorn. 'This is a shabby attempt.'

'I do not understand you . . .'

'Oh, I think I do. You were here this morning, asking to see my patient. You turn up again, not three hours later, with an injury that begs my attention. Is there no length to which you will not go to be in the company of Captain Ross?'

'I assure you,' protested Kit, 'I had no such aim in coming here. My finger is all but severed.'

Atticus Lambe regarded her red hand for some moments while her finger throbbed. 'Your little scheme has failed; I discharged Captain Ross at noon. And that being the case, you may come in.'

There was a dreadful smell in the church: excrement, blood and under it all the sweetish smell of incense. Someone moaned, incessantly, low voiced, behind canvas curtains. Wooden pews had been covered with tick mattresses and a soldier lay on each, bearing their wounds from Cremona. Each man lay under his own pool of light from the stained glass, the jewel colours masking the stains of their dressings; the red of blood, the brown of excrement, the yellow of pus.

Atticus Lambe picked up two chairs and set them beneath a broken window. Kit sat in the white light; Lambe sat opposite her and took her hand into his lap. Painfully, she uncurled the fingers – all had been cut when she clasped Taylor's dagger but none as grievously as her littlest one.

She found it hard to look at the wound – the finger was cut to the quick and she could see white bone. Lambe took a fresh kerchief to clean the wound. 'I just saw a sergeant with a pierced eye,' he said, speaking to the cut. 'What do you know about that?'

She winced. 'Nothing, sir.'

'Hmm. This is not a day of action, and yet two men have come to me injured and bleeding. What am I to suppose?'

'I cannot tell you, sir.'

'He will lose the sight in his eye.'

Kit swallowed. Taylor had always disliked her; now she would be his implacable enemy. 'Will he be discharged from service?'

'No.' Lambe seemed pleased. 'I have given him a patch. Men have fought with greater lacks than an eye. He had not much beauty to spoil, but his judgement of distance will be affected. So you may take solace in the fact that in battle he may well die all the faster.'

She met his gaze. He looked down at the cut again. 'How did you come by this wound?'

Kit thought fast. 'I drew my sword in haste, and my hand slipped.'

'Ah. And lost your sword in the process, I see.' He looked at the empty scabbard at her waist. 'Your sergeant told me much the same story, except he contrived to put his eye out when drawing his dagger. I doubt our enemies have much to fear from you; you seem to be doing their job for them.'

He threw the stained kerchief into a basin. Beyond it she saw a collection of instruments: pliers, knives and even a little saw. 'Well: your finger is all but severed and since you have been obliging enough to start the surgery for me, I should just nip the thing off.'

She looked him in the eye and raised her chin a fraction. 'Very well. If it is beyond you to mend it, take it.'

Her gambit worked. 'Of course I can stitch the thing. But a choice lies before you. I can take the finger, cauterise it and you will go on your way. Or I can save the finger, and you run the risk of infection and a higher amputation later. Which is it to be?'

'I will keep the finger.'

'Very well.'

She watched him closely, anything to distract herself from the terrible, probing pain. Anything that meant she did not have to watch the sewing needle, curved like a tooth. In the end, she could not bear it. 'May I not have something for the pain?'

He looked at her as if he had beaten her at a hand of cards. 'We have nothing to give you. Our supplies have diminished so much as to be kept for more *serious* cases. But you may pass out soon enough from the pain.'

Kit nodded. Had Ross had to lie thus, awake, while Lambe dug the bullet from him? Or did an officer's stripe buy a spoonful of laudanum?

So she sweated, bit her lips and watched Atticus Lambe. The grey eyes like water over pebbles, the black pinprick pupils that focused on her finger – the scroll of his ear, the ash-blond hair cut close into the neck. He was young – not more than five and twenty – and would have been handsome if he had not been so thin. His cheeks were hollow, his white wrists protruded some inches from his frock coat – he was too thin, too tall, too gangly; like a pale summer spider. His skin had a strange grey sheen to it; in fact he seemed all of one colour, for his teeth, skin, eyes, all were pearly grey, and his medical frock coat was of the same hue. He sweated with the effort, despite the icy mountain breeze whipping through the broken window. She knew that he saw only her finger – that she was not a human, but a challenge. He disliked her, she knew, but at this point he would have done anything to save this finger. As he worked, she found herself reluctantly admiring him. He had a prodigious skill.

At last she was stitched and bound and he unfolded his long body. He took off his pince-nez and pushed them into his breast pocket. 'You'll keep a good scar,' he said, almost friendly. 'But you'll keep the finger too.'

She stretched out her aching arm, flexed the other fingers. 'I don't know how to thank you.'

He considered her. 'Oh, I think you do.' His gaze was an awl, probing her as closely as the needle had done; urging her to understand something. But before she could reply, the surgeon had turned away from her. 'Take the bed in the Lady Chapel. The nurses will bring you gruel.'

'I'm to *stay*?'

'Yes. The first twelve hours are crucial for the incubation of any infection. By morning we'll know if we need to take your hand.' And he dismissed her with a wave.

Kit laid herself down on the little bed in the Lady Chapel as she'd been bidden. She looked at the frescoes curling about the white walls – more haloed saints. Exhausted by the events of the day, she slept, and the saints of the mountains watched her.

She was woken late in the evening. One of the nurses, a pimply boy sporting a butcher's apron, brought her a dish of thin gruel.

Her stomach growled, and she spooned it down, but she could not help but think of her pig, and his blood pudding, and his sides made of pork, and his legs made of ham, and his back made of bacon. She could almost smell him – she was *sure* she could smell him.

There was a murmuring at the door, and she could hear a voice – Mr Morgan, with his voice as up and down as the Welsh mountains from which he hailed, and that heavenly smell again. She heard her own name, then Lambe's voice, curt and flat, but acquiescent. She strained to listen but the door closed, nothing happened, and she drifted again.

The next time she woke, she thought she dreamt, because she saw a little table set by her. A little silver candlestick stood sentinel, with a fine white candle burning. A crystal glass stood on the other side, brimming with rich red porter. On the table was set a shining pewter plate, not a battered army tin but round and true as the moon. It was piled with pork, done to a turn, with crispy crackling shining with fat and the plate swimming with rich gravy. Kit propped herself on her elbow, her hand throbbing anew, but she hardly felt the pain. She threw back the coverlet, and made to rise.

But at that moment Atticus Lambe entered the little room. He took his glasses from his nose, flipped his coat tails out behind him and sat down at the table. With his grey eyes fixed upon her, he took a good drink of his port, took up his knife and fork and tucked in to the pork. She watched as he sucked on the bones, chewed on the flesh and his grey teeth snapped the crackling. He ate every morsel on the plate, his eyes never leaving her, the pupils now huge and round. There was something obscene in the way he savoured the meat, and swilled his mouth with the wine. Then, finally, he crossed his cutlery, drained his porter, and left without a word, his grey eyes on her to the last. He left the detritus there, and the heavenly twin smells of meat and wine, to torture her dreams.

She lay back, as exhausted as if she'd fought him physically. She did not sleep again, but waited until the hospital was quiet, and even the groaning man had ceased his cries. The candle guttered and died and now only the saints' gilded haloes could be seen as she rose in the silver moonlight and crept from her room. She would not spend another night in the power of Atticus Lambe.

Chapter 18

And to drink the King's health in the morning . . .

'Arthur McBride' (trad.)

No one wanted to miss the battle of Luzzara.

After months of waiting, of missteps and manoeuvres, they were to meet their enemy face to face. Men rose from their hospital beds in the little white church, boys joined the Imperial forces from the streets armed with pitchforks and their Sunday coats dyed red. Marlborough had told them that the streets were paved with gold and booty. Kit did not care for booty, but knew that she was near the end of her personal quest. Every company, including Tichborne's, was to be at Luzzara. This time there would be no mistakes. There was no clandestine strategy; this was out and out battle in the open, just as Kit had always imagined it. Here, she would find Richard and fight side by side with Ross.

He was now fully recovered and they seemed back on their old footing, but they had shared that moment at the aqueduct and it had made them brothers in arms. They rode together; they camped together by the fire. Joy and optimism returned, O'Connell got out his fiddle again and played the old favourites: 'The Humours of Castlefin', 'John Dwyer's Jig', 'The Maids of Mitchelstown'. Kit kept her song inside – there was only one ballad for her, and there was to be no singing except that once, by the aqueduct, half in, half out of the freezing water, and then only to save a life. She was glad, so glad, that Ross had lived, that their friendship had survived. The only difference was Atticus

Lambe, trundling sullenly behind on his medical cart like some Grim Reaper. Whenever his grey eyes fell upon Kit she felt chilled. She vowed never to get sick and need his ministrations again.

Kit had never seen so many souls gathered in one place as she saw on the battlefield of Luzzara. This was a plain between the River Po and Lake Garda – a true battlefield, a vast open space; granted, it was pitted with ditches and channels, and low fences and high bushes, but it was an interrupted plain where the Alliance forces and the armies of the Two Crowns faced each other, lined neatly, leagues apart.

Kit waited on the hill with the Scots Grey Dragoons. She clasped her reins with her tender right hand – still bandaged but better – and narrowed her eyes across the plain. A ribbon of blue wreathed the slope opposite, punctured by spears and colours with standards. Immediately before her was the martial figure of the Duke of Marlborough; in his helmet and his armour and his silken cape and his Order of the Garter, blue as the sky. But she turned her eyes from him to look along the ranked redcoats, stretching as far as the eye could see, left and right. She could not see Richard. In fact, she had not seen nor heard of him since Cremona, and she was beginning to wonder whether she had imagined him. But she had to believe he was here, was one of those red skittles on the hill. She lowered her musket from her shoulder, took out her case knife and made one last notch on the stock. Two hundred and eighty-five days without Richard. Today she would find him.

There was a long, tense silence – the horses shifted and tossed their heads, the partisans wavered in their lines, the muskets shimmered as they were brought to the shoulder. In that moment, sitting high above the battlefield on Flint's back, she was a girl again, back in her cotton gown at the top of Killcommadan Hill, the sun warm on her back. She was ready, poised in the moment when she'd tipped forward, hung between balance and motion, just before she started to run. Then the cacophony; the trumpets sounded the attack and the drummers began their battery, the cannon rolled forth. Flint pricked her ears, ready too. And Kit spurred her on.

It was one of the most perfect moments of her life. The wind rushed by her ears, blurring the sounds of battle; her eyes streamed. She drew her father's sword, and it shone above her in the sun. The sounds of thousands of feet and hooves on the field was like nothing Kit had ever heard – clods split and spun from the earth – soil was in her mouth, gunpowder in her nose. She was invincible. She gave an incoherent battle cry as she hurtled down the hill towards the enemy, slashing with her sword the French cavalier who rode straight at her. He fell from his horse at last and she found another, then another, crazed with battle, drunk with it. The French foot soldiers were under Flint's feet; she cut them down where they stood. The world had collapsed to red and blue; red were spared, blue she put down. Then, out of the corner of her eye, through the chaos, she saw a man in a red coat fighting like a Catherine wheel, his sword at full length, turning like a dervish.

Richard.

She put up her sword and slid from the saddle. Somebody shouted. She ran through the ranks. Now she could see him clearly; his brown curls fell over his face just as they used to. She was so close now – close enough to see those green eyes she'd almost forgotten. Her mouth opened to scream his name. Then there was a flash, a cloud of bitter smoke and she was punched backwards though the air, lifted from her feet. There was a nameless, awful pain at her hip. Then blackness.

Kit woke to see a silver creature crouching like a spider on a table by her bed. The silver creature had a snubbed silver snout with one nostril, a long broad back, and leathery, spindly limbs like a daddy-long-legs. It was a creature from a nightmare, its silver skin tarnished, its smell acrid like urine. As her dreams fled and she began to wake, she realised what was on the table at her bedside. It was her silver prick.

She tried to sit, could not, her heart racing, her thoughts spinning in horror. She did not know where she was, or how much time had passed, knew only that she was on a bed, alone, in a stone room. There were no plaster saints floating above her head, so she was not in the church-turned-field-hospital at Arco. She looked down at her body, bandaged from chest to thigh, and grew cold. Atticus Lambe had stripped her and treated her and found out her secret.

All of the safeguards, all the deceit she'd practised for months, training her speech and her manner and her deportment, and it was her own body which had given her away.

Her truckle bed was right in the centre of the room, with a little table by her head. Her uniform was folded neatly over a nearby chair like a shed skin; she was wearing the linen shift and ragged red cross of the field hospital. She remembered then; the battle, the euphoria – then Richard, and the explosion. She'd been injured, for there was a pain in her hip acute enough to make her want to vomit when she moved. She forced herself to think. So she had been unmasked, and by Atticus Lambe, a man who had proved himself her enemy.

Her father's sword was propped tidily by her uniform, her sheathed dagger placed neatly on the top of her pile of small clothes. Her musket – which had been in her hand when she'd fallen – was gone; and with it, all notion of time passed. She'd fallen off the calendar into this stone well – presumably, somewhere above her head, there were sunlit lands where time carried on.

There were no other patients with her – if Lambe had told no one, she could dispatch him. Battle was one thing, but cold-blooded murder? Could she do it? Her own body answered the question – when she tried to rise again she could not, for her bandaged right leg would not move at all – responding to her efforts only with a searing pain from hip to foot. She lay back, exhausted by even this tiny exertion. She was trapped.

She heard feet moving around overhead, and for what seemed like hours she waited. At last he came, first an arm appearing in the doorway, holding a firebrand high; then the doctor himself, pale and malign under the hissing torch.

'Where am I?'

Atticus Lambe set the torch in an empty bracket. 'You are in the fortress of Riva del Garda. My Lord Marlborough has commandeered the upstairs chambers for his war rooms, and I have been given the cellars for my hospital.'

'Where are the others?'

'What others?'

'It was a mighty battle. I cannot be the only injured man.'

He looked at her. 'But you are the only injured woman.' He rolled his sleeves up beyond his long white wrists. 'The wounded soldiers are in the wine cellars. Because of your particular . . . needs . . . I reserved this dungeon especially for you.'

He drew up a stool next to her, his eyes lit by the torchlight as she had never seen them. He laid the back of his cold hand on her forehead, and she shrank from his touch. 'No fever,' he said. 'That is good.' His hand moved to her cheek, and he pushed a cold thumb through her lips. It tasted sour. 'Of course, one sees it now. Plump lips. Those eyes, shaped and coloured like a cat's. Snub nose, freckles, white skin that has never seen a razor. Red curls. Such a pretty boy. Pity.'

She wished he would go. She wanted to think, to plan, and she could do neither under his gaze. His eyes travelled down her body. 'It was very interesting, operating upon a woman again. I have not opened up a dame since I was at Saint Bart's. And they were corpses, of course.' He sniffed. 'Mostly whores. I once opened one up with a child inside.' He broke off and smiled pleasantly.

'But why am I taxing your patience? You will never need to know this. Childbearing is not in your stars.'

She shuffled on to her elbows with an effort and studied his face. Was he mad? Did he *not* know she was a woman?

'I mean, of course, that although you are female, you will *never bear a child.*'

He sat back, as if he had played an ace at the card table. She watched him, numb with shock, her dry lips working. *Never bear a child.* The surgeon gave a merry laugh. 'Forgive me. Let me begin at the beginning.' He folded back the coverlet and raised her gown. 'The musket ball entered your body here at the hip.' He pressed on the place where blood had seeped through the bandage, and a fiery pain shot through Kit. 'It chipped the ball joint and travelled into the womb, rupturing the lining. I removed the bone fragments from your hip and staunched the bleeding in the uterus wall. I sewed the womb as, you will remember, I once sutured your finger; no mean task, I assure you, for it is as thick as cow's liver.' Kit shook her head, dazed – was he actually expecting her to congratulate him on his tailoring? 'I did an admirable job, but the rupture will never allow the implantation of a viable foetus.' He replaced the covers, stood and brushed his coat, as if she had infected him somehow. 'Well; I imagine you wish to be alone with your thoughts.' He extinguished the ring of torches, one by one, and left her in total blackness.

She cried then. She cried from loss; not the loss of Ross or Richard or even Kit the soldier, but the loss of her future children, children she had never known she'd wanted until now.

After that Atticus Lambe would come to her each day, draw up a chair as if he were to begin a cosy fireside chat, and then torture her with his words. At these times his eyes were black, his pupils huge, the pale grey of his eyes diminished to the tiniest halo about the darkness. She thought to herself – *he is mad*. He would talk, constantly, of Captain Ross – never by name, but always as 'him'.

'I thought about letting you die.' He spoke matter-of-factly. 'You were bleeding profusely. It would have been so easy to let you bleed out. And then you would never see have seen him again.'

Kit swallowed. She tried to adopt his dispassionate tone. 'Why didn't you?'

He did not quite look at her, but changed the subject. 'He had a wife, you know.'

Kit was startled. 'Ross?'

'Yes. He met her at Oxford. She was his tutor's daughter. Our tutor, of the Greek language. We sat in his room, Ross and I, and what times we had!' His wistful face looked almost pleasant. 'Our tutor would tell us of Jason, and Hercules, and Achilles the great hero of Troy. He would tell us of the love the Greeks held for each other – a higher love between men, of the mind as well as the body – not the grubby rutting of men and women.' His lip curled. 'But he was stolen from me, by that chit of a don's daughter. His family was against it; second son, destined for the Church or the army, but still the apple of their eye. But he married her anyway. Diana, she was called. A delicate thing. He settled her on his estate in Renfrewshire with his mother. By the time he bought his commission Diana was with child. The bull had got a calf on his heifer. Then he went to Flanders and the child came early. Diana's doctor was a village quack, and mother and babe died on the childbed.' Again, the passionless delivery, with just a hint of professional scorn. 'He blamed himself for being absent, for moving her from Oxford, where she would have had access to the best medical minds.' He sniffed. 'And since then he has fought every campaign they would give him. Trying to get himself killed. So of course, because he courted death, Fate turned every blade from him and he dodged every bullet.'

Kit thought of Ross at the walls of Cremona, taking a case knife from a French body, cutting his own hand with the blade so it might never harm him again. She said, in the same spirit of candour, 'I think, now, he cares to live.'

'I think so too. But only since you came along.' There was real pain in his voice. The surgeon looked down on her. 'Do you think you saved him that day?'

She did not need to ask which day. The retreat from Cremona. The aqueduct. Arthur McBride.

'You *do*,' Lambe said accusingly. 'You think you saved him. But you didn't. *I* saved him, not you. You pulled him from the mud, which is an office that a mule could render him, but it takes a man of science to save a life. Did you know he'd stopped to wait for you? I heard as much as he raved. "Kit," he'd say, "catch up." Patients say all manner of things. I could tell you more than a priest.' His eyes bored into her, and she wondered what *she* had said in her delirium. 'He turned back for you and got himself shot. You weakened him. You are the heel of Achilles. His weak spot. I understand. You think you're in love with him.'

'By God,' she said, suddenly understanding. 'If I am not, I know who is.'

He flinched, as if slapped; stood, and stalked from the room.

She lay back, her heart thudding. *The heel of Achilles*, he'd called her. This she did not understand, but she understood 'weak spot' all right. Had she compromised Ross at Cremona? Had the same thing happened to him at Cremona as happened to her at Luzzara? Both of them had run to the aid of a loved one. Did Ross, then, have feelings for her? She did not know – but she knew one thing for certain. Atticus Lambe loved Captain Ross. And Atticus Lambe was jealous of Kit Walsh.

Kit considered the nature of such a love. Lambe was convinced that the love between men was a higher thing, prescribed by the Greeks. What if he was right? What if it was not a low thing – a cooper's beefy hand on the thigh, the 'coney-catchers' of Dublin docks sniffing the air for young untried boys – but a thing of nobility, as lofty as the sacrament between man and wife?

If Ross had feelings for her, they must have been of the nature of the Greeks – for he believed her to be a boy. Had he changed, after the death of his wife, to find himself unable to love a woman again? It seemed a long stride from marriage and consummation with a woman to the love that Atticus Lambe desired, the love that had once been so graphically described to her by Maria van Lommen. Or had Ross developed feelings for her because he knew, on some level, that she was female? It was all so confusing, but her last waking notion was one even more discomfiting. Was she, as Lambe maintained, in love with Ross?

In the first days in her hospital-prison Kit had no way of knowing which hours were passing, but in time she began to distinguish day from night by the faint noises of the outside world. When carts went rumbling over the drawbridge and children played about the moat, it was day. Then, too, she heard footsteps over-head and the groans akin to those she'd heard in the sanctuary at Arco, and knew that Lambe was dealing with his patients in the cellars. When jug-bitten soldiers sang in the street, or an owl hooted in the keeps, it was night. She began to think of the outside world as a place she would never go again. She did not know whether the regiment missed her, whether Lambe had told them of the woman who'd been masquerading in their midst, or even whether the Grand Alliance had won the battle of Luzzara.

Outside in that world people were divided into petticoats and uniforms, and were identified by which one they wore. But she learned in her dungeon that character had nothing to do with a person's sex. The self inside was clean and white like the core of an apple, and it mattered not whether the apple's skin was red or green. She was still herself, still Kit. She wondered whether love too was not a matter of sex, but was attached to a person. Was Kit the woman as lovable as Kit the boy?

She realised too, over the next many days and weeks, how much she needed Atticus Lambe; and that he needed her as much as she needed him. Now she knew his secret love he sought her out. He was her saviour; but she was also his. Many times she thought about telling him about Richard – that she just wanted to find her husband, then she would leave and never trouble him again. Might he let her go, might he even help her, in order to be free of her? But something stopped her. She did not want him to bend his malign gaze on Richard. So she held her tongue, as Lambe loosened his.

In many ways, he did right by her. He changed her dressings assiduously and fed her gruel with his own hand. But although he gave her nothing but food and water, he medicated himself constantly from the ranks of little green bottles he kept in a cabinet in the corner of the dungeon.

The first time she caught him at this, he'd held a little green bottle aloft, as if drinking her health. 'The Greeks again, you see,' he said, drily. 'They gave us all the greatest elements of our civilisation. Socrates gave us philosophy. Hippocrates medicine. And Paracelsus gave us laudanum.'

Reality dawned. All those men he'd treated, he'd cut open with only a leather strap to wring in their hands and a stick to bite in their teeth. The limbs he'd taken with his saw, the musket balls he'd dug from sinewed flesh, the incisions he'd made; all with no relief from the pain, because Lambe was feeding his terrible addiction. 'You have been keeping it for yourself,' she breathed.

Lambe turned his head, very slowly, and focused his eyes on her. The pupils were huge again. 'No,' he said, forming the words carefully, hissing like the torches. 'Not all of it. I gave some to *him*. My love cannot suffer pain.'

She had to ask. 'You really think Ross is of your . . . persuasion? That he loves like the Greeks?'

Here Lambe blinked and frowned. 'I think he would. I think I could make him love me – but you have been turning his head. But soon you will be gone,' he said. And she knew then, he would never let her leave his dungeon.

Getting dressed was the most painful process she had ever had to endure. She could barely lift her right leg into her breeches, for the hip joint seemed to have no power, and her wound began to bleed again, an ugly dark stain soaking through the bandage. She could not face strapping on the silver prick, so tucked it in her saddlebag. She leaned on her sword as a crutch. This time she would not skulk out of his hospital – oh no. She must see Lambe's face. For she had a deal to make.

He came down in the evening as ever and saw her dressed and sitting on the bed. He paused for a moment, but said nothing, setting his torch in the sconce as he always did. He turned and she rose to face him.

He raised his chin. 'You walked out of my care once. You will not do it again. You will stay until you are well, and when you are well, I will have you discharged. You will be shipped home to whatever little province you hailed from.'

'I am going,' she said measuredly, 'to walk up these stairs and out into the world. I will commend your care and rejoin the dragoons. I will leave you to your devices and you will leave me to mine.'

He stared at her, his pupils angry black pinpricks. She could not be sure that he had heard her. 'I am going now,' she repeated. 'And you will not prevent me.'

'No!' he shouted, his voice booming about the dungeon. She turned, painfully, leaning on her sword. 'You will keep my counsel, and I will keep yours.' Her voice sounded weak, and her accent very Irish, as it always became when she was tense. 'For if I have a secret, you have one too. Your secret lives in a bottle, and it keeps you alive. You cannot be without it.' She stood as straight as she could bear. 'I have the ear of the Duke of Marlborough himself. What will he say, I wonder, when he knows you have been leaving his men in pain to feed your wants?'

Atticus Lambe drew back his lip. 'The duke will not listen to a woman! He will not give you an audience when he knows how you deceived him!'

'Except he does not know, does he?' she whispered. 'I do not think you have told anyone. I think you have given it abroad that Private Walsh is gravely injured, but not that he is female. I think you were purchasing time, deciding what to do, deciding if you could bring yourself to kill me.' She moved closer to him, so they were almost nose to nose. 'There is no reason why you may not kill me now. I am too weak to resist you. You could restrain me easily, stab me with one of your instruments; pretend I have died of my wounds. I am in my uniform. You wouldn't even have to go to the trouble of dressing my body.' She shook from the effort, steeled herself to look into the pale eyes. 'You cannot do it, can you? You cannot take a life. You are too good a doctor.' She spoke calmly. 'If you'd been there with Ross's wife and babe, you would have saved them, would you not, though it ruined all your hopes?'

Almost imperceptibly, he nodded, his eyes blinking once.

'Return to your profession,' she urged gently, 'and I will return to mine.' She held his gaze.

He dropped his pale eyes first. 'I have patients to attend to.'

'Goodbye, Mr Lambe.' She held out her hand, the hand he had stitched. 'And thank you for your care of me. I hope not to trouble you again.'

He took her hand with no pressure, his fingers limp and clammy. He met her eyes with a brief flicker of a glance. 'Goodbye, Mr Walsh.'

It would do. Kit walked up the stone stair, painfully, into the light.

Chapter 19

And he pays all his debts without sorrow or strife . . .

'Arthur McBride' (trad.)

Ross and the dragoons welcomed Kit back warmly; Sergeant Taylor
alone stood apart. She had been gone for almost three months.
Captain Ross had been told, on repeated enquiry, that she was
gravely ill and on the brink of death, and could have no visitors
because of the risk of infection. When the captain restored her
matchlock musket to her, she carefully carved four score notches
on the stock – another eighty days without Richard – while she
listened to the regiment's news. Luzzara had been a victory for
the Grand Alliance, but the French had had their revenge at a
skirmish at Cassano, on the Adda river close by Milan, and that
battle had claimed a nobler casualty than she. The Prince of Savoy
himself had been injured and had returned to Austria for treat-
ment. 'He's been abed as long as you have, Walsh,' said Hall.
'The leech loves royal blood too.' Now the prince was back in
the saddle – his recovery keeping pace with Kit's – the dragoons
were to rejoin him back at Rovereto to launch their next offensive:
the capture of Mantova. 'Furious as a wasp in a bottle, is the
prince,' said Southcott, 'and determined to have Mantova back
from the French.' When Kit asked Captain Ross whether Atticus
Lambe would be travelling with them, he told her that he would
be staying at Luzzara with the injured until they were well enough
to travel, but would join them for the next engagement. 'You owe
him a great debt,' said Ross.

'I do indeed,' said Kit grimly

As she rode away from Lambe's clutches she thought, almost incessantly, of her conversations with him. While in his dungeon-hospital she had thought only of getting out alive, of seeing Ross again, of finding Richard. But now she was safe, she returned again and again to the revelation that she would never bear a child. Sometimes she wondered whether he had lied to her to play games. But when she thought of the rest of their discourse she was as sure as she could be that he had never lied to her about matters medical. The body was his only truth – he could not harm, only heal. He had spoken of Ross's wife and child, and the particulars of their deaths, with dispassion; there was no reason to suppose that his assessment of her own injuries was anything other than cold fact.

She had never particularly wanted children; when newly married she had assumed, without much excitement, that children would one day follow; children who, in her idle daydreams, wore her face or Richard's like little mummers' masks. She had only really wanted to share her life with Richard. But now she felt she had truly lost something. And now she was a man again, breasts bound painfully once more, the silver prick resting uncomfortably on her scars, and under it a ruptured, useless womb, completing the strange hybrid she had become.

She watched Ross constantly. He was solicitous, ever present, he smiled, his gaze lingered on her a little too long. She asked herself whether he perhaps saw her as a son, but their ages were not so different for this to be plausible; and she began to be convinced that it was Lambe's sickness that ailed him. That Ross loved her as a boy thrilled and disgusted her, but just as much, she questioned her own feelings. Was it possible to love two men? Did she still truly love Richard? And if she did, why could she not remember his face?

As they neared Rovereto it was coming to high summer. The trees had cast off their white capes to show green leaves, the sky was blue instead of silver. She marked a momentous notch on her musket; three hundred and sixty-five days without Richard; an entire year. It had been summer when he'd left Kavanagh's, and it was summer again. But the sun and the mountain air were good physicians – every day she became stronger. Her hip still pained her, especially at night, but every day she would walk on it for a league or two, leading Flint, to strengthen her wasted limbs.

On their last night in the mountains before descending into the town they came to the very spot where she had slept in Ross's arms on that deep midwinter night. Now she sat a little apart from him when they ate their mess of stew. Hearing of their approach, camp-followers had joined them from the town, and a dragoon called Foreshew was reunited with his local love. Soldier and lady announced their intention to have a 'camp marriage' and Ross, as the captain of the troop, was to officiate. He conducted the mock ceremony in good heart, and watched the couple share a shortbread and jump over two crossed swords, but as the newly-weds kissed, Kit read in his face some indefinable pain.

After the wedding Ross sought her out, sitting beside her on a fireside log. There was an odd silence, but she knew how to break it.

'Who was Achilles?'

He looked surprised. 'Achilles,' he said, recovering quickly, 'was a hero of the Trojan war. He slew his enemy Hector at the gates of Troy. Then he himself was killed when Hector's brother Paris shot him in his heel.'

His heel. Kit chilled, remembering what Lambe had called her.

'Legend had it that he was invincible everywhere on his body except at that point. You see, when he was a baby, his mother Thetis dipped Achilles in the River Styx, a river that was supposed to afford invulnerability. But she held him by his heel, and the magical waters did not touch that point.' He stretched long booted legs before him. 'Christ, I have not thought of such things since I was in my Greek tutor's rooms at the House. I remember . . .' There was a pause. Would he say more? Would he talk of that tutor's daughter, that tutor's grandson? But he stopped himself with a little laugh. 'Such stories have little relevance to you, I suppose.'

She wanted to say, *Not at all, I am living it, we all are.* The siege of Cremona, the siege of Mantova, the siege of Troy. Instead she said: 'An uncomfortable position to be in. You feel safe, but you are not.'

'No,' he said. 'Not safe at all.' He looked at her intently, in a way she wished he would not. She wished his features were ugly; his cheeks marked with pox, his manner brusque, anything that would make what she must do easier.

She rolled in her blanket next to him. They did not touch; she was close enough to him to feel the warmth radiating from his body but they had never been farther apart. Nearby the newly-weds shared a rug and she had to listen, wide awake, to their amorous groans and soft laughter, knowing Ross heard them too. Did he truly want her that way, believing she was a man?

She turned on her back, her hip shooting with pain, plugged her fingers into her ears and made a vow by the stars. She would be a good wife, in her heart as well as her deeds. She resolved, when back in Rovereto, where the whole regiment were to be billeted until the upcoming siege of Mantova, that she would find Richard at last. Now she admitted to herself that she had not tried as hard as she might – she had loved the army for itself, loved being a soldier, loved the adventure she had once craved on a quiet Friday in Kavanagh's bar. And had she loved Ross a little? Lambe's accusations rang in her ears with the distant bells of the mountain church.

But that was past. Now she must do what she should have done months ago. The following morning, as soon as they reached Rovereto, she would go to Richard's captain, to Tichborne himself. Those months gone by shamed her, and she dared not question too closely why she had not gone to Tichborne before.

However, the next morning, she had no sooner thrown her pack down on her tick mattress in the covered market before Tichborne's aide came to her and summoned her to his master. Kit's hands shook as she buckled on her sword. Had Mr Lambe told Tichborne her secret? As she walked the well-remembered path through the marketplace, still with a slight limp at her hip, she racked her brains to think what else the most senior of captains could want with her.

Captain Tichborne had taken over an office in the silk market, and was writing at his desk with his adjutant at his shoulder. He was hatless, and his bald pate had turned rosy with the sun. Kit was reminded of the moment in the Golden Last, over a year ago now, when she had signed her life away to join the army. Then, as now, a bottle and two glasses stood by for a toast. Must she drink to the queen when she ended her army career, just as she had when she'd started?

But when Tichborne looked up he smiled.

'Well, Mr Walsh,' he said comfortably, laying down his quill. 'I am glad to see you returned to us, and well mended, it seems.' He nodded at her leg. 'It falls to me to give you some good news. Your captain has recommended you, for your actions at Cremona, in his and the late Colonel Gossedge's cause, for a promotion. It is my pleasure, therefore, to confer upon you your sergeant's stripes.' He laid four little stripes made of plaited brocade on red felt on the top of his open ledger. 'Find some good woman of the town to sew them on for you. Most ladies will do as much for a kiss, eh? What?'

Kit stared at the little stripes. 'Your health, Sergeant.' The adjutant poured two glasses, and jumped back. 'The queen!' said Tichborne, and Kit downed her tot for courage. 'Captain Tichborne?'

'Sergeant Walsh?'

Her new name would take some getting used to. 'Could I ask you about a man of yours? His name is Private Richard Walsh.'

Tichborne's pale brows lifted. 'A relative?'

'My brother, sir.'

'A brother!' He was all pleasantness. 'Well now. We'll take a look at the muster. Adjutant!'

The adjutant sprang forward once more, with a scruffy scroll. Tichborne spread it on his ledger and pointed down the column of names with a stubby finger. 'Walsh, Walsh, Walsh.'

This is it, thought Kit, her blood thrumming in her ears.

'Yes, he's here,' he said.

She swallowed. It could not be so easy. 'Here in Rovereto?'

'Yes. He came back with the rest after Luzzara.'

'And where do your men stay?' she asked breathlessly.

'Some are at the castle. But many are billeted on private houses now – they have been in the town for many months. Their time is largely their own until we lay siege to Mantova. All I can tell you is that he's . . .' he checked another manifest, '*not* on the watchlist tonight so he is free to roam the taverns.'

'But . . . which ones?'

'Sergeant Walsh,' said Tichborne, leaning forward conspiratorially. 'I am not your brother's keeper. What!' He shouted with laughter. 'Not your brother's keeper!' He waved her away, still laughing.

Kit wandered into the late afternoon sun, dazed, the little brocade stripes lying limp in her hand and her belly warm with grappa. She wanted to run straight to Ross to thank him, but she knew she must not. The taverns were not yet open, so there would be no seeking Richard until sundown. She had no need to find a seamstress to sew on her new stripes, for she'd been sewing for her mother since she was a child. But Tichborne's suggestion had put her in mind of Bianca Castellano. Surely there could be no harm, now, in a visit after all this time? The girl's misplaced passion for her must have been transferred to some other likely fellow. But still she tucked the little stripes in her pocket, for a sergeant was a better prospect for marriage than a private, and she had no wish to raise the girl's hopes again.

She walked steadily in the direction of the church and came at length to the house she remembered so well. The door was opened by a tall, shambolic figure who stepped blinking into the light.

It took Kit a number of heartbeats to recognise Signor Castellano. She remembered Bianca's father all those months ago – groomed, fleshy and florid, his attire costly and correct in every detail. Now he was thin and gaunt, his skin had a grey pallor, his hair was unpowdered and greasy, escaping from his pigtail. His eyes were bloodshot, his cheek unshaven. When he recognised Kit his eyes narrowed with fury.

Kit's insides shrivelled with misgiving, but she made her enquiry. '*Grussgott*, signor. Is Signorina Bianca at home?'

Signor Castellano breathed as heavily as a squeezebox. 'There is no one here by that name.'

'But . . .'

'I know no one of that name.'

Kit took a step back. Had Bianca died? 'My condolences, sir, if you have lost . . .' Castellano reached out and grasped her by her stock, knocking the breath from her. He pulled her close to his face and she could smell his sour breath. 'I told you once,' he hissed through yellow teeth, 'that I would cut you. Now get you gone from my door before I fetch my knives. I will chine you like a boar and sell your pluck in the market.' He threw her into the street, and slammed the wooden door shut before she could say more. As she picked herself up and dusted down her uniform, she felt the strong instinct, born from months in the army, that she was being watched.

Perplexed and unsettled by the encounter with Castellano, she set out to trawl the taverns. There she was greeted by her fellow dragoons, who had been given the news that she was to be a sergeant. The approval was universal; to a man they believed her promotion would free them from the tyranny of Sergeant Taylor. They pounded her on the back, shoving a bottle of grappa under her nose. Kit downed glass after glass, and by the time all her fellows had bought her a drink, she was warm with happiness and hope. Then the thought that the last time she'd been in this tavern, nine months past, she'd stumbled across the nasty little scene played out between Sergeant Taylor and Bianca sobered her suddenly. A lovely young woman, too young to die.

Just then, the door opened and Kit looked up as a beggar woman entered, cradling a bundle. The landlord went to shoo her away and Kit turned back to her companions. But the beggar began to shout and claw at the landlord, pointing over his broad shoulder at the table of dragoons. She broke free from his burly grip, rushed over to Kit and thrust her rags under her nose. 'This is yours!' the woman cried, and dumped the bundle in Kit's lap.

Kit looked down at a tiny but perfect child, wrapped in a filthy grey shawl. She looked up at the beggar woman, expecting some trick for coin, and was stunned to recognise Bianca Castellano.

The girl was skeleton thin, the violet eyes that had been so striking now seemed deranged. Her black curls, once so lush and neat, were as greasy and tangled as a bellwether's fleece. 'This is your child,' insisted Bianca, tears in her voice, as Kit gazed at her, horrified. She reached out a thin hand, childlike itself, and tweaked back the shawl from the baby's crown. There, fiery and unmistakable, grew a tuft of red hair.

The dragoons cheered and laughed, barracking and jostling Kit. She could have laughed too if it wasn't so sad. She, a woman who could never have a child, now, incredibly, held a babe in her arms that could be her own, with porcelain skin and red hair, reaching up to her face with a tiny starlike hand. For one moment of madness she almost believed it, then reality asserted itself. She stood, holding the child carefully, and drew Bianca away from the jackals at the table. 'What happened to you? Where are you living?'

Bianca looked at her with hollow eyes and Kit understood. She was living nowhere. 'Come,' said Kit.

She crossed the tavern with her cloak covering the baby and Bianca in the crook of her other arm. 'Landlord,' she called. 'A room for this lady.'

The burly landlord did not raise an eyebrow. 'That's one way to celebrate becoming a sergeant, Mr Walsh,' he said. 'Two pfennigs an hour, a schilling for the night.'

Kit dug in her pouch. 'A sovereign for a week,' she said.

Upstairs, she seated the girl on the bed, and stood before her, still holding the baby. 'Bianca. What happened? What do you mean by coming here to me?'

'This is your child,' the girl insisted. 'Don't you remember?'

'Think, Bianca,' Kit urged. 'I never lay with you.'

'You *did*.' She was crying now. 'You came to my house. You paid court to me – you came when my father was from home – you paid me sweet compliments. You talked with me, about our future, and then we . . . you . . . lay with me in my parlour. It was as beautiful as paradise. And now we have been blessed with a child. A red-headed child, the image of you.' She nodded to the little bundle Kit held. 'Now you must marry me – you will, now, my Kit?' Her claw-like fingers reached to Kit's coat and clutched a handful of the cloth.

Kit wanted to laugh at the ridiculousness of the situation – but Bianca's distress was too palpable; and the story was so terribly sad. She knew she could absolve herself in a moment, by removing her jacket, but she had already been discovered once by Atticus Lambe, and was now more jealous of her disguise than ever. 'I did visit you,' she said slowly. 'And I did come when your father was from home. But I never tempted you with even a word, Bianca. We never so much as kissed.' Kit looked in the eyes that had once sparkled with promise, and now were flat and fathomless and dead like the orbs of a skull. The girl nodded sadly. 'Yes,' she whispered. 'You are right.'

The child began to keen a little, and Kit gave the bundle back to Bianca. Bianca cradled it tenderly, and offered it her breast. She was horrifically thin and wasted. A phrase the potmen at Kavanagh's used to use came to Kit: 'even the tide wouldn't take her'.

Kit walked to the window to confront her own reflection. What she saw made her turn back. 'Red hair,' she said. 'Taylor. The child is Taylor's.'

Bianca looked up, fear and relief written on her face. 'Yes,' she said. 'She is.'

Kit sat next to them, on the bed. 'What happened?'

Bianca lowered her voice. 'I went to seek you, that last night, to take my leave. I wanted to tell you that I would wait. I saw a redhead, in the uniform of the dragoons, but when he turned it was Taylor. I told him that I was seeking you, and he became enraged. He dragged me behind the church and . . .'

Kit sat in silence, remembering how she'd envied Bianca once, with her gowns and jewels and her fond father. Now she knew that women were not safe in their fortress of petticoats. Taylor had laid siege to her, stormed the citadel, and left her in tatters.

'I do not know what to do,' whispered Bianca. 'I am at the end of my wits. I saw you at my father's today – I go each day to see if he will see me, or . . . or her.' It was the first time she'd mentioned the baby's sex. 'But he always turns me from the door. There is nothing for us. I am ruined.'

'How have you lived?'

'I have begged from house to house, sometimes from the regiment, sometimes the eating houses. Once I started to show they put me on the turning stool, you know – and after that my disgrace was universally known and no one would help me.'

Kit was horrified, remembering the dreadful trial she'd seen on her first day in Rovereto, nine months ago. 'Could your father not prevent it?'

The enormous eyes looked up, surprised. 'He was the one who elected me for the turning. I thought I would lose her.' She held the child close and Kit shook her head at the inhumanity of it. Bad enough to sit on the stool alone – but with a child in the belly . . . 'I'd been sheltering at the church, but when the baby came the priest turned me out.' Kit remembered the church at Arco where Mr Lambe had stitched her together again. So the church would shelter soldiers but not a mother and child. Sanctuary indeed. 'So we sleep in the open, for now, but when winter comes . . .' There was no need to go on.

Kit was appalled. She had not given Bianca Castellano a single thought for the many months away from Rovereto, until Captain Tichborne had suggested a local woman might sew on her stripes. She had blithely gone to seek Bianca for her own ends. She had not given any credence to the depth of Bianca's feelings – she had assumed that because she was not a real man Bianca's was not a real attachment. Kit had used her, hurt her and used her again. It was time to be called to account.

Kit felt in her waistcoat and brought out the purse that Marlborough had given her, soft leather in royal blue, with Marlborough's arms stamped upon it in discreet gold. She handed the purse to Bianca, who emptied it on to the bed.

'Five pistoles!'

'Yes,' said Kit. She still had her coins from Kavanagh's and her pay and Richard's would be enough to get them home to Dublin.

'I cannot take this.'

'Yes you can.' Kit took a breath. 'The child is mine.'

'I beg your pardon?'

'She would not be in the world were it not for my selfish actions. So she is mine. Let it be universally known. I hereby swear that I will bear the living of her.'

'Are you sure? This is a great undertaking.'

'Yes.' She knew, now, there would be no child for her and Richard. She thought for the first time of what this might mean.

And there would be one benefit in her acceptance of paternity – although she was not proud of this private and selfish motive. Such an admission, publicly known, would prove beyond doubt that she was a man. It would work against the dark alchemy of Mr Lambe if he chose to start some rumour before she could complete her search for Richard.

Kit ran down to the bar and ordered some soup and stew for Bianca and then carried it up the stairs herself. Bianca placed the babe on the pillow to sleep, while she ate ravenously. Kit could not watch her hunger, and turned again to the window. 'Taylor,' she said. 'Have you been to Taylor?'

Bianca looked up from her plate, mouth dripping with sauce. 'Of course you have. That is why you came to me.'

She turned and looked at Bianca, Bianca looked down and bit her lip. Before the eyes dropped Kit read something dreadful there – a new shame. 'Did he . . . *dare* to insult you again?'

'Yes,' said Bianca dully, 'while the child cried in the gutter.'

Kit felt an all-consuming rage. Yes, she could walk away now, having housed and fed mother and child. She could ignore Taylor's transgressions, find Richard and go. But then Taylor would go unpunished. Bianca would be sport for him, sport he did not even have to pay for, not like the plump whores in the taverns with their flashing satins and inviting eyes, who would not lie with a soldier unless he pushed a coin into their bosom. Kit spoke before she could change her mind. 'In the morning I will make a reckoning with Sergeant Taylor.' Taylor's time had come. All his million little offences to her, the bell, the pig, the thousand insults and petty hardships to her and her fellows, paled next to the dark crimes he had visited on Bianca and his own child.

'No,' Bianca said quickly. 'You may not challenge him – you will be arrested.'

'Not now. I am lately made a sergeant, and may challenge one of my own rank. Rest easy,' Kit said grimly, 'I will avenge you.'

She tucked Bianca into the only bed, next to her sleeping baby, as if she were a child herself. The girl's great eyes were already closing. The food and warmth had done their work. Bianca spoke sleepily, slurring her words. 'Did you ever find your brother?'

'No. I know he is here in Rovereto somewhere.'

'If you do this thing for me, I will find him for you. I can go anywhere in this town from sewers to palaces – I have become invisible.'

Kit could well believe it. 'Sleep now,' she said tenderly.

She leant and kissed them both. The baby's cheek felt like a peach under her lips. Bianca looked up as she received her salute, with the ghost of a smile about her lips. 'Our first kiss,' she said, so sadly that Kit could not meet her eye.

The baby shifted in her sleep, and uttered a little cry. 'Does she have a name?' Kit whispered.

Bianca was silent, and for a moment Kit thought she might already be asleep. But the whisper came back. 'Not yet. I did not dare name her in case . . .'

Kit thought she understood. Bianca was afraid to love her daughter, in case she was forced to let her go. She knew then that Bianca had faced the horror of abandoning the baby, like the foundlings in the valley, probably tens or hundreds of times. 'You should give her a name,' she said. 'She is safe now.'

Bianca lifted her dark head. 'What is your given name?'

Kit hesitated. 'Christian.'

'Then I shall call her Christiana.'

Kit lay back on the little rug on the wooden boards and laid both hands on her barren stomach. She looked out at the starless dark. There was now a child in the world who bore her name.

Chapter 20

For if you insult me with one other word . . .

'Arthur McBride' (trad.)

In the morning, before it was even light, Kit sewed on her sergeant's stripes by the candle's end, as mother and child slept in a close circle on the bed.

She strapped on her sword by first light, and stepped out into the street. As she walked through the market square she passed by the silk post and a shout stopped her in her tracks. 'Sergeant Walsh.'

It was Captain Ross, framed in the doorway like an avenging angel, his eyes burning blue. 'A word.'

Kit followed her captain into the timbered counting house with a sinking heart. Ross paced the office, his hands clasped behind himself over the skirt of his coat, the knuckles white, as if he were too angry to leave his hands at liberty.

'I thought to congratulate you on your promotion today, but I find I now must address you on another subject.' He stopped pacing and fixed her with his eyes. 'It has come to my notice that you are now a father. Is that true?'

Kit fastened her gaze on the door jamb, to the left of his face. She could not look at him, but nodded curtly. When she had agreed to shelter Bianca she had not anticipated this particular interview.

'I heard that you insulted a young woman last time we were billeted upon this town, and she has now given birth to a daughter. Still correct?'

Now she must speak. 'Yes.'

Ross shook his head as if reeling from a blow. 'You disappoint me, Walsh.'

She swallowed the lump in her throat.

'In my mind there is a healthy case for your stripes to be taken away, before they are even sewn. But I am told I am in a minority – I am told that these things happen in the army, to likely young fellows such as you, when a large number of young men are billeted on a town. And I am sure you did not mean to compromise the lady?' There was a question in the statement – a plea for her to mitigate her behaviour, to absolve herself.

She was silent – there was nothing she could say.

'I must say, Kit, that your silence does not become you. I say again – you have disappointed me; you have disappointed me gravely. I know you have no father to teach you better, but I had thought – hoped – that I myself had given you some guidance.' Kit shifted her feet. This was horrible. 'I assume you intend to support the child?'

'Yes.'

'Have you offered the lady marriage?'

'No.'

'I see. Well, I cannot guide you further. You are a grown man. Have you considered the lady and her position? Do you have any notion of what life holds for her now?'

She could not be angry with him for his defence of Bianca and his censure of the careless young buck that had ruined her bound her to him more than he could ever know. She was mortified that they must now be so estranged. 'You have a shining army career ahead of you, if you will grasp it. I will say only this by way of advice. A wife does not have to be a burden. A wife can be the greatest blessing ever afforded to a man.' His voice broke a little; she made the mistake of looking at him now, and for the desolation of his expression she bled for him.

'I cannot offer her marriage,' she whispered, 'however much I wish to.'

'I see.' His face was stone. He pulled his coat straight. 'Well, then, there is nothing left to say. You are dismissed.'

There was nothing she could say. She had agreed to support Christiana, and that was that. Let Ross detest her; it was better that way; as soon as she found Richard she would be forced to desert her post anyway, and would disappoint him even more gravely. But the disapproval in the blue eyes brought tears pricking at the back of her own. She swallowed hard, and went to seek Sergeant Taylor.

She found him at the Gasthof, washing his breakfast down with a drink. She watched him for a moment through narrow eyes. He ate and drank with relish, like a man with nothing on his conscience. He wore an eyepatch now, to cover the injury she had given him, and it added to his air of menace. He drained his cup and banged it down, resting his arm along the table. Kit walked forward, drew her dagger and stabbed it down into his sleeve. The drinking hand was now trapped. Taylor looked at the dagger and slowly, slowly up at Kit. 'Walsh,' he growled. I'm celebrating. Won't you join me?'

'I am certain,' said Kit coldly, 'that no actions of yours deserve such celebration. Unless you plan to acknowledge your responsibilities, and the blessings of a new life?'

'Ah, so she brought her whelp to you. Clever little bitch.'

'Do not,' said Kit though her teeth, 'describe Signorina Castellano in such terms.'

'Well, she is clever,' protested Taylor equably. 'The red poll gave her the idea, I suppose. Besides, the brat could easily be yours – you were sniffing her skirts last winter, as I remember. And you owe me something; your handiwork ruined my beauty.' He indicated his missing eye. 'The jades are more reluctant to lie with me now, but the little Castellano will always be grateful.'

'Stand up,' said Kit, yanking her dagger from his sleeve. 'Stand up, damn you.'

Sergeant Taylor stayed where he was but swivelled on his stool, regarding her with his single eye. He bared his teeth and barked like a dog.

Through the long interrupted night while Christiana had keened and cried, and slept again, Kit had imagined how Taylor would react to her challenge, but had not once imagined him barking at her.

'As a child in Manchester,' he began in his flat North Country voice, 'for years I could not sleep for the neighbour's talbot. It barked from dusk till dawn, from one year to the next. My dad was a grocer, had a keen knife, and one night I could take it no more. I got up and slit the dog's throat, and threw the body in the Irwell.' He spoke to his half-full glass, never once looking up. 'I wouldn't have been more than eight. I've slept well ever since, until you came along, Walsh. You bark around my feet wherever I go like a little talbot pup. No – for that's a good English breed; a little Irish terrier, that's you. Now give me your message and be gone.' He swallowed the last of his drink with relish, and held the glass high for another.

'I bring you a challenge, and nothing else.'

'You really are a tiresome cur, for we've had this conversation before. You may not challenge a superior.'

Kit pulled him to his feet with an effort – he was a stocky, solid fellow. She shoved her shoulder, with the stripes upon it, in his face. 'That may be; but I'm damned sure that Sergeant Walsh may challenge Sergeant Taylor.'

Taylor eyed Kit's stripes. A fiendish grin spread across his face. 'Ah,' he said, bowing as one would to royalty. 'I did not know. I congratulate you.'

'Save your compliments,' hissed Kit. 'Just name your time and your place for us to meet.'

Taylor spat and kicked his stool away. 'I've always thought the day would come when I must shut you up. I've nothing better to do now,' he said, 'and I've had my breakfast.' He retreated into the snug for a while, and spoke low voiced to some of his fellows. *Arranging his affairs, no doubt*, thought Kit, twitching with impatience, and wishing she'd done the same. She had given Bianca her purse, so she and Christiana would be well for a twelvemonth or so; perhaps she should have left instruction for her coin, and her sword, and a letter to Maura, and something to tell Richard. But she wished also, with a tiny pang, that if she had indeed spoken her last words to Captain Ross, they had not been in anger. 'Come on, *Sergeant* Walsh,' said Taylor, almost genially. 'Time to silence the barking.'

Duelling was not against the law of the army, but it was frowned upon. So Kit and Taylor headed tacitly to the accepted place where duels were fought. The Turk's house was an ornamental eastern palace left over from Venetian rule, with pointed windows and delicate traceries, and its own slim stone bridge across the river. The Forbato bridge, which connected the Santa Maria quarter of Rovereto with the Venetian quarter, was always quiet except on market days, and because it was outside the bounds of the city, did not fall under the laws of the *comune*.

Kit and Taylor walked in an odd, almost companionable silence. It was too early for many folk to be abroad; only the birds were waking, the morning mist creeping up the mountains, the gilded peaks still crowned with summer snow.

The Forbato bridge was a delicate thing, and it was hard to believe that it had carried all the soldiers that had ever come and gone from the town. It formed an impossibly high pale arch that spanned the gorge.

Having no seconds, Kit and Taylor drew and presented their own swords, exchanged them for examination, swapped them back. They took off their red coats and left them at either end of the bridge.

At the coin toss the queen's shilling tinkled high in the air, shining and spinning as it fell, and Kit chose the city side of the bridge. She was defending Bianca, the princess and her citadel, against an incursive ogre. Kit took her stance; weight spread, legs apart, knees bent, sword in hand. Taylor stood at the other side of the bridge like a squat troll. She would save this rare place from the likes of him. On that summer dawn Rovereto, with the bridge and the gorge and the snow-capped mountains and the blue cypresses and the cascade and the castle above, was the most beautiful place in the world, and he had despoiled it. With a roar of a beast he ran at her; she ran at him and they met in the middle of the bridge with a clash.

It had never once occurred to Kit that she would lose the duel with Taylor – she was shimmering with anger on Bianca's behalf. She had almost forgotten that deadly figure she had seen from the cathedral in Cremona, cutting through every Frenchman in his way. But she remembered him with the first strike of his sword. She almost sank to her knees with the force of it. He was not a sergeant because he could shout, or because the men feared him; he had risen because he was a good fighter. Kit imagined him on those Manchester streets, so rough that even the dogs got their throats cut, scrapping his way to the top of the dung heap that had birthed him. Each subsequent ring of his sword on her father's blade told her the same thing.

Desperately, breathlessly they fought; their swords speaking for them as they hacked and slashed. She had not picked up her blade since Luzzara and her unpractised muscles were slow to remember their skill. If she had thought that Taylor's faulty sight would affect his swordplay she had been mistaken. She got one lucky strike to Taylor's sword hand and he dropped his weapon, stumbling to one knee – but at once he grabbed the blade of her sword to help himself up and yanked it from her hand. Pouncing, she picked up Taylor's blade from the ground and weighed it in her grasp – now she must fight with his heavier, regimental blade while her own father's sword shone wickedly in Taylor's meaty paw.

Round and about, tiring, her hip pained her; she stumbled once, and it was enough – following up his advantage he was upon her at once, crushing her sword hand on the balustrade of the bridge – the regimental sword hanging over the abyss and the jade-green River Leno far below. Her hand drained of blood, grew limp, opened; and Taylor's sword fell into the void. The combatants locked eyes, both taken aback, long enough to hear the sword plunge, many heartbeats later, into the Leno with a faint splash.

Just as Taylor raised Sean Kavanagh's sword high, the sun rose over the mountains. Blinded, Taylor stepped back, mistimed the kill-stroke and hit the stone balustrade of the bridge, the blade sparking and shuddering from his grip. He shook his stinging hand, cursing, and Kit moved at once, grabbing the haft of the sword as it fell. The blade calmed in her hand – *a sword that cuts you once can never hurt you again*. She took up her father's blade, and now she was above and Taylor below. She plunged it through his shoulder and into the timbers of the bridge – nothing fatal, but enough to pin him like a moth upon a card. 'Yield,' she said, low and hard.

Taylor squinted up at her with his one eye, breathing through the pain and the defeat. And yet he smiled. He seemed disinclined to rise, so, as honour dictated, she took her sword from him and gave him her hand. But still he lay there, saying nothing, and smiling. He seemed to be waiting. She backed away from him, breathing hard, with a strong sense of foreboding. There was a shout, and footsteps boomed over the bridge. Then Taylor's face crumpled theatrically and he clasped his shoulder, groaning. Kit turned, too late, for she was already surrounded by half a dozen men, the men Taylor had spoken to in the Gasthof. They had her arms and her throat. 'Sergeant Christian Walsh, you are under arrest for causing injury to your superior officer.'

She struggled like a tiger. 'Unhand me,' she cried. 'I am a sergeant in the dragoons, his equal in rank.'

Taylor rose, breathing hard, his bleeding teeth bared in a smile. He shrugged as best he could. 'Ah, Walsh, forgive me. I did try to tell you that I was celebrating, did I not? You see, I too was decorated, for my bravery at Luzzara. You see, while you were being coddled in a hospital bed, I fought through the French lines. So you,' he swaggered despite his wounds, 'just fought a duel with Sergeant *Major* Jebediah Taylor.' He took a pair of epaulettes from his pocket and waved them at Kit. 'Haven't had a chance to get 'em sewn yet. Was going to ask a local woman. Know anyone, Walsh? *Know anyone?*' He laughed, and coughed, and laughed again, holding his shoulder, but more in mirth than pain. Kit lunged for him, but Taylor's cronies were upon her, forcing her down until her knees cracked. Heavy irons were clapped upon her wrists and ankles.

As she half-walked, half-stumbled back to town between her captors, her irons trailing and sparking on the rocky path, she could hear Taylor shouting from the bridge, his voice echoing through the valley.

'By God, I'll sleep well tonight, Walsh!' He barked twice, as he had done in the Gasthof, and then howled, his eerie cry echoing about the valley, a dog unmasked as a wolf.

Chapter 21

If you do you'll be flogged in the morning . . .

'Arthur McBride' (trad.)

Kit was imprisoned in the dungeons of the north tower of Rovereto castle, where the miscreants of the regiment rotted until their punishments could be carried out.

She walked about her new home like a caged lion, her fingers trailing the damp walls, a journey that took her just ten heartbeats. She fell over a little table and two crippled chairs, both missing a leg. At night – she guessed it was night – she slept on the floor, shivering. Presumably outside it was still summer. But in this pit winter had taken up camp, crouched in the old stones, and never left. She was alone, for most men were too canny to be sent to prison when there was a siege to lay and booty to be collected. She wondered whether she would still be here when the dragoons marched to Mantova. The thought depressed her spirits almost more than anything else.

There was no prospect of escape. The only door in the dungeon was set high in the wall to be reached only by a rope ladder, which had been removed as soon as she had climbed down it. The circular chamber was entirely dark, with slick, damp walls growing with some type of moss and lichen. She thought of herself as some sort of maggot or caterpillar, living in the dark, waiting for her change.

The court martial had been brief, and presided over by a Major Caradew, an officer Kit did not know. Tichborne and Ross were nowhere to be seen. She thought she knew the reason for their absence – Tichborne had just shown the ill-judgement to promote a private with criminal tendencies, and Ross . . . well, Ross had made his feelings about her very clear.

She had stood impassive as Major Caradew had spoken her sentence; Kit would keep her rank, for in a time of war a sergeant could not be spared. She had been given a light enough sentence; she had expected a discharge, but instead she had been given two hundred lashes. She was to be flogged in the castle courtyard, and, as was her privilege as a sergeant, only in the presence of fellow officers, not the general company. In many ways she had been lucky – she would not lose her rank nor her commission, but she would lose her skin. Flogging was a horror, a flaying open of the back that left a man as skinned as a beef steer at a tannery. Flogging was the punishment everyone feared. She had heard horror stories along the road; a man whose back had been turned to scarlet ribbons which fluttered behind him like a pennant. Another flogged down to the spine so the white bone showed, a third who had had to sleep on his stomach for the rest of his life.

But Kit would rather shed her skin a thousand times than her jacket. More terrible to her in her sentence than the words 'Two hundred lashes' were the words 'the prisoner is to be stripped to the waist'. Once they took off her coat, tore off her shirt and unbound her breasts, she was lost.

She had been close, so close, to finding Richard. 'He's here somewhere,' Tichborne had said. And now, before she could complete the quest, she would be unmasked, and sent home.

Her flogging was to be in two days, and she knew that one of them had passed for she had been thrown two parcels of food by a cheery guard who would usefully shout 'breakfast' or 'dinner' as he threw them down. She contemplated trying to grab him, tying him up with her belt. She still had her sword, so she could dispatch him straight; but she was not the type to kill in cold blood. Besides, the castle housed Marlborough and Savoy too and would be guarded to the hilt.

After the second parcel the grille was opened and the rope ladder let down. 'Christ,' said a voice that set her heart beating. 'Bring me some more lamps. And a bottle and a bird while you're about it.'

She heard a faint protest from above, then the voice cut it short. 'Do it.'

Ross set the lamp he held down on the little table, and Kit, blinking, saw her prison for the first time. There had been a Bible with her all this time, lying loose leaved and curled with damp on the table – a Bible and no light to read it by.

She felt great joy to see Ross, but was ashamed of her hovel, of the damp and the dark and the smell of piss and worse. The lamp was the only light, so his eyes were tawny like a hawk's, his hair bronze and the reds and golds of his uniform leached to saffron and black. She studied this new Ross, guardedly; remembering the last time they'd spoken, his coldness, his anger. She wondered what he would say first – then she would know. He looked about him wryly. 'Well,' he said. 'As lodgings go, it is not the *best* appointed I have seen.'

She smiled. He was not the angry martinet from the silk post, this was the Ross who had joked with her along the road. 'Flint misses you,' he said.

She smiled, to cover a pang. 'And I her.'

'Kit,' he said, and the word sounded lovely in his mouth – at the silk post it had been all 'Mr Walsh'. Ross sat forward, his face serious. 'You will soon be mounted on Flint again, riding at my shoulder to Mantova. We'll have some fine old times again, I assure you. The siege of Mantova will be a famous victory. Take your flogging like a man, and when it is over all will be as before.' He sounded overly hearty, trying to cheer her.

She looked at him sadly. How little he knew.

Ross misinterpreted the silence. He sighed, and shook his head. 'I have never wanted to disobey an order until this one. I wish I could take you out of this place, help you escape. But the army has been my life; and something in me will not allow it.'

'I could give a name to it,' she said, low voiced. 'I would call it honour.'

He looked at his feet. 'Whatever it is, it prevents me. I cannot let you escape.'

'And I would not like you as well as I do if you did.'

He seemed taken aback, but bowed a little. 'I have, however, commuted your sentence – you will now receive one hundred lashes, not two. Your punishment, however painful, will be a gesture only. I told Major Caradew there were mitigating circumstances.'

Her heart beat slowly and painfully. 'What circumstances?'

He stood. Outside the circle of light she could no longer see his face, but his voice echoed around the tower. 'Kit. I am not proud of the way I spoke to you when last we met. I was . . .' he searched for the words, 'angry and disappointed.' The words he found did not seem to be the ones he sought, but he went on. 'I was troubled that my . . . that one of my men would act so; it seemed a deed without honour, and not like you. I believed you had more than a modicum of respect for the fairer sex. Furthermore, I sensed that some of our mutual experiences – I am thinking in particular of the valley of the foundlings – had furnished you with the knowledge that the coming of the army can bring particular hardships to women, hardships of which I felt sure you would not wish to be a part.'

She thought of baby Christiana. 'You are right. I would never act so.'

'I believe that now,' said the voice. 'I made enquiries among the men and learned two things.' He paused in his pacing, at the edge of the light. 'I discovered that you challenged Taylor, believing him to be of equal rank to yourself, and that he practised a deception upon you – no,' he held a golden hand high in the dark, 'not of an overt nature, but a deception of omission to conceal his promotion, which is a falsehood of its own kind. Moreover, I heard it said that you and he fought over an offence to the mother of your child. I questioned Southcott and Hall and they told me that they had seen you defend the same lady from Taylor's attentions nine months ago in this very town. Further enquiry at the Gasthof provided me with the information that you challenged Taylor on behalf of the lady and her child. A red-headed child, Kit.' He sat at the table with her once more, and clasped his hands before him. 'The red hair of two men in my troop; yourself, and Sergeant Taylor.'

She said nothing, but looked at his hands. The fingers long and strong, the nails square and short, a faint silver line across the back of one hand. 'I ask you now; is the child Sergeant Taylor's?'

How she wanted to tell him then! But she had made a promise to Bianca; and could not now link her reputation with another man, and certainly not a man such as Taylor. She framed her answer carefully. 'If someone asked a question of you, sir, taking into account all you said just now, and asked you for an answer that would compromise a lady and make an already vexing situation harder for her, what would you say?'

He thought for a moment. 'I would probably say, Kit, that I can make free of my own business, but that honour prevents me from making free of a lady's.' He looked at her. 'And so? Does the child belong to Sergeant Taylor?'

She met his eyes – a tiny candle burned in each. She said, in a voice heavy with meaning: 'I can make free of my own business, sir, but honour prevents me from making free of a lady's.'

He held her gaze for a moment and then nodded. 'Then I owe you an apology. I should have trusted in your character – I should have trusted you. You have acted like a man of honour and I most heartily beg your pardon for suggesting otherwise.'

Her hands lay on the table so close to his; a paler colour of butter, with tapered nails and the heavy scar on her little finger. A woman's hands – it seemed so clear to her – why could he not see? She moved her scarred little finger to touch his in forgiveness, when the grille in the door above slid open with a clang. 'Captain, sir? Your vittles.'

Ross rose from his seat; a tray was passed down with a roasted chicken upon it, a jug and two clay cups. Ross set the tray before Kit and went back for the two lamps the jailer handed down. She turned her attention to the heavenly chicken and tore it limb from succulent limb. She ate without shame, for she'd had nothing worth eating since the night at the San Maurizio when Bianca had dumped Christiana in her lap.

Ross watched her indulgently. 'Good?'

'Marlborough himself must never have had so fine a bird,' she said, through a full mouth.

'You've made short work of him,' he said, for the carcass sat before them, picked clean, standing jagged like a bone crown.

She tried a jest. 'So will I look, come tomorrow,'

Ross's smile dropped from his face too soon. He poured the contents of the jug into the clay goblets, and raised his cup to his lips. 'A few bad moments, Kit, that will be all.'

She drank and the liquor kindled her throat and belly. She suddenly felt free with Ross – free to abandon their rank and speak as the brothers they had been. There would never be another time. She cocked an eyebrow. 'You sure?' she asked, very Dublin. He set down his cup. 'Yes.'

He stood and unbuttoned his jacket, then in one fluid movement he pulled his shirt over his head and turned his back to her. 'This is how sure I am.'

She stood too. 'When?' she said.

'Many years ago – in Spain. I was a young ensign.' He glanced over his bare shoulder. 'You are wondering, I expect, what my crime can have been. Nothing quite so honourable as yours, I am afraid. It was instead the crime of a tired young puppy who had spent his pampered youth in feather beds. There, Kit; now you know the worst of me. I slept on my watch. And I have never done it since.'

She looked at his gilded back in the light. It was broad and finely muscled and smooth. No, not smooth – there were scars there, laid across it like tiger stripes. She looked closer, reached out.

Now with his back turned she had the courage to touch him – the cold pads of her fingers stroked his warm flesh, so softly she thought he must not feel it. She gently traced the silvery lines, the map of his past pain.

He flinched a little.

'They don't still hurt?'

'Not a whit,' but his voice sounded jolted; by the memory, or her touch?

'Did it hurt then?'

'The whip stung a little.'

He was trying to spare her but there was no need – she did not ask for herself, for she knew the lash would never touch her; she would be taken in hand as soon as the ensign stripped her. She asked for *him*, she wanted to know what *he* had been through.

He pulled his shirt back on, almost trapping her hand in the linen; she pulled it away, as if stung. He called for the jailer brusquely, as if he did not trust himself. She felt sure, then, that he did love her, that he had always loved her; as boy or woman, it did not matter. She wished she could frame some farewell, that she could take leave of him properly, thank him even. But such declarations would make no sense to him – he fully expected to have Sergeant Walsh back in his dragoons directly after the flogging.

'I will see you tomorrow,' he said in farewell, and met her eyes at the last. 'Everything will be as it was.'

But she knew that it would not.

Kit's surroundings were much improved by Ross's visit. She wondered just how much he had paid the jailer, for she was allowed to keep the candle with two tallow wicks to spare, she had a venison mess for her dinner and a pot of porter instead of small beer.

She tried to read the Bible, to look for some comforting homilies, but she happened upon the passage that Ross had read as a eulogy to the dead children in the valley of the foundlings. *The fruit of the womb is a reward. Like arrows in the hand of a warrior, so are the children of one's youth. How blessed is the man whose quiver is full of them; they will not be ashamed when they speak with their enemies in the gate.'* She shut the book and put it under her head as a pillow to keep her head from the damp floor. As she drifted to miserable sleep she realised she had never even learned Captain Ross's given name.

In the dead of the night she was awakened by the grille of the door sliding back with the familiar clang. She raised her head. The candle end still burned. She blinked awake. 'What's amiss?' she called to the jailer, her voice a crow's croak after the wine.

'Visitor,' he said. 'You are popular tonight.'

Kit's heart speeded – he'd come back! Now she could say, at last, what she'd meant to say. Her delight lasted no more than a moment. 'Woman this time. I suppose you'll want more lamps again,' said the jailer grudgingly, with the resentment of one who'd never been handsome enough for his courting to benefit from illumination. Bianca Castellano climbed down the rope. Kit hurried to help her. 'You shouldn't be here.'

'Nor should you. I told you not to challenge Taylor.'

'It needed doing. Where is Christiana?'

'With Marta, the innkeeper's wife at the Gasthof. She is kind. She has taken to Christiana – she lost six of her own. And Andrea, her husband, has given me employment at the inn.'

'Mary and Joseph,' exclaimed Kit, 'he doesn't let you serve those jackals, does he?'

'Marta won't let them near me.'

Kit smiled. 'Don't let Andrea take all of your money.'

'I've hidden it.'

'Good girl. Bianca . . .' Could she tell Bianca that by tomorrow she would be packed off to Ireland, and that was if she was lucky? She did not know what punishments awaited a woman who had made a fool of the English Army, of the great Marlborough himself. She might spend all her days in a cell like this one. So she held her tongue and studied her visitor.

Bianca looked better, and fuller in the face, and had something of her old spirit. She was in a new gown, much mended, but clean. Her hair was brushed and neatly braided. But she had an air of excitement and agitation, and looked about her as if hunted. 'What is it?' asked Kit. 'Not Taylor?'

'No.' She shook her head. 'He has not been near me. I hear he's lost the use of his arm, though, so he cannot for the moment fight.' *Nor pin me down again* was the unspoken line.

'Then what?'

'It's just . . .' She fixed Kit with her great eyes. 'I have found your brother. I have found Richard Walsh.'

Kit's world somersaulted. Joy and fear gripped her innards; the physical sickness of something she'd been longing for coming to pass. She stared at Bianca, for some moments hardly breathing, hardly moving. Then she breathed out all the air that was in her lungs. Time to shed her skin.

'Not my brother,' she said. 'My husband.'

Chapter 22

And you dare not change them one night . . .

'Arthur McBride' (trad.)

Kit had told Bianca all. Of Kavanagh's and Maura, and her marriage, and the night when Richard was pressed. Of the inn of the Golden Last, the wrong Mr Walsh. Of the voyage, of Genova, of the Madonna della Fortuna, of Maria van Lommen, of Captain Ross's training. The journey to the mountains, Cremona, Luzzara, and her trials at the hands of Mr Lambe. Then her return to Rovereto, all in search of her husband.

There was long silence, then Bianca uttered the first words she'd spoken in an hour. 'I hope,' she said bitterly, 'that he is worthy of such love. To transform yourself, to come all this way, to put yourself in harm's way; it is extraordinary.'

Kit smiled briefly. 'I know why you would ask such a thing. But some men are honourable,' and it was Ross that she meant. 'Can you get a message to Richard?'

'I had another notion,' said Bianca. 'You go to him yourself.' She held Kit's gaze, her eyes glittering with meaning.

Kit understood. 'No.'

'Listen to me. There are two maids in this room. Will that dolt on the door know which one leaves?'

'*No*,' said Kit firmly.

'It is the only way, and you know it. You escape your sentence and you find your husband.'

'Bianca. Think. What will happen to you if they find you here in my stead?'

'I told you – I am nobody now. A beggar. You can tie me up; I will say you overpowered me. They will kick me out of doors, that is all.'

Kit looked at her, and saw how much the girl needed to help.

'Kit. Let me do this. My tale did not end happily. Yours can.'

She nodded briefly. 'Very well.'

Bianca glanced up at the high door in the wall, and the grille that was closed at present. 'What about the guard?'

'He never comes unless he's called, or he has food for me. And that won't be till dawn. What time did you come?'

'After the tavern. Midnight.'

'Then we have time enough.'

In the light of the candle and the lamps, Kit and Bianca changed clothes. A soldier and a maid became a soldier in a shirt and a maid in a petticoat. Then, for just an instant, two naked women; the same; not the same. Kit picked up the warm unfamiliar garments from the floor – the petticoats, the stockings, the camisole and corset. Her fingers fumbled on the clothes hurriedly – a prurient guard could see them half dressed without suspicion, for he expected them, she was sure, to be in the act of love; but two naked maids would require explanation. The clothes seemed strange to her – so many strings and ties and buttons, so many ways to deceive even in a simple sprigged peasant frock – a stomacher to narrow the waist, a stuffed roll to fan out the skirts, a laced corset to keep the breasts high, in its own way as restrictive to the breath as her own wrappings about her bosom. And for Bianca, the bandeau about the breasts, the waistcoat padded about the waist and the curious silver prick were just as unfamiliar.

There was a difference in height so Bianca was a little swamped in the uniform, while the skirts of the sprigged muslin were a little short for Kit and the bodice a little low for decency; but these, said Bianca, were all faults on the right side. Shoes were a problem; while Bianca could fit her narrow feet easily into Kit's long cavalry boots, Kit struggled with Bianca's button boots – they pained her feet but they must be worn, as the skirts rode high above her ankles.

There was no looking glass so they became each other's lady's maid. Kit braided Bianca's long hair and tucked it into the regimental collar, winding the dirty white stock around the plait. No artifice could make black hair red, but the candlelight confused all colours well enough. There was the tricorn of course, but to wear it inside would excite more suspicion than it suppressed.

The power of costume was amazing – Bianca looked, if nothing like Kit, utterly convincing as a man – her gaunt little face and huge eyes appeared youthful but not feminine. 'Now you,' said Bianca.

She seated Kit on the broken chair and worked by lamplight. She loosened the leather tie on Kit's hair and ruffled it loose. She combed it with her fingers, and cracked the candle wax off the strands. Kit felt the unfamiliar silky weight about her bare neck and shoulders. The curls, remembering, sprung up about her collarbones – she had not realised how long her hair had grown in its tight queue, all those months that she had been imprisoned by Mr Lambe. It was near as long as Bianca's and had retained its fiery colour – glowing with a copper sheen in the lamplight. It was, all of a sudden, a woman's hair again.

Bianca seemed to think so too. 'I will fasten my combs into the crown,' she said, 'but leave the long lengths falling about your bosom.'

It seemed odd to be spoken of in these feminine terms, but Kit sat patiently. Bianca's practised fingers twined the top section of her hair into curlicues and puffs to be secured with the simple tin combs still warm from her own head. Bianca seemed happier – she had an explanation, now, for her rejection. At last she stood back. 'Pinch your cheeks,' she commanded, 'and press your lips together.' Kit obeyed, and Bianca was silent for a moment.

'Is it all right?' asked Kit, impatient. 'Will I do?'

'Yes,' said Bianca, wondering. 'More than that. You are beautiful. How did I not know? How could I not have seen?'

Kit laid a finger over her lips. 'If you did not know, then, God willing, nor will anyone else.'

Kit tugged at her bodice; Bianca slapped her hands away smartly. 'No; leave it,' she said. She knew too well, now, what could distract a man.

'The musket must stay behind,' said Kit. She'd made a last notch on the stock – three hundred and seventy days without Richard – but had no further need of her calendar; tonight she would see her husband again.

'And what of the sword?' asked Bianca, dangling it from her hand, unaccustomed to its shape and weight. '*You* cannot wear it.' But Kit took it from her, gripping it firmly – the sword which was the only legacy of her father – the only thing remaining in her world that she and he had both touched. The sword she had brought with her to Kavanagh's and hung over the bar in temporary retirement, only to see battle again at San Columbano, Cremona, Luzzara. Yet Bianca was right – it did not fit; what, was she to carry it in her ribbon sash? Or conceal it somehow under her skirts? Escape would be difficult enough without such an encumbrance. No: she now had to be as convincing a woman as she had been a man – swords were not for maids. One hand under the haft, one under the blade, she handed it, almost with ceremony, to Bianca. 'Please, if all goes well with you' – she did not need to elaborate on what this meant – 'see this conveyed to Captain Ross of the Scots Greys. He was my commander, and showed me great . . . kindness.'

Bianca looked at her swiftly but said nothing; she merely

repeated the name, nodded and hung the blade awkwardly in her buckler. 'I will write you at the Gasthof,' promised Kit. 'I meant what I said about Christiana, she is mine, and will always have my support.'

Bianca waved her hand. 'Christiana and I will be well, never fear. Now heed; I have written down the direction for you. Your husband is living in the Santa Maria quarter in a private house.'

'In a private house!' That explained why Kit hadn't found him, nor would she have, for however long she trawled the taverns. Kit took the direction, neatly written on a scrap of paper, and tried to push it into a pocket which wasn't there. Then, in a gesture that seemed a world away, she tucked the paper into her bosom. She embraced Bianca and kissed her firmly on the cheek. 'I have a sister,' she said. She blew out every candle but one – and tied Bianca loosely to the chair with her back to the door. In the low light she hoped the guard would simply see a figure in a dragoon uniform slumped in a chair in a hopeless attitude, and not look too closely at the figure in the sprigged gown who needed his hand to climb the rope ladder.

Her heart thumping, Kit called for the guard, and heard the scramble and slap of the rope ladder being thrown down. Kit had to remind herself, as she climbed, not to be agile; she forced herself to take his grubby hand to help her up. He hauled her up to the doorway and set her on her feet. She thanked the guard, low voiced, trying to avert her eyes; but as if drawn she looked him, fatally, in the face. He looked at her intently and she thought she was lost – but all the time he was looking at her chest. The bodice of Bianca's dress strained tight, and her bosom was bolstered almost to her chin. The breasts that had been her biggest liability were now her greatest asset. The guard actually licked his lips. 'Lucky bugger,' he muttered under his breath.

She swept past him hastily, as a shy little miss might, and scuttled up the stone staircase and through the courts she had last seen as a prisoner. Being a woman felt so different – she felt lighter by the weight of her uniform, had not realised what ballast she had been carrying for the last year. Below her waist she felt remarkably free – between petticoats and stockings her legs were unencumbered and she felt the relief of being without her silver appendage. Her gait was different, and she realised her deception had made her walk differently – maybe all men walked so to protect their member. But above the waist she felt constricted, by the tight lacings pressing her chest so between the corset and the fear she could scarcely breathe. She felt colder too – Bianca's cloak was light, and with her hair swept high and her bosom exposed, the mountain breeze was fresh about her throat and ears.

At every gate she expected to be stopped; she wanted to shrink into her cloak and pull her hood close over her head, but she knew Bianca's instincts were right; she should keep her assets on show. Every guard opened his door for her, or lifted his pike to his side; some even bowed, or paid her compliment, and all of them raked her with their eyes. She felt fearful of those glances – she was afraid of being Kit again. No one, now, would challenge her to a duel, or call her out, or swing a sword at her, but those glances meant she was prone to other dangers, the kind of dangers that had beset Bianca Castellano.

One more gate to go; she even recognised the guard on the postern gate, but he too looked no higher than her bosom. She passed under the portcullis, every nerve tingling, expecting the heavy iron teeth to fall upon her and slice her in two. But she was across the moat and away into the night. The constant moon shone down knowingly, witnessing her escape, betraying her by lighting her figure for all to see. Then the little alleyways claimed her with their friendly shadows.

She was Mistress Kit Walsh again, and she was free.

Chapter 23

He always is blessed with a charming young wife . . .

'Arthur McBride' (trad.)

Kit crossed the Forbato bridge, the bridge where she had fought the very duel with Taylor which had seen her imprisoned. At the centre of the bridge, with the River Leno whispering beneath her, and the fall thundering at the river's bend, she took the paper from her bodice and paused in the moonlight to read it: Via Ranier, 17. Her heart thumped; her palms were damp though the night was chill. She stood still, and breathed deep, and something shrivelled within her with misery. This was not how she should be feeling, but how could you teach yourself to be joyful?

She hurried across the Leno before she could turn back, and walked along the bank, reading the street directions painted on the huddled houses. There: Via Ranier. The white houses huddled on the bank of the river; had Richard looked from the window of his lodging house at dawn three days past, he would have seen his wife, in dragoon's clothes, duelling with her colour sergeant.

At number seventeen Kit raised her fist to the door, but her hand fell – she could not knock, not yet. There was a light at the window, despite the lateness of the hour, and she pressed up to the cool glass.

It was a perfect domestic scene. A man and a woman sat at a small scrubbed table. Between them stood a candle, a jug and two tankards. The table was small, but it was as if even this distance was too great for them to be apart, for they joined hands across the table. The woman was of middle years, handsome, plump; she smiled into the man's eyes and laughed softly at his remarks. A little dog sat at his master's feet, white and scruffy, wagging his stumpy tail, wearing an expression of adoration akin to his mistress's. The man was younger, plump too, and not wearing a uniform. Kit's heart leaped – it was the wrong house. Richard wasn't here at all. But she peered again, and something caught the corner of the man's eye and made him turn.

She leapt away, and pressed her back to the plastered wall, breathing heavily. She wanted to run. But there could be no running now. To go to that door, to knock and seek entrance, was the hardest thing she had ever had to do.

When he opened the door he knew her at once. In her head she still looked like a soldier, but to Richard she must look as she'd always done. He stood back as if slapped, his countenance white as paper. 'Kit!' he stuttered, and her name sounded strange at his lips; so familiar, yet not. He drew her in over the threshold, the first time he'd touched her in over a year. 'What are you doing here?'

I came to seek you. The words rolled around her head, but she could not speak. His accent was just the same, so like her own, and it sounded to her like home. The room was warm but she was shaking. She could not take a step – and it was the woman who rose and helped Kit to her own stool.

Kit could see now that the woman was a good many years older than she – that she had a pleasant open face, a florid complexion and glossy black curls falling from her lace cap. She frowned and her fingers pleated the rough silk of her skirt. The expression of worry sat oddly on her; she had a face made for smiles. As if in a dream Kit heard a murmured intimate conversation: '*Who is she, amore? – It is my sister from Ireland.*' His lie was a sibling to hers; *my brother, my sister.* The lady's smiles returned, she made some polite greetings which Kit heard not at all, bobbed a curtsy, and tactfully left the room to prepare some refreshment.

Now a true husband and wife sat here, at either side of the jug and the candle, but with none of the affection that had warmed the former tableau. The scruffy white dog settled himself on Richard's feet and stared at Kit with naked hostility, growling.

Kit looked at her husband for a long moment. He was stouter, and his hair was longer and tied at his nape in the army style, a style that did not suit him. His features were a little blurred, his jawline softened into jowls. His green eyes were the same, if set a little deeper, and he looked prosperous, guilty; cornered. Not at all a ravenous battle-ravaged foot soldier, but rather a wealthy urban burgher. She surveyed the topography of his face coldly – he had been living here in comfort with his *frau* while she had suffered on a snowy mountaintop and in a dank hospital in Luzzara and in a dungeon at Rovereto? She wondered how she looked to him.

There was so much to ask. But now she had found him, she had just one question. 'Who is she?'

He sighed, and she hated him then. 'Chiara Anselmino. She is a widow, of good standing in the town.' He had always had a fondness for respectability – he would not even kiss her in the churchyard until they had passed the lychgate – and she could see that he was wondering how the sudden appearance of a wife would affect his standing.

'Did you ever love me?'

He did not answer her directly. 'Kit – I did not think to ever see you again. And I am changed – from top to toe. I am a different man. I am a soldier now. Every campaign I fight might be my last. Death is everywhere, and when you don't fight, you want something to love, something to live for. And now, I'm to head to Mantova under Brigadier Panton, perhaps never to return. Battle – it's a dreadful thing – you don't know, you can't know . . .'

'Battle!' she interrupted. 'Don't speak to me of battle. I know it better than you, for it has been my constant companion these twelve months.'

She told her story for the second time that night, leaving aside all references to Captain Ross except in passing. The other thing she left out of her incredible tale was her barrenness. Whether it was true or not, she did not want to seem less of a wife to Richard – she did not want to compete with that ample *frau* in the pantry who could doubtless have a litter of babies if she wished.

Richard listened to her at first open mouthed and then, as she talked about the army, began to interject. 'Ah, Gardiner. I served under him at Chiari.' 'Don't tell me about the Spanish musket. I know its little ways. The flintlock always sticks on the third fire.' 'Riva del Garda – I took a fever there myself.' They were almost, almost, friends again; unthinking, she drank from the goodwife's cup, once she even laughed. As if he detected a distant call of truce, Richard said, hesitantly: 'Kit, I must ask you. How did you find me? Is our . . . relationship . . . generally known?'

She looked at him, scorn reawakening. 'No,' she said. 'I gave it abroad that you were my brother. But know this – if you are living with that dame as man and wife you are guilty of bigamy.' He looked towards the parlour door and she knew the truth. He was married. 'One word to Tichborne and you will be discharged directly.' She spoke harshly. Ever since she'd taken that first step over Kavanagh's threshold to follow Richard into the army, she'd looked upon their marriage as a Holy Grail, and all the time he'd been living here, sipping quietly from a clay cup.

He went whiter than he'd been when he'd first laid eyes on her. And then she could see exactly what this life meant to him – this house, this jug of wine, this dog. This woman. *Their* marriage had been an illusion. This was *real*.

'Did you even write?' she asked, plaintively.

'Kit,' he said, shaking his head a little, the smallest smile playing at his lips. 'You know I have never been one for letters.'

And there it was. That one sentence: the useless, don't-blame-me defence, the things-just-happen-to-me attitude, told her then of the magnitude of her mistake. Was *this* what she had followed across oceans and mountains and plains? She looked in his green eyes, searching. She tried to find her Richard in there – the Richard who had first kissed her when she was making a bed in Kavanagh's, who'd chased her about the dining board, and tickled her until she screamed, the Richard who had taken her virginity in their marriage bed. He dropped his eyes and she knew the truth. She could not find him – *her* Richard was not there.

Suddenly she was blindly furious. She could have hit him then – not a fishwife's slap but a blinding swinging cut with the blade she no longer owned – the blade she had taken up for him and then given up for him. Instead her fist landed on the table; the cups and jug jumped, the candle guttered, and the dog began to bark. The woman came back into the room, brow furrowed under her lace cap. Richard sprang up, hands outstretched, soothing her, encouraging her out of the door. The intimacy of that little conversation was the final straw for Kit. For the first time since Dublin she dropped her head on her crossed arms and wept. All the time she sobbed, Richard sat across from her, shifting awkwardly like a stranger. He had no comfort to give her, not even a pat such as he gave his dog.

At length she raised her face, and dried her cheeks. She was surprised to find she felt better; despite what she'd been through, she still had herself. She looked at Richard. There was no accusation in her gaze now, just curiosity. 'What happened to you after that night at Kavanagh's? I want to know.'

His tale mirrored hers – he'd gone to the Golden Last, then Genova, then the mountains. It transpired that they'd passed by each other several times: Richard had been in Villafranca where Lieutenant Gardiner had fallen in the castle's fountain, drunk. He'd been in Rovereto when Marlborough had come to town, and he'd been, as she knew, in Luzzara. And he'd been with the sappers to undermine the bridge in Cremona. 'I did not think I would come back from Cremona,' he confessed. 'It was only after that siege that Chiara and I became serious. Conflict instructs you in what counts the most.' He'd forgotten to whom he spoke, his eyes shining. 'Until then it was just dalliance.'

'I could put her on the turning stool, you know,' Kit said. 'Spin her until her guts spill out of her mouth. I could cut her so you wouldn't want her any more. Take her nose, like they do to the whores. I know how, I know how to use a blade.' She was crying again, ugly sobs, as ugly as the words that spilled unbidden from her mouth. 'You are not married in truth,' she said. 'Not married in the eyes of God. The priest – did your widow pay him well to perjure himself?'

'You are right,' admitted Richard. 'But what I have here has more substance than our union, even though we were blessed by God. I believe, Kit, I *truly* believe that I will love Chiara for all of my life, and therefore God, at the end of it, will forgive me.' He sounded more definite about this than in any pronouncement she had heard him make in his life, including his wedding vows. For a moment, Kit did not know what to say. His words stopped her in her tracks. He pressed on. 'Kit,' he said gently. 'We did not know each other really. Did we? We were the youngest creatures in our house – a beautiful colleen, a likely young chap, under the same roof. We united because it made sense. You always took the lead. Chiara and I, we are more like partners.'

She had not known he had seen so much. How strange that he'd found happiness with a foreigner – home-loving Richard, who'd never been outside Dublin. She used to speak French to vex him, and he would pin her down and kiss her till she stopped. And now he was married to a Roveretani, and would likely never go home again.

'How is Maura?' he asked, as if catching her thoughts.

'She told me to come.'

'*Did* she!' The first real smile.

With the smile, he was once again her old Richard, and she loved him again. She was suddenly terribly sad, awash with self-pity. What a waste. 'Such hardships,' she said. 'Such hardships I have endured. I near drowned, many times. Froze my very marrow on the mountain. Almost lost a finger, took a musket ball in the hip . . .' She could not go on, could not tell him what else that shot had done. 'What did I do to deserve this? Have I not been dutiful? Have I not done everything that could be asked of a wife?'

Richard dropped his head. 'And more.' He looked about him, sadly. The little house, the glazed windows, the widow's homely alpine furniture. And above his head, through the wattle and plaster of the ceiling, a comfy bed with linens and a tick mattress and stuffed pillows. His marriage bed. His home. 'Is it your will,' he said, 'that I return with you to Ireland?'

They looked at each other. Here was Kit, there was Richard, sitting across the cups and the dying candle. All fury spent, all passion long gone. Kit did not want to be this woman. She'd only just begun to be who she could be. 'No,' she whispered. 'I will keep your secret.' She sat a little straighter, straight as she'd sat in the saddle as a dragoon, and dried her tears. 'Commend me to your wife,' she said, 'and say I had to be on my way.'

At the door he touched her arm. 'Is there anything you need?' he asked.

There were so many answers she could have given.

'You need money?'

'No!' She spoke vehemently. She did not want to take anything from him.

'What will you do?' It was the first flicker of interest he had shown in her future.

'I don't know.'

'Kit,' he said gently. 'I did love you. Once.'

She closed the door on him. She would rather not have known.

Chapter 24

Intending no harm but meant to pass by . . .

'Arthur McBride' (trad.)

Kit spent the rest of the night on the Forbato bridge, watching the scene played out in the lighted windows of 17 Via Ranier close by.

She saw the widow return to the table, distressed, and sit down. Kit could imagine her words. *Who was that dame? She is no sister of yours.* She saw Richard, lying easily, making conciliatory gestures, palms down; the widow shaking her head, crying. Kit watched him placate her, in a way she knew well. His desire for an easy life had always made him persuasive when he was in the wrong. He came to Chiara, kissing her gently like a child, touching her constantly as he had not dared to touch Kit.

She grew angry again. Richard was fighting for this marriage – should she not have fought for hers? She had spent the last year fighting. How could she walk away now? If she could take him home, in time she would feel once again the feelings that dragged her over oceans and over mountains. She would return tomorrow and drag him before a tribunal – stake her claim and let the officers deal with him. *Let them have one more night together*, she thought. *Tomorrow, we'll see.*

Richard was on his knees now, contrite. *Forgive me, forgive me, she means nothing.* The little dog, adoring, jumped at him, covering his face with fond licks. The dog was a powerful ally; he carried the action; for both lovers laughed, and when they sobered, the day was won.

The widow looked down at Richard doubtfully, then fondly, wanting to believe his love. He got to his feet again and held out his hand. She, too, got up, hand in the small of her back, wincing, arching her body, eyes screwed tight, belly out-thrust.

Kit's world stopped. Started again.

Pregnant. The widow was pregnant.

Now Kit felt the cold. It was in her bones, her eyes stung with it. A baby. There was to be a baby at 17 Via Ranier. Another soldier's bastard. Chiara was a 'respectable woman' – she remembered Richard's odd insistence. Now she understood. He had known Chiara was with child. If she let them be, the soldier's bastard would be a legitimate child, born, for all the world knew, in holy wedlock. By walking away she would save another babe, another Christiana, from the mountainside. Kit could find it in her to take Chiara on in a fair fight, but she could not destroy a family. At 17 Via Ranier the candle, carried by some careful hand, left the lower room dark and in a moment warmed the upper window of the bedchamber. The dog, abandoned by his beloved master in a darkened room, pierced the night with a heart-rending howl. Kit turned away and walked across the bridge.

Now she wanted to go to Ross. She wanted to steal into the officer's rooms above the silk post, wake him from his sleep. And tell him what? What did Captain Ross want with Mistress Kit Walsh? A bedraggled, half-frozen grubby woman with lank candle-fat hair, sitting on his coverlet and telling him a fantastical tale. How would such a woman compare to Kit Walsh, Ross's brother in arms, his battle-fellow and partner in war? What could a woman offer to a man who loved men? She must concede and stand aside. And even if Atticus Lambe had been wrong about Ross, even if the captain could love a woman again, Kit was still married in the eyes of God. Those saints of the mountain did not mean so little to her that she could disregard their almond gaze.

She could not go to Ross but she needed a friend. She tore a handful of bitter grass from the verge as she went, and in the bleak half-light made her way to the regimental stables.

Here her luck turned: for the dragoon guard at the door who sat musket at shoulder, was, in fact, fast asleep. She crept closer; she recognised the man, a fellow named Fulford who had twitted her several times about her red hair.

There he sat, stockinged feet crossed, as if he were at his own fireside. Why, she thought, would Tichborne give Fulford the dead watch anyway – it was the time at which the most stalwart man was most likely to tire, and Fulford was no stalwart. Thinking like a soldier gave her courage. She took the private's musket from his limp hand, and butted the stock into his temple just above his ear. She felt no guilt; she was saving him from a flogging.

She stepped over the unconscious soldier, relishing the familiar smell of the stables; the warmth, the steaming flanks, the shifting hooves. She knew Flint's hocks at once. Placing her hand on the grey coat, she trailed her fingers from tail to nose, whispering the mare's name. Flint turned with a delighted whicker, tossing her head with a keen look in her liquid eye. Kit allowed herself a moment to lay her cheek on the warm neck. Flint knew her at once, despite her strange attire, and mouthed at the clump of grass in her hand.

She took Flint's rope head collar and led her past the unconscious guard. The sight of his boots, down at heel and leaning together by the door jamb, made her pause. Of all the accoutrements of a man she missed her boots the most. When Richard had asked her what she'd wanted she had not thought to ask him for the boots from his feet. But here were a pair of army-issue boots, down at heel, leaning together at the doorpost. They fitted remarkably well. She thought of leaving Bianca's button boots in their place, picturing the foolish Fulford's face as he groggily tried to push his toes into them; but she did not want to jeopardise her flight. The jest cheered her though.

To take the horse and the boots gave credence to the story of her desertion – Dragoon Kit Walsh, who escaped a flogging by dressing in the clothes of the mother of his child, and stole his grey and a pair of boots to aid his flight. Once safely outside the stable she mounted Flint with some difficulty, but once she dug the scuffed heels into Flint's sides, they were away, and nothing had changed. She galloped across the Forbato bridge for the last time and, without turning to look in Richard's window, threw Bianca's shoes in the river.

It was nearly dawn. In her cell, Bianca would be thrown her breakfast at the change of the dawn guard, and taken up for her flogging. 'I hope he is worthy,' Bianca had said of Richard. Had she, too, seen Richard with his widow? Had she changed places with Kit not so that Kit could achieve her happy ending, but break with a man who was *not* worthy?

Guilt sat like a stone weight in Kit's stomach. In her hurry to get to Richard, she had not thought enough of what would happen to Bianca. What if the soldiers kept her as a plaything to be passed around the castle? Kit could not betray Bianca's sacrifice by putting herself in danger again, but as dawn broke she rode across the river and up the hill above the castle. There, sheltered by trees, she watched two of Captain Caradew's men enter the castle to collect her from her cell. Then a general commotion, a ringing of bells, and suddenly Bianca was at the gate. Holding on to her gaping uniform, she was flung into the dirt by two guards, followed by a gob of spit.

Kit waited until Bianca had picked herself up, and hurried, head down, into the same alleys that had hidden Kit the night before. Bianca was free too. Then Kit turned Flint's head down the valley, kicked her sides and galloped away from Rovereto and Richard.

As she rode away from the camp, she began to relax. She had no real idea in what direction she was going, and seeing a cart approaching on the winding road ahead, she started to slow down to ask. But soon, far sooner than her eyes could make out the features of the figure on the box, she knew the driver. He was wearing a grey hurricane cloak and a slouch hat, and his pale hands held the reins of the black coach pair like the figure of death himself. Dr Atticus Lambe.

The road clung to the vertiginous mountain. Lambe could not turn at all in his bulky medical cart and she could not turn back now without drawing attention to herself. She rode on, drawing her hood over her eyes. As they grew closer, closer, she could not help seeking out the grey pale eyes with the black pin pupils that she had looked into so often.

But Atticus Lambe's eyes swept over her without a flicker of recognition. She was a woman, and she was beneath his notice.

She breathed out with relief. She was a free woman and could ride wherever she wanted. She was truly alone for the first time in her life, and she didn't think she had ever been quite so unhappy.

PART TWO

The Fan

Chapter 25

In the finest of clothing he's constantly seen . . .

'Arthur McBride' (trad.)

Venice was a place that had to be seen to be believed. It shone in the setting sun; a cluster of fantastic palaces crafted from stone as delicate as lace, domed churches like upturned grails and bell towers like jade-topped spears. All this booty was huddled on islands split by silver canals, to be reached only by a looking-glass lagoon. Venice was as beautiful and insubstantial as a dream.

But Kit was bound for the less salubrious harbour at the Arsenal, a crenellated haven guarded by stone lions, their gape-jawed faces gilded by the dying light. By the time the ferry made landfall the sun was low in the sky, a great red ball sinking into the lagoon.

As Kit guided Flint on the slippery planks of the wharf, the city turned from rose-gold through bronze and copper to the base metals of night; the last act of the alchemist sun. The harbour was abuzz with activity: soldiers, tradesmen, whores, rope-makers, caulkers, carpenters, mudlarkers. Here too she saw ostlers and horse traders, buying and selling. Flint followed her obediently but with shaking legs, glad to be on firm ground at last. Kit paid a lad to mind the mare.

Venice, as she knew from Ross, was a neutral power, so she'd expected ships of all colours in the haven; but the cross-trees seemed to be flying the standards of France. Undaunted, she switched to her mother tongue and enquired about a passage at a schooner called the *Banc D'Arguin*. The ship sat low in the water but looked sturdy enough. It was tricked out in the blue and gold of the French colours, and had a mermaid for a figurehead. She talked to a shipman hanging on a rope like a monkey.

'Where are you bound?'

'Plymouth,' he said briefly.

It would do. 'Have you a berth to spare?'

'If you've cash to spare.'

She swallowed. 'How much?'

'Fifty francs, thirty schillings or two guineas.'

Her face fell. *'Merci bien.'*

'De rien, madame.'

In the hours that followed she walked up and down among the skeps and nets as the light fell and the tar torches were lit, the acrid smell poisoning the air. Desperate to distance herself from the painted jades, she made proper enquiries to each shoreman and boatswain; but the gravity of her situation soon became clear. Passages from this golden city were as costly as the city itself. Even the quality were anxious to leave the war-torn region; on one jetty she saw a whole family in jewel-coloured silks, standing patiently on the dock in size order like nesting dolls. They had enough money, clearly, to go wherever they wanted; the passages Kit could afford went only as far as the next port.

With a sick feeling she faced the fact that she did not have nearly enough in her money belt to take her home, let alone to buy a berth in the hold for a horse. She sat on the seawall, watching the ships unfurling their sails for the evening tide, the great hulls moving out on to the red water until their giant forms became tiny specks in the sun's scarlet path. The wealthy family processed past her and up the gangplank of the *White Hind*, a caravel bound for England. Kit watched as the walkway was taken up and she was left behind.

She sat on, the stone still warm under her skirts, and rued the money she'd lost. Those coins that clustered in a warm metallic jumble in her waistcoat or in the money belt which had jingled between her thighs where her balls should have been. She regretted now, bitterly, that she had not asked Richard for a purse. She cursed that she had spent her family's treasure on this year-long fool's errand. For a moment, watching the red coin of the sun disappear into the lagoon, she even rued the purse from Marlborough that she'd given to Bianca for Christiana's keep. Five pistoles could have bought her a passage to Dublin in style – she could have bought her own sloop – but she could not set her own comfort against the life of a child.

Men had beggared her. She had spent a fortune seeking Richard, and she had taken on Taylor's child. She vowed there and then, in the port of Venice, never to be the dupe of a man again. She was strong, she was resourceful, she was a trained soldier. She was still Kit.

The transaction was difficult and protracted; but after much wrangling she had a good price for Flint from the Venetian ostler. The trader was as hard as stone – eyes like jet and a bristle on his cheek like filings of iron. Her efforts were hampered by her scant knowledge of the Veneto dialect and more so by her deep reluctance to let Flint go – her last link with the army, with Ross, and her constant companion. Kit did not kiss Flint, or stroke her velvet nose; she turned away, and could not look back.

As she blinked back the bitter tears, she felt a pricking at her nape. She had felt, ever since she donned a gown again, that she was somehow more noticeable than when she hid under an anonymous uniform. But this was different.

She stood still at the centre of the bustling wharf and then turned on the heel of her boots. Could someone have followed her? Sergeant Taylor vowing revenge? Or the pale spectre of Atticus Lambe? She shook her head to dislodge her fears. She would take the money from Flint to the schooner she had applied to first, and beg to make up the cost of the passage aboard by doing needlework or cooking or cleaning. But as she turned to go, she caught a white flash out of the corner of her eye.

In the crazy shadows of the torchlight was a golden carriage, its gilded paint alive with reflected flame, curlicues and carvings vital and animated, cherubs seeming to puff their cheeks and move their wings. Four black horses, steaming and stamping, stood obediently in the traces. But it was the passenger who held her gaze.

A fancy gentleman, plump and bewigged, leaned from the carriage. His beckoning hand wore a glove, and the snowy fingers spun a gilt coin dexterously between them. A little golden sun in a glove as white as cloud. She was back at Killcommadan Hill, back fourteen years, back to a time when adventure meant a roll down a green hill and a sovereign proffered by a white hand. As if in a dream she walked forward; to see the same face under a different wig, a wig in the latest fashion. And something else was different too. The fancy gentleman addressed her in French.

'You need money, Bess?'

Here was a man offering her money; a man who had changed her life for the better once before.

'I am a respectable woman.'

'Respectable women need money too.'

Warily Kit dropped her hand to where her sword should have hung, but he tucked the coin away, folded his white hand over the door, and regarded her with great interest.

'Are you leaving or arriving?' he asked, still in perfect French.

She answered him in kind. 'Leaving. As fast as I may.'

'Pity. I myself have just arrived. My work here has just begun.'

'And mine is ended.'

'You need a passage?'

She nodded.

'Where to?'

'Plymouth.'

'You're English?' he said, in that language.

She was stung. 'Irish,' she said, very Dublin.

'I too! Better and better.' He leaned a little farther out of the window. 'I will tell you a secret; I hate the English almost as much as I hate the French; and I love the Irish, naturally, for they are my countrymen. Don't tell.'

'Who would I be likely to tell?'

'The Queen of England.'

Kit snorted. 'You are trifling with me.'

'I am in earnest, I assure you. She and I are closely acquainted.'

She looked at him doubtfully.

'Shall we be friends? Why don't you sit in my carriage, and then we may take our ease.'

She raised her chin a little. 'We cannot be friends when we are not properly introduced.'

He clapped his hands. 'Quite right.'

Kit considered. She did not want to go by the name Walsh any more – let Richard's widow use it. She decided to try the gentleman's memory. 'Kit Kavanagh.'

He did not display a flicker of recognition. 'You looked as if you were choosing your name.'

'I was.'

'You have many names, Bess?'

Kit Kavanagh. Christian Walsh. Kit Walsh. 'Three to date. Four with your addition of Bess.'

'I too. I am James Fitzjames Butler, 2nd Duke of Ormonde, 13th Earl of Ormonde, 7th Earl of Ossory, 2nd Earl of Butler.'

She inclined her head.

'So, we are introduced. Now will you sit in my carriage?'

The four black stallions were buckled to the traces, ready to go; the reins were taut, the drivers, in full livery, ready on the box. 'Uncouple the horses first,' Kit said.

'Now, why would I do that?'

'Because you might be a slaver, or worse. I only have your word that you are a nobleman. If you want to talk, let's talk. But uncouple the horses first.'

She expected him to be angry, but he spoke again, although not to her. 'Pietro. Stand the horses aside.'

His man climbed down from the box. 'What shall I do with them, Your Grace?'

'I don't know, man,' said the Duke of Ormonde testily. 'What does one do with horses? Give them some oats or something. Then hand this lady in.'

Kit watched as the horses were released and wooden chocks placed behind the gilded wheels. If she'd still had pockets she would have put her hands in them. The silent coachman handed her into the carriage. The interior was another riot of gilt, and the cushions saffron yellow, like the yolk of an egg. She settled herself. 'What do you want of me?'

'I want you to have dinner with me.'

'Why?'

He waved one gloved finger from side to side. 'I will tell you at dinner.'

She set her chin. 'I need a reason first.'

'The best reason for taking dinner is that one is hungry. Are you not hungry?'

She was. All she had eaten along the road was a meal a day in the taverns where she'd stayed, always keeping some coin back for oats, always mindful of the passage to be bought at Venice.

He smiled. 'I'll tell you what. You come to dinner with me, in the finest palazzo in Venice. You hear my proposal. If you don't like my proposal, I will bring you here in the morning and buy you a passage directly to Dublin myself. What do you say?'

She considered. He had once given her a coin and asked little in return. He had let her go in peace then, might he not do so again? He had not molested a fresh girl of sixteen, and with her new instinct for these kinds of things she sensed that, with Ormonde, it was as it had been with Lambe. Whatever the duke wanted from her, it was not her body.

'I have a condition,' said Kit.

His smile widened. '*You* have a condition?'

'I amuse you?' she asked.

'You have no money for your passage nor a place to stay. You are in a two-shilling dress that's three weeks on. You are sitting in a golden coach with a duke of the realm and yet *you* have a condition. Yes, you amuse me; I like you more and more.'

'I had to sell my horse. I want her back.'

He knocked his cane on the roof. A face topped by a tricorn appeared at the window. 'Get Miss Kavanagh's horse back,' he said.

'She's the grey at the ostler's by the French schooner,' began Kit, but the duke stopped her with a wave. 'He knows. He's been pursuing you for the better part of the afternoon. You can no more clip him from your heels than your own shadow when he's been ordered to follow. Give a fair price,' he told his man. The tricorn bobbed and disappeared. 'Oh, and Pietro,' called the duke, as an afterthought. 'Meet Madame Berland off the Paris ship and tell her to get back on board and go home.'

Then the Duke of Ormonde held out his hand for her to shake just as the horse dealer had an hour past. As Kit took it she understood; Ormonde was a horse dealer too.

Chapter 26

As we went a walkin' down by the seaside . . .

'Arthur McBride' (trad.)

The carriage rolled forth along a broad thoroughfare by the lagoon, Flint trotting happily on a leading rein behind. Kit's eyes followed the *White Hind* sailing to England, now a mere speck on the horizon. This time she watched without a qualm. She could own it now; she had never really wanted to go home.

She was torn between the vista at each window and the intriguing character opposite. Ormonde regarded her openly, so she had no qualms about scrutinising him. He was of middle years, perhaps the age that Sean Kavanagh might be now, had he lived. He had a smooth, florid complexion, and plump cheeks; his eyes were so deep set that Kit could not determine, nor could she say with any certainly many years after, what their colour was. His wig, in the latest fashion, was piled high at the crown and flowed long to his breast. He wore a coat of the finest velvet, the colour of ox blood, and breeches of moleskin tucked into boiled leather boots. The cut of his clothes was faintly military, but each one of his diamond buttons would pay the entire regiment of the Scots Greys for a year. He stood her gaze with amusement, but said, after a little, 'There are better vistas to be had,' and nodded to the window. They were passing a beautiful palace as white as flummery. It was ornamented with a delicate filigree crown of stone, and a hundred windows shaped like little roundels and staring like eyes. And beyond this confection of a city, hanging in silver swags and ruffles like a backdrop at the playhouse, hung the distant mountains, their peaks burnished in rose-gold. The mountains where she'd been just days ago, where Richard dwelt with his new wife and where Ross slept in his officer's billet. Whatever Ormonde had to offer, at least she was still in the same country as Ross and the same sun set on the captain too. She wondered whether Bianca had given him her sword, and what he'd thought of the gift. Did he carry it? Or did he cast it away? Did he mourn the loss of his beloved companion Kit Walsh, or did he think Sergeant Walsh a coward and a deserter, a milksop who had turned his coat and run rather than face the lash?

The carriage passed between two pillars into a vast paved square, scattering a flock of leaden pigeons. Pietro opened the door.

'We must leave the horses here,' the duke said.

'Why?'

'You'll see.'

Stepping down from the carriage with the aid of Pietro's cold hand, she did see. There was no more road to travel, only water. At the marble quayside, a black boat, curved like a Saracen's blade and low-slung in the water, waited for them. She stepped in and settled on the scarlet cushions opposite the duke. Pietro doffed his tricorn and the boatman, with the aid of a long skinny pole, pushed off from the mooring.

They sailed silently into the mouth of a vast channel, flanked by a domed church on one side, and another palace on the other. The boat slid silently, but there was noise everywhere, chatter, singing, even music as fiddlers and pipers played in the other boats. The boatman slid expertly between all the other traffic on the canal, and Kit marvelled at the other passengers – dressed in silks and velvets, loaded with jewels, most of them were masked, their eyes glittering, watching her. It seemed as if the fabulously opulent palaces that ranked the canal watched her from their glass roundels, too, the windows now lit from behind by candles and glittering chandeliers.

At length, at a breathtaking curve of the canal, they came to the most beautiful palace of all, a rose-pink façade with pillars and capitals of snowy marble. The boat sailed directly into the bowels of the palace, between ornate wrought-iron gates that opened at their approach as if by magic.

Kit, slightly unsteady on her feet, followed Ormonde into a vast marble atrium, across a pied and polished floor and up a wide marble staircase. Halfway up the stair she was confronted by a full-length mirror, and by some trick of another mirror set in the landing behind her met a multitude of her own reflections, diminishing into infinity, like the ranks of a female army.

She had not seen her likeness since the polished silver looking glass at Maria van Lommen's house in Genova, and the image she had seen there had been set like amber in her mind's eye for over a year. She still expected to see a soldier when she looked in the mirror. The reality was different.

She looked like a ragged whore. The dress, made and over-mended by an innkeeper's wife, had been in fashion when the *frau* was a young bride, before her spreading flesh had split the seams and her workaday tasks had scuffed the muslin. Above the faded cloth Kit was paler than she remembered, and thinner– her collarbones jutted forth and the ridges of the top of her ribcage showed at her chest above the swellings of her bosom. Her waist seemed painfully thin in the gown compared to how it had appeared in the bulk of the uniform, but her arms, by contrast, were strong and well muscled.

Her face, though, was the revelation: so thin, so pale; violet shadows beneath the eyes. Her lips were still full, and now too full for her sunken face, as if she had been struck about the mouth. Only her eyes were the same, green as the Liffey, deter-mined, fringed by glossy dark lashes, and framed by dark brows.

'You're lucky,' Aunt Maura had once said. 'Redheads' lashes are usually as pale as straw.' She did not look lucky. Her skin looked pinched and thin across the bridge of her nose, but the same scattering of freckles sprinkled her cheeks as they had since childhood. She could see the blue of her veins, as if the blood ran cold and too near the surface of her skin. Her hair was dark auburn with grease and grime, the candle fat she had used to smooth it back into a queue sticking to each strand, the careful braids and buns Bianca had made on the top of her head now sitting muddled and tangled like a bird's nest. She saw no promise in the face – nothing that excited her in the way it had evidently excited Ormonde. The duke appeared in the mirror behind her. 'Don't get used to her,' he said enigmatically. He did not spare his own reflection a glance; she knew then that he had been raised with mirrors, that they clothed the walls of his house like tapestries. More than that; he inhabited his own skin perfectly, like a well-fitting suit of clothes.

They continued up the stair and into a great salon on the first floor lit by a hundred candles, reflected in a quintet of crystal windows. The canal outside was now black and gilded like a slick of oil, and the perfect palaces opposite watched them with candlelit eyes. But inside was a far finer sight, a table set for two by the window, groaning with fowl and fishes and sweetmeats.

'Pietro,' said the duke, 'see that we are alone.'

Kit sat down uninvited, and at once began grabbing and gobbling and chewing. There was a great round silver plate before her, with a ring of dressed birds arranged upon it. She grabbed one, dismembered it, and tore it with her teeth. She would have eaten it whole if she could.

Ormonde watched her indulgently as if she were a favourite lapdog. 'Good?'

She nodded. 'What is it?'

'A dish of doves.'

'Doves.' She smiled through her mouthful, but did not stop eating. Doves. What else would they eat in a city like this?

Ormonde took nothing himself, but served them wine from a basin of ice sunk into another little table at his elbow. She gulped it like water and it rushed up her nose – unlike the rough red army wine it was as yellow as straw and fizzing with a million tiny crystalline bubbles. The duke watched every mouthful she took, every bone she sucked, every finger she licked intently. But she ate her fill, undaunted. At length she stopped, sat back and belched loudly as she would have done in uniform.

'So,' she said, her new devil-may-care confidence bolstered by the food and wine. 'I've eaten your dinner. Suppose you tell me what you are doing here?'

Ormonde placed his glass down on the table carefully. 'Do you ever play chess, Bess?' He rhymed playfully, but his eyes were serious.

She recalled Marlborough's chess set in the Castello at Rovereto, and the pieces he'd placed on the map for the Prince of Savoy – white king, black king. 'I have seen it played,' she said truthfully.

He sat forward, and took up two silver-capped salt cellars in his beringed fingers.

'So you must know,' he said, 'that the objective is to place the king in check. Two evenly matched opponents will go along merrily at the outset, losing a few pawns perhaps, then a bishop or a rook here and there; sometimes a knight is lost in the action. Then slowly, imperceptibly, the play slows, clots, and solidifies.' He placed the little crystal towers together, abutting, trapped. He looked up at her. 'You have heard, perhaps, of the war that is raging in the mountains?'

'I have heard a little about it,' she said drily.

'The Duke of Marlborough has been trooping up and down the country, with the Prince of Savoy at his elbow, but Louis of France has been matching him at every turn. Perhaps you heard, too, of the capture of Maréchal Villeroi, the French commander?'

She remembered every detail. 'Somewhat.'

'Even the capture of Villeroi availed us nothing; they replaced him with De Catinat, then Villeroi escaped and was reinstated, and on we go. Now they have their citadels, we have ours, and no one can move. Stalemate.' With his forefingers, Ormonde pushed the salt cellars together so they chinked like wine glasses. 'We have entered what is known as the endgame – the last stage of the conflict; something audacious must take place; something brave and unexpected. You ask me what I am doing here? I have been sent by Queen Anne. I am here to break the stalemate.'

She looked at the salt cellars, and back at him. 'And what am *I* doing here?'

Ormonde sat back and clasped his hands across his waistcoat. 'Bess,' he said. 'I want you to be a spy.'

'On whom?'

'The French.'

'For whom?'

'For me. For the queen.'

She took his first answer. 'For you.'

He inclined his head. 'Very well. For me.'

She felt, for the first time, a frisson of danger, twin to the one she had felt in the castle of Riva del Garda when she had become Atticus Lambe's night-time confidante. *Having told me this much, he will never let me go.*

'You will summer at my house on Lake Maggiore. You will put yourself entirely in my hands. I will train you and mould you to become someone else.'

'Why me?'

'You speak perfect French. You are clearly brave.' *You have no idea*, she thought, wryly. 'And,' he said simply, 'you are beautiful, and will be even more so when I have finished with you.'

This was a strange thing to hear after so many months in

uniform, and after seeing her rag-and-bone reflection, but it was not wholly unpleasant.

'Who would I become?'

'You will assume the identity of a French countess – a woman who came here with her husband and lost him to an ambush on the road. You will shed your low birth and become a noblewoman. You will forget your low manners and become the model of decorum. You will walk like a lady, not a laundress. You will speak English with a French accent, and French with no accent at all. You will sleep in a feather bed every night. You will be clothed in silk, bedecked in jewels. Your hair will be dressed and perfumed and burnished at night with a silken cloth. You will learn the history of your family by rote, right back to the days of Charlemagne. And at the end of three months, when my cater-pillar has become a butterfly, I will test her wings, and if I find her ready, I will release her into the French court, there to flutter and settle and hear what foolish men will tell a beautiful woman. Then I will make your fortune.'

Kit considered. She had become well used, in the last year, to dissembling, to acting the part of someone else. And she knew that given the choice between returning to Kavanagh's as a single woman, and staying here and fighting on somehow, she would stay. For the siren call of adventure rang out to her, from a great distance, barely audible but sweet as a bell. She felt as if her choice was inevitable, as if she was caught at a point of no return. It was thus that she'd first met Ormonde, poised at the top of Killcommadan Hill, and had started to fall and could not stop.

Kit took a sip of wine, her hand shaking a little. 'How exactly will I be tested?'

Ormonde steepled his hands together, and touched his fingers to his full lower lip. 'There is to be a great ball in the city of Turin, in three months' time, for the name day of Prince Eugene of Savoy. He holds the ball every year and is determined to hold it this. It is to be a display of Allied power and opulence, and our confidence that we shall hold the region. At the ball will be the Duke of Marlborough,' she detected a slightly cool tone when the duke mentioned Marlborough's name, 'also the Landgrave of the Hessians, and every officer of the Grand Alliance.'

Kit choked a little, mid-swallow. Princes and counts and landgraves and dukes, all were as nothing to his last utterance. *Every officer of the Grand Alliance.*

Ross. She would see Ross again. Her cheek paled, and warmed again to a blush.

'I'll do it,' she said.

'I thought you would.' The duke raised his glass and drank with his eyes never leaving hers.

Chapter 27

Says Arthur, I wouldn't be proud of your clothes . . .

'Arthur McBride' (trad.)

Kit threw open the shutters, and the sunlight streamed in.

She had lain in bed late, and while she had been sleeping spring had fled and the dog-days of high summer were here, warm and balmy and bearable because of the cool breath of the mountains.

She had had three nights in a feather bed – Ormonde had kept that part of his promise already – and not for the first time she pitied poor Madame Berland, who had been turned around at Venice and shipped back to Paris.

Kit and the duke had spent that first night in Venice, then travelled for a day and a night in Ormonde's coach, with Flint cantering behind. Kit would have ridden, but Ormonde seemed inclined to become better acquainted with his new asset.

She blessed, now, her first instinct to conceal her soldier past from Ormonde. If he knew that she had met Marlborough and Savoy at close quarters he would not risk placing her in a room with them, and would summon back poor Madame Berland on the next ship. It was not so unlikely that her disguise would work; it was not so great a leap to hope that the female Kit could kiss hands with Marlborough and even Villeroi unrecognised. So she kept her peace, and invented, instead, a history for herself which had more than a kernel of truth.

She told Ormonde of her life at Kavanagh's, and her new husband, and Richard being pressed into the army. How she had followed him to Genova, and sought him in Rovereto, Cremona, Luzzara, Riva del Garda and Rovereto again.

'And did you find him?'

She did not have to counterfeit; her eyes filled with tears. 'No. I heard he was to join the regiment of Brigadier Panton in the siege of Mantova, but more than that I could not discover. All I know is,' she chose her words carefully, 'the husband that I married was nowhere to be found in Rovereto.'

'Take heart,' the duke said easily. 'He may survive this yet, if you do your office well; and then you may take a pot of gold back to Dublin for him.' He looked at her with approval. 'I made a good choice,' he said, as though her quest was to his credit and not hers. 'You have to be brave indeed to follow camp, and come so close to conflict.' She thought of her mother – had she been brave, too, to follow Sean Kavanagh from France to Ireland? 'It benefits our cause, too,' Ormonde went on, 'that you are so acquainted with the campaigns and manoeuvres of our forces.'

They had arrived at their destination at night, driving for what seemed like hours along the shore of a vast silver lake. At the little lakeside town of Stresa, the carriage drew to a halt on the foreshore and the final stage of the journey was undertaken by boat. Pietro silently conveyed Kit and Ormonde across the lake. Too tired to speak, Kit had first seen the Palazzo Borromeo through half-closed eyes, a great torchlit frontage perched on a rocky island in the middle of the dark water.

Now, in the first light of day, she could see the true glory of the place. This was the Isola Bella, a beautiful island indeed. The palace was perched atop at least ten terraces of gardens, green parks set in white marble balustrades, covered with carefully tended flower beds and hanging baskets, and shaded by shaped and clipped trees hanging with jewel-like fruits. White peacocks strutted on the lawn, arranging their snowy feathers to spread and air in the sunrise. The sound of gently plashing fountains reached her ears and a wonderful scent rose to her nose; myriad flowers opening in the morning sun like the peacock tails. Beyond the terraces the slopes of the mountain met the serene blue lake like the silken fall of a bishop's cope. Above their peaks a perfect V of geese flew across the buttermilk sky, honking. Kit laughed with them; it was incredible.

There was a knock at the door. Pietro stood there. 'His Grace's compliments, and would you join him on the terrace?' She looked down at herself, fingered her lace nightgown. 'Like this?'

His face was immobile. 'Like that.'

She padded obediently after him, her bare feet chilling on the marble.

As in Venice, apart from Pietro, there seemed to be no servants in the place at all. This told her more eloquently than the duke ever could just how secret their undertaking was. She had become so convinced that the place was deserted that when a raucous voice called to her at the foot of the marble stairs she actually jumped. A golden cage stood at the bottom of the grand staircase, and a large multicoloured parrot clung to the gilded bars with his pliant, ugly feet. 'Silly slut!' he shrieked.

She smiled. Pietro did not. She looked at the bird. The parrot cocked its head at her and blinked its beady black eyes. 'Oysters?' he asked kindly. 'Not for breakfast,' said Kit. The gaudy bird looked gratified, and pressed home his advantage. 'Church Hill,' he said. 'Damned Jacobites. Like rats in a trap.'

Kit, the Jacobite's daughter, felt suddenly cold, and walked away, following Pietro to the lakeside terrace. The duke was leaning on the balustrade with both hands, the curls of his wig brushing the stone. A china cup stood next to his right hand, and he took sips from it without using the handle. He turned at her approach, smiling, brimming with barely concealed excitement as he dismissed Pietro.

'You like the place?'

'It is the most beautiful place I have ever seen.'

He inclined his head. 'It was named after Isabella, whose husband, the Count of Borromeo, built the palace for her. Ironically, she was a dog-faced slut; fortunately her namesake surpasses her.'

His language made her feel oddly at home, as if she was back in the regiment. She walked over to the balustrade, the sun already warming her through the flimsy nightgown, but he drew her back.

'Come away from sight,' he said. 'You do not yet exist. Come inside.'

He took her into a vast hall, cool after the heat of the morning, and guided her to the middle of the polished floor, positioning her in the centre of a many-pointed star tricked out in marble. Far above her head hung a vast chandelier. The morning sun struck the brilliants, teasing the unlit candles.

Ormonde walked around Kit, as if she was a horse he would buy. He did not speak for a while; then he said: 'I will be frank with you; I have never attempted such a deception before. But I am confident that you are just the raw material we need. Your looks, your courage, your natural intelligence . . .' Kit had never received so many compliments with so little warmth attached; it was hard to feel gratified by his remarks.

'You will put yourself entirely in my hands,' the duke declared. 'You may ask me as many questions as you wish. I am your tutor, but I am not your master. You are not my creature. I am not your better. At dinner we will converse as equals, as a duke and the countess you will become. We are partners in this. And if you do what I ask of you, we will both achieve our heart's desire.' She wondered, intrigued, what his was; she knew her own.

'I will strip you down, take away everything you are and build you up into an entirely new person. Only by this will our scheme succeed. But make no mistake. I am not your friend. I like you, Bess, I do. You remind me of myself, and I prefer my own company to anyone else's. But if you fail,' he stopped before her face, 'I will not shield you. I will deny you more times than Saint Peter – we never met, I never knew you, you never came here. Equally, if you are captured you may deny all knowledge of me. I will offer no censure, nor take any offence. We will walk away from each other without a backward glance. Do you understand?'

She nodded, not cowed by his honesty: at last, a man who spoke straight. She liked the arrangement. She believed that if she did as Ormonde asked he would do right by her.

'But we must build on a foundation of total candour. The story you told me in the carriage. Was it a complete account of your adventures? Did you leave anything out?'

Her stomach shrivelled. But she met his gaze. 'No.'

'Do you have anything to ask me before we begin?'

'Yes. What do I call you?'

'Remember, from now on we are equals. You will call me at all times by my given name, which is Fitzjames. Let us try it.'

'Fitzjames,' she said shyly.

'Good. Now, come here. Time to be a newborn babe.' He placed his hands on the facings of her nightgown and tore it from shoulder to hip.

It fell to the floor, leaving her completely naked. She stood stock still, as if on parade, determined not to flinch. She did not even move to cover herself. She did not think that he would force himself upon her. He echoed her thoughts. 'Do not be uneasy; I am not going to fuck you. I have no interest in your body whatsoever. These,' he flicked her nipples, and tugged at the red fleece of hair at her groin, 'are my tools. I am merely taking an inventory.'

He looked at her skin, touching her with a fingertip as if she was alabaster. She did not flinch. 'White as bread underneath the grime.' He touched one stiff nipple. 'Brown as ale.' He squeezed her upper arm. 'Too muscular.'

Would her muscles give her away?

'Worked your passage to Genova, did you?'

'Yes,' she said.

'Too much swabbing. These arms need to relax, and soften.'

Kit breathed out in relief, and felt a brush at her ribs.

'Too thin.' He touched her cheek. 'Dry, and a little weather-beaten.' Then he touched her hip, but gently, where an ugly starburst of a scar sat upon her hip bone. 'What happened here?'

She thought fast. 'I sustained an injury. A stray musket ball in the hip as I followed the camp.'

'At Cremona?'

'Luzzara.'

He nodded. 'Trouble walking?'

'Not now.'

'Can you dance?'

'Never tried, but for the town hop.'

'Never mind. You will.'

The duke raised his eyes higher. 'Hair. God meant it for red, I suppose; hard to see beneath the veneer of grease. Smells like a fleece.' His frank assessments hurt her no more than his earlier compliments had pleased her.

'Well.' He lifted her gown from the floor and draped it about her shoulders again, as if covering a statue for the winter. 'Good. Now I am not your tutor but your physician; and here is my prescription. You must bathe in water today, and scrub with tallow soap to cleanse your skin and hair. I have directed Pietro to purchase lemon and alum for lice – we do not need pests about our person. Thereafter you will bathe in milk daily, to restore the lustre to your skin. Have you heard of Cleopatra, Bess?'

She had not.

'Another queen – a great beauty. She bathed in asses' milk. I cannot offer you that, but these hills are lousy with kine, and they will provide. You must clean, comb and polish your hair, and dress it as best you can. Is all this clear?'

She nodded. 'Then you will join me for luncheon in the morning room by the lake, and there you will eat your fill as you will three times a day in all. Buttermilk, cheese, fowl – cream on your porridge and all things rich and healthy. All my produce comes from these fertile slopes of the mountain.' He waved his hand to the vista with a proprietorial air. 'We must have you plump as a partridge – fill your breasts, so they may fill your gowns. And when our outward shows are achieved, we must work upon the most crucial organ – your mind. But that is for later.' He rang a small silver bell. 'Pietro has run a bath for you in the bathhouse by the lake. Everything you need is there, and a work gown to dress in too. You will notice there are no servants here except Pietro. For now, you must wash and dress yourself, but once my servants return you will never have to dress yourself again – never tie a shoe, never fasten a button. Your life will change utterly.'

The bathhouse by the lake was a little paradise – mosaic tiles in blue and green and gold wreathed around the walls like steam, and a sunken square bath in the Roman style waited for Kit filled to the brim. Kit sank into the water up to her eyes. She had not been in a bath for over a year. She took the lump of tallow and scrubbed herself into a lather, soaping her shoulders with a linen cloth. She washed everywhere, all the time looking out at the glorious summer lake and mountains and not quite believing where she was. She washed herself three, four, a dozen times until her skin was rosy red and squeaked to the touch. Then she completely submerged herself in the bath, scrubbing and rinsing her hair, first with soap, then with lemon and alum. Rising from the water, Venus renewed, she squeezed the water from the dark red mass of her hair, and wrapped herself in the long linen cloths.

She saw a grass-green gown, the brocade glowing in the sun, draped across a chair like a shed snakeskin. She left it there for now and went to sit, just as she was, in the late morning sun, with a heavy comb of carved ivory in her hand.

The blunt fringe she had cut across her eyes in her chamber in Kavanagh's was quite grown out now, and the hair curled in long tendrils about her face. The locks had grown back in swags and hanks and curls, now clean and bright as copper, every filament snatching at the sun. She sat on, when she was done, letting the warm wind dry her hair, listening to the music of the bees, and the strange alien cries of the peacocks. When the little church at Stresa began to ring the angelus she got up reluctantly and went back to the bathhouse.

With the aid of a large looking glass she piled her hair on the top of her head with half a dozen jade combs that she found in an inlaid chest, leaving one long length under her left ear, curling the lock round her hand. She examined the effect – her hair now glowed with the colour of carnelians, her eyes were as jade as the combs, and she smoothed her dark brows into fashionable arcs. Her cheeks were, it was true, a little ruddy from her soldier days so she rubbed a little of the oil of olives into them, and slicked a little on to her lips, which she bit to redden them.

Then she put on the grass-green gown, a 'work gown', the duke had called it. Indeed, it was simple, but it was still a thing of wonder. It was heavy with brocade, and she laced herself into it with difficulty – no wonder the quality needed a maid – pushing her breasts upward so they sat fashionably, two pale half-moons, under her chin. She examined herself in the glass – her reflection resembled her no more than the ragged girl she'd seen on the Venetian stair. She threw a towel over the mirror, and went to wait outside. Unable to sit comfortably now, she stretched out on the warm stone, luxuriously, until Pietro's shadow fell across her.

On the terrace, the duke sat under a shaded awning, the table before him piled with pyramids of fruit and crystal glasses, and, in a salver of ice beside him, a pile of oysters.

The Duke of Ormonde looked at Kit wearing an expression she could not read.

She stood in front of him, her confidence draining. Then she asked, 'What do you think?'

Then he smiled. 'I think,' he said, 'that you will be of more use to the cause than any soldier in Marlborough's army.'

Chapter 28

We take great delight in our own company . . .

'Arthur McBride' (trad.)

By nightfall Kit was the Comtesse Christiane St-Hilaire de Blossac.

After their luncheon by the lake the duke took Kit to the very top of the palace, where no one could overlook them but the lake gulls. Above the windows sat a gallery, which could be reached by sliding wooden ladders, and all around the gallery a regiment of books lined the open shelves. The place smelled like a schoolroom.

Ormonde sat her at the secretaire, before a scroll of paper and a quill and inkpot.

'Have you letters?'

'Yes. I can read and write. My Aunt Maura taught me . . .'

She did not finish the sentence, for he pressed his forefinger to her lips. 'No. She does not exist. There is no Aunt Maura, no alehouse in Dublin, no missing husband. Forget all that, and Ireland too. You have never set foot there.'

'Then who am I going to be?'

'Who are you?'

'I do not understand you.'

'The best falsehood is the truth. Who are you?'

'Kit Kavanagh.'

'Farther back.'

For the first time in years, she used her christened name, the name her French mother had given her.

'Christian. I'm Christian.'

'In French, Christiane,' he said. 'It's a start.'

He paced to the window. A little fishing smack was tacking across the blue lake. 'When I said that the best falsehood is the truth, did you understand what I meant by that?'

'No.'

'If I call you Liliane or Marie-France, and someone calls that name in a crowded room, you will not answer, nor even turn your head, however carefully you have been prepared. But if your name really is Christiane, and someone calls you by it, you will reply. If you are asked to sign your name to a document, the unwary will begin to write the first few letters of their own name, not their alias, before they remember. But you, you are Christiane, so you will write Christiane. Equally, it is easier to lie about a past that marches closely with your own.' This she understood, for she had done just this when she had lied to him about her past year. 'So I am going to construct your identity from your own life. Now: let us consider your mother, and your French heritage.' He clasped his hands behind his back. 'I want you to cast your mind back; remember all you knew of her.'

Kit, her eyes on the little boat on the lake, thought about her mother in fine detail for the first time in years.

'What was her name?'

She breathed out as she spoke the name. 'Heloise de Blossac.'

'Who was she?'

'An enameller's daughter from Poitiers. She met my father when he was on a French campaign, and followed him home to Ireland. By then she was with child.'

'You?'

'Me.' The parallels were striking. Her mother and her, following a man across the sea.

'No more children?'

'None. She didn't even want me.' It did not hurt, now, to say what as a child she could not have uttered. 'She hated me.' Perhaps it was a blessing if she could not have a child – better not to bring a daughter into the world, to bring her up alone. 'She just wanted my father.' Kit realised she was speaking of her mother as if she was dead, but for all she knew, her mother was still alive, well into her middle years and living . . . where? On the farm still? Or had she gone home to France, now that there was nothing left of Sean Kavanagh but the blood that nourished the grass on Killcommadan Hill?

'And your father died?'

'At the Battle of Aughrim.'

His eyes flickered briefly. 'And you hated your mother?'

'Yes.'

'Well, now she's going to help you. We will have you as a native of Poitiers. It is provincial enough and far enough away from Versailles for the court not to be closely acquainted with your bloodline. Now, what do you know of the town?'

'Nothing. Except for the fact that they must make enamel – she had a jug of my grandfather's, one of the only things she brought with her. It was a lovely thing.'

'Your grandfather's name?'

'Jean Christophe Saint-Hilaire de Blossac. He was rich; his trade did very well, and the family became gentry.'

'And your grandmother?'

She thought hard. 'Marianne. Marianne Valmy. A *curé*'s daughter.'

He nodded. 'I'll work on the rest. For today, a *comtesse* would know about politics.'

He told her, in far more detail than Ross had – and this time with the aid of books and maps, instead of a stick and a puddle of mud – the origins, notable battles and strategies of the War of the Two Crowns. Following his pointing finger, she could see at last exactly how far she had travelled about the boot-shaped peninsula, back and forth over the mountains and lakes, and could see how crucial the northern cities – Milan, Mantova, Turin – were as counters in the game. They stood sentinel, ranged like outposts along the border, keeping France at bay. 'Do you see?' said Ormonde. 'If they break through this line, the forces of the Two Crowns could gain the whole peninsula, and overrun the Empire.'

He told her of the major players on the chessboard; of how enemies Louis of France and Eugene of Savoy were raised together at the Palace of Versailles, inseparable boyhood friends. 'Louis refused to give Eugene preferment to the army, so Eugene went to fight for his uncle the Emperor, and now they are on opposite sides. Eugene's first language is French,' said Ormonde. 'So he will know at once if you dissemble.'

Kit swallowed. She could not tell Ormonde that she had once stood with the prince, no more than an arm's length apart, on the tower of the cathedral in Cremona – that he had taken her prisoner from her grasp and thrown him to his death.

'He is the finest test for you,' Ormonde declared. 'If we take you to his name-day ball and he recognises you for a fraud, then nothing is lost – you would be a birthday jest from an eccentric English *milord*. If he takes you for a French woman, we know that you are ready to go to the French court at Mantova, and meet Philippe d'Orléans, nephew to Louis of France, and Villeroi himself.' Kit swallowed nervously. She cared not for Philippe d'Orléans, for he would not know her from Eve; but Villeroi – how much had Villeroi seen her? She had been there at the *maréchal's* capture. He had looked on her, but had he seen?

Of Marlborough, Ormonde was dismissive. He referred to him as 'Jack Churchill'. 'He is all brawl and bombast,' he said. 'He will crack a walnut with a battering ram. But Villeroi, he is a different matter. They say he talked himself out of captivity. He

is of formidable intelligence.' She remembered the *maréchal* nego-
tiating with Captain Ross even with a knife to his throat.

'And I am to deceive him?' she asked plaintively. 'To pluck out
his strategy?'

'No, never in this world.' Ormonde shook his head.

'But . . . you said that I am to find out what the French intend!'

'But you do not *ask*,' said the duke firmly. 'You *never* ask. Your
only office is to be charming and beautiful, and show an interest
in these men, and show as much animosity to the forces of the
Grand Alliance as you can convey without arousing suspicion.
Information will come to you, but if you dig for it, you are mining
a barren seam.'

Kit spent the following morning, as she had been instructed, on
her person – she slept late, bathed in milk, dressed her hair and
oiled her skin. Then after luncheon she climbed to the tower,
and found Ormonde surrounded by open books, maps and reams
of paper closely written in his flourishing hand. He sat her down
at the secretaire and coached her in her new bloodlines, the region
of Poitou-Charentes, the house where she'd lived since her
marriage and, of course, her imaginary husband. Once he'd been
through her history, telling her the story of her own life as if he
were Aunt Maura telling her a tale, he tested her, correcting her
and prompting her, until she was word perfect.

'Which river flows through Poitiers?'

'The Clain.'

'What was the name of your townhouse?'

'The Hotel Poitevin.'

'To which saint is the cathedral dedicated?'

'Saint Pierre.'

'Walk me home from the cathedral after mass.'

'From the square, you take the left way into the rue Chasseneuil,
past the Jardin des Plantes. The hotel is on your left.'

He nodded. 'Good. I would take you to Poitiers myself if I could; but even with my carriage and a change of horse it is time we don't have. Savoy's name day is in just under three months.' Kit's stomach lurched – there didn't seem time to get prepared, to assume an identity in such detail. But then she remembered another self, the Kit who had simply cut her hair and put on a suit of clothes. She had been a man before she'd gone down the stairs, with no such tutoring.

Ormonde, ever businesslike, pressed on. 'What is the name of your husband's military order?'

'The order of Saint Louis.'

'Where did you meet him?'

'At the house of my Aunt Hortense at Angoulême. He taught me to shoot with a bow in her pleasure gardens.'

'Where did he serve?'

'Cadiz and Vigo Bay.'

'And there we are on a firm footing, for I served there too and can furnish you with more details than I care to recollect.'

This was a new Ormonde to Kit. She wondered whether his experiences in battle had set him on this path to clandestine warfare, to prefer the battles that were fought in ballrooms and salons, with words and whispers.

'Is everything clear so far? We will go over everything again, each day; but do you have any questions?'

'Just one.'

He inclined his head, like his parrot.

'What is my husband's name?'

'Remember what I told you. Truth is the best falsehood. What is your real husband's name?'

She felt a small pang. 'Richard.'

'Ri-shard.' He said it the French way. 'Perfect.'

'Why perfect?'

'Because of the Lionheart. Richard I of England, a native of

Poitiers. What better name for a Poiteven? "The Vicomte Richard Saint-Hilaire de Blossac".' He spoke the name like a herald. 'It sounds well. You should have a motto, too. What shall it be?' The duke spoke to himself as if he did not expect Kit to be of any use in the matter of Latin epigrams. But she spoke up at once.

'I have one.'

He looked surprised. 'Shall we use it?'

She shrugged. 'Truth is the best falsehood.'

'Don't shrug,' he admonished. 'It is not the gesture of a lady. Tell me your motto.'

'*Virtus Ipsa Suis Firmissima.* Truth relies on its own arms.'

There was a pause. 'Well, that certainly fits,' said Ormonde. 'We'll take it.'

Ormonde would ruthlessly interrogate Kit not only on the subject of her own bloodlines, but also on those of Louis of France. 'A French countess would learn these bloodlines at her mother's tit. Let us begin again.' He took up a great book and paced behind her. 'The House of Capet.'

'Hugh Capet, Robert II, Henri I, Philippe I, Louis VI, Louis VII, Philippe II, Louis VIII, Louis IX, Philippe III, Philippe IV, Louis X, Jean I.'

'The House of Valois.'

'Charles Comte de Valois, Philippe VI, Jean II, Charles V, Louis I Duke d'Orléans . . .'

'. . . Jean, Count of Angoulême . . .'

'Jean, Count of Angoulême, Charles, Count of Angoulême, Francis I, Henri II.'

'The House of Bourbon. The bloodline of the current King Louis himself.'

'Robert Comte de Clermont, Louis Duc de Bourbon, Jaques Comte de La Marche, Jean Comte de La Marche, Louis Comte de Vendôme, Jean VIII Comte de Vendôme, Francis Comte de Vendôme, Charles Duc de Vendôme, Antoine de Bourbon, Henri IV, Louis XIII, Louis XIV.'

'Yes. And finally the House of Orléans.'

She looked up, askance, suspecting a trick. 'Only Philippe d'Orléans, the first branch of his tree.'

'Precisely. The very prince who holds court at Mantova; enough.' Ormonde shut the book and threw it among the papers on the secretaire. 'We must do what we can to stop the French marching all over the map.'

But despite Ormonde's hostility to the French, his tutelage on the subject of her home and family worked a strange magic on her. Though she felt fully Irish, she was half French. She'd paid no mind to that other half she carried with her always like the obverse of a coin, but now she thought of the people of Poitiers, that far-off unknown town. Did they know that this war was being fought in their name? She had no quarrel with them, they had not injured her, those citizens going about their business, making their enamel. She did not hate the French; but she had chosen her side, had killed for the Grand Alliance more than once. Then a thought occurred.

'Fitzjames?'

'Christiane?'

'What of my husband? My . . . counterfeit husband?'

'What of him?'

'Well – am I to say he is back in France? Or must they suppose he is in the French forces, behind the lines?'

'No. He will be dead.'

'He's dead?'

'Will be. Remember your future tense.' Ormonde was a stickler for grammar, insisting that a *comtesse* would speak with exactitude. 'He is not dead *yet*.'

He would say no more, so she had to be content.

Ormonde's education was all-encompassing. He covered every detail. He would open his strongbox and scatter a fortune in stones willy-nilly on the secretaire: tiaras, jewelled collars, sparkling orders hanging from their ceremonial ribbons like mini-constellations. She could not put a single jewel back in the box till she had learned its value and described the cut of the stone, the nature of the setting. At these times he would show her a sparkling diamond collar with a matching bracelet and earrings like two miniature chandeliers. 'These diamonds are from Versailles,' he said. 'They belonged to Anne of Austria, who was . . .'

'Louis XIV's mother,' supplied Kit, wondering, if that was the case, how Ormonde had come by them.

'This set will be yours,' he said, 'if you succeed in your mission.'

She looked up at him, her hands full of the bright jewels, suspecting a jest. But his deep-set eyes, all colours and none, were in earnest. 'Truly,' he said. 'They are currency around the world, wherever you choose to go. Their tender is accepted everywhere. But for now, tell me the cut and cost.'

On one of the only rainy days of that summer, Ormonde invited her to sit with him in the small parlour on the *piano nobile*. They sat either side of the empty fireplace in the glorious little room, enamelled with white and gold, and in between them was a little table, holding nothing but a long box. The box was a pale rose in colour, edged in gold, and wedge shaped, tapering slightly at one end. 'Take it in your hands and open it,' he said.

Inside was a fan. Kit took it out and spread it, carefully, with her left hand. It had ivory struts chased in gold, but the fan itself was made of thick cream paper, a humble material but made priceless by the artistry of its decoration. It was exquisitely painted with a scene of a woman with powdered hair in a sky-blue dress sitting in a leafy arbour playing a lute. Her lover, in a mauve frock coat, sang to her from a sheet of music. The scene was beautifully rendered, and even the tiny music notes had been picked out with a brush that must have been the width of a hair. She turned the fan over – the back was plain but for a tiny basket overflowing with flowers, every leaf and petal just as lovingly painted. The fan was edged with tiny gold sequins, stitched on to a narrow ribbon, like miniature coins. She turned the thing over again, opening it, closing it, letting it hang from its golden tassel. It was the most beautiful thing she had ever held in her hands. 'Is it for me?'

'Yes.'

'*Thank* you, Fitzjames.'

'The pleasure is mine – but it is not a gift.' He smiled. 'Would you thank an armourer who hands you a musket? It is a tool, a weapon for your new uniform. Or perhaps it is better to think of it as a quill and ink, for really it is a means of communication.'

'It is?'

'When you opened the fan with your left hand, you told me to come and talk to you. When you closed it and struck it against your left palm, you told me to write to you. You have just told me to wait for you, when you touched the gold lace edging. Then, when you changed the fan to your right hand, you told me that I was imprudent.'

She closed the fan and hung it from her hand by the tassel, her arm at full length, as if she wanted the thing away from her.

'And now you have closed it and left it hanging, you are telling me that we will continue to be friends.'

Kit's head spun. 'Will all those at the ball know these signals?'

'Not all of the officers, of course, for some of them rose from the rank and file. But a gentleman will know.'

A gentleman. Ross. Kit's cheeks heated at the thought that she could send Ross such clandestine messages. *Come and talk to me. Write to me. Wait for me.*

'Let us try,' said Ormonde. 'Hold the fan to your right cheek to say yes, to your left to say no.'

Patiently, he coached her: to open and close the fan rapidly told a companion that he was cruel; to hold the fan over the left ear told a suitor the holder wished to be rid of him. To hold the handle to the lips invited a kiss. 'Most of these, of course, will not be necessary; but you must know them so that you do not send communications accidentally. Besides, these messages will be useful to us at the ball. You can signal to me if you are in trouble. Now you try.'

She rose and followed him to the middle of the room, then they stood facing each other as if they were about to dance a measure.

'Tell me,' he said, 'that we are being watched.'

Kit thought for a moment, then half-opened the fan over her face.

He nodded. 'And now that I have changed.'

She held the fan to her hairline, and slid it across her forehead, but then she fumbled and dropped the fan, the ivory struts falling on to the marble floor with a smart tap. She bent at once, flustered and apologetic, but found her reaching hand trapped under Ormonde's boot. He stood on her fingers, firmly and deliberately, hard enough to hurt. He stooped, and picked up the fan, before he took his foot away. Kit straightened, wringing her hand furiously, biting her lip in vexation.

'Do not,' said Ormonde, 'ever, stoop to pick something up. If you drop a fan, a kerchief or even a diamond, it is for someone else to pick it up for you. You are a countess.' He held out the fan to her, then snatched it away. 'Who are you?'

'La Comtesse Christiane Saint-Hilaire de Blossac,' she said sullenly, to the marble floor.

Ormonde cocked his earlobe with his forefinger. 'I beg your pardon?'

She looked him in the eye, chin high, haughty. 'La Comtesse Christiane Saint-Hilaire de Blossac,' she said.

'Better. Now it is your turn. Send me a message.'

Kit rested the fan on her lips. Her hand still hurt. *I don't trust you.*

He laughed. 'And you are right not to.' Then he sobered. 'Come, let us be friends,' he said kindly. 'We will stop for the day, ready ourselves for dinner.'

She made a reverence to him and he to her, as he always insisted they should when they met or parted. She could feel him watching her walk away. She stopped and turned.

'Fitzjames?'

'Christiane?'

'What does it mean when you drop your fan in front of a man?'

He looked at her speculatively. 'It means that man owns you.'

She smiled a tight little smile, nodded faintly, and left the room.

Kit's days were spent in the tower room, rehearsing her identity with the Duke of Ormonde, who spoke to her like a benevolent schoolmaster. Her evenings were spent at dinner and cards with 'Fitzjames', who treated her as a noble companion. The lessons, though, never ended. Ormonde taught her to eat with a fork as well as a knife, to sip her wine from a crystal goblet, to laugh without snorting, to bite without showing her teeth, to flatter with delicacy. After a convivial dinner at the little table by the lake, she would learn to play piquet and bezique in the warm summer evening, with gold-edged playing cards. Ormonde taught her to gamble like a lady, with low stakes and high risk.

During the day they spoke English, and Ormonde encouraged her to remember her mother's tricks of speech, speak with her accent and flutter her hands like her. At dinner she and 'Fitzjames' conversed in French, still served by Pietro alone.

So Kit lived a strange existence, in the vast and glorious Palazzo Borromeo, with a master, a man and a parrot. Pietro was a man whose face she could not describe, even an hour after she had left his company. He was bland, shadowy, unrecognisable; a common fellow with no significant features or idiosyncrasies to mark him out. He was every man and no man, and, as such, a perfect servant to his master, whose business was so decidedly his own. Pietro would only speak if prompted, and had no conversation.

The bird, by contrast, would shriek at her like a ballad seller, to get her attention as she passed – and though it alternated between calling her a 'silly slut' and a 'damned Jacobite', she felt they had a certain rapport. He had only a few utterances in his lexicon, but his inflexions gave his vocabulary a world of meaning, as did the cock of his head and the ruffling of his rainbow feathers. Ormonde had told Kit from the start that he would not be her friend, despite his evening pleasantries, and his taciturn servant was clearly of the same mind; so the parrot was the only friend she had at the Palazzo Borromeo.

Now and again she had a day of leisure, when Ormonde took the boat to Stresa, where he kept his carriage in livery. Kit would wave to him from the atrium, and when she could no longer see him, she would turn and run like a child, skidding on the gravel, into the gardens. She would wander the alleys, she would dangle her hands in the cool fountains, watching the crystal water playing on her soft, lady's hands, the calluses and chapping of soldiery smoothed away. She would breathe in the jasmine and the oleander, the honeysuckle and myrtle. She would look across the straits to Stresa, where ordinary people went about their business, innocent of the deception being practised just across the water.

After she had been over the gardens Kit would take herself into the house and stroll through the cool grottoes entirely decorated with seashells, trailing her fingertips over the rough walls. Then she would climb the marble stairs and spin through the empty ballroom, breathing the scent of beeswax, and wander the painted salons, loving the solitude after a year of living cheek by jowl with three score men. She could not imagine the Palazzo Borromeo peopled with glittering guests, chattering and laughing and dancing. That summer, it was hers.

On these days when her time was her own, she bathed in the milk that Pietro brought to the bathhouse, and her skin was once again supple and clear and white as the milk itself. She ate alone on the terrace, finishing every dish that was placed before her, and emptying her glass. Ormonde's regime was working: the hollows in her cheeks had filled out and the shadows under her eyes had gone, for she slept well in her feather bed. Her arms had softened and rounded again, the hard dragoon muscles relaxed into feminine contours. Her waist was still as slim as a whip, but her bosom had filled, and she could no longer count her ribs. She practised her broken English even to herself, until her Dublin brogue was almost a memory. She breathed in the mountain air every day, and would doze in her schoolroom like a cat in the shade of the terrace. She did not know where Ormonde went on those days of absence, but he would leave at dawn and return at dinner. He would never speak of these trips, any more than he ever spoke about himself; but she was in no doubt that he was laying plans for her emergence into society. From time to time, she would go to the little boathouse, to see the rowing boats bobbing at their moorings. She never took one out – it would not be seemly for her new persona – but they reassured her that she was not a prisoner. If she got too frightened, she could run.

One night, Ormonde greeted her with a rank of green bottles on the dinner table. The bottles wore chains about their necks and wore gold-lettered labels about their stout bellies. 'French champagne,' announced Ormonde. 'Tonight, I will teach you to drink.'

At first they drank at the table. The wine was very good – clean and sparkling. It didn't feel like real drinking. She had another, and another. After all, she'd spent enough time in taverns with the dragoons – she was sure she could hold her grog. She forgot to eat. She was warm with happiness. She would see Ross again, clothed in diamonds, and they were friends, 'Fitzjames' and she, whatever he might say.

Somehow, they ended up sitting on the lake shore in the warm summer night, with the bottles between them, their fat glass bottoms pushed into the shingle, looking out into the night at the omnipresent moon on the water. Kit squinted happily against the stars. They were Ormonde's diamonds – her diamonds – with the black looming shapes of the mountains below. She thought of Ross where he slept in those dark heights. She raised a glass to him silently. Ormonde caught the gesture and they were suddenly toasting everyone they could think of; at first, reverently, Anne of England, Eugene of Savoy, and Leopold, Holy Roman Emperor.

Then they toasted Louis of France and his nephew, the pretender Philippe. One name was not mentioned; its absence shouting louder than the rest. But, unexpectedly, Ormonde raised his glass once more. 'To Jack Churchill,' he crowed, standing unsteadily. 'Fuck him!' The mountains bounced the obscenity back to him, loud enough so Marlborough himself, in his battle tent, could surely hear it too.

Ormonde refilled their glasses. 'Do you like music, Christiane? It is a subject we have not yet discussed.'

Kit thought, fondly, of Dublin, where there was music on every corner of the Liberties. Looking out at the velvet night, she told Ormonde of her favourite songs: 'The Humours of Castlefin', 'John Dwyer's Jig', 'The Maids of Mitchelstown' – the music which had sailed with her on shipboard, had climbed with her up the mountain, safe in the belly of O'Connell's fiddle.

'Hmmm,' said Ormonde. 'There is something lacking, then. I

know these ditties and I love them too, for I am Irish; but this is not music as the cream of the French court understands it. I must open your ears . . .'

'As you have opened my throat.' She laughed, emptying her glass.

'But music is out of my stars. I have found you a tutor.'

She clasped his arm in protest. 'But *you* are my tutor.'

'But I need someone who can teach my nightingale to sing.'

'I *can* sing!' She needed him to know that. She did not want their lonely, lovely exile to be disturbed. She pointed her finger at Ormonde's fine lace jabot, to underline her point. 'I can sing. I once sung someone back to life.' Ross, it was Ross she brought to life, and she mustn't mention Ross. But she needed Ormonde to know she could sing. It was suddenly very important that he should know. She would sing him 'Arthur McBride', just as she had sung to Ross, so he should know that she was not a country mouse. She opened her mouth to sing her sweet song across the lake. But instead of a song flooding forth she puked over Ormonde's fine lace jabot.

She saw his eyes spark in brief anger like the flint of a matchlock, then knew no more.

Chapter 29

And the same to you gentlemen, we did reply . . .
                                        'Arthur McBride' (trad.)

When she awoke, Kit's head pounded. Her mouth was dry as sand, her eyes grainy and slow to open. She stumbled to the window and threw open the shutters, gulping the mountain air.

Just as she was, in her nightgown, she walked out through the gardens, the gravel of the yew walks hurting her feet through her silken slippers. She welcomed the pain. Anything to take her mind off her roiling stomach and throbbing head.

She would go to her favourite spot at the headland, a great fountain with numerous grottoes carved out of it, harbouring stone seashells and cherubs and dolphins spouting water. It was a place where Kit Kavanagh could go unobserved, before she resumed her labours as Christiane St-Hilaire de Blossac. But to her annoyance, someone already sat there.

It was a lady, but a lady of singular appearance. She wore a coat and breeches of dark gold silk, buckled kid shoes, and her powdered hair was caught back in a neat queue tied with a black bow. She was dressed, in short, as a man.

The lady turned at her approach, and spoke in English. 'I cannot decide,' she said with a heavy accent, 'whether it is too grotesque to be beautiful, or too beautiful to be grotesque. What is your opinion?'

'I *think* it is beautiful,' Kit ventured, practising her new broken

English, 'but surpassed by the vista beyond.' She gestured to the view that could be seen through the cataract – the lake, the mountains.

'There we agree,' said the lady. 'I keep telling Fitz he should rip these fountains out, but he always says he does not want to offend the Borromei family.'

Kit was more and more intrigued. *Fitz*. She studied the lady. She was very pale and not unattractive, but she had an oddly shaped skull with a domed forehead, and a pronounced overbite to her jaw which gave her a faintly canine look. The lady unfolded her long limbs and stood. She was uncommonly tall – taller than Kit, taller than Ross. She held out a hand.

Kit was about to shake it heartily, then remembered, just in time, that she should offer her hand to be kissed. The lady saluted her proffered fingers in the proper fashion. Kit, as a countess, opened her mouth to present herself first, as was proper for one of superior rank. But she did not get the chance.

'Lucio Mezzanotte,' said the stranger.

'La Comtesse Christiane Saint-Hilaire de Blossac,' said Kit faintly.

The lady smiled. 'Bravo. You remembered. But with me, you can be Kit Kavanagh if you please. Fitz has told me everything. I am here to teach you music.'

Why did Ormonde go to such lengths to maintain secrecy, if he was to blurt all to this beanpole of a woman? 'But I thought that my lord duke – Fitzjames – said he was to be my tutor in all things.'

The lady snorted. 'Fitz can barely play the spoons. He needed a master, and here I am.' *A master*. Kit smiled to herself at the identification 'Shall we repair to the music room? I cannot hear myself think by these infernal fountains.'

Kit stole sideways glances at her new tutor as they strolled back to the palace, past the flower beds and the sauntering peacocks. She was so slender, with snake hips and a swinging gait. Her cheek was smooth as a babe's, her lips and cheeks rouged, her brows were plucked into two high half-moons and a heart-shaped patch rode high on one cheek. But what betrayed her the most was the necklace at her throat, some sort of pendant of glittering glass in the shape of a raindrop, a long curling tail coiling about the ribbon that held it. A silly mistake.

'As we are now so much in each other's confidence,' Kit began tentatively, 'I wonder if I might make a suggestion.'

'Of course,' said the lady. Her voice was like Bianca's, the same accent of these lands, the same high and piping timbre.

'This is a personal matter. It is just that once I dressed as a man . . . for a mumming,' Kit said hurriedly. 'I would pad my waist a little to hide my slim shape, and rub a little potash on my jaw each morning, to give the impression of the beard that I lacked. And I left off my jewellery.'

The lady stopped and turned, turning dark eyes upon her, squinting slightly through her long lashes against the sun. 'I have not the pleasure of understanding you.'

'I do not mean to offend. Remember, I, too, dissemble, and to assume another character takes time; Fitzjames is teaching me how to best present myself, over many weeks, to better work my deception.'

The finely plucked brows drew together. 'And what is my deception?'

'That . . . that you are a man.'

For an instant Kit thought she'd angered her; then she laughed, throwing back her head, opening her mouth to show very small white teeth. 'But I *am* a man.'

Kit studied him, her mouth agape. Everything about him was womanish – he had no more beard than she, and the tell-tale knot of muscle at the throat, the lack of which she had always been at pains to disguise under her army stock, was entirely absent.

'But,' she blurted, 'you *can't* be.'

'I am, though.' He collected her confounded expression, and relented. 'I am not being entirely fair. I am not wholly a man, but I am no woman either. I am a *castrato*. I was castrated in my youth to preserve my voice.'

'Your voice?'

'My singing voice. In Florence, where I was born, the practice is common. There is a shop by the Duomo with a sign above – "here we castrate boys".' He plucked a scarlet flower from a shrub and began to shred it, as he walked, with his long white fingers. 'Your Protestant faith has not reached us in Florence; we are Catholics to the bone and are ruled by the law of the Church. The Pope, God guard him, decreed that no female should sing in a Church choir. So the Church recruited boys, boys with sweet girlish voices. These boys, Kit,' he turned to her, 'these boys can sing fit to pierce your soul, they can describe, in one soaring, sustained note, the ultimate solitude of God.' He walked on again with his short footsteps. 'But boys lose their voices when they gain their beards. So, if you are poor, and your son has a promising voice, you can make your fortune. I cannot blame my father.'

Kit struggled to follow. 'Your father?'

He shrugged, like a man. 'We were poor, and I had a promising voice.'

'What did he do?'

'He took me to the backstreets, to the shop with the sign. They put me in a warm bath, and fed me opium until I was drowsy. Then they took a huge pair of iron pliers, black as a crow's beak. They are called *castratore*.' He bit his lip, stopped. 'They stitched me up, but I still bled for a sevennight. I was nine years old.'

Kit was silent, appalled.

'But,' he went on breezily, 'my voice was preserved. It is a substantial gift. And now I thank my father every day for what he took from me, and what he gave me.' He glanced at her, proudly. 'I am an artist. Lucio Mezzanotte is celebrated all over the world. I sing in the greatest opera houses – La Fenice. La Scala. Even your own opera house in London.' As he strutted and crowed Mezzanotte reminded her of the white peacocks. 'That is where I met Fitz. I was presented to the queen.'

'But,' Kit said hesitantly, 'there must be other . . . lacks.'

She did not know how to frame the question – was he like a woman, down *there*, or was there anything remaining of the man he had been?

'You are speaking of the act of love? One can still participate. There are ways. But I cannot perform the man's part in that particular performance. And, of course, I cannot have a child.'

'Nor I,' said Kit, feeling the loss once again like a blow. She had no woman's part, he no man's. They were both halfway creatures.

'But we can still love,' said he.

'*Yes*,' she said fervently, unguardedly. 'And hate.'

There was a silence as they rounded the yew walk, and the bittersweet scent of the leaves enveloped them.

'Do you hate the French?' It was Mezzanotte's turn to question her.

She considered. 'No.'

'But you fight them.'

'Yes.'

'Because you have been told to? Because your commanders do?'

Marlborough. Ross. Ormonde. 'I suppose that is so, yes.'

'I want them all dead.'

She considered this brutal statement, so at odds with the view they enjoyed.

'Not because I hate them. But because I love my country. And

I want it back.' He cast the shredded flower he held on the gravel walk. 'Love is the best reason to fight, not hate.'

She thought of Dublin, of Kavanagh's. 'I love my country too,' she said, heartfelt.

'England?'

'Ireland.'

'Ah, Ir-e-land.' He gave the word three syllables. 'Like Fitz.' Mezzanotte flicked a glance at her. 'Perhaps you love it here, on this enchanted island? Do you?'

She considered. 'Yes,' she said. And it was true.

'Then fight for that,' he said.

Kit worked with Mezzanotte every morning, in the ornate music room on the *piano nobile*, which she came to love more than any other room in the house. Mezzanotte, ordering Pietro about as if he were Ormonde himself, caused the instruments to be uncovered so Kit could admire the carved and enamelled spinets and harpsichords, crouching on their golden legs like an exotic menagerie. He had the place filled with flowers from the garden, and ordered that the great glass doors that opened out on to the sun terrace should be thrown open, so that they could overlook the lake.

The castrato was excellent company; witty, kind and prodigiously talented. He sat Kit down with him on the scarlet upholstered stool by the harpsichord, and took her hands. 'Do you love music?' he asked, searchingly.

Mezzanotte seemed to deal in absolutes – love or hate were his business with nothing in between. Kit answered promptly, remembering Ormonde's question of the night before. 'Yes, of course.'

'What kind of music?'

Kit did not name her favourites as she had for Ormonde, for she was sure those Irish tunes would be unfamiliar to a Florentine. 'Jigs, hornpipes, ballads.'

'You sing?'

'I used to sing a catch or two in the alehouse.'

'Sing to me now.'

Uncertain, her voice small, she sang a verse of 'Arthur McBride'. She did not think of her father but remembered instead singing it to Ross, in the aqueduct at Cremona.

> *Oh me and my cousin, one Arthur McBride*
> *As we went a walkin' down by the seaside*
> *Now mark what followed and what did betide*
> *It being on Christmas morning . . .*

She choked and stopped. Mezzanotte patted her arm. 'Good. There's something there we can work with. Emotion is no cause for shame – emotion drives the performance. Use it.'

He strummed a chord on the harpsichord, his long white hand spanning an octave of notes with ease. 'Unfortunately your repertoire cannot help us; the songs with which you are acquainted would be wholly unfamiliar to a French countess. Now listen: I will teach you one simple song to play, to accompany yourself on the harpsichord. This is *"O cessate di piagarmi"* by Alessandro Scarlatti.'

He struck the keys with artistry and ease, and what she heard made her ashamed of her homely ditty. She looked at the castrato, wide eyed. 'I could never play like that!'

'Such a standard will not be expected of you,' said Mezzanotte with his characteristic lack of modesty. 'But La Comtesse Christiane would doubtless know how to play a little. It is most suitable for a high-born lady to learn such an instrument. One can sit straight backed with decorum – and since the hammers pluck the strings in the belly of the instrument, there is little exertion. Myself, I don't really like the instrument – there are no dynamics to be had – hammer hard or soft at the keys, you will hear the same result. But pipes and violoncellos are not suitable for ladies to play. Nothing in the mouth, and nothing between the legs.' He winked lasciviously and Kit smiled and relaxed.

But in the course of the morning her tongue recalled almost all of her army swearwords as her fingers fumbled, slipped from the keys and made crashing discords. Rather run down the hill into battle than this. 'It is impossible,' she said, but Mezzanotte was philosophical. 'Never mind,' said he. 'We have time.'

And they did. Kit now rushed through her toilette every morning, and hurried to the music room. Half of her morning was taken up by Mezzanotte playing for her, and testing her on the names of composers, pieces and arias. Then they would take iced sherbet on the sun terrace, and talk companionably. Afterwards they would work on the Scarlatti and Kit's singing. Mezzanotte soothed her doubts. 'In all likelihood, you will never be asked to play,' he said. 'But if you are, you must be able to give them a piece.'

'And if they ask for another?'

'They will not. Young ladies are far too delicate to play more than once.' He winked. 'To play twice might quite overcome them.' Kit smiled to think of what she had been through in the last year, and what Bianca had endured, and to think that there were some ladies in the world who must be protected from straining their voices or delicate digits.

'Besides,' continued Mezzanotte with ill-disguised scorn, 'there will be plenty of other young ladies panting to delight the company.'

Slowly the palace was being peopled, for Mezzanotte had brought with him a string quartet from Venice, where he had lately been performing. After a day at the harpsichord he began to bring them to the music room. Kit admired their dedicated, serious professionalism and their unquestionable skill.

She began to develop her own preferences, and favoured the

new composer Antonio Vivaldi above all. Mezzanotte saw it and was pleased. 'You will become a true connoisseur in time,' he said.

On the third day Mezzanotte met her at the music room door. 'No music today,' he said. 'Time to dance.' He led her down the great stone stair to the ballroom. The parrot greeted them at the foot. 'Silly slut!' he screeched. Mezzanotte did not miss a step. 'Don't worry,' he said drily, 'he's talking to me.'

Ormonde waited for them under the great chandelier. He greeted Kit warmly, and she was relieved, for she had not seen him since the night when she'd puked over him. He and Mezzanotte were clearly intimates, for Ormonde greeted them both with the same warmth.

Mezzanotte's quartet gathered and tuned their viols, and Ormonde and Mezzanotte stripped each other's coats, as if they were about to duel. Then the viols struck up, and the lesson began.

It was a strange ball for three, and they danced until they were flushed – even Mezzanotte's pale skin took on a rose colour beneath the rouge. Kit was pulled and pushed through the stately, ancient dances; the minuet, the pavane, the gavotte, then dances of the latest fashion; the sarabande, the *rigaudon de la paix*, the *gigue à deux*.

Her partners were as different as they could be – Ormonde stately and solid, but rhythmic and quick to the change; Mezzanotte supple as a willow, hopping lightly from foot to foot. 'It is well that you have such disparate partners,' said Ormonde, 'for if you learn to dance with me and this silly slut, you can dance with anyone.'

Kit looked to Mezzanotte, but he smiled and cuffed Ormonde affectionately, setting his wig back upon his forehead. *The parrot*, thought Kit. Silly slut. She wondered how many times the castrato had been here to this palace by the lake.

They watched her in turn – whoever did not partner her walked about the couple, tapping a length of cane on the floor in time to the music like a dancing master, correcting a stray foot or arm with a tiny tap, calling out the change. In the aptly named *folie d'Espagne*, Ormonde took Kit to task in a manner that had her wondering whether he had guessed her past. 'You are marching like a soldier. Take sliding, mincing steps.' 'Stay on the balls of your feet, the heel should not touch the ground; you are not on parade.' 'Shoulders back, you are not carrying a musket.'

Mezzanotte was more tactful; his concern was not deportment but musicality. 'Feel the rhythm – your toes should touch the parquet on the off beat.' 'Take your time in the turn – you should face your partner by the end of the sustain.' 'Your movements should mimic the dynamics, at the crescendo, make the gestures bigger – at the diminuendo, smaller.'

For her part, Kit watched them. They seemed the firmest of friends, finishing each other's utterances, an intimacy that seemed born of long acquaintance. Once she happened to mention the court of Mantova, when she enquired after the likely number of couples who would be gathered at the French court. Recollecting their secrecy, she looked quickly to Ormonde, but he nodded to her and answered her unspoken question. 'Mezzanotte is safe. He is bound by the strongest bond of all.'

That night, as his quartet played and as Kit and Ormonde drank their champagne by the terrace, the fine muslin curtains billowing in the breeze, the stars studding the night outside, Mezzanotte sang for them for the first time. The notes, pure and clear as a chime, strung together like priceless jewels, floated over the water, soaring higher than the mountains. The words of the aria, as simple as the tune but written with untold artistry, pierced Kit's heart.

Dove sei, amato bene!
Vieni, l'alma a consolar!
Sono oppresso da' tormenti
ed i crudeli miei lamenti
sol con te posso bear.

Where are you, beloved!
Come to console the soul!
They are oppressed by torment
and my cruel laments
alone with you I can bear.

Mezzanotte was singing of Richard, of Ross, of his own beloved Florence, of his manhood, of everything that had ever been loved and lost. Kit had to hurry from the room, holding her head high so the tears would not fall until the door closed behind her. She found her way to one of the downstairs terraces and let her tears fall into the lake. Each one silvered as it fell, swelling and stretching like the glass drop that Mezzanotte wore.

When she had recovered she went in search of the castrato, to tell him that she had not understood before. To tell him he was indeed an artist. The dining salon was quiet and dark – her companions must have retired. Kit crept past the parrot and to the foot of the stairs, but the bird never missed a trick. 'Like rats in a trap,' he remarked.

She climbed the stairs softly to Mezzanotte's room, the oriental chamber on the *piano nobile*. The door was ajar and she pushed at it gently – it swung wide. There lay Mezzanotte, naked, prone across the tangled bedclothes, fast asleep.

The bone-white lengths and curves of his body were so pale as to make the very sheets look dun. One hand was crooked behind his head, the other reached out, in sleep, to his companion. Rooted to the spot, her eyes were drawn inexorably to his groin, and there his white manhood lay across his thigh, tiny as a child's, with two sad empty pouches, useless and flaccid, hanging below. Another man, naked too, sat on the side of the bed in contemplation. Mezzanotte's outflung hand touched his side. He was hunched, looking out though the window at the silver lake. This man was stockier, the rolls of his naked flesh settling down his body like candle grease. His hair was black and grey like that of a brindle cat, and shorn short to be worn beneath a wig with comfort. Kit backed away, and as her slipper struck the door frame, he turned and looked at her. It was Ormonde. She was never sure, afterward, if he even saw her; but she flinched as if struck, turned and ran. She did not run from the debauchery; but from the look of utter desolation on Ormonde's face, like that of a soul in Hell.

Safe in her own chamber, Kit went through the motions of her night-time routine, the strokes of the comb through her hair, the polishing of her locks with a silken cloth, the oiling of her skin, the careful placement of her day clothes in the armoire. She stood for a moment, naked and silvered, by the window, as she'd once done in Dublin, the night before she'd donned her soldier's coat. So Ormonde and Mezzanotte were lovers. But what could be the nature of their love? The first time the duke had seen her, all those years ago at Killcommadan Hill, he'd asked to see her tail. Perhaps Ormonde loved men, but loved the bodies of women, and Mezzanotte, in his halfway state, fulfilled all of his desires? Ormonde had never shown her the least interest, so he must have Atticus Lambe's predilection for men, and yet Mezzanotte was not fully a man. Perhaps it was true: love was attached to a person and not a gender. If so, would Ross still love her now the boy had become a woman?

Chapter 30

You've only the lend of them as I suppose . . .

'Arthur McBride' (trad.)

Ormonde never spoke of Kit's discovery, but the castrato seemed to feel free to talk of 'Fitz' with her in a way he had never allowed himself to before. It was in her mind to tell him of Ross, but something always prevented her. Besides, nothing could stem the flow of Mezzanotte's confidences. He told of how he had met Ormonde in London, of how they spent as much time together as Ormonde's campaigns would allow, and always summered here in Italy. When Mezzanotte told her how he suffered when Ormonde returned to his wife and children Kit wondered whether men were capable of a parallel love for men and women both; or whether, for a man of Ormonde's position, a marriage to Emilia Butler, Countess of Ossory, had just been an expedient way to secure his titles and produce his heirs.

'Fitz came to every one of my performances in London,' said Mezzanotte fondly. 'He did not miss a single night.' He fixed his dark eyes on Kit. 'For that is when he first loved me,' he said simply, 'when I sang.'

'He loves you, then?' she asked, with the same candour.

'Oh yes,' he said. 'He does not want to love me, and his love makes him cruel. Sometimes he uses hard words to me, beats me even. That is because he struggles. He is a duke, he has his sons, and *her*.' That single syllable was all he would say of Lady Ormonde. 'But he gives me little gifts to make amends. He brought me this from the Royal Society.' Mezzanotte held forth the glass drop he wore about his neck. The shape of a tear, with a long tail curling about the ribbon on which he wore it, its bulb shone as if it had a tiny star trapped inside it.

'It is beautiful,' said Kit.

'Yes. It is not art but science, and science is rarely beautiful, don't you find?'

'What is it?'

'It is a Prince Rupert's drop. Molten glass, dropped in a pail of cold water, makes this raindrop shape. It has a hard exterior – you may beat the bulb with a hammer to no avail – but the inside is unstable because of how it was formed in the water – the outside cools more quickly and hardens but the inside is a mess of contrasting forces. It holds a secret – as we all do.' He winked. 'Its secret is, that if you clip off the tail, the drop will shatter and disintegrate into dust.' She looked at it – it seemed to capture the sun. 'Fitz gave it to me for he said it reminded him of me – that a man is nothing without his tail.'

Kit was shocked, but Mezzanotte smiled at the drop fondly. 'You see? He is a mess of contrasting forces too. Even when he gives me a gift he has to hurt me. A kiss and a blow.' He centred the Prince Rupert's drop over his heart. 'Fitz is like a child. You cannot indulge him by becoming upset. I hung it on this ribbon and wear it every day to show him that I am strong, tail or no.'

That summer on the Isola Bella passed swiftly and pleasantly. Kit changed, but the change came hard. She'd been a woman for nineteen years and a man for one, but oddly it seemed those periods weighed the same when hung in the balance. It took her time to unlearn to be a man, and learn to be a woman again. It took her some weeks to cease to spit, and smoke, and swear, and shrug, and thrust her chin forth combatively when she spoke. It took practice to learn to blow her nose on a kerchief instead of her sleeve and to walk with small steps, instead of pounding the ground when she walked.

And now, Prince Eugene's name day, the day for her new persona to be tested, loomed sickeningly close. Kit lay awake, burning with nervous excitement in the warm summer night, her eagerness to see Ross again tempered by fear of giving herself away.

With one week to go, Ormonde met her at the foot of the stairs, took her arm and turned her about. 'I have something for you. It is in your chamber.'

Kit followed Ormonde through the airy passages and the great empty salons. At her chamber he stood aside and let her open the door.

At first she thought there was someone in the room, but as she approached she could see that it was a gown, dressed upon a wooden mannequin, a beautiful dress of duck-egg blue silk rimed with diamonds that glittered like frost, with a froth of white lace at the throat and a waterfall of the same lace at the sleeves. The silk was so stiff with embroidery and crystals it could have stood on its own, and so wide that the dress seemed to take up all the considerable space between the bed and the armoire.

'It is a Rockingham mantua,' said Ormonde into the silence. 'One of the costliest gowns in the world. It is made of Oris tissue, and woven with real silver thread. You will wear this to Savoy's name day, and you will wear it tonight.'

She walked around it. There were blue silken ribbons all down the back of the bodice, tied in a complicated cross-weave. She gently lifted the skirts and saw a cane frame below the petticoats to make the skirts stand out. 'It looks impossible to put on.'

'You have hit upon the very point,' said Ormonde. 'You cannot put it on alone. Clothes for the nobility are specifically designed so that they may only be donned with the help of servants. They like it. It makes them feel rich.' He walked forward, and flicked the bodice lace with his beringed fingers. 'Six women are coming to dress you. Henceforth they will be your personal maids.'

Servants. Kit played with the ribbons. 'You have taught me to mix with the quality; but how do I behave with servants?'

'That is the least of your concerns. Behave exactly as you like; the worse you behave, the better it is. You do not need to make any allowances, or consider their feelings.' Ormonde spoke as one who had grown up with such attitudes. 'When the time comes to put on the mantua, they will undress you. Just stand naked as you did for me. Do not cover yourself. They are not people, so there is no need to feel shame. They will do the rest. They are all from Stresa across the water, but speak enough English to do your will.' He turned to leave.

'And, saving your mother's nation, if you do anything peculiar, they will naturally ascribe it to your being French.' He closed the door behind him.

Kit was left alone, with the gown. She stood behind the thing and looked in the looking glass. She looked like a countess. The dress was a ridiculous, wonderful thing, but it scared Kit. It was her new soldier coat.

The Rockingham mantua, which was to be worn for the name day of a prince, had its first outing for the benefit of a very different man indeed.

Ormonde had received a letter at breakfast which he read over twice before pocketing it. All day he looked pent up, distracted and twitchy. He did not concentrate on Kit's dancing or her afternoon tutelage, and she was left to recite the bloodlines of the royal houses of France and the streets of Poitiers by rote, while he stared from the window, fidgeting, expectant.

In the late afternoon he abandoned her and went down to the ballroom, to sit in his favourite chair. 'Church Hill!' squawked the parrot at his master, and she knew then that it was Marlborough the bird had meant all this time.

Ormonde sat in his throne until nightfall, requiring no refreshment or company. He stroked his chin, and waited. Kit and Mezzanotte played a hand of bezique, talking in the hushed murmurs that seemed to be required. After dark there was a knock at the great doors and Pietro opened them. A man in full military uniform entered and marched to the gilded chair. He wore the uniform of a brigadier, but his face was blackened with gunpowder, his clothes rent, and he bled at the knee.

The duke sat a little straighter and removed his fingers from his chin. He regarded the man without speaking, until the soldier bent his knee and bowed. 'My lord duke,' he mumbled.

'Brigadier Panton,' said Ormonde. 'I have waited a long time for you to come to my door.'

I'm to head to Mantova under Brigadier Panton, Richard had said. *I might never come back.* Kit dropped her cards on the table with a soft patter. Neither man seemed to notice. The brigadier stood up. 'You might offer me a drink at least,' he said. 'I've ridden all the way from Mantova.'

Ormonde lifted a solitary finger and Pietro was at Panton's elbow with a decanter of Madeira and a glass set upon a tray. The brigadier filled the glass, emptied it, filled it again.

'Well, Jeremiah. I take it that all went as I told you it would?'

The brigadier took another swig of his Madeira. He did not quite meet Ormonde's eyes. 'Yes,' he mumbled. 'It was a fucking shitstorm.'

Ormonde nodded with satisfaction, but without surprise. He sat forward, elbows on knees, hands steepled before his chin. 'Then let me tell you what is going to happen. You will finish your drink, then Pietro will take you upstairs to your chamber. There you will find a new suit of clothes, for I do not care for my guests bleeding all over my parquet. Then you will come to dinner and you and I will talk about the next step, and I will explain to you precisely why, this time, we will be doing things my way.'

Pietro appeared again and steered Panton from the room. Ormonde tipped his head back and rested it on the gilded chair-back. He gave a long, happy sigh. 'It begins,' he said.

Kit ate little at dinner. She drank slowly, and she listened while Ormonde and Brigadier Panton spoke together, heads close, low voiced, through the half-dozen courses. For this evening at least, she and Mezzanotte were both women, neither expected to comment upon matters of war. Kit heard snatches of the conversation, and Mezzanotte, after a few attempts to draw her out, kept his peace in the face of her tense silence. She heard of the Grand Alliance plan under Marlborough to besiege Mantova, and take it back from the French. With a sinking heart, Kit realised that the campaign was an unmitigated disaster. The losses had been catastrophic. At one point Brigadier Panton, exasperated by some enquiry of Ormonde's, broke out with 'God, no – we lost just about every man.' Kit put her fork down. Richard dead – staring up at the branches and the rooks with sightless eyes. Richard half in, half out of the lake – that lake of death which formed the natural moat for the city of Mantova, the lake where she'd seen her first dead body, and her second and her third. She sat like a china doll, pale and sightless in the Rockingham mantua, and waited as dolls do. Directly after dinner she sought Ormonde in his study. He was writing rapidly at his desk and did not even look up as she entered.

'No.'

She had not even spoken. 'You do not know what I would ask.'

'Panton commanded your husband's regiment. Panton besieged Mantova. All his men are dead. You think your husband is among them, and you want to go and rummage on the battlefield, like a scavenger, to see if you can find his corpse.'

'You *have* to let me go.'

'You are mistaken.'

'I will be back within the week, I *swear* it,' she pleaded. 'You have my word, as . . . as an Irishwoman!'

He put down his quill. 'Christiane . . .'

'No!' She lost her temper. 'Not Christiane. Kit Kavanagh. Kit Walsh.' The pretty French accent was gone; the strong Dublin tones were back. 'And my husband, Richard Walsh, could lie dead on the battlefield.' She stopped, took a breath. 'I have to *know*.'

He spread his hands. 'I will have the rolls of the dead conveyed to me here. Then you will know soon enough.'

But she wanted to see him with her own eyes, not read his name on some manifest. She wanted to know whether he had suffered. If he was alive she would let him be. But if he was dead she could not leave him there on the battlefield for the crows to peck at. Faithful or no, he deserved the proper rites.

She fell to her knees. 'My lord duke. I *beg* of you.'

'Get up.' The words fell like blocks of ice. 'Countesses do not beg.' Ormonde's eyes were flint, as she had seen them once before when she had puked.

She rose, begged his pardon prettily, took her leave of him as a countess takes leave of a duke, and took comfort in his smile and satisfied nod. Then she went to her room and packed her things.

There was no one abroad in the grey pre-dawn as she crept down to the boathouse. She struggled with the heavy oars at first, but at length she found her rhythm and rowed rapidly across the lake, the breeze riffling the smooth surface of the water, the clouds little puffs of cotton above. As she rowed around the gardens she saw her favourite fountain, with an extra statue – a white figure with long pale limbs, wearing a white chemise and a white periwig, blank eyes fixed upon the mountains. The statue turned its head and watched her row. It was Lucio Mezzanotte, seated in his favourite place. How much did he know of her request of Ormonde? Would he betray her to his lover? After a long, long moment, the figure raised a white hand in valediction, and she knew it would be all right.

Her flight might have ended once again at the livery stable, but Kit had been there many times with Ormonde. The duke had insisted that Kit should become used to riding sidesaddle, and so Pietro would row them into Stresa and they would visit the livery stables. Ormonde would pick out his favourite mare, and Kit would ride Flint, who always greeted her with a delighted whicker. They'd take a turn about the lake in the pleasant sunshine. The vista was so breathtaking, and Ormonde's company so pleasant, that she could almost forget the dreadful discomfort of the pommel, and in time became as swift riding sidesaddle as astride.

So when she came to the stables in the pearl-grey dawn, the ostler tacked up Flint without a word and led the mare out. Kit, remembering Ormonde's instruction on dealing with servants, did not offer explanations, but stood erect and haughty as she waited for her mount, chin high, thanking the stable boy with the merest nod.

She led Flint through the empty daybreak streets of Stresa. Part of her education had been to understand the geography of the various regions of this peninsula, so she had no difficulty in choosing her direction. Soon she was on to the Brenner pass and away to Mantova.

Chapter 31

To the Devil I pitch you, says Arthur McBride . . .

'Arthur McBride' (trad.)

Three days of riding, from Stresa to Milan, from Milan to Brescia, from Brescia to Mantova. Not so long a ride, not so great a distance; and yet she'd come much farther than she'd ever thought a mortal could travel. For she had journeyed all the way to Hell.

When she was a young lady, newly come to Kavanagh's and beginning to look at books, Kit had once seen an etching of the Inferno. There, in the Underworld, were pale bloated corpses on an inky plain, branches curling above like claws and grotesque creatures feeding on the dead. The print had been enough to keep her in her pew in church every Sunday.

The battlefield at Mantova resembled it exactly. She had followed the plumes of smoke on the horizon, and by the time she had arrived at the long plain in the shadow of the castle it was all over. Had the last man died when she was sleeping in the hedgerow last night? Had the muskets fallen silent when she saddled and watered Flint this morning? Or had the gun carriages rolled away as she approached, rumbling unseen down other roads? No matter. It was finished; and the artillery was as silent as the redcoats that littered the field. Those corpses, powdered with the soot of the shot that had killed them, lay in a low dark haze of the same acrid fog, shrouding the scene. Colour seemed leached from the field, like that black and white print of long ago. Even though it was still summer this was a world where no flower lived or bird sang. Here the grotesque creatures feeding on carrion were the camp-followers and local peasants, dressed in dun rags, pulling rings from fingers, and 'Agincourt teeth' from mouths to sell to apothecaries; even splitting stomachs with their stilettos to look for coin in the very pluck of men. Their labours only added to the gore.

There was no colour here save red: the colour of the soldiers' coats and the colour of blood. The field stank like a slaughter-yard. The pall of mist rolled out on to the lake, and above it hunched the city, proud and smug and untouched, besieged but unbroken.

Kit, dead eyed, tied Flint up in a small copse and joined the scavengers. She was so exhausted from her ride she could have lain down among them, but she could not rest, not yet. As if there had not been enough blood, the pitiless mosquitoes feasted on her flesh, and she had barely the energy to flick them away. Then began the gory business of looking into each lifeless face. To begin with she would close the staring eyes – she could not bear the jealous stare of the dead at the living – but in the end she gave up. There were just too many.

Some bodies were face down in the mud, so she turned them with her foot. Not him. Not him. To keep her horror and grief in check she began to count the bodies she'd turned carefully, aloud, as if she were in the schoolroom. One hundred, two hundred.

Her skirts slowed her for the blood had turned the bottom foot of her petticoats scarlet better than the dyer's. She found a knife and cut off her hampering skirts, leaving the circles of stained linen where they lay like a great bloody bandage.

Somewhere a woman was keening, howling like a beast in fathomless grief. Kit chilled at the sound – a mother? A wife? A sister? She turned and a voice close by said, in English, 'Poor little mite, he does not know his master is dead.' She looked up too see a little, scruffy dog, a dog that had used to be white, but now was muddied and bloodied. He sat on the chest of a sprawling corpse, howling as if his heart would break. She stumbled over.

Kit could not howl. No tears came. Nothing. She sat, slumped, looking at the face she'd once loved, and Richard looked past her, unseeing, to the branches and the rooks.

After a long time, she did not know how long, she got up. She closed this last pair of eyes, and kissed the cold forehead. She began to drag Richard into the undergrowth. The dog bit her and worried at her sleeve; she brushed it aside – he troubled her no more than the mosquitoes. With Richard's musket and her bare hands she dug a shallow grave in the soft summer earth, smelling the scents of home, of the farm, of the ploughshare when it bit through the earth. Perhaps all earth was the same wherever a man lived. But what a barren crop she planted in this foreign soil.

When Richard was covered, every bit of him, she knelt and prayed. She could remember only the Hail Mary, but it would have to do; she said it three times for the Trinity. She could not remember any hymns so she sang 'Arthur McBride', from start to finish.

Now she did lie down, on Richard's grave, and slept on the soft dark earth. She was woken by a furious whinny – two peasants were cutting Flint's leather rein from its branch; one fellow at the head collar, one fellow already on the mare's back.

Kit took up Richard's bayonet, and with the skill of long practice, she pulled the man from the saddle in such a way that he knocked his companion to the ground. Foot on throat, she dispatched them both in a moment, pushing the bayonet through their yielding, concave bellies. Still she felt nothing. She left them lying there, bleeding and twitching.

She tried to pick up the dog but he barked at her furiously, backing away on his haunches. 'Stay, then,' she said, not caring – and left him sitting on the barrow of earth. Without looking back she vaulted on to Flint and away. There was nothing to look back for.

The return to the Palazzo Borromeo was a race. What if Ormonde had renounced her as a bad lot and a runaway and had abandoned their plan? Now Richard was gone, she was free – she had to see Ross, had to know whether he could love her. He seemed everything now – her future. Without him there was nothing. She had to go to Savoy's name day.

As she rode through the night she tortured herself with the thought that the palace would be empty, Ormonde's chair covered in a dustsheet, the Rockingham mantua boxed in a chest between tissues of cool silk. But at Lake Maggiore Pietro was waiting for her at the jetty with his blank retainer's expression. Flint was handed on to a page from the livery stables, and Pietro rowed her, without greeting or interrogation, back to the looming palace.

Kit crept across the marble atrium like a guilty maid. The parrot perked at once, and shouted 'Like rats in a trap!' Kit thought of the soldiers at Mantova, of the siege-gone-wrong, the rats in a trap, and was suddenly poleaxed by grief. She still had her courage, though. The hour was late, but if Ormonde was not abed with Mezzanotte he would be in the small office, writing his letters and plotting his plots. Better to face him at once.

She strode across the vast, dark ballroom, the moonlit muslin drapes whispering and billowing at the window. When the voice came, she was so startled she almost tripped.

'I've seen you before.'

Ormonde was sitting in his golden throne, still powdered and bewigged and dressed for dinner. His eyes glittered like jet. He was very drunk.

'What do you mean?'

'In Ireland. You thought I'd forgotten, but I hadn't. I never forget.'

She stood as still as a statue, the moon turning her to alabaster. She hardly breathed.

'You were in my destiny. Even then.'

Kit could not speak. She was frightened of him for the first time – more than that – terrified.

'We were meant to do this thing. For England, for all of us. And you had to jeopardise it; for what? A rotting corpse? Yes – I know all about your husband.'

She swallowed the tears fiercely. She would not let him see her cry.

'Let me look at you.'

She stood for him as she'd done once before, on the marble star under the chandelier in the middle of the ballroom. She would not strip for him this time, but stood just as she was. Her travel gown was ruined, the petticoats, the pantaloons, the stockings all soiled and shredded. He walked around her as he'd done the first time. He lifted one of her hands to the moonlight, the hand that had dug a grave. 'Your nails,' he said, almost without reproach. He looked up to her filthy face, 'your skin,' and to her hair, matted with grave dirt, 'your coiffeur. Are you injured?'

'No.'

'The blood?'

'Not mine.'

He walked to the polished dining table, littered with the detritus of dinner. He took the embroidered silk runner from the table, and placed a handful of hefty pomegranates in it. Five, six, seven. Then he wrapped them in a parcel. Kit watched with fascination and dread. He came to her with the bundle, and he swung it round his head.

The first impact knocked her over. Then she could do no more than lie there as he rained down blows upon her with all his strength – a dozen strikes before she lost count. He avoided her face, but concentrated on her torso and back, knocking the breath from her. She coughed and retched, her breath burning, her ribs afire.

At length he stopped, exhausted, and tossed the bundle away. The pomegranates burst from their silken bundle and rolled glossily away across the marble, spacing out in the moonlight's path like little planets.

'We will not speak of this,' said Ormonde, out of breath. 'We will resume our work tomorrow, and everything shall be as it was.' Then he strode from the room.

She lay there after he had gone, her cheek on the marble star below the dark chandelier, and let the tears seep from her eyes at last.

Chapter 32

Temper your steel in the morning . . .

'Arthur McBride' (trad.)

At daybreak Kit limped to the shutters and threw them wide. The sun shone as bright as ever, the water was still as blue as the sky and the pleasure boats scudded unheeding across the water. The church bells rang from their onion spires and cowbells clanged their secular counterpoint from the mountain slopes. Everything shall be as it was, Ormonde had said. And it almost was. But there, chill as that unmistakable freshness on the breeze, was that first breath of autumn. Richard was dead, summer was dying, and Savoy's name day was in less than a week.

Kit took in a deep breath to quell her fears. As she filled her lungs her ribs pained her. She stripped off her nightgown and looked at her naked body in the long looking glass. There was not a bruise on her. But for the pain, she might have imagined last night's beating.

Everything shall be as it was. Her routine was exactly the same: in the mornings she would carry out her toilette – her hair and skin, once washed, could be seen to have survived her adventures tolerably well, but she must work hard, now, to restore her hands to their pampered whiteness; they were scratched and grazed, the nails broken and ingrained with dirt. She washed them repeatedly, trying to erase the memory of those terrible hours on the battlefield. However, her young body began to recover. She was a soldier, she was resilient – she had been knocked down before, and got up again.

Lucio Mezzanotte seemed anxious to rehabilitate his lover in Kit's eyes. 'He is a good man at heart,' said the castrato in the privacy of the music room, 'but he cares so much. This enterprise of yours could be the making of him. He spent years in Ireland, kicking his heels in the backwaters (begging your pardon). If he breaks the deadlock at Mantova, it could be his chance to find preferment with the queen.'

Kit listened, unmoved. She did not hate Ormonde. She did not even blame him for beating her. She had disobeyed him, and jeopardised her safety and his plans. But she did begin to wonder, more and more, what kind of man she served.

For Ormonde's part, he treated her exactly as before. They danced together, dined together, even laughed together. They would play cards, and listen to Mezzanotte's arias. And every afternoon after luncheon, they were alone together in the tower. He never laid a hand on her again, except to kiss her fingers, or help her into a carriage. She never connected the hand that held hers with the one that had dealt her blows. As her ribs recovered and she could walk and breathe without pain, she could almost forget he had beaten her, almost forgive.

The only change in him, for those last days before Savoy's name day, was that his tests became even more rigorous. She was no longer frightened of him, but she feared failure, and applied herself to his interrogations with all the faculties at her disposal.

'Tell me all you know of Eugene of Savoy.'

She looked out of the windows at the mountains, as if the answers were writ there. 'He was born in Paris.'

'Where?'

'At the Hôtel de Soissons.'

'Go on.'

'His mother was Olympia Mancini, his father Eugene Maurice, Count of Soissons, Count of Dreux, Prince of Savoy.'

'And what is particular about his mother?'

'She was the mistress of Louis' father, Louis XIII.'

'And?'

'It was said that she was a witch.'

He smiled a little. 'Continue.'

'Eugene adored his mother above all others, and in fact, we boast a mutual acquaintance; my own *grandmère*, Liliane Saint-Hilaire de Blossac, was lady-in-waiting to her at Versailles.' She hesitated.

Ormonde sensed her disquiet. 'Do not trouble yourself about this falsehood. Olympia Mancini was out of favour and long gone before Savoy was old enough to look at women. And when she was in favour she had a revolving carousel of ladies – the pretty ones were the first to be dismissed. Go on.'

'Young Eugene was raised at Versailles with the young Louis XIV. They were the best of friends.'

'Yet now they fight on opposite sides. What caused their schism?'

'The king wanted Eugene to enter the Church because of his poor physique, but Eugene longed for an army career. He petitioned Louis for a commission at nineteen, but was refused.'

'In what manner?'

'Louis dismissed him from the court for meeting the royal gaze. He said that no one else ever dared to stare him out so insolently.'

'Then what?'

'Savoy transferred his allegiance to the Emperor Leopold I at the court of Vienna, but was tested immediately when he was tasked with defending the capital against the Turks. He crushed them at the Siege of Belgrade, where he took a musket ball to the knee.'

'Which knee?'

She considered. 'The left.'

He nodded. 'Good. And then?'

'Then he met his partner in warfare.' She glanced up at him, warily. 'The Duke of Marlborough.'

'Jack Churchill,' sneered Ormonde.

'Yes.'

He shut the book he held. 'I think you are ready. I have written to Savoy to tell him that your husband is working for us behind the French lines. He hates Louis with that particular passion we reserve for those we once loved.'

She watched him replace the volume on the shelves. 'If you pull this off, and you will, you will gain your heart's desire.'

The phrase sounded oddly clumsy and old-fashioned on Ormonde's lips. She reckoned she had done enough to achieve it by now. But first you had to know what it was. She had thought it was Richard all this time – it had taken her longer to find out that it was Ross. All she wanted now was to see him again – beyond that she did not know. She looked at the duke, hoping he was right. 'Fitzjames? You once said I could ask you anything.'

'You can. The question is, *may* you.'

'Then can I, *may* I ask, what is your heart's desire?'

'I want to prove to the queen that cunning trumps bombast. I want to replace Jack Churchill and see him brought low.'

'Why? Why do you hate him so?'

A pause.

'You said I could ask.'

'But I did not say I would answer.' He changed the subject. 'Tomorrow, think only of this: whatever happens, you will be travelling back in the carriage with me after the ball. We play for low stakes in Turin.' But higher ones in Mantova, thought Kit. 'The worst that can happen there is that you are unmasked as a fraud, everyone laughs at my jest for the prince's name day, and my reputation as a buffoon is assured. It does not matter.'

It sounded as if it mattered more than he owned. Now she thought she knew the answer to her question. Ormonde had been passed over for the office Marlborough held. Ormonde had once been a great general, and now whiled away his summers surrounded by women and eunuchs. What he wanted most of all was to be taken seriously, to be reputed as Marlborough was reputed, not as a voluptuary, nor a jester, but as commander-in-chief of the forces of the Grand Alliance.

The night before Savoy's name day she could not sleep. What made her restlessness worse was the knowledge that she must. Dark shadows beneath her eyes always angered Ormonde. She tried to recite her lessons, but could only remember the roll call of the regiment of the Scots Greys, Queen's Royal Dragoons. The names of the Bourbons and the Capets and the Valois eluded her but she could remember without difficulty Southcott, Hall, O'Connell, Wareham, Swinney, Rolf, Noyes, Crook, Page, Dallenger, Kennedy, Lancaster, Farrant, Gibson, Laverack. Names not as noble as the Bourbons, but all good men and true. She could even remember their given names, all the Johns and Jacks and Jameses – except for Captain Ross, whose given name she had never learned. The dragoons went trooping through her sleepless mind in their red coats on their grey horses. But of the streets of Poitiers, the great hotels and pleasure gardens of Paris and the life of Eugene of Savoy she could remember nothing.

Badly frightened, Kit rose in the true dark of the small hours and lit a lamp. She sat at the little dressing table and took up a stub of lead pencil. Spreading the fan wide she wrote, as faintly as she could, on the reverse. She crammed the writing small, each ivory strut dividing her remarks under the headings *Prince Eugene of Savoy*, *Count Wirich Philipp von Daun*, *Victor Amadeus II of Sardinia*, *The Prince of Anhalt Dessau*; all the dignitaries Ormonde had warned her she might meet. She scribbled tiny words that could be cues, the name of an eldest son, a youngest daughter, a well-fought campaign, a favourite summering place. Then she closed the fan upon its secret, huffed out the candle and repaired to bed for the last remaining hours of night, little comforted by her actions.

Chapter 33

For the day being pleasant and charming . . .
                                        'Arthur McBride' (trad.)

On the eighteenth day of October, at seven of the clock, a golden carriage drew up at the Palazzo Reale in Turin, the royal residence of the House of Savoy. Seated inside were James Fitzjames Butler, 2nd Duke of Ormonde, 13th Earl of Ormond, 7th Earl of Ossory, 2nd Baron Butler, accompanied by the Comtesse Christiane St-Hilaire de Blossac, to attend the name-day ball of Prince Eugene of Savoy.

The duke was wearing dark gold satin and a long periwig of iron grey. His Order of the Garter sparkled through the tumbling curls like the Pole Star peeping through cloud. But his magnificence was nothing in comparison to his companion's. The *comtesse* was a true, timeless beauty. She was wearing a priceless Rockingham mantua of nacreous duck-egg blue silk, the colour of the duke's garter ribbon, and the gossamer sheen of the fine tissue captured the moonlight. The stomacher was worked with crystals in curlicues and florets and the fleur-de-lis which betrayed her origins. The skirts were so wide that the *comtesse*'s consort was obliged to sit on the other side of the carriage, for half a dozen petticoats and a stiff cane frame left him no room. The gown had been laced at the back with blue satin ribbons, tied and tightened by no less than six maids. Two miniature diamond chandeliers hung from the *comtesse*'s ears, lengthening the lobes with the weight of their worth. A simple sky-blue ribbon was tied about her swanlike neck, but below it was fastened a diamond collar of such price that it would have bought the carriage and four that conveyed it. The *comtesse* sat straight as a ramrod – she had no choice for a carved wooden busk sat between her breasts – she could not have slouched like a soldier even if she had a mind to. Two perfect half-moons of bosom were bolstered so high as to rest beneath her collarbones. Her locks were powdered white as snow, and built up over pads of horsehair to add another two feet to her already considerable height. Not a single red hair showed under the powder, not a freckle showed through the lead-white make-up. Her red brows had been painted out, and other higher brows, crescents of perpetual surprise, had been painted in an inch higher. Her cheeks were rouged in small, doll-like circles, her lips were stained with ceruse, and a heart-shaped patch rode high on one cheek. From her outward show, she bore no resemblance to Kit Kavanagh, one time dragoon of Her Majesty's Scots Greys. The *comtesse* even wore a wedding band under her the wide weave of her lace mitten, something Kit Kavanagh had not worn for over a year.

As they pulled up before the entrance the duke laid a hand on the countess's arm, quite kindly. 'Remember,' he said, 'whatever happens, you will be travelling back in this carriage with me tonight.' And then the footman was at the door, the steps were let down and the *comtesse* was handed out of the carriage.

Kit laid her lace-mittened hand on the duke's glove, and walked up the paved way to the entrance between ranks of burning torches as tall as she.

Turin seemed a city made for giants; the great dome of the Duomo loomed over this titanic and perfect square, three sides of which comprised the Royal Palace of Savoy. The palazzo had a vast frontage of snowy marble and was the biggest building Kit had ever seen, with perhaps a thousand square-paned windows molten with torchlight. Two mighty statues of long-dead Savoyard cavaliers reared on either side of the huge oak doors, which were thrown wide open in welcome for the exalted guests of tonight's entertainment.

Inside, there was a press of people, enough diamonds to blind the sight, chatter to burst the eardrums, and heat and music to overwhelm the senses. No wonder, thought Kit, that women of quality swooned, in such gowns, in such gatherings. She gripped Ormonde's arms as she toiled up the magnificent marble staircase into a huge cathedral of a ballroom, with a coffined ceiling studded with gilt bosses like morning stars. Far below, a floor of polished ebony, inlaid with geometric shapes of ivory in stark contrast, reflected the glory above. Kit's embroidered slippers slid on the floor as if she skated on ice – dancing on such a surface, she thought grimly, would be well-nigh impossible.

But there was no time to fret. Almost at once she was introduced to a trio of Savoyard nobles – Count Wirich Philipp von Daun, Victor Amadeus II of Sardinia and the Prince of Anhalt Dessau. There they stood, resplendent in their velvets and satins, their powdered hair immaculate, their long royal features so alike they could be kin. Three pairs of eyes looked down three sharp-bridged noses. For a moment, she was tongue tied – her stomach turned somersaults, and she wanted to run. This was a huge, a terrible mistake. She could not do this. But then their formation as they fanned out before her reminded her – she opened her fan coyly before her face and dropped her eyes to the pencilled scrawl. As rank dictated, she greeted Victor Amadeus first. *Victor Amadeus of Sardinia*, said the fan. *Became Duke of Savoy aged nine. Remodelled the Palazzo Reale. Put down his rebellious citizens in the 'salt wars'. Persecuted the Vaudois (Savoyard Protestants). Married to Anne Marie d'Orléans.* 'My prince,' she said, lowering the fan. 'I must compliment you on the new façade of this palace. It is better than Versailles, I believe.'

Three haughty faces broke into smiles, and Kit breathed again.

She greeted the Prince of Anhalt Dessau next (*ninth of ten children, introduced the iron ramrod to the Prussian corps, married to Anna Louise Fohse*) followed by Count Wirich Philipp von Daun (*born in Vienna, son of Field Marshal Wilhelm Graf Daun, one son named Leopold*). Then the trio of princes parted like the acolytes they were to reveal the Prince of Savoy. He was not just the centre of their circle, but the centre of the room; for that one evening he was the centre of the universe, the satellite planets revolving around him. If Louis of France had reserved the soubriquet of the Sun King, then Savoy was the moon, the white king of the chess set. He was magnificent in silver tissue from head to toe; even his vertiginous wig was set in silver curls like an angry ocean, with a silver tricorn perched on top like a boat. Waterfalls of silver lace fell from his cuffs to his knuckles, and in place of his sword he held a silver cane topped with the eagle of the Habsburg monarchy. But under the magnificent array she recognised his diminutive person, and his rabbity face.

As Ormonde made the introductions Kit recalled the last time she had met the prince – those terrible few hours at the top of the Duomo in Cremona, watching the clouds of rising stone dust as the French sapped the bridge to the citadel, watching the blue coats in the cathedral square confound the red. Then, Savoy had had the Maréchal de Villeroi under his hand, the *maréchal* who had escaped to later hold Mantova. Then, Savoy had worn his half-armour and his sword, his face framed by a short periwig. Then, she'd worn her red coat and tricorn, and her face had been caked in the mud of the aqueduct, the mud of the Romans. But still, still . . . Heart thudding, she felt Ormonde's arm bear her forward.

Savoy looked her up and down. '*Comtesse,*' he said. 'You are an ornament to our name day. France's loss is our gain.'

'May I not be the last of France's losses,' she said, 'nor your Imperial gains, Highness.'

He smiled in the way she remembered, his two coney-teeth protruding slightly over his lower lip. She sank into a deep curtsy, the mantua pooling about her in a mass of blue silk, then rose and moved away as the next dignitaries stepped forth for presentation. She risked a look to Ormonde as she took his arm, and he gave an almost imperceptible nod. But the ordeal was not yet over. For the tall and splendid man before them turned and the conspirators found themselves under the eye of John Churchill, Duke of Marlborough.

But nothing would put Ormonde out of countenance. He nodded coolly, and spoke first. The exchange was so cursory it could have passed over a drover's cart.

'Jack.'

'James.'

The two men locked eyes as if they squared up for a bar fight. Then Marlborough's eyes broke from Ormonde's and raked her appreciatively. Just as she had with Savoy, she remembered the last time she had seen him. Bloodied and muddied, just returned from Cremona, she'd received his purse and his commendation. She held her breath. Would he know her? Kit heard Ormonde say, 'May I present the Comtesse Saint-Hilaire de Blossac?'

'You *certainly* may,' said Marlborough. 'She speak English?'

'Better than your French,' said Ormonde.

Marlborough took her hand and kissed it with a smack. 'Charmed, I'm sure.' But his eyes soon returned to Ormonde. It would take more than a decorative countess to divert them from their rivalry. Now she saw them together she was reminded of a cat and a dog – Marlborough was a big, golden, forthright gun-dog, eager, tramping through battlefields as a dog would roll in the dirt, crossing oceans as a dog would plunge into a millpond. Ormonde was smaller, sleeker, feline; his ways were circumspect, winding his policies like a ball of yarn, weaving his way through the court as a cat would through the legs of a chair.

Marlborough barked first. 'Christ's wounds, you're like a ghost in this company. We have not seen you this many a month. Screwing and Jewing in your palace, I suppose. Where *have* you been hiding?'

'Oh, I'm always around, Jack,' said Ormonde, pleasantly. 'In plain sight, for those with the wit to see me.'

'Haven't had much time for blind man's buff, James. Been fighting the Frogs. Beggin' your pardon, ma'am.' Marlborough nodded to Kit, who favoured him with a smile. The two dukes continued to bait each other, and Kit, neither expected nor required to participate, felt free to look around the room.

And then, for the first time in three months, she saw Captain Ross.

For just a moment, she could not breathe. She had remembered him, in her mind's eye, in every detail – the way his dark hair grew, the length of his limbs, the curve of his cheekbones, the breadth of his back. In this company of dukes and princes he stood above them all – the best-made man in the assembly. But he looked deeply unhappy – his dark brows were drawn together, his expression was guarded, his gaze low under the fringe of his lashes. She saw with a leap of joy that he still had his old trick of pressing his full lips together and releasing them again when perturbed, but he had acquired a new habit too. He tapped his hand continually on the hilt of his sword – not to the beat of the music, but to some odd internal rhythm of his own. Kit did not heed the rhythm – she was looking at the sword. She would know it anywhere; for it was her father's. Kit began to breathe again, heavily, the blood mounting to her cheek, rendering the rouge superfluous. So Bianca had given Ross Sean Kavanagh's sword, and he had worn it for remembrance. He loved her still. She let go of Ormonde's arm.

Her steps were borne inexorably towards Ross; her new, dainty steps, her slippers kicking out the skirts of the mantua as she had been taught. As if her movement caught his eye he raised his gaze to her and their eyes met. She had forgotten this one thing – how truly blue his eyes were, bluer than the lake that had been her home these past three months. Now, she thought, now he will know me. But though his gaze held a dozen emotions – surprise, question, gratification – there was not a modicum of recognition in it. Her way was blocked – Ormonde claimed her once more, this time to talk to the Landgrave of the Hessians. *Charles I, Landgrave of Hesse-Kassal*, said the fan. *Has a vast army of fearsome mercenaries he lends out to foreign powers. Married to his first cousin Maria Amalia of Courland.* Suppressing her impatience, Kit spoke to the landgrave prettily, asking a woman's questions about his forces, concealing Kit Kavanagh's knowledge of warfare, shivering prettily at the might of his armies. Out of the corner of her eye, she saw Ormonde greet Brigadier Panton, and carry him off to the saloon for a hand of cards. She was free to excuse herself and seek Ross again.

The hour struck midnight, and she could see the captain at one of the open embrasures. He was alone, but she could not converse with him for they had not been introduced. He turned back into the room, observing the company, then he found her among the throng and caught her eye. Determined now not to miss her chance, she walked towards him, and past him, and deliberately dropped her fan. Ross pounced like a heron, folding his tall frame to pick it up. She watched him tensely; it was a gamble, for what if he spread the thing and read what was written there? But he handed it back, folded as it had fallen. 'Your fan, madam.'

She nodded to him in thanks and there was a charged silence in which the music seemed to fade. Then she remembered: their ranks were now reversed; she must speak first. A dragoon must wait for his captain to address him, but a mere captain may not speak to a countess. It was not for him to introduce himself to one such as she.

She stood straight. 'I am La Comtesse Christiane Saint-Hilaire de Blossac.' He bowed deeply. 'Captain Ross, of the Royal Scots Grey Dragoons.' His voice was just the same. He took her hand, and she was transported back to her cell in the Castello at Rovereto, at the moment of their parting, when he had stripped off his shirt and shown her his scars. She had touched his flesh then as she touched it now. He *must* know her. But he released the hand and straightened. She felt herself avoiding his gaze, fearing that under the wig, and the accent and the make-up, her green eyes would give her away.

'And now we are introduced, *Comtesse*, we may dance. Will you be mine for the minuet?'

She nodded, concealing her nerves – the minuet, with its complicated walks and tricky rhythms, had been her nemesis, driving Mezzanotte to despair.

She took the floor with the captain, in the very centre of that great cathedral of a marble room, and there was a silence. The minuet was an exhibition dance, with just one couple dancing at a time, and the eyes of the whole room were upon them. Then, as the dance floor was a leveller of rank, the countess and the captain honoured each other, with a bow and a curtsy. She tried to slow her breathing and her heart, and to remember her lessons; she must remember to lay her hand lightly on the captain's, to dip and rise in time to the music. She must move her feet on the first beat, wait the second, then step on the third, fourth, fifth, wait the sixth, then begin again. Ross brought the same careless elegance to the dance as he did to his riding. They achieved the first round without error, and Kit began to relax. This was just as well, for Ross seemed inclined to converse.

'Would you prefer to speak in French or English?'

'You speak French?' She was surprised, for she remembered well translating for him at Cremona.

'Execrably.'

She smiled. 'Ah, these English schools,' she teased, very French, 'where they take away a little boy and send back a man. The *lycées* of Paris are kinder; they let our sons grow under the civilising influence of their mothers.'

'And yet I adored my own foundation at Rugby. The education I received there was only lacking in one regard.'

She dared to meet his eyes, questioning him.

'In the tuition of French.'

They were parted by the dance, and Kit executed the z-shaped promenade as she had been taught, eyes now locked with her partner at all times as the dance required. Then they came together once more, linked elegantly at the wrist, to take a turn about the floor.

'Better to try English, then.' Kit was relieved – her voice was very different now and no trace was left of her Dublin brogue. But he had heard her speak her perfect Poitevan French before, in Cremona, *in extremis*. A man does not forget such a moment.

'I see you wear a sword, even at an entertainment such as this,' she said. 'Do you fear for your life?'

'It has become a habit.'

'Even among such a company?'

'Always; besides, my sword is the insignia of my profession and the most precious thing I own. It was left to me for safe keeping.'

She hugged this to herself; he had forgiven Kit Kavanagh. She wanted to ask more, but it would not do to press the point so soon. There must be, as Ormonde had instructed her, small talk before greater matters could be discussed. 'You said you were a captain?'

'Yes, of a company of horse.'

'You must have been in some dangerous situations, I imagine?'

'Some so dangerous that certain of my men were put to the trouble of saving me.'

That she knew very well. 'And do you save them in turn?'

He sobered, not joking now. 'We save each other.'

Their dance ended with the longed-for, daring finale when the partners hold both hands – the most contact allowed in any dance. He clasped her hands firmly, but his face was set. The lovely, easy manner that had made her heart rise like a swift had gone. They honoured each other, then he almost ran from the floor as the next couple took their place. He took a glass of champagne from a liveried servant and tossed it back.

She followed him, took a glass for herself, and asked, 'Why are you angry?' The question stopped him in his tracks.

'Am I angry?' He looked in his empty glass.

'I think so, yes,' she said gently.

He turned to face her and looked at her, directly. 'Because my men deserve better. We are marching up and down, and we are diminishing little by little, waning like the moon. With every campaign we lose another one or two. And we are lucky. Our task is largely reconnaissance,' she remembered the dragoon law so well, 'so we escape, betimes, the heaviest losses. But at Mantova, one of our regiments was all but wiped out.'

The ghost of Richard and his black earth and his white dog was so present, suddenly, that she could not speak.

'I may speak of it to you, of course, but not to my superiors. Loyalty is all, and I have always been loyal; but something needs to break the . . . the . . .'

'Stalemate,' she offered.

'Yes!' His eyes glittered. She could see he was very drunk, more so than she had ever seen him.

'I lost a man at Mantova,' he said, sobering again. 'A man called O'Connell.' She spilled her champagne a little. O'Connell, the big black-eyed Irishman. O'Connell, who had turned a blind eye when she had struck Sergeant Taylor, O'Connell who had played the fiddle so that it wrung her heart from her. 'I spent my own shilling to send his medals back to his wife, for there was no money to be had. How many shillings do you think this night cost?' Ross gestured about him, his sweeping arm taking in the gilt, the chandeliers. 'It is all for show – it is a mask. Look how rich we are. Look how secure the Grand Alliance is. And yet we are not.' He took another brimming glass from a passing servant. 'We took a beating at Mantova, so all is not as it seems.' He drank thirstily. 'I have the feeling you are not as you seem, *Comtesse*.'

Her heart thumped. It was right that he, who knew her the best of all, should be the one to find her out. 'Who is?' she said lightly.

'I see you wear a wedding ring.'

'The insignia of my profession and the most precious thing I own,' she teased, echoing his earlier words.

'And yet there is no Vicomte Saint-Hilaire de Blossac?'

She knew the patter. She knew what she should say: *My husband lives, he fights for England's cause behind French lines*. But she missed her cue, ignoring Ormonde speaking in her head like a prompter. She lowered her eyes. 'Not any more.'

He looked at her sharply, his eyes wide. 'I am sorry. Was your loss recent?'

'In some ways it seems as if it were a year ago,' she said truthfully, 'and in other ways, just a week.'

'I am sorry,' said Ross, genuinely contrite. 'I am a fool. I have had overmuch to drink, and I *am* angry, and I insulted you. I took your grief for complacence. And God knows it is not a mistake I should make, for I too have lost.'

'A bereavement in the family?'

'My wife. And my . . . son.'

It was the first time he had told her of his wife. How salutary that he would share with a woman, in the first hour of acquaintance, something he would not share with his brother in arms. Kit was learning much about the difference in the sexes.

'But that was not the loss of which I spoke.' He looked down to the sword, and Kit followed his eyes. She could not miss this opportunity. She steeled herself, and then asked, 'Are you speaking of the former owner of your sword?'

He looked at her with surprise. 'I am.'

She licked her lips. 'Is he dead?'

'No, not dead. Gone.'

'It sounds as if you loved him,' she ventured.

'*Love*,' he said with a bitter laugh. 'A woman's word.'

'Is it?' she asked. 'Then can you instruct me? Can you describe the regard you felt for this man?

'Forgive me,' he said. 'I did not mean to deprecate your excellent sex. It is just that this is such a difficult bond to describe to someone who has not been a soldier. You ride with someone by day, and sleep by them at night. You spend more time together than man and wife. You cheat death every day but at the same time feel more alive than you have ever felt. You feel bone-shaking terror at one moment, and the next you are laughing fit to burst with merriment. And through all of this you fear most for your brother, for you would do anything for him, and you would give yourself to the Reaper before you give up a hair of his head.' He tapped the hilt of Sean Kavanagh's sword. 'Thus I felt for my brother that is gone.'

For a moment she could not speak. 'That sounds like love to me, Captain.'

He smiled sadly. 'Perhaps it is. But it is a love of the mind and heart – there is nothing of the body in it. It is not the love which, saving your presence, a man would feel for a woman. Only in such a partnership can a man achieve his heart's desire.'

There was Ormonde's phrase, Maura's phrase; trite but true. She understood then, singing inside with joy, that a union with Ross could offer the best of both worlds – he would love the person he had fought with, his brother in arms, and he would love her as a woman, with a physical bond. 'And is that your heart's desire, to have such a partnership?' His answer suddenly mattered, so much.

'Sadly, that is one of the privileges of peacetime. For now I would like the French to be beaten, with minimum losses to the Alliance. Then I will ride for the horizon; and beyond that, perhaps, such happiness awaits me.'

From across the room she saw Ormonde signalling discreetly. There was so much left to say, but she could not frame a goodbye. Instead she said, ridiculously, fervently, 'I hope you stay alive.'

He smiled. 'And I wish the same to you. And if we both manage it, I would see you again,' he said.

'You will,' she replied, hardly breathing, praying it was true.

Ross raised her hand to his lips and kissed it tenderly, on the flesh of her scarred little finger, the one that had been all but severed. She felt the kiss through the lace, through the skin, right to the very bone of her. Then he checked and stared at the hand, his fingers moving to the scar, searching, feeling the deformed joint. He turned the hand over, looking at the finger through the lace mitten. Then he looked her in the eyes. He opened his mouth to speak, but she snatched her hand away and ran.

In the carriage Ormonde was cock-a-hoop. 'Got 'em!' he said. 'Even Jack Churchill! "May I . . ." "You *certainly* may." The great booby! And on whom did you test your persona while I was closeted with Panton? I saw you dancing with a handsome captain.'

'Some cavalryman,' she said airily.

'And I take it he did *not* know you as Irish.'

Until the last moment, she would have sworn he did not. 'No.'

Ormonde clapped his hands together. 'Capital!' He threw his head back against the velvet seat and laughed until the tears spouted. 'The English Army,' he said. 'The finest cunts in

Christendom!' He wiped his eyes. 'Now all is ready. You are ready. Panton is ready.'

Kit wanted to enquire what Panton had to do with their scheme, but could not stem Ormonde's triumph. 'Now for Mantova,' he said. 'Now, we are in the game.'

For a moment Kit was horribly afraid, a visceral bowel-opening fear such as she had never felt in battle. The fear that made her want to wrench open the door, jump out, and run back to Ross. The moon was on the wane; soon it would be a sliver, and then? After tonight, and that conversation with Ross, she knew what she had to do. Not for Ormonde, or for Richard, or even for the English Army; but for Ross. She would break the stalemate. She would do what Ormonde wanted, and in the peace that followed she would have a fortune and freedom, and she would spend both of them finding the captain again.

Chapter 34

And you'd have no scruples to send us to France . . .

'Arthur McBride' (trad.)

The day after Savoy's name day Kit slept the day through. Ormonde let her be. But the day after that, his preparations acquired a new direction. He trusted that she knew her history and her cultural references by rote, and now he concentrated on the unexpected, training her to improvise her way out of a conversational impasse. Then these improvisations themselves would be rehearsed, until he felt her identity would hold water.

'Ah, but *Madame la Comtesse*, if you are from Poitiers you must know Antoine de Rouvroy; he was the Haute-Maréchal of Poitou-Charentes.'

'Yes,' Kit replied without hesitation, 'we dined with him and his wife Viviane. She was just then churched with their first daughter, Marie-France.'

'And you must know Jean Marc-Charpentier, of the Angoulême Charpentiers.'

She foundered. 'Yes, of course, but . . . it was a long time ago . . .'

'No,' said the duke, wagging an admonitory finger. 'Never claim an acquaintance with a name that cannot be verified. It is the easiest way to trap a charlatan. The names I have given to you are well-known scions of Poitevan society; if anyone asks you of another person, say you do not know them. They may be trying to trip you. Now: what do you say if someone sails in an unexpected direction?'

Kit laughed prettily and fluttered her hands. 'My lord, all these questions! I expect a catechism from my priest, not from a great general! Come, you must tire of my prattling; tell me of your adventures in the Veneto.'

'Good. And if they persist?'

She pressed her lips together, and her eyes filled easily. 'Forgive me; my husband so lately dead; my spirits are quite overcome.'

'Excellent. No true gentleman will press you further.'

Kit's confidence rallied a little, but one gaping hole in her education troubled her.

'Fitzjames?'

'Christiane?'

'How did my husband die? The *vicomte*, I mean? And when?'

'All in good time.'

On the day before Kit's planned sortie into the French court at Mantova, Ormonde gave her a purse of gold nobles. 'What is this? My pay?'

He smiled. 'Not yet. You will get your diamonds when the task is concluded; it is not yet begun. No, this is to ease your path – bribes, my dear Christiane, bribes.' He closed her hand over the purse. 'You are there for one reason and one reason only; to find something out with which I can break the stalemate. Once you know something – any hint that is dropped, the slightest intimation of what their strategy shall be from hereon in – you will need to engineer your extraction.'

'How?'

'That is up to you. Contrive to send me a message, or Panton – that is where the money comes in.'

She had an idea. 'Can I take Flint?' Flint would carry her away from danger, and towards Ross's horizon.

Ormonde stroked his chin. 'Has he ever been in a team?'

'He is a she. And no – she has always been a cavalry horse.'

'Hmm. I was going to suggest matching her into a four and having her pull the coach. But we cannot risk that. We need speed at your arrival.'

'Why?'

'Because you will be pursued.'

Kit grew cold. 'By whom?'

'By Panton and his division.'

She sat bolt upright. 'What?'

'Christiane. We have to sell them the story. You will arrive at Mantova pursued by Alliance troops.'

'But . . .' she blustered. 'I didn't know this.'

'Because I didn't tell you,' he said calmly.

'But . . . you cannot just thrust new gambits upon me!' she protested. 'It is the day before I go to Mantova!'

'At this point in the game,' said Ormonde smoothly, 'you will be told as little as possible about your infiltration. That way you will react to the situation with perfect conviction.'

'What will they be pursuing?'

'Christiane . . .' Ormonde's voice held a warning.

'What will they be pursuing? Me?'

'Your passenger,' he said, 'and the dispatches he carries.'

'My passenger?'

'All in good time.' He spoke soothingly, as if she was a child.

She was silent for a time. Then: 'Fitzjames?'

'Christiane.'

'Can I trust you?'

There was a pause. 'You asked me that once before.' He smiled his buccaneer's smile. 'I refer you to my earlier answer.'

'Can I?'

'Trust this. Your life is as precious to me as it is to you.'

She looked doubtful. 'Truly?'

'Well . . . almost.' The smile again. 'Let us say that I want this deception to work as much as you do. I will not fail you in this.'

She said nothing.

'Now go to Mezzanotte. He is waiting in the music room. Your last music lesson, remember?'

Kit rose unhappily and descended the staircase. The parrot, spying her, clambered up his bars with aid of beak and claw and screamed: 'Like rats in a trap!'

'Quite,' replied Kit soberly.

The night before her departure for Mantova Kit sat down at her dressing table to write two letters. She wrote to Bianca Castellano, to thank her for giving her sword to Captain Ross, to enquire after the health of Christiana, and to send a few gold nobles from Ormonde's purse for the baby's care. She had made an undertaking to support the child, and she would continue to do so. Then she wrote a letter of blithe falsehoods to Aunt Maura, telling her that all was well, and she would see her soon. Then she wrote a letter of terrible truths to Signora Chiara Walsh, 17 Via Ranier, Rovereto, to tell the widow that Richard was dead. Then she took to her bed, to lie wakeful for the rest of the night.

At the grey dawn, hollow eyed, Kit allowed herself to be dressed in her travelling clothes, a gown of holly green crape, with a matching cape and a tiny tricorn hat to perch upon her powdered hair. She had left off the Rockingham mantua, but it was to travel with her in her trunk. She said her farewells to Lucio Mezzanotte and she put three letters in his long white hand. 'Will you see these conveyed? In the name of friendship?'

He looked at the three fat little packets. 'Only if you swear that there is nothing in these dispatches that will compromise Fitz.'

'I can promise you that,' said Kit. She had to admire such loyalty, however misplaced. 'I am merely putting my affairs in order.'

The castrato shuffled the letters like the cards they had so often played together. 'You think you will not return?'

'Who knows?' she said.

There seemed nothing else to say, so they embraced. She nodded at the parrot, her other erstwhile companion. 'Goodbye,' she said.

'Damned Jacobite,' said the parrot.

Kit did not have the spirit to converse with Ormonde on the way to Mantova; and he too seemed little inclined for conversation. Kit was preoccupied with the danger she would face in the French court, but Ormonde too seemed jumpy and nervous on his own account. He seemed changed; as changed as his carriage. The coach had been freshly enamelled in blue and gold and gilded with the invented cognisance of the St Hilaire family and the fleur-de-lis of France. When the carriage finally stopped after many hours of travel Kit's stomach gave a sudden lurch. She glanced out of the carriage window, but did not recognise the little town. There was no great citadel, no lake. 'Are we there?'

'No,' said Ormonde, breaking his long silence. 'This is Castellucchio, just outside Mantova.'

She looked at him sharply. 'Why have we stopped?'

He did not quite meet her eyes. 'We are here to pick up your passenger.'

The passenger. 'Who am I to convey?'

'This is where I leave you. *Bonne chance*, Christiane.'

'Wait!' She clawed at his sleeve. 'Who is to be my passenger?'

But Pietro helped the duke down the steps and shut the door smartly. Ormonde turned and answered through the open window. 'Your husband,' he said. 'Who else?'

She gaped at him in horror; but he smiled faintly, nodded and turned away. 'Fitzjames?' she called. 'My lord duke?' But he was walking off across the little piazza before the church, scattering pigeons as he went.

She forced the door of the carriage, and made to get down, but a gloved hand held the door closed, a broad torso in a red coat blocked the light. Her jailer stooped and dipped his head in the window.

It was Brigadier Panton. 'I'm to ask you to sit tight, *Comtesse*,' he said. 'Not long now.' And he turned his back to her, the broadcloth of his coat blocking her sight, deaf to questions.

She tried the opposite door of the coach but it was locked, and besides the carriage was parked so flush to the city wall that the door would not have opened anyway. *Like rats in a trap.* There was nothing to do but wait as she'd been instructed, fuming. A pox upon Ormonde; she'd always known at heart he could not be trusted. She wanted to kick the doors open, and knew she could do it too; but she forced herself to sit still and listen.

She could hear a commotion in the square, a man screaming in protest. Then heels dragging on cobbles, a sword drawing, a slash and a thud. Then the light streamed in the window again, the carriage door was opened, and a figure bundled in. But it was not Panton.

The passenger wore a uniform of French blue, complete with gold buttons, white stock and polished boots. He was of middle height and middle age. He was also very, very dead.

Kit scrambled from her seat, and pressed herself to the other side of the coach.

The brigadier appeared at the window again. '*Comtesse*, meet the *vicomte*,' he said, with his characteristic sneering laugh. 'My company will pursue you to the gates of Mantova, and our artillery will lay down some covering fire.' He must have seen her face. 'Do not upset yourself. My men have been instructed not to hit you. With the will of God and a following wind, the French will let you into the citadel.'

'But . . .'

'No time for discourse. Ormonde drilled you, didn't he?'

'Yes, but . . .'

Panton slammed the door. 'Yah!'

At his shout the coach and four took off, hurtling through the piazza and the town gate, and towards the lake with the city floating upon it. She passed the plains where she had buried Richard, and, holding herself braced against the sides of the carriage through the careening, speeding chase, allowed herself to look at her second dead husband.

He lay slumped in the corner of the carriage, his side slashed through his coat and through his skin to show the shambles of his innards tangled like blue snakes. His face was a dreadful greenish white. His lifeblood, leaking from his side, made no impression at all on the red velvet of the seat as it was the same colour. She looked at the dead face, the eyes as brown as hazelnuts. Was this man perhaps thirty? Younger? Did he have a wife and child back in France? Was he even French, or was he some poor English foot soldier who'd been selected to die for Ormonde's scheme? She reached out in the rattling, lurching carriage, and as carefully as she could closed his eyes. The eyelids were still warm beneath the pads of her fingers. She put a hand to his heart. There was no beat. But there had been, till a moment ago. He was still warm. The slash, the thud. They'd killed him just now, in the street.

She hunched as far away from the corpse as she could, and gazed from the opposite window.

The gates of Mantova's great castle came closer and closer. Now she could see the drawbridge, and the blue blobs on the battlements and at the vast studded gate resolved into soldiers. From somewhere behind, Panton's thundering cavalry began to fire, the muskets deafening. The sound woke her up, as if she'd been in a dream. *You are a soldier*, she told herself. She sprang into action. Steeling herself and choosing the moat-side window in the lee of the gunfire, she leaned from the carriage as far as she could. She shouted in French: 'For God's sake, let me in! My husband is dead and they will kill me too!'

The soldiers now had faces, white blobs with gaping mouths, shouting and gesturing. The gates remained shut. She tried again. 'In the name of King Louis and the Duc d'Orléans, open the gate!' And then a miracle: the gates opened for her. Panton's men ceased their fire, fell back and wheeled away to safety on the other side of the lake. The gates clanged closed behind. She was inside the citadel of Mantova.

Chapter 35

And we have no desire strange places to see . . .

'Arthur McBride' (trad.)

On a grim October day, in the driving rain, a funeral procession crossed the rain-silvered piazzas of Mantova.

The procession was heading to the funeral of the Vicomte Richard St-Hilaire de Blossac, a noble fellow with a promising military career, who had been tragically killed in the company of his young wife, before he could join the French generals at Mantova. The sun dared not show his face – even the heavens were hung with black.

There were few mourners for the unfortunate *vicomte*; just a few military men, their voluminous black rain cloaks parting occasionally to reveal glimpses of their uniforms, splitting the dark, blue like lightning. To be truthful it was hard to notice them, for at the head of the cortège walked his widow. Of all the dreadful consequences of the *vicomte's* untimely death – that he would never again see a sunset, or hear an aria, or taste a Chablis – the most grievous was surely that he had quitted the company of his young wife. She was a rare beauty dressed all in black, her waist greyhound slim, her plain satin gown scattered with jet and bejewelled with raindrops. Her hair was high and powdered white, a single long ringlet twining down the full décolletage. A tiny black veil, embroidered with tiny black stars, both concealed and revealed a face of transcendent beauty.

Erect and dignified, the widow St-Hilaire de Blossac led the small cortège from the Palatine church of Santa Barbara across the green grass of the Cortile della Cavellerizza, under the Porta Nuova and through the fractured rain-sheer reflection of the Palazzo Ducale, in the direction of the Castillo di San Giorgio.

The *comtesse* looked devastated by grief, but in actuality her grief was spent for the moment. Now she had but one concern uppermost in her mind – to reach the shelter of her new apartments before the rain washed the powder from her red hair.

Safe in her chamber Kit sank down on the chaise before the mirror, exhausted. It did not matter that the spots of rain had mottled her powder and given her russet spots, like an African cat. But still, she took up the powder and the horn and puffed at the rusty patches herself. She could not be easy showing her red hair any more – she associated it so much with Kit Kavanagh. The Comtesse Christiane had white hair, always immaculate. Only when she was satisfied that her hair was white once more did she survey the ruin of her face in the looking glass.

She'd been taken by surprise at the strength of her own grief. At the counterfeit funeral, she had collapsed entirely. She had listened, initially, to the priest's intonation in formal Catholic French and Latin, but the words of the funeral service took hold of her, jostling with the other words in her head, the names of the generals at her shoulder, their wives, their sons, their birthplaces. Kit did not have her fan with her, so was relying on her overcrowded brain, and it was easy, at first, to keep her dignity. But the words of the funeral service insinuated themselves into her ears, and the altar boy who had been given a silver franc to sing the Te Deum had a sweet and soaring voice, recalling Lucio Mezzanotte to her mind. At the paternoster, she slid the wedding band from her finger, the mock wedding ring she had worn only for the last three months, and laid it on the cold marble tomb. And then she gave in.

She forgot about the Comtesse Christiane, and was suddenly herself, crying, really crying, sobbing uncontrollably. She cried for the unknown soldier, the corpse from the carriage and for his mother his sisters and his daughters and all those who had loved him; those that did not have a grave to visit and would likely not even be told about his secret and necessary death. Then she was crying for Richard, and she could see him as she'd known him, back in Dublin, when she'd loved him without reservation. She cried for the days when the handsomest maid in the village married the handsomest boy, when words meant what they said, when dances were hot and inexact and sweaty and bore no resemblance to the stately minuet. Feeling wrung out, and empty of tears, she took a deep breath. She felt, oddly, that it was Richard who had been given the rites he deserved. She felt much better, but looked much worse. She took up the alum paste and then set it down again. There was no profit in her trying to repair such a wreck herself – she had no skill with face-painting. She rang a silver bell for her maid.

Kit had been given a small, comfortable apartment in the Castillo di San Giorgio, one of the oldest parts of the Ducal Palace set upon the edge of the glassy green lake. As well as the many smooth and silent servants who were at her disposal she had been given a dedicated maid to wait upon her, a minor Mantovani noblewoman with good French named Livia Gonzaga.

As Livia painted and powdered, Kit thought over the events of the last week, unable to believe she had already been in Mantova for seven days. After her dreadful, precipitate arrival she had been helped from Ormonde's carriage by a brace of guards and taken to these very rooms. She had been fed and rested, by a kindly Mantovani nun who gave her a black gown and the news that her husband was indeed dead. Placid now, and genuinely numb, she had allowed herself to be cleaned and dressed, and then a man came to her rooms, an erect and impressive man of middle years who introduced himself as Louis d'Aubusson de La Feuillade, Duc de Roannais and *Maréchal de Camp* of the French Army.

Louis d'Aubusson, she recited to herself; *joined the French Army at aged fifteen, raised his own regiment of horse and fought in the Nine Years' War, all before he reached his majority. Knows everything there is to know about the army. Be careful.*

Gently, he asked her about her husband, his family and his service record, and she was able to reply in detail and with a quiet dignity. He nodded throughout, and then he said: 'And now, the delicate matter of your husband's funeral. I implore you, *Comtesse*, to understand that in no way would I address you on such matters if the *vicomte*'s family were at hand. But as they are so far away in Poitiers the unhappy task falls to me to ask you about certain particulars. I assure you, madam,' he went on, 'that even though your husband passed away on foreign soil, he will be given all proper rites. The medals that were pinned to his chest – would you like to keep them or is it your will that they be buried with him?'

In the carriage she had barely noticed the medals pinned to the corpse as if it were a tailor's dummy. Ormonde had been thorough indeed. But she was not put out of countenance – Ormonde had laid it down that Richard St-Hilaire would wear the Order of St Louis and had won the St Martin medal at the Battle of Catinat.

'It is my will that he be buried with them,' Kit said. Who knew where Ormonde had got them? Stolen, stripped from another poor corpse? Let that unknown soldier keep them to honour him in his cold grave.

Louis d'Aubusson nodded. 'And now, if you are equal to the exertion, I would very much like to present you to the duke.'

Kit nodded, rose shakily and accepted his arm. The *Maréchal de Camp* escorted her deep into the belly of the palace, where a pair of twin golden doors opened to admit them into a painted chamber as big as a basilica. There were giants painted all over the walls; giants wrestling in epic bouts, huge leviathans wreaking havoc, titans toppling pillars of stone as if they were wicker canes, chaos in epic scale upon the walls.

Blue-coated gentlemen sat at long trestle tables set with golden candlesticks, nibbling tidily at their food, talking in polite undertones, accompanied by a string quartet. Thanks to Mezzanotte she recognised the piece – an air by François Couperin – and the quality of those who played it. The ball at Turin had been a grand affair, but Kit saw that the French did not stint themselves any more than the Alliance. The war, and Richard's field of death, seemed a long way away, even though that grim plain was visible from the window. This was a feast fit for a king, and a would-be king sat at the head of it. This, then, was Philippe, Duc d'Orléans, nephew to the King of France.

Born at the Château de Saint-Cloud, she recited under her breath. *He was paid two million gold livres to marry Louis XIV's bastard daughter. His mother slapped his face in the full view of the court for agreeing to the marriage.* But now the man who had been the court joke at Versailles was a player in the game. Louis had chosen his nephew as his heir.

Resplendent in blue and gold, wearing a full-length wig of glossy chestnut curls, the pretender sat a little apart from the company on a golden dais. Servants in blue livery conveyed morsels to him from the board upon a golden tray. He waved his food away and held out his hand to Kit, his royal ring uppermost. She knelt and kissed the three feathers of the fleur-de-lis as Ormonde had taught her. 'Rise,' he said, and she stood before him, risking a look into the royal face. Philippe had a strong nose, ruddy cheeks and full lips. He would make, she supposed, as good a king as any other.

'*Madame la Comtesse*,' he said. 'I grieve for your loss.'

'I thank you, Your Grace.'

'Our prime concern is for your comfort here, until such a time when you may be safely conveyed home. Your husband will be buried with all honours due to such a faithful servant of France.'

Her eyes began to prick.

'I will instruct my own *abbé* to conduct the service for you. D'Aubusson will arrange everything.'

Kit curtsied low, and Orléans gestured to his man again, picking up the leg of a capon from the little gold tray and tearing at it with his teeth. It was a curiously brutal gesture, as voracious and destructive as those of the giants on the wall. Beneath the veneer, thought Kit, we are all animals.

Back at her apartments D'Aubusson settled her solicitously into a chair. 'The *maréchal* will come to you tomorrow, madame,' he said, 'with news of the arrangements for your husband's interment. My lord *duc* has agreed that he shall be given the honour of resting in the Mausoleum at the Palatine church.'

Kit barely heard the details of her husband's funeral. The maréchal Villeroi, the meeting she had dreaded. If the *maréchal* knew her for the dragoon who had helped to capture him in Cremona, her mission in Mantova was over. Kit plaited the black crape of her skirts between her fingers. She must find out whatever she could as soon as possible. 'You are very kind to concern yourself with my affairs – you must have so many other more pressing duties?' Her voice rose interrogatively, framing a question.

'Your husband made a sacrifice for France. What could be more important than his committal to God? Besides, we are not very much occupied at present. We are watching and waiting.'

She dropped her eyes and raised her handkerchief. 'My husband was so eager to join your enterprise. He would so have longed to ride out at your next manoeuvre . . .' But D'Aubusson rose, and nodded. 'I'll leave you now.'

She barely slept, and in the morning Livia had barely finished her new mistress's toilette when the *maréchal* was announced. Kit steeled herself, and turned from the mirror. But a very young man entered, in a spruce uniform of blue and gold, followed by an even younger man in cavalry livery.

The first man bowed, and she invited him to sit. '*Madame la Comtesse*, I am Ferdinand, Comte de Marsin, Deuxième Maréchal de France.'

Second Maréchal of France. This man was Villeroi's deputy. Kit breathed again, and racked her brain for information about this minor nobleman who had been given such a significant promotion. *Born in Liège. Moved to Paris at the age of five. Ambassador extraordinaire to Felipe V of Spain. Unmarried, but had a secret bastard daughter to whom he is peculiarly attached, with a Spanish noblewoman at the Escorial. Had the child conveyed to Paris. Fought at Speyerbach, one of the battles we claimed for Richard . . .*

Fortunately, the *maréchal* was too tactful to want to discuss Speyerbach. He expressed his condolences prettily, and took her proffered hand. She studied him carefully. He was young and handsome, but walked with a rolling gait which reminded her of her own injury, and when she invited him to sit, he sat with one leg straight forward, the knee locked. He apologised, immediately, for his posture, which was necessitated by an old injury from a musket ball. A shame, Kit thought, that she could not mention her own injury at Luzzara. But it seemed she had no need of such a connection; De Marsin showed the same kindness and solicitude as d'Aubusson and the *duc* himself. Kit's relief was short-lived, for his conversation soon took a dangerous turn.

'I know your home town of Poitiers well,' he said. 'I had an uncle down there, he used to take me boating on the Clain.'

She smiled sadly. 'I, too, used to take the pleasure boats in the summer. There's a church at the turn of the river, the Baptistère Saint-Jean . . .'

'I know it!' he said, animated. 'A truly heartbreaking vista.' Then he looked down. 'It is of Poitiers I wish to speak to you.

In the absence of your good family, the Duc d'Orléans has honoured me with the task of settling your husband's affairs. I have taken the liberty of writing two letters on your behalf containing the sad news of your husband's death. One to Poitiers and the other to Paris.'

Her heart began to thud. 'But my dear *maréchal*,' she gasped, 'I cannot put you to such trouble.'

He waved his hand. 'My dear madame, it is no trouble, I assure you. The letters are already written and as I am fortunate in my secretary – I did not even put quill to paper.'

'But . . .' she blustered, 'perhaps it would be better if I conveyed the news to my *belle-mère* and *beau-père* myself upon my return . . .'

De Marsin clasped his hands together. 'I regret, *Comtesse*, that I can make no promises at this time of your being able to return home in the immediate future. We find ourselves, madame, at a crucial stage of our conflict, and to convey you at this time across the border – well . . .' his elegant shrug was expressive, 'I could not guarantee your safety, and not for worlds would I place you in danger.'

'But . . . to receive such news in a letter . . .'

'Be comforted, madame. I have addressed the letter not to your husband's excellent parents directly, but to the Haute-Maréchal of Poitou-Charentes. I expect you are acquainted with this gentleman?'

'Indeed,' said Kit, picking up her cue, even in her panic, as adroitly as an actress. 'We dined many times with Monsieur Antoine de Rouvroy and his wife Viviane.'

'Quite. I have asked M. Rouvroy to pass on this sad news in person, along with my assurance that you will be home in the bosom of your family as soon as possible.'

He turned to the young fellow in the corner and beckoned him. Kit had forgotten the presence of the liveried boy, but the fellow bounded forward when summoned with an eager step. 'This is Jean-Jacques. He is our speediest fast-rider and has been an army messenger for a brace of years despite his youth. He has been given my instructions to take this dispatch directly to Poitiers.'

Kit looked at the young man with a sinking heart. He was positively twitching with constrained energy. 'I cannot take your fastest man from you.'

'It is no inconvenience – he would be taking the road to the Massif Central and thence to Paris anyway. It would be no hardship, Jean-Jacques, to break your journey in Poitiers?'

The young man bowed. 'None at all, *Maréchal*. 'Tis on the way. Change horses at Poitiers anyway.' His speech was as staccato as hoofbeats.

De Marsin spread his hands. 'You see. And in Paris he will deliver another dispatch on your account – your husband's passing will be entered in the rolls at the École Militaire, and his death registered at the Invalides. In this way – if you forgive me mentioning such a low matter, but in the absence of your *beau-père* I must – you will very soon be in receipt of your widow's pension.' He jerked his head to the eager lad. 'Jean-Jacques rides faster than Boreas – he will be back within the fortnight.'

'Week's more like it, sir.'

The Maréchal de Marsin took his leave before Kit could protest further, taking his fast-rider with him.

As the door closed she laid her forehead on the cool smooth wood. De Marsin had been implacable – the letters had been written, and to object further would be to betray herself. Kit swallowed; she had just one short week to find out what she needed to know before the news came back from Paris and Poitiers that would unmask her, condemn her and likely send her to the gallows: *There is no such person as the Vicomte Richard St-Hilaire de Blossac.*

She recalled her answers in the interview; she had, she was

sure, answered convincingly. Then she thought of the *comte* – how he had seemed. She remembered how he had sat. How he had looked at her.

The interview had not been entirely hopeless. She had seen something interesting in the Maréchal de Marsin's expression – of the three great men she had met in Mantova, he alone had seemed susceptible to her beauty. Orléans himself had his eyes on the throne and nothing else – D'Aubusson was military to the backbone, utterly correct in his behaviour and bearing. But this young *maréchal*, with his florid speech and fervent eyes, had seemed to hang on her words. She sensed that his romantic Gallic heart had been captured by her persona of the young abandoned widow, and he had cast her as some tragic heroine. In this limbo, waiting for the next great push, he had the leisure to lend his heart for a time. She decided, there and then, that the *maréchal* Ferdinand de Marsin would be her key to unlocking the stalemate.

She stood at the window when they were gone, and watched Jean-Jacques the fast-rider leave the gate. She saw his tricorn dip as he opened his leather satchel and checked the dispatches in his bag. Then he straightened, gathered the reins, looked along the road, the top of his tricorn aligned like an arrow. He jerked his spurs into his mare's flanks, and she shot forth as if from a bow, thundering along the causeway and across the bridge and the lake. Ormonde must have known this too – that they would send to the École Militaire in Paris to register his death, and have his service record entered in the rolls at the Invalides. Ormonde had known, then, that she would have a finite time to discover what she must and escape. He must have known that as soon as a reply came from Poitiers or the Invalides, she was done for.

'Livia,' she asked of her lady-in-waiting as they walked, 'who would you like to rule here? The Alliance or the French? You may speak freely – do not allow my personal allegiance to weigh with you.'

Livia looked up from her ribbons, her eyes and mouth wide.

'You are surprised that I asked you?'

'No. I am surprised by the question.'

'Won't you tell me why?'

'Because, *Comtesse*, begging your pardon, we do not want the Alliance or the French. We want to rule ourselves.'

Kit's days at the Castillo di San Giorgio began to take on a rhythm. Every morning she gazed from her window across the lake to the causeway, looking out with dread for the blue and gold messenger's livery of Jean-Jacques. What would these kindly, courtly men do to her once she was unmasked? What tortures would they devise for a spy, for a woman so wanton she would dishonour the very idea of a fallen French hero for her own ends? She must find out what she needed to know before Jean-Jacques returned – but equally, she must leave the city before he arrived.

Each day, she went to visit her husband's tomb accompanied by Livia. The marble of the coffer remained plain, no name, no date, no rank carved with chisel on stone. After a few days she guessed they were waiting for proof of the life and service of Vicomte St-Hilaire de Blossac. She would walk back through the city each day, watching the Mantovani go about their business, unruffled, it seemed, by the occupying force. She detected a certain resignation in their day-to-day tasks; not an indifference exactly but an acceptance – today they were ruled by the French, tomorrow perhaps by the Alliance. Their jewel of a city had been coveted for centuries, and would be for centuries to come; meantime there was bread to bake and wood to carry.

At her apartments Kit was left very much to herself. She was given every comfort, but took her meals in her room, spent her hours reading or sewing, walked only to her husband's grave and back and saw no one but Livia Gonzaga. She began, quietly, to panic. How was she to infiltrate the court, and find out what she needed to know, if she was isolated so? She knew why she was being left alone, and admired the French command for their solicitous consideration. She had a complicated relationship with Ormonde but had always trusted his judgement – now, for the first time, her trust faltered a little. The duke had not known or guessed that the flower of the French court would respect a widow's mourning to the extent that she would be excluded, almost entirely, from court life; and the nightly entertainments that sent faint phrases of music to her window, or lit the sky outside her casements with bursts of coloured fireworks, went on without her. So when La Maréchal Ferdinand de Marsin visited to see how she did, she welcomed the young count almost more effusively than was respectable. She must talk to him, she must make some headway; for all the hours she spent at her needle or her prayer book Jean-Jacques the fast-rider spent pounding the road between Paris and Poitiers. 'My dear *maréchal*,' she said, jumping to her feet, 'I am glad to see you indeed. Might I persuade you to take a turn about the palace? I must confide in you that I tire of these four walls.'

He looked a little taken aback, then smiled. 'I fear that the courtyards are now parade grounds, and not for the world would I subject you, in your current sad circumstances, to the scrutiny of low men. But,' he said quickly as her face fell, 'I think I may have the ideal solution. May I?' He offered his arm and she took it gratefully as he led her from the room.

He took her along panelled oak passageways where ranks of dark portraits, the image of Livia, looked down their long Gonzaga noses at her. At length they reached a low door in the wall. The door was unremarkable, and could have led the way to a cellar or garderobe, but it did not. Kit emerged into a green quadrangle surrounded by a colonnade of delicate marble pillars.

It was a secret garden, fragrant with roses and honeysuckle, in the very belly of the castle. 'This is the garden of Isabella d'Este herself,' said De Marsin, with a reverence that made her like him. The garden was its own little universe; the sun warmed the little stone courtyard even on this autumn day, and by some audible accident the harsh French commands of the drill sergeants could not be heard. The sky over the garden was a serene square of blue, the colour of the Virgin's cloak.

'It is beautiful,' Kit said.

'It is yours – for the duration of your stay,' said the Comte de Marsin. 'I will personally vouch for your privacy and stand a man at the door. Here you may take the air whenever you wish, and be entirely alone.'

Kit walked forward to one of the roses and cupped the bloom in her hand. The last thing she needed was more solitude. She spoke carefully. 'You are all kindness, *Maréchal*,' she said gratefully. 'This garden will suit me perfectly in times of reflection. But to say the truth, I also need some diversion, to take me out of myself; to help me to . . .'

He moved closer to her, and his shadow joined hers. 'To forget?'

She turned quickly. 'No, not that. Never that.' She laid a hand on his arm, shifting her body closer so her bosom all but touched his sleeve. She bit her bottom lip delicately until she was sure he was looking at her mouth. 'I express myself ill; forgive me. I am so little used to company now. What I meant to say is that I crave a distraction, not to allow me to forget my dear Richard, but rather to let me know that it is still possible to dance, to laugh, to hear sweet music, to eat with relish. Even if I cannot do these things yet myself, I can see them in others and know that one day, perhaps, it will be possible to live . . . and love, again.' Now she raised her eyes to his, pleading, promising.

It was a risk, but it had worked; De Marsin was caught like a fish on a hook. He faltered, and moved towards her fractionally, his gaze fervent. 'My dear madame, in that case allow me to invite you to join me in His Grace's presence this very night; there will be an evening of diversion; nothing comic nor soldierly but a gentle entertainment, which no person of discernment would deem unsuitable even for a lady in mourning.'

She took his hand, lowered her head and kissed the fingers she held, her lips lingering on his flesh. 'My dear sir,' she murmured to the hand, 'you are all goodness.'

When she released his hand De Marsin looked at it as if it was not his. He almost forgot to bow, did so just in time, and said, 'I'll leave you now. Until tonight.'

'Until tonight,' she agreed, and made sure she watched him wistfully until he was out of sight.

Kit's heart beat fast below her bodice that evening as she took her carriage to the Palazzo del Te, but she need not have worried that she would be a target for deprecating glances. It was dark by the time she reached the palace, and the Sala dei Giganti was lit only by hundreds of candles. The frescoed giants retreated to brood and wait, into the dark beyond the flames. There were a hundred gilded chairs set before a wooden stage, encircled by scores of musicians clutching viols. She could barely find De Marsin in the gloom, but before long he was at her side, and found a seat for her beside him. 'You see? We meet under the cover of night,' he said. 'No one will remark upon your presence.'

'Why the gloom?'

'We are to have a treat. *Le Duc* has charged his *chef de ballet* to recreate that most famous of ballets – the *Ballet of the Night*. It was this very ballet which gave our Royal Majesty Louis the name of the Sun King, you know, when he danced the role of Apollon aged just fifteen.'

Kit was well prepared. 'My grandmother had the honour to

wait upon the king's mother for some years – she was there at the Louvre on the night when His Majesty first danced the role.'

'It must have been a sight to see,' whispered De Marsin. 'Louis was quite the proficient, you know, and the Duc d'Orléans has inherited his uncle's partiality for the dance. Alas, the king himself is now lost to the art; he retired from the ballet some years ago due to an infirmity.'

Ormonde had expressed it differently. 'The Sun King is now a fat fuck,' he'd said. 'He and the sun have about the same girth.' Kit sat down, with the rest of the glittering gathering, wondering how an evening spent in silence could help her discover what she needed to know. Every single little light was extinguished, like someone putting out the stars. A hush fell over the company, the viols struck up, and a trapdoor sprung open in the wooden stage, letting a shaft of light burst through. A figure rose as if by magic, with a headdress of sunrays radiating from behind his head. His costume was made of cloth of gold, he wore sunbursts at his wrists and knees and on his feet were gilded shoes, with fashionably high French heels. The audience clapped and clapped, but not for the young slim dancer in the golden clothes. They clapped for Louis – as if time had folded back on itself and the young king was here. They were witnessing anew the birth of the cult of the Sun King, who had come to earth to sponsor his heir's claim. Kit looked across to Philippe of Orléans, sitting in his gilded chair, watching the sun figure hungrily as if he had the alchemy to exchange the wooden chair for a golden throne.

A narrator spoke from the shadows, turning Kit's attention back to the stage.

'As the light arises from the sun, still in the fire of its dawn, Honour follows its luminous train. In its wake ever follow Grace and Victory.'

As he spoke their names other figures appeared to dance about Apollon, bearing laurel wreaths and palm leaves and sceptres, all the symbols of power.

Kit found herself caught up in the spectacle; less for itself than for the feeling that something immense was about to happen, to which this ballet was merely an overture. Those words spoken by the narrator rang like a prophecy. But of what? If she could not find out, she was finished.

She sat through the hours that followed, holding her lower lip in her teeth. The rather sedate music from half a century ago had not the power to move her half so much as 'John Dwyer's Jig' or 'The Humours of Castlefin', nor did the grace and lyricism of the dancers tug at her heart. But her self-pity overwhelmed her so much that she had little difficulty in presenting De Marsin, when she turned to him at the final note, with a faceful of tears.

He touched one of them. 'You are crying. I should not have brought you. Forgive me.'

'There is nothing to forgive.'

'But you are upset.'

'Say rather inspired,' answered Kit fervently. 'Oh, *Maréchal*, who could not love our king and our country? Who could not wish for the Sun King's heir to sit upon the throne of Spain, and,' she looked up at him through her lashes, taking a guess, 'of the Empire too.'

He did not contradict her. 'I assure you, madame, that day will come; and sooner than you might think.'

She smiled tightly, her thoughts racing. Could it be true that the French would be so foolhardy as to cross the mountains and invade the Holy Roman Empire, with no better foothold in the north than Mantova? But the lamps were lit once more, and there were loftier claims on De Marsin's attention. Philippe of Orléans raised his beringed hand and beckoned. The *maréchal* bowed and kissed her glove. 'My master calls,' he said. 'Our leisure time is at an end; time for the business of the evening.'

'So late?'

'Time is growing short. Our preparations must be thorough.'

'I hope you plan for our enemies to be brought low, and for my husband to be avenged.'

'Trust the *duc*, madame. I assure you, our plan cannot fail.' He looked as if he would say more, then checked.

Kit had been a soldier long enough to know when to sound the retreat. 'Do not say any more, my dear *maréchal*. But let me say, for my own part, that I beg you not to place yourself in the teeth of danger. You have been so good to me. I have already lost a husband. I could not bear to lose such a friend.' She laid her hand on his arm.

He swallowed. 'I have called for your carriage, so that you are not put to the trouble of conversing with strangers. Allow me to escort you to the gates.'

She inclined her head to hide her frustration. She might have tried how far her widow's plight might have taken her with others in the room. But the evening had not been entirely hopeless, for De Marsin took her arm tenderly, and guided her out into the evening with the solicitude of a lover. At the gates of the Palazzo del Te a carriage almost clashed with her own and the drivers traded insults; the strange carriage pulled ahead and stopped before the ranks of burning torches with a crunch of gravel. She and De Marsin stood aside as a cohort of important men in blue militaries disembarked – one of them, the most decorated with brocade and medals, checked when he saw De Marsin and hurried over to greet him. Kit's heart stopped.

It was Maréchal Villeroi, the commander-in-chief of the French Army, and the very man she and Ross had captured in Cremona.

Pulses, thudding, Kit shrank into De Marsin's shadow.

'My dear De Marsin, well met,' exclaimed Villeroi. 'Is the Duc D'Orléans within? Shall we begin our council?'

'We were waiting for you, *Haute-Maréchal*.'

'Then let us wait no more.'

Kit's carriage had stopped behind Villeroi's, and Livia stepped down to greet her mistress. Kit crept away discreetly, hoping that De Marsin would forget about her in the face of his other priorities; that she could mount to her carriage, and make her escape. But his chivalry would not allow it.

'I must beg for a moment, *Haute-Maréchal*, to carry out the labours of Venus before we give ourselves entirely to Mars. Allow me to present the Comtesse Saint-Hilaire de Blossac, whom I promised a hand into her carriage.'

Villeroi bowed, and Kit curtsied, keeping her face low and her eyes on Villeroi's boots, praying that De Marsin would say no more.

'The *comtesse* has made a great sacrifice in our cause, perhaps the greatest; she lately lost her husband, the Vicomte Richard Saint-Hilaire de Blossac, Knight of St Louis.'

'I regret I did not know the gentleman.' Villeroi's voice softened. 'Of St Louis, was he?'

'He had that honour, *Haute-Maréchal*, while he lived,' said Kit to the ground, quietly.

'I too am a brother of that order,' said Villeroi, touching a medal at his lapel with a metallic tap. 'It is strange that I do not recall hearing his name.'

She raised her eyes from his boots to look at the medal – the same order that had been pinned over the still heart of her counterfeit husband. It was a mistake.

'But I know you, surely, madame,' exclaimed Villeroi, peering at her face in the torchlight.

Kit forced a smile. 'I think not, sir,' she said hurriedly. 'I am sure I would remember our meeting.'

'Have you been at Trianon? Or the Salle du Petit Bourbon?'

She shook her head. 'We lived very quietly, at Poitiers; we were not often at court.'

'But I could swear . . .' Villeroi's voice tailed away. He smiled. 'Well, there. It is salutary to remember that even if he commands a hundred thousand men, a man may still be made a fool by one beautiful woman.' It was said with great gallantry, and Kit smiled again, but the *maréchal* had already forgotten her and taken De Marsin by the shoulder, ushering his deputy into the palace before the younger man could take his leave of Kit. Shaking, she climbed into her carriage unaided and settled back into the cushions, heart thudding painfully. The ballet of the night was over.

Kit had to endure an anxious few days. To the dread of the messenger's return from Paris was added a new fear: that Villeroi would suddenly remember where he had seen her before. But no sergeants-at-arms came to her door, and her fears were a little abated when she saw Villeroi's carriage leave the city to return the *haute-maréchal* to the eastern front; but she was still no nearer any certain knowledge of what the French had discussed at the *Ballet of the Night*.

A week passed without a dinner, an entertainment or even a card game; then De Marsin's man came at last with another invitation. There was to be a regatta on the lake; a valedictory celebration for the officers before their imminent manoeuvre. The Maréchal de Marsin would be honoured if the Comtesse de Blossac would accompany him as his guest. Kit glanced at the rolling clouds once more as she answered in the affirmative. *Before their imminent manoeuvre*. She had been in Mantova for fourteen days. The troops were getting ready to leave. Tonight might be her last chance to discover where they went.

Livia found her a magnificent black gown from her own Gonzaga coffer. It had a stiff rebato of jet beads behind the head and a stomacher of dark gold satin. She requested that Livia weave jet beads and dark golden chains in her powdered hair, built up higher than she had ever worn it, and in the curls and waves Livia pinned a little ship, fashioned in ebony and with sails of gold tissue, to honour the spirit of the regatta.

The *festa* was to begin at sundown, and the lake was already red by the time Kit was escorted across the drawbridge. On the foreshore the Maréchal de Marsin waited for her in a barge bravely painted in gold and blue. He was wearing a smile and his dress uniform, with a full wig of snowy white. He offered her his hand, and she stepped into the boat beside him.

Night was falling, and a thousand torches were lit on stakes all round the lagoon, and in the boats themselves numberless silver-backed candles gave the impression of floating constellations. The lake was dotted with painted vessels, all grand and gilded, but none so great as the barge that carried Orléans himself, which was fashioned like a golden swan. Orléans sat in the helm of the boat, self-possessed and impassive; so well bred was he, thought Kit, that it was impossible to divine whether he was enjoying the spectacle or not. There was another even bigger barge in the very centre of the lake, carrying a small orchestra and all their various instruments. A corpulent singer rode with them dressed head to toe in flowing golden tissue folded almost like a toga. 'The *chanteur* represents Olympia,' De Marsin whispered.

'Goddess of Mount Olympus,' supplied Kit.

'And a symbol of the Gonzaga.'

'Ah.' She listened to the song carried across the water, as high and clear as the alpine bells she used to hear across the lake at the Palazzo Borromeo. She could tell from the singer's tone that he was a castrato, though he had not the quality of tone, for her taste, of Mezzanotte. 'Purcell,' she said, identifying his song. 'An odd choice, the music of the enemy?'

De Marsin turned to her, the candle flames in his eyes, and something else – a light of mischief? 'Perhaps that is the point. Perhaps we want them to know that anything that is theirs can be ours.' He nodded across the lake.

Her practised eye caught the glint of a musket barrel in the trees. She could barely prevent herself from ducking down and shouting a warning, as she would have done in the dragoons. But she sat still and narrowed her eyes – there was definitely a red coat in the trees, and another, and another. 'My Lord Orléans has uninvited guests,' she said, as calmly as she could. She could see, now, that they were in no immediate danger; she knew the English matchlock could not shoot this far. Kit surveyed the redcoats. Now she looked closely she could see quite a number of them in the undergrowth and posted about the lake. The soldiers leaned on their bayonets and watched the French disporting themselves. She thought then how dangerous this was – to make a trivial *festa* such as this directly before the serious business of warfare. And then she realised what De Marsin had said. *We want them to know that anything that is theirs can be ours.*

This was a show. This was a statement of the glory of France, and their comfort and ease in Mantova; everything had been considered and planned, not just for the pleasure of the French officers, but for the humiliation of the Alliance. The Purcell was a part of it – many of the men would recognise the piece. Mantova was a place that had been besieged twice by the Alliance in vain, a citadel for which thousands of soldiers had died. For which Richard had died. The dark blister of his grave lay in the very copse that now sheltered the redcoats, outside the city walls, no headstone, no honour, while the counterfeit Richard lay within the walls entombed in noble marble. She could do this, she could succeed in this mission, for the sake of both of her dead husbands, and for Ross, who lived and breathed.

The guests all moored their boats and came to shore for a great feast laid out on golden boards. In the centre of the fruits and sweetmeats sat a magnificent centrepiece, a castle cunningly wrought of sugar, sitting at the bottom of a model mountain.

She turned to the *comte*. 'Olympus again?'

The *maréchal* smirked. 'If you will. And perhaps the temple of Olympia sits below?'

But something was wrong. The castle was a great white edifice around three sides of a sugar piazza, with a thousand sugar windows of square gold leaf. It seemed oddly familiar. Then it struck her, like a thunderbolt. She had been to that castle, that castle made of cake and confectionery. She stared at it until her eyes blurred – expecting to see a little gold leaf coach draw up before it, and for a little sugar duke to climb out and hand down a sugar countess dressed in blue. As she watched, Orléans cut the castle with a sabre, the dark cake within a death slash down the architrave of the Palazzo Reale in Turin.

She clasped De Marsin's arm and set down her cup of punch. He turned to her, with concern. 'Madame? Are you quite well?'

'No.' She looked up at him, her eyes wide with appeal. 'I am not well.'

He looked about him. 'Come,' he said, 'you must be seated.' He led her to a low wall.

'Have you a fan?'

She remembered the fan she had left in the Palazzo Borromeo. 'No. Soon I will be well.'

'I will call for your maid.'

'No!' Louder this time, but he was already gesturing to one of his men. 'Fetch the *comtesse*'s woman.'

Cursing inwardly, she drew him down by her. Now she had left only the time it took for Livia to walk from the castle.

'Sir,' she said, 'I will be frank with you. I am terrified for my safety. It is clear that you are to embark on some great enterprise, and I am to be caught in the midst of it.'

'Trust me, madame,' said the *maréchal* soothingly, 'you will not be harmed. I give you my word.'

'If I could tell you, sir, how many men have sworn as much to me on their word. What is a word? May not a promise be spoken, and as easily broken?'

He straightened. 'But I think the word of a *maréchal* of France, madame, may be trusted.'

She laid a hand on his arm. 'If you could only tell me a little of what you go to do . . . You have come to mean so much to me.' She drew back her hand, as if she had said too much. '*All* of you brave gentlemen, so much like my dear husband.' She pressed her black glove to her lips.

His profile, as he looked over the lake, was impassive. He had been happy to dally with her when he had been kicking his heels, but now his mind had shifted to war. If her feminine wiles were no use, what had she left? She racked her brain, rehearsing once more in that strained silence everything Ormonde had taught her of the Maréchal Ferdinand, Comte de Marsin. *Born in Liège. Moved to Paris at the age of five. Ambassador extraordinaire to Felipe V of Spain. Unmarried, but had a secret bastard daughter to whom he is peculiarly attached, with a Spanish noblewoman at the Escorial. Had the child conveyed to Paris.*

A secret bastard daughter, to whom he is peculiarly attached . . .

'*Maréchal*. Ferdinand.' She gave her voice a tremor as she spoke. 'I have lost my husband. But we both knew it might be God's will that a soldier would die – such is a fighting man's lot. But I have a child in Poitiers. A daughter called Christiana. She is very young, I was only just churched when my husband was commanded here to Mantova, so she stayed with my mother and wetnurse away from battle and danger.' She gripped his arm again. 'Please, *Maréchal*, tell me I will return home safe. Tell me I will hold my child again, and feel her little hand close about my finger as it used to do.'

It was very dark now, but she could sense that De Marsin's head had turned towards her.

'I have a daughter too. She is the delight of my eyes. She is why I fight.'

She said nothing, but pressed his hand now in fellow feeling. *Know when to stop*, Ormonde had said.

She heard him exhale, very quietly, and held her own breath. Here it came. 'The mountain is the Superga hill in Piedmont,' he said, low voiced. 'And the castle of sugar, it is the Palazzo Reale in Turin.'

So she had been right. She turned to him, eyes wide. 'You are to take Turin?'

'In a sevennight, with forty thousand men.'

She swallowed. *Turin.* She had been right – the French looked to the Empire; Turin was Eugene of Savoy's headquarters and home. It was audacious, it was brilliant. Turin stood at the gate between the Empire and France – with the taking of Savoy's own city the Franco-Spanish would control ingress and egress to the peninsula – they could choke it at the throat and take the rest of the boot to the south at their leisure. 'And will you prevail?' It was a whisper.

'We cannot fail. Please be assured. There is no danger. The Duc de Vendôme has made a counterfeit sortie south, to Castiglione, and the Alliance is pursuing him, leaving Turin defended by only one regiment of cavalry – the Scots Grey Dragoons. The city is ours for the taking.'

Kit's head spun. Ross and his dragoons stood alone between Turin and forty thousand men. But in order to save him, she must first leave this city alive. 'And if Mantova is no longer defended . . .'

'But you will not be in Mantova,' said the Comte de Marsin. 'You are to be conveyed to Genova tomorrow, and from thence to Poitiers. You shall embrace your daughter again, I swear it.'

Kit dipped her head and kissed his hands, and the tears in her eyes were genuine. Relief, sheer relief.

As she raised her head she saw her lady-in-waiting approaching. Livia walked along the foreshore, the great castle rising at her back, in a halo of torchlight.

The *maréchal* rose and bowed. 'Rest easy tonight. I will take my leave of you early tomorrow.' He handed her to her feet; she bowed to him and walked as calmly as she could by the side of Livia Gonzaga, bursting to tell the true princess of this place that she and the ghosts of her family would soon have their city back again.

In the morning Kit looked about her apartments one last time, checking each armoire and drawer, even though Livia had packed for her. There should be no trace of her left here, nothing that remained of her mission to Mantova save the one anonymous corpse in the Santa Barbara. She glanced from the window one last time, and what she saw stopped her heart.

There, speeding across the causeway as fast as an arrow, was a tiny figure of blue and gold on the fastest horse in the French army. Jean-Jacques. The messenger. She had almost forgotten him.

Kit turned and ran down the stairs, pell-mell, through the court-yard and into the waiting coach. She took leave of the Comte de Marsin almost too swiftly for politeness, snatching her hand from his lips, and pressing it to her own, letting her eyes fill with hasty tears. 'Forgive me, *Maréchal*; you have been so kind. It is the emotion; I think I must just leave you now – no farewells.'

He nodded and stood back, but his hand still rested on the door of the coach. 'I understand. I wish you the joy of your reunion with Christiana.'

She looked up, confused in her hurry and panic. 'But *I* am Christiane.'

He looked puzzled. 'Your daughter,' he prompted gently.

She pried his hand gently from the door. 'My dear *Maréchal*, if you have any parental feeling, let me go now so she may be in my arms all the sooner.'

He let go of the door, and bowed his head. She kissed her hand to him as the coach turned about the courtyard, agonisingly slowly. As the four stepped out on to the drawbridge she could actually hear the hoofbeats of the messenger's horse on the causeway, galloping towards them. She shrank back in her seat but her eyes were drawn inexorably to the carriage window; she could see Jean-Jacques now, thundering closer, closer, till the hurtling carriage actually passed him. As they swept away across the lake and she looked back at the floating city she had left, he was pounding at the gates.

Now she turned away, to the road, grim faced. The carriage had picked up speed, but it would not take Jean-Jacques long to tell De Marsin how he had been tricked. While they were on the eastern road she was in danger.

Time was of the essence. She knew there was a heavily wooded copse between the lake and Castellucchio, the little town where she had been given her counterfeit husband. Once the carriage fell dark with the cover of trees she sprang up. Fumbling with the lacings at her waist with shaking hands, she freed herself from her voluminous skirts and petticoats and shed them like a skin. She clambered out of the window in her stockings and bodice; the rushing wind tore down her hair and blasted the powder from her face in little white puffs. Grabbing a handful of the coachman's coat she pulled him from the driver's box, and he fell tumbling to the ground with a cry and a sickening crunch. Clambering into his place, she tugged on the tangled reins with all her strength. She had never driven a four before, and it took her some time to rein the team to a jog, then to a stop, and she tied the reins hurriedly – too many reins – to the pommel. She jumped down and ran back to the unconscious coachman and stripped him as quickly as she could, struggling with his dead weight. He was a burly fellow, but his clothes would have to do. She stripped in the freezing forest down to her pantaloons, and pulled on the coachman's shirt and breeches and coat, her frozen fingers remembering the male buckles and ties and fastenings. Then she reached up to her hair, tearing the horsehair pads from her coiffure, flattening down her own locks stiff with powder, and scraping them back as she'd used to. She crammed the coachman's tricorn on her head and ran back to the coach, clambering up on to the driver's box and gathering the reins again.

She had no idea what to do. What if the horses would not go for her? What if they stood here, grazing, till the *maréchal* and his men came? Heart thudding, she raised the heavy leather straps and brought them down on the back pair's rumps, shouting, 'Yar!' The four stallions took off like racehorses, and she nearly toppled back over the box. Gradually, muscles straining, she steered them to Castellucchio. Then, instead of taking the road to Genova, she drove the horses on to the Brenner Pass, the lakes and the Palazzo Borromeo.

Chapter 36

And bade it a tedious returnin' . . .

'Arthur McBride' (trad.)

'Turin? When?'

Kit stood before the Duke of Ormonde, in the great marble hall of the Palazzo Borromeo.

The palace seemed different now to its summer self – the lake outside was grey as pewter, the mountains silvered with the first snows. No pleasure trippers tacked on the rilling water, and even the peacocks in the gardens were mute with autumn sullenness.

Only Ormonde was unchanged. He sat in his gilded chair like a king, Kit before him in her coachman's coat and tricorn like a lowly supplicant.

She calculated. It had been three days since the Maréchal Comte de Marsin had told her the French would besiege Turin in a week. 'In four short days they will begin the attack. But perhaps sooner.'

Ormonde stroked his chin. 'Why sooner?'

'A messenger came from France as I was leaving, bringing information that would unmask me as a spy. They know I know, so they may mobilise sooner.'

Ormonde shrugged. 'It is no small thing to mobilise an army. They need time.'

'But they need the currency of surprise.'

'Yes,' he said, measuredly. 'Yes, they do.'

She stood, awkwardly, shaking out her aching arms. This was not at all how she had imagined this interview. Would she be rewarded now, and dismissed? Would she be offered safe passage to Dublin, or given leave to go where she wanted? Would she be free to find Ross and reveal herself?

She had expected congratulations, perhaps even an embrace. She had expected a flurry of activity, of dispatches, of summonses for Panton, Tichborne or even Marlborough. But Ormonde stretched like a cat. 'Well done,' he said. 'And now I imagine you would like to bathe, eat, and take your ease. Change into some pretty clothes. Coachman to countess, what?' He laughed but the laugh did not chime true. She was unsettled by his ease.

'What will you do? Tell Marlborough?' She could imagine how Ormonde would enjoy it – bringing the duke here, telling him that he had managed to discover with the aid of one woman what Marlborough's ten thousand men had not.

He tapped his teeth with his fingernail. 'I will consider.'

'Do not consider overmuch. It will not take them long to find the owner of these clothes in the woods.'

'Leave it with me,' said Ormonde, dismissively.

'But . . .'

'Kit. Leave it with me.' She was jolted by the use of her true name. She raised her chin. 'So I am to be Kit Kavanagh once more?'

'Oh, I think so. I think the Countess Christiane has served her purpose, don't you?'

At dinner she felt a little better. She had bathed, dressed in a copper brocade gown and eaten her fill. She also sported the diamonds that had once belonged to Anne of Austria, to remind Ormonde of what was due to her, now she had done as he'd asked.

From Mezzanotte she had received the congratulations and embraces so markedly lacking from his lover. Dinner was relaxed and the three of them talked easily of anything but the approaching siege. Kit told herself that this must be because Mezzanotte was present, but she did not wholly believe it. Ormonde had always shared his secrets with the castrato.

Still, she waited till Mezzanotte had begun to sing, before she questioned Ormonde. Her voice hung in an odd limbo between the countess and Kit. She no longer knew who she was, her accent odd; now Poitiers, now Dublin.

'Where is Marlborough at present? How quickly could he get to Turin with his forces?'

'Very quickly, if he was so minded. He is on the Superga hill, overlooking the city, taking command of his latest mistake: the general retreat to the Po valley.'

'I see.'

'What do you see?'

She was silent.

'We do not need to put away our candour,' he said, 'now that our mission is ended.'

'I understand why you are manifesting little urgency. If Marlborough is already sitting on top of the city he can reinforce it as soon as he may.' It was all right. Ross and the dragoons would be safe.

Ormonde ran his finger around the rim of his glass. 'Kit. I am not going to tell Marlborough.'

'Not?'

'No.'

'Someone else, then? Panton? Tichborne? I understand you don't want to hand the credit for the salvation of Turin to your enemy, but . . .'

'Kit,' he said again. 'I am not going to tell *anyone*. Not a single member of the Alliance forces. Not a general, not a dragoon, not a foot soldier, not a drummer boy.'

She listened to the exquisite song, her world crumbling. 'Why?'

'Come, come,' said Ormonde, drumming his fingers gently on the linen tablecloth. 'You know why. I have taught you well. You tell me.'

'Because,' she said slowly, 'if the Alliance has no warning, the French will take Turin.'

'And then?'

'Marlborough will be blamed.'

'And?'

'Relieved of his command.'

'Precisely.'

'Then you will petition the queen, and take his place as commander-in-chief of the Grand Alliance.'

Ormonde sipped his champagne, his eyes veiled. 'A very interesting conjecture, Kit. I cannot, of course, confirm these fantasies.'

'But they are true, are they not?'

He regarded her. 'Think, Kit. Do you really want me to say yes?'

She did not. She didn't want to know such dangerous information. She was reminded of Atticus Lambe, in the hospital dungeon of Riva del Garda, revealing his addictions and peccadilloes. Suddenly afraid, she rose from the table, and opened the double doors, Mezzanotte's heartbreaking aria pursuing her.

> Dove sei, amato bene!
> Vieni, l'alma a consolar!
> Sono oppresso da' tormenti
> ed i crudeli miei lamenti
> sol con te posso bear.

As she left the salon she felt a prickling at her back, the prickling of Ormonde watching her, convinced that his comfortable candour was derived from his certain knowledge that she would not leave the palace alive.

She shivered under the coverlet, her teeth chattering. She was cold with horror and dread. The thought of Ross, of all the dragoons, those good men, her friends, defending the citadel of

Turin alone, sickened her. She could see them in her mind's eye, surprised by attack, fighting valiantly, failing, falling, cut down by the French. Another crushing defeat that made the ground slippery with blood; another Aughrim, another Mantova. Sean Kavanagh. Richard Walsh. Enough. *You don't have to wait to be rescued*, Aunt Maura said in her head. *Go and rescue him*. And this time it was Captain Ross that she meant.

Kit got up and lit her candle, and, in the warm light, she dressed herself as best she could. Now unused to the task, her shaking fingers fumbled with her lacings. She needed elegance but also practicality; so she chose a brocade carriage dress in saffron velvet, and a heavy travel cloak. She had no time to dress her hair, so she scraped her own clean hair back and chose a powdered wig from her wig stand. She fastened the diamonds at her ears, wrists and throat, for her credibility would depend on her magnificence, and besides, they were rightfully hers. Rapidly, remembering the artistry of Livia Gonzaga, she made up her face with white alum, with ceruse on the lips and cheeks. There was no time for a patch. She picked up the fan that had been her prop and stay, and set it down – it was useless to her now. She wished she had a sword instead. She wished she had her uniform again. She had dissembled every day that she wore it, but now that suit of clothes seemed more honest than a gown. She longed for her heavy felted coat, for the facings and lacings and boots. The wish reminded her.

She fell to the floor and looked beneath the bed. There they were – her dragoon's riding boots, which had been waiting there, patiently, for her to remember them. She pulled them on gratefully and they were well hidden beneath her skirts.

There was a faint knock at the door. She froze for a moment. 'Just a moment!' she called breezily, as she threw her heavy cloak behind the bed, tore off the wig, hauled the coverlet over her pack and threw her night chemise over her travel clothes. Taking a deep breath, she opened the door a crack.

It was Lucio Mezzanotte. He walked in and took her by the shoulders. 'Christiane. Kit. You should leave this place.'

She stripped off the chemise.

'Ah.' Mezzanotte closed the door behind him, and sat down on the bed. He watched her as she replaced her wig and collected her cloak. 'You have anticipated me. Christiane . . . forgive me. Kit.'

'It does not matter what you call me,' she said, her voice hard. 'Whoever I am, I am not a fool.'

'He is going to kill you,' said the castrato.

Kit stopped packing. Started again. 'I know.' But still it was chilling to hear it stated like that.

'Where will you go?'

Kit fastened her pack, hesitated. How much should she tell Mezzanotte? 'I don't know.'

She turned back to him – he looked at her, amused. 'Take this.' He waved a silver flask at her. 'It can get cold on the mountain, and it might take you some time to find Marlborough.'

She stepped forward and took it gratefully. 'And what will *you* do? Surely you must leave him now?'

Mezzanotte looked up, his eyes enormous in his long pale face. 'Why? I love him.'

Kit shook her head. She could not articulate the reasons, if he did not know them already.

'He has done worse than this,' said Mezzanotte. 'Before I even met him. I always knew what I loved.' He fingered the Prince Rupert's drop about his neck, the glass greedily imprisoning the lamp flame. 'He told me once that when he was a young general in Ireland he fought the Jacobite infantry for King William.' Kit leaned back against the door, suddenly weak. She fixed her gaze on Mezzanotte where he sat on the edge of her coverlet, just as Maura used to do when telling a tale. 'He had the rebels completely exposed and surrounded. The Jacobites surrendered, and they started to run. They threw away their weapons in order to run faster. But Fitz fell upon them with his cavalry and slaughtered them all as they tried to get away. He said the grass was slippery with blood. He said that, to this day, this place is known locally as the "Bloody Hollow". All because of him.'

Kit went still. 'Where was this?' but she knew the answer.

'Oh, I don't remember. Some hill near his estates in the east. Some funny long Irish word.'

'Killcommadan?'

'That's it.'

Kit closed her eyes, feeling the ridges of the door against her back. Ormonde. Ormonde had killed her father. Sean Kavanagh had been one of those fleeing Jacobites. His sword – her sword – was one of the weapons that was thrown down in surrender. Sean Kavanagh's blood had made the grass slippery in the Bloody Hollow. Was that why she had met Ormonde on Killcommadan Hill that day, when she was little more than a child? Now she understood too that his infernal parrot had, all this time, been repeating his master's boasts. *Damned Jacobites. Like rats in a trap*.

She could not speak for her white-hot anger. But Mezzanotte did not seem to notice. 'Fitz said he made his fortune that day,' he went on. 'He says if he had not done what he did, he would not have been brought to court, and he would not have been at the opera with the queen, and he would never have met me.' Then the castrato registered Kit's expression. 'He is not a bad man.'

She pushed herself away from the door and grabbed her pack. 'I am going. Let him try to stop me if he will.' She felt as if she could kill him with her bare hands.

'He will not even wake.'

His voice, weary but certain, stopped her in her tracks. 'How do you know?'

'Juice of the poppy. Opium. I told you they fed it to me in

Florence when they took my manhood. I have been using it ever since.' She turned to look at him and saw an expression she recognised in his eyes. His lids were heavy and hooded, his pupils enormous. She had seen that same look on Atticus Lambe. 'It has been my constant friend,' confessed Mezzanotte. 'And tonight, it is his. Fitz sleeps in a poppy field. You have until dawn at the least.'

Kit's simmering anger abated somewhat. 'What will he do to you?'

'I? I know nothing of your flight. I will wake beside him, none the wiser.'

Kit could not leave Mezzanotte like this. 'Tomorrow he may spare you. But he will smash you one day,' she warned. 'You'll shatter under his hand, like that drop you wear.'

Mezzanotte grasped his pendant. 'I know. But I would rather die under his hand than live under someone else's.'

Kit tiptoed down the great stone stair, and past the parrot's cage. In the dark he was just a grey parrot, the gaudy feathers leached of hue, dreary and dun; headless at present – his head tucked under his wing. She thought she had got past without a final insult but the bird took his head from under his wing and screeched, 'Damned Jacobite!' She winced, hoping the screech did not penetrate the sleep of the poppy. 'And proud of it,' she hissed.

She walked past, then stopped and turned. On a sudden whim she twisted the gilded catch of the cage and the door swung open. 'Go on,' she said. The parrot gave a throaty chuckle and cocked its head at her, fixing her with eyes like black beads. It shifted its ugly clawed feet, but made no move to fly. She regarded it for a moment, then understood. 'Not you too,' she said. 'Well; please yourself.' And she shut the cage door again.

Chapter 37

For we were the lads who would give them hard clouts . . .

'Arthur McBride' (trad.)

Superga hill. Superga hill. Superga hill.

Kit repeated the direction to herself over and over, in time with
Flint's hoofbeats, like a litany.

She had expected a slight incline, a little rise in the terrain, but
when she and Flint finally reached it they found themselves toiling
up a vast and looming mountain. Mare and rider were exhausted
beyond measure, having already ridden for a night and a day. Flint
had had no nourishment save some wayside grass and water, and
Kit's only sustenance had been periodic nips from Mezzanotte's flask.

Their climb was not made easier by a red river flowing down
the green hill – hundreds upon thousands of cavalry and foot, in
their red coats, pouring down the slope like a cataract, in retreat.
They seemed in spirits, these men, swaggering and joking; some
doffed their hats to her, some sang a catch, some whistled. She
loved them, these soldiers, really loved them. She wanted to shout
at them all, *Turn back!* But she had no authority – she must find
Marlborough, had to find Marlborough.

As she climbed, the view unfurled beneath her like a Turkey
carpet and she realised her adventures had come full circle. She
had begun this coil by rolling down a hill on Ormonde's orders;
now she climbed a hill against them. She kept her eyes high – the
climb, the climb was all – she would not fall again.

At the crown of the hill stood a marble mausoleum, eerily

reminiscent of the one in Mantova where she had laid her counterfeit husband. She thought fleetingly of him. Had the French dug him up by now, and thrown him in a pauper's grave? Or had they let him lie?

At the little chapel she slid from Flint's back, and rested her head for a moment on her sweating lathered neck. She breathed the sweet smell of hay and horse, and tied the mare to the wrought-iron gate of the tomb. There she read the names of long-dead Savoy princes, a roll call of skeleton emperors and bone kings. But beyond the white tombs was a collection of red tents, brave and warm and alive, their fabric walls moving with the wind, as rosy and animate as the tombs were pale and dead.

Marlborough's tents.

Kit threw back her cloak so that the diamonds at her ears and throat caught the sun, pressed her lips together, pinched her cheeks and straightened her wig. The current Prince of Savoy was probably between his silken sheets in the white palace below, the palace where she'd celebrated his name day. If she failed today, he might soon be laid to rest here in this cold stone bed.

Kit walked forward to the fluttering tents. Their pennants were blowing in an easterly, in the direction of the doomed city, pointing in warning. In the centre of the circle of red sat two men at chess. At first she did not recognise Marlborough, for he was jacketless, his red coat laid beside him on the grass. His opponent was in a like state of undress, in his shirtsleeves, his coat laid aside. He too was unfamiliar at first, but when he looked up she could see that it was Lord Mark Kerr, a commander she had seen at the castle at Rovereto, and again in the lines at Luzzara. Both men watched her approach, and, she noted with relief, both got to their feet. She must, even after the ride she had undertaken, still look like a lady, if not a countess. She did reverence to Marlborough first, then Lord Mark, but spoke as she curtsied, mindful of pressing time.

'My Lord Marlborough, I have some vital intelligence for your ears. The French intend to take Turin by surprise, and use the city as their bastion to take the rest of the peninsula, and annex it to France.'

'What?'

'I swear it, my lord. I have been at the court at Mantova, and had it from Maréchal Ferdinand Comte de Marsin himself.'

'Turin?' Marlborough frowned. 'They would not dare brave the lion's mouth. They have passed it by a thousand times – it is held by Savoy and always has been.'

'Held securely?' asked Kit pointedly. 'Or by one regiment; the Scots Grey Dragoons?'

Marlborough's eyes narrowed. 'How do you know this?'

'I told you. I have been at the court of the French.'

'And you are now in their pay?'

She shook her head. 'No, sir. I am on the side of the Alliance, through and through. I urge you to fortify the city. The French could, even now, be riding into the valley.' She repeated herself. She became more voluble, more insistent; she was losing their attention, and began to shout like a fishwife.

Lord Mark came closer to her and sniffed. 'She is a foolish drunken woman – I can smell brandy on her breath.'

She took a step back – it was Mezzanotte's brandy he'd smelled.

'No,' said Marlborough slowly. 'She *is* a French *comtesse*. I saw you, did I not, at the palazzo yonder with Ormonde.'

'The Duke of Ormonde?' interjected Lord Mark, exchanging a significant glance with Marlborough.

'Aye,' said Marlborough grimly, and his demeanour changed. 'What scheme is this, madam? Tell me the meaning of this falsehood, or I will have you clapped in chains, countess or no.'

She looked about her desperately. She wished she had the purse he had given her to show him – the purse with his own arms stamped upon it; but she had given it to Bianca.

In desperation she tore off her wig and took up Marlborough's coat from the grass. She put it on, buttoned it and faced him, hitching the gown to show her soldier's boots. Now, save the skirt, she was the same Kit who had faced him in Rovereto, when he had rewarded her.

'I am no countess,' she said. 'I am Kit Kavanagh, of the Royal Scots Grey dragoons. At the castle of Rovereto you once gave me a commendation for bravery and a purse of five pistoles, for coming to the aid of Colonel Gossedge at Cremona.' She went to the duke and took his hands, looking up into his face, appealing to him using both her soldier's forthrightness and her feminine wiles. 'You used to call me "the pretty dragoon".'

Marlborough looked at her for five dreadful heartbeats – then his face changed. 'Lord Mark,' he said, in a low voice that rang like a bell. 'Call the officers. Fall in the trumpeters. Halt the men and bring them back.'

'But my Lord—'

'Do it, Kerr. For I would rather trust this lady than any man in my army. And for Christ's sake, man, put on your jacket, there is a battle to fight.'

Chapter 38

And we have no desire to take your advance . . .

'Arthur McBride' (trad.)

Kit learned that day what a true commander was.

Marlborough had only to stand at the crown of the hill and before the trumpets had even sounded, the red tide that had flowed down the hill like lava congealed, halted and reversed, to surge back up the hill and surround its commander. Marlborough waited until all the company was crowded about him before he held his hand high for the trumpets to cease. He stood on a stone tor that marked the very summit of the hill. His height was already remarkable, but the stone he stood upon made him a giant among men, and he spread his arms in welcome like Christ about to make his Sermon on the Mount. But at the same time he looked more humble than usual. He had ordered Lord Mark to dress himself, but he had left off his own coat, and spoke to the men as one of them.

'I have it on authority,' he said, 'that the French are even now marching upon Turin. Their retreat was a feint. They are returning in number – above forty thousand men will march on the city below. We will not let them take it. For if they take Turin, home of our dear friend and ally Prince Eugene, they have a stronghold on the edge of the Empire and will overrun the peninsula. And we will *not* let that happen.' He opened his arms again, to show his shirtsleeves. 'You see, brothers,' he said. 'I have no concealed armour. I am equally exposed with you, and I require none to go where I will refuse to venture.' Kit looked around at all the rapt faces – every soldier listened attentively, no one stirred. 'Remember you fight for the liberties of all Europe, and the glory of your nation, which shall never suffer by my behaviour; and I hope that the character of a Briton is as dear to every one of you as it is to me.'

Deafening cheers almost drowned the last of his words, and he was taken up by the redcoats nearest him and carried shoulder high. Tricorns were thrown high, songs and catches were sung, and Kit felt her heart swell – she wanted to cheer too – she wanted to be one of them. She learned then, for the first time, why the English Army was so devoted to Marlborough.

The duke's ensign approached and had to shout above the cacophony. 'My Lord Duke, the prince is come.'

Marlborough was set down; the trumpets sounded once more, the sergeants shouted. The merry band of revellers fell into lines and the lines into regiments and the army, calm, professional and deadly, formed before Kit's eyes. What must she do now, in such a company? God willing, Ross would now be safe, for this army of thousands would descend to defend the city. Marlborough was due to meet his commanders in his tent; what would Kit Kavanagh do now? How could she serve? She looked down, out of countenance, not sure where to put herself. Marlborough swept past her on his way to his tent, his spurs striking sparks on the rocks underfoot. He stopped, turned. 'Coming?' he asked.

Kit looked up. 'Me?'

'Of course. Don't stand there gawping.'

'The point is, surely, to wait.' Eugene of Savoy was striding up and down the tent, his wig, his skin and his whole person given a scarlet hue by the sun leaching through the red fabric. 'If De Marsin finds the city heavily defended, and the French vanguard is repelled at once by great numbers, they will retreat. What we want is for the French to think that Turin is theirs for the taking. Let Vendôme come from the west, and Orléans and De la Feuillade and Maréchal Marsin from the east, let them all come. Let them gather in the valley – all of them. Our divisions, and yours, will wait in the hills here at Superga and at the Po and fall upon them. They will be like rats in a trap.'

Rats in a trap. Kit heard Ormonde's phrase in Savoy's mouth, like a death knell. The Jacobites. The English. Now the French.

Marlborough tapped his nail on his teeth. For a time he did not answer. 'I see the sense in what you say,' he conceded. 'But equally, if the French come at force, and charge through the gates, they may take the city before we can act. Only one of my regiments defends the city – the Royal Scots Greys, ringed about the walls.'

Eugene too thought for a moment. 'The Hessians are at Castiglione, close upon the city. Let us command the landgrave to march his men to Turin with all possible haste and stealth, to enter the city secretly, and in great number, but at the rearward to defend the gates from within.'

'And outside the gates?' asked Marlborough with some heat. 'What of the dragoons in the valley, who defend the walls? I have never yet left a regiment of good men to die like lambs at Eastertide.'

'You would prefer that the French retreat, intact, to try their chance again? Or do we finish this? We have been stuck in stalemate for long enough now. Time for the endgame.'

Ormonde's words again. Kit's heart sank. She knew which way the wind was blowing.

Marlborough shook his head. 'I cannot condemn those men to certain death.'

'And what of their commander? Captain . . .'

'Ross. Captain Ross,' said Marlborough. She loved the duke at that moment for knowing his men so well.

'What would he say, if you gave him the choice and offered him such glory?' pressed the prince.

Marlborough's eyes found Kit, over the heads of the officers. 'I would have to say, knowing their number as I do, that any one of the Royal Scots Greys would face death with a glad heart, and consider it an honour.'

Savoy nodded. 'Very well,' he said. 'Let a message be sent to Captain Ross. He must defend the gates, and engage the French outriders as best he can before he is delivered. For my part, I will send a fast-rider to the Hessians. If the Duc de Vendôme is bringing his army from Garda they must be let pass. I will tell the land-grave that it is my pleasure that he come to the aid of the queen's dragoons.'

Marlborough inclined his head. 'Very well.' He nodded smartly and marched from the tent, followed by his officers. Kit hesitated a moment too long and missed her opportunity to leave under the cover of the English officers.

She shrank back into the folds of the tent, and from the shadows watched Prince Eugene write an order, and seal the dispatch. He held the letter high, the sealing wax still congealing with an acrid smell, when a rider appeared at the tent flap. He collected the scroll with a brief bow and a click of the heels. 'For the landgrave of the Hessians, at Castiglione,' said Savoy, 'with all possible speed.'

Kit waited for Savoy to take up his pen once more, for the scratch of the quill, the plop of the wax, the hiss of the seal and the smell of the tallow. But there was nothing. She peered around the tent swag, past the Imperial officers, and saw Savoy sit back in his chair and tap his stubby fingers on the arms. The sun shone outside once more, turning him a demonic red again. His rabbit teeth held his lower lip, and his eyes were veiled. She had seen that expression before; when he had thrown Maréchal Villeroi's aide-de-camp from the cathedral tower in Cremona.

Savoy's deputy, whom she recognised as Florian Von Habsburg, voiced her thoughts for her. 'Shall I send for the second rider, Highness?'

'No.'

Von Habsburg looked puzzled. 'Highness, forgive me, but I think that speed is of the essence.'

'We will not be needing a second rider.'

'But Highness . . .'

'Yes?'

'You told Lord Marlborough . . . another rider would be sent. To warn the dragoons.'

'Florian. If they look at all prepared the French will know they have been forewarned. We need to let this gambit play out.'

'But . . .'

'My city, Florian. My command.' Savoy rose and swept from the pavilion.

Kit forced herself to count ten rapid heartbeats before she too slipped from the tent. She walked as quickly as she could to Flint, who was cropping grass next to Savoy's mausoleum. She vaulted on to the mare's back as best she could in her riding skirts and turned Flint's head towards Turin.

Chapter 39

All hazards and danger we barter on chance . . .

'Arthur McBride' (trad.)

Kit passed scores of redcoats, some drilling, some taking their ease; some feeding their horses, some cleaning their muskets, some playing with their dice. They waited, in their practised, various fashions, for the bugle's call. She galloped through the ranks, heedless of the catcalls and greetings. For her the trumpet had already sounded.

In time she was beyond the red sea and taking the winding mountain roads down to the plain. There she passed carts and wagons and mules, carrying wine and grain and salt, the traffic on the *corso* carrying on as ever – the tradesmen to and from the city unaware of what was about to befall Turin. By some accident of geography she could no longer see the city and began to doubt her direction. She stopped by a sparkling cataract to give Flint a drink, and held her mouth under the stream. She dare not stop for long, for the urgency rose in her chest, filling her throat, choking her.

She put a foot in the stirrup. Flint was in a lather, dancing and skittering, and Kit stooped to screw her right stirrup iron tighter. Just as she bent forward a sharp crack rent the sky above her and Flint jerked back her heavy head. Instinctively Kit kept low and spurred Flint forward; she remembered well the sound of a musket, and the report of the discharge bounced about the mountains. The French must be closer than she thought.

The chance shot gave the exhausted pair the spur they needed for the next few miles. She must be in time; not just for Captain Ross but for all the men she'd fought beside. Morgan, who'd brought her a plate of pork to the hospital in Rovereto. Southcott, who'd taken her side against Sergeant Taylor when she'd rescued Bianca in the street. And not just them, but the dozens of other men she'd been privileged to call friends and brothers.

Now the domes and spires of Turin reappeared, seemingly farther away than ever. She was now in the low hills above the plains, and could see the entire vista before her – the shining citadel, the darker walls encircling it, and something else too. She could see now red coats dotted about the walls at intervals, like drops of blood on a crown of thorns.

She pulled Flint to a stop. She had already been fired on once – should she cross the river and approach the western gate? Or enter the Palatine gate directly from the exposed plain?

Then her attention was captured by a sound – a sound that her body remembered before her mind did. The loose stirrup began to sing – a barely perceptible ringing timbre, sweet with threat. The metal was vibrating, in a steady regular rhythm. Suddenly she was back in Kavanagh's alehouse, with Sean Kavanagh's sword singing the same metallic song in the bracket above her head. The sword and the stirrup both sang of the coming of an army – thousands of boots striking the ground in time, marching nearer.

She looked to the hills up to her right, and saw a dreadful sight. A skyline dark with soldiers then pouring and tumbling as the line descended at a rush, only to replaced by another rank and another.

This was not the red tide she had seen marching up the Prospect road that day, but a blue tide, closing in on Turin like a tidal wave. For a moment she could not tear her eyes away. Then she dug her spurs into Flint, hard, and rode like the devil down to the plains.

From then on it was a desperate race. The French outriders had already closed with the standing cavalry, the red coats fighting with the blue. The plain was now flooded with bluecoats, surging forward on the city, an awesome, terrible sight – so this was what forty thousand men looked like – more souls than she had ever seen gathered in one place. In despair she spurred Flint harder – she had to find new reserves of energy, to press forward; she had to find in that thundering desperate race the soldier within her, under the petticoats and layers of silk and lace. The red ribbon around the walls shredded, entangled with the blue, was trodden down. She felt sick as she saw the red horsemen fall. Not *him*, she prayed, let it not be *him*. Where, in God's name, was Marlborough?

And then a miracle: a trumpet sounded from Superga hill; and a red wave gathered at the skyline, swelled and broke. And front and centre, there was Marlborough, his blond wig streaming out behind him, thundering down the hill on his white charger. *There* was a leader, first into battle. *I require none to go where I will refuse to venture*, he'd said. *There* was a general, not a man like Ormonde who would skulk in his palace, like a cat upon his cushion. The French turned in confusion, turned and fought. The dragoons, let be, streamed inside the gates.

The French, pinned between the English and the river, fought like cornered rats; as Kit approached, some of them ran and jumped into the river, to be swept to death or safety. But she had eyes for nothing but the crumpled red coats lying on the battle-field. She urged Flint across the river, then slid from the mare's back. She stumbled forward and breathed again the scent of death. Aughrim, she thought. Mantova. Da and Richard. Once again she looked into each dead face, turned each lifeless body with her boot; a dozen, two dozen. Some faces she recognised, some she didn't.

She carried on her dreadful task as the crows wheeled overhead, as the battle raged on the other side of the river; this time there was no scavenging. Likely the searchers watched, greedy eyed, from the city, waiting for the English to retreat so they could pick at the corpses. Just one redcoat, in the far distance, bent over the bodies.

Kit straightened up, but then she saw him not probing pockets or slitting stomachs for coin, but pressing his ear to each chest searching for the greatest treasure of all – a heartbeat. And if he did not find one, gently closing unseeing eyes with his long fingers. As she watched he straightened up; only one man of her acquaintance was so tall and straight and had a fall of hair so dark. Only one man she knew wore Sean Kavanagh's sword.

She walked to him as if she strode through water. He looked up, as if he had dreamt her.

'Christiane? *Comtesse*? What do you here?' He ran to her, half angry, and gave her a little shake. '*Comtesse*? Come to shelter. Here's no place for a woman.'

She wanted to protest. But it *is*. A battlefield – why not? Every place is a place for a woman. She knew then that it was not the soldier in her that had made her ride so hard, it was the woman, Kit Kavanagh, a woman just as strong as the dragoon she had been. Women were not soft and weakened creatures fit only for decoration and gentle pastimes. They were Maura, running an alehouse while dying of a lump in her breast, they were Bianca, raising a child in a town that thought her a whore, they were Kit Kavanagh, riding into battle to save a man she thought might love her.

Unable to answer his question, unable to speak from relief, she went to him, took his warm face in her cold hands and pressed her lips to his, as hard as she could, needing to feel that he was alive, that he breathed.

For a moment, he kissed her back, just as hard. Then he drew back. 'This is folly,' he said, and she did not know whether he meant the embrace, or the place in which she'd chosen to bestow it. 'Come.' He took her by the arm, and pulled her with him, stumbling to the postern over and around the red bodies. She pulled back. 'What of the dragoons?' she asked.

'Safe inside,' he replied, 'I was looking for survivors.' He hammered on the city gate and shouted the words: *'Nemo me impune lacessit!'* The gates opened before them, and he took her hand and pulled her through them.

Inside the citadel, the scene was scarcely calmer than outside. Foot soldiers ran hither and yon, cavalry trotted back and forth, artillery carts brought ammunition to the already loaded barbican. Every coat was the red of the English or the bronze and black of the Hessians. The battle raged outside the walls, but here Kit was among friends.

In the middle of the chaos, she stood facing Captain Ross holding both of his hands as if they were at the church door. She could think of nothing sensible to say. 'You stayed alive.'

'I told you I would try. As did you.'

'And I found you.'

'As you said you would.' He shook his head, incredulous, as if waking from a dream. 'I have so much to ask you.'

She laughed, shakily. 'And I have so much to tell.'

She stepped forward to kiss him again, but felt, all of a sudden, other eyes upon her.

'Comtesse!'

She turned to see Brigadier Panton pushing through the press of red coats towards her, a Hessian guard at each shoulder.

'Comtesse Christiane Saint-Hilaire de Blossac,' he barked, 'you are under arrest, in the name of the queen, for infiltrating Her Majesty's army as a spy for the French.'

Chapter 40

Now mark what followed and what did betide . . .

'Arthur McBride' (trad.)

As Kit languished in jail, for the second time in her life, she was not, to begin with, unduly concerned. Ross was alive, she knew that Turin was safe, she knew that Marlborough was her ally. There must have been some misunderstanding. Panton had said she was a French spy; he meant, of course, a spy *for* the English *upon* the French. He of all people knew how hard she had travailed in the English cause – had he not placed her in a carriage with a dead man, and shot at her, to see her through the gates of Mantova?

She remembered the report of the musket, snapping from the mountains, as she rode to Turin the previous day. *Someone shot at her.* Her mind slowed, clockwork wreathed in treacle, sticking, juddering, gathering pace again.

Slowly, shivering with something other than cold, she pieced it all together. Ormonde, once he found her gone, had her followed by Panton, his lapdog, with instructions that she was not to reach Marlborough. But Panton had failed to catch her, and then failed to stop her reaching Turin. Now she was in company he could not kill her in cold blood, she must be silenced in another way. Ormonde always had a contingency plan. She was to be captured, her story twisted, her word tarnished. Ormonde's own words came back to her, as clear as if he was in the cell with her. *If you are discovered, I will wash my hands of you.*

By the second day she knew that no one was coming for her.

That was the day she took the diamonds from her ears and wrists and throat and pushed them deep into her bodice. She thought of Ormonde. Now the cat had woken, and stretched and tempered his claws.

On the third day the door was thrown open, and she dared to hope her salvation was at hand; but she was merely taken from her cell and bundled into a barred wagon. Her pleas to send a message to Marlborough and Ross fell on deaf ears. She shifted her bruised body and repeated her message in English and French, and even the Florentine of Mezzanotte, but to no avail – she was in the belly of the Empire now, and she had no German.

Blinking in the daylight she could see from the slabs of daylight between the bars that she was being taken from the rearward gate of the city out into the mountains. She held the bars and breathed the air, inhaling cold terror. God forbid she was being taken back to Ormonde.

The reality was no less frightening. The barred wagon stopped at a vast stone monastery. As she was dragged out of the carriage the wind whipped about her skirts, rooks rose and cawed from the numerous dark towers above, and a flurry of snow whirled about her head. As she pulled her travel cloak close she thought that it must be a year since she had huddled in the mountains above Rovereto, with her head on Ross's chest, lulled to sleep by the beating of his heart.

She was taken across the courtyard, a guard at each arm, and into a cavernous room with an altar at one end. Rows of soldiers sat upon pews as if she was to serve mass.

'Pray stand for our honoured judge; Johan Wilhelm, Elector Count Palatine of Neuberg, Duke of Ulich and Berg.'

This was not a church; this was a courtroom. She scanned the crowd for Ross, or even Marlborough. There were plenty of English and Imperial uniforms but she could not see a single dragoon. Kit set her mouth in a grim line. She had worked in an alehouse long enough. She knew a stacked deck when she saw one.

Kit sat where she was bidden between her two guards, on a raised bench in full view of the court. She watched the very grand figure of her judge enter the chamber.

The Elector Palatine was a man of middle years and middle height; he wore a silver wig which curled about his long, lupine face. An ermine robe peeped from beneath his ochre cloak, as if indeed he were a wolf beneath his clothes. He seated himself at a high bench behind a lectern, and spoke in a growling voice, his tones carrying up the pillars to the cross-ribs of the ceiling, rolling around the church like a thundercloud. Kit felt, as she had so many times in the past year, that a storm was coming – but this day the rain would rain on her alone.

'Let me see the accused.'

Kit now stood as all others sat, clasped in a bruising hold about her upper arms by her two guards. She wondered how she looked to them all – her gown travel stained, her wig disarranged, her make-up streaked.

'I see you have many names,' said the Elector. 'Christian Kavanagh. Kit Kavanagh. Kit Walsh. La Comtesse Christiane Saint-Hilaire de Blossac. How is this court to address you?'

Kit raised her chin. She was finished with aliases. When she spoke it was with her full-throated breathy Dublin brogue. 'Kit Kavanagh will do me very well, my lord.'

'You call me "Honoured Judge". Place your hand on the Bible, and swear to tell the truth in God's name.'

She put her hand on the cool leather binding of the volume that was handed to her. It could have been any book; for all she knew it was a collection of the tales Maura told her. 'I do so swear.'

'Kit Kavanagh, you stand accused of spying for the French, to the detriment of the cause of the Grand Alliance. You will hear the case against you, and then you will be given the chance to speak to the charges. You may sit.' Kit sat down, heart beating rapidly. She genuinely had no idea what to expect. How could Ormonde indict her without implicating himself? 'A true bill has been entered against you by one Brigadier Panton on behalf of the English Army. You are accused of spying on the command of the Grand Alliance on behalf of the command of the Franco-Spanish army, and to further their nefarious efforts to infiltrate and overwhelm the citadel of Turin. How do you plead?'

Kit was silent – she had never been inside a courtroom, did not know the form of words; she had not, in all of Ormonde's assiduous tuition, been prepared for an eventuality like this.

The Elector sighed faintly. 'As the defendant, you plead guilty or not guilty.'

'Not guilty, Honoured Judge.'

'The first witness shall be called.'

Kit sat down heavily on the hard pew, waiting for the inevitable. She knew who the first – perhaps the only – witness would be, but was still not wholly prepared to see him again. When Ormonde entered she hardly recognised him in his army uniform. His coat was as red as blood, his buttons gleaming gold, his facings as white as the snow that fell softly against the stained-glass windows. But he did not make the mistake of looking as if he'd had a new uniform tailored for the occasion. His breastplate bore the scars of battle, his scabbard was scuffed. He had judged it perfectly – the sybarite had stayed at home, and the general had come to court. She hated him at that moment.

Then she wondered – her greatest secret, concealed and untold, kept even from Ormonde himself, when should she reveal it? She had worn a uniform with more glory than he, she had been in the heat of battle, not watching from the crown of the hill as the Jacobites slipped on their own blood. Surely her service, in the Alliance's cause, would put her loyalty beyond doubt?

She watched Ormonde as he looked about the court, serious, unsmiling, and she kept her counsel. Her military career was the one card she held, and she'd watched enough card games in her time to know how the game was played. He would not know yet, from her lips, that she had changed his queen for a knave.

It became evident that she was not required to tell her story. Ormonde would tell it – as a nobleman his account would necessarily be deemed more believable.

'My lord duke,' began the Elector, 'the court thanks you for your testimonial.'

Ormonde inclined his head. 'I will do any office, great or small, in service of my country,' he said nobly, hand upon his sword.

Except fight like an honest man and a soldier. Kit pressed her lips together with an effort and kept her peace.

'Would it please you to tell the court where you first met the accused?'

Kit thought that she could see a chink in the clouds. What would Ormonde say now? What could he say? If he admitted that he had created the perfect spy, to undermine Marlborough and put himself at the leadership of the Alliance, then he must admit his own treachery. What confection would he create for the court? That he had taken a poor girl into his house? That he had felt sympathy for one of his countrymen, marooned in a foreign land?

'I met her at the port of Venice.' Ah, thought Kit, *then it suits you now to forget our meeting on Killcommadan Hill*. 'She was trying to board a ship to leave that state.'

'Was she successful in this endeavour?'

'No: she did not have the money for the passage.'

'How did you come to speak to her?'

'I beckoned her over to my carriage.'

'Why did you do that?'

'I was taken by her.'

'By her beauty, I suppose,' said the Elector, as one who is tone deaf might speak of music.

The men barracked and Ormonde half-smiled. 'I will not perjure myself – by her beauty, yes; but by something else.'

'What else?'

'She spoke perfect French. It seemed to me that she would be ideal for my purposes. I offered to stand her dinner in Venice, and become better acquainted with her.'

'You discovered she had a French mother?'

'Yes, Honoured Judge – from Poitiers in the Vienne.'

'Is this true?' The Elector turned at last to Kit.

There was little profit in denying it. 'Yes, my lord.'

The Elector took up his quill. 'French mother,' he said aloud, as he wrote. He looked up again, this time at Ormonde. 'And where had the accused been immediately prior to your meeting?'

'She told me she had been at Rovereto, in Trentino. She believed her husband was stationed there, and she had followed him thus far from Ireland.'

The Elector turned back to Kit. 'Did you seek your husband at Rovereto?'

'I did.'

'But you did not find him?'

Kit thought about the little house at 17 Via Ranier, and Richard sitting hand in hand with his widow, a jug of wine between them, the little white dog at their feet. Then Richard, dead and cold with the same white dog howling on his grave. What use was it now to besmirch his memory with the stain of bigamy? He was dead, let him rest. 'No,' she said. 'No sign of him.'

'So, my Lord Ormonde,' said the Elector. 'You bought the accused dinner.'

Yes, Fitzjames, thought Kit. *What will you say now? The cat is in a corner.* She felt confident for the first time. She had something to hold over him. She could tell the court that he had recruited her as a spy, to overturn Marlborough – he would be disgraced. She would be freed.

'And?' prompted the Elector.

'I made her an offer,' said Ormonde.

The soldiers jeered again, and Ormonde's face was suddenly still. *Aye, my lord*, thought Kit, *they would not treat Marlborough thus*. The Elector held up one hand. 'Am I to understand, my lord, that you solicited Fraulein Kavanagh for bedsport?'

Ormonde smiled now. 'No, my lord. I am a married man.'

'The brothels are full of married men.'

'Perhaps I should have said, then, that I am a man of honour. I made her quite a different offer.' The court was now silent – you could have heard the drop of a tailor's pin. 'I asked her to become a spy.'

Kit looked up, mouth agape.

'A spy for the Grand Alliance?'

'Of course. I was of the opinion that the war in these lands had reached a stalemate, and I decided that I would aid my noble successor the Duke of Marlborough.'

Kit snorted, and earned herself a stern look from the Elector.

'How did you plan to aid the duke?'

'By gaining certain information that would further his cause. I was always fighting the war, always in my own way.'

Kit could remain quiet no longer. She leapt to her feet. 'Lies!' she shouted. 'Ormonde was working against Marlborough all along – he wants to be commander-in-chief of the Grand Alliance and works only for Marlborough's disgrace! Ask him! Ask him!'

She was wrestled back to her bench before she could say more, and the Elector fixed his sea-grey gaze upon her. 'Fraulein Kavanagh. If you cannot keep quiet during the testimonies, then you will be returned to your cell and the trial will take place in your absence. You will have a chance to speak in good time, but by God, if you do it out of turn, I will take that chance away.'

Kit sat back, her heart racing. *Truth is the best falsehood* indeed. Ormonde had followed his own motto – he had told the truth as far as it went but with a vital twist – he had claimed to be fighting *for* Marlborough, not *against* him. And for that one crucial detail, it was his word against hers.

'Go on, my lord duke.'

'I offered Miss Kavanagh a deal – I would educate her, feed her, clothe her. She would assume the persona of a French countess, and infiltrate the French court at Mantova to discover the strategy of the Two Crowns. If she did this for me – and for Marlborough – I would free her with a fortune.'

'Is it your belief that when you first recruited Fraulein Kavanagh she had every intention of doing what you asked?'

'I believe she wanted to make her fortune. So yes, I believed she would follow my orders as far as they went.'

'And it is your belief that, after a time, she changed her allegiance from the Alliance to the Two Crowns?'

'It is.'

'In your opinion, when did that happen?'

'She left my care briefly, just after the siege of Mantova. Information from one of my deputies, Brigadier Panton, led her to believe that her husband may have died at the siege. She left my house that night, against my wishes, to seek him on the battlefield.'

'And did she find him?'

Ormonde blinked twice and looked down with respect and regret; the consummate actor. 'Regretfully, I believe she did.'

'And yet she returned to your house?'

'Yes.'

'What change had her dreadful discovery wrought within her?'

'I believe a very great change. She was out of sorts, hostile where she had once been amicable, full of malign humour.'

'And did her character remain fixed in this attitude?'

'No. She then became tractable once more, and we resumed our studies.'

'To what reason do you attribute such behaviour?'

'I believe now that that is when she had decided that she would change sides. I think she felt that her husband had been let down badly by the Alliance's strategists, and that her own journey and her travail had come to naught. I believe she decided that she would revert to her mother's blood and throw in her lot with the French.'

'When she saw her husband's body at Mantova?'

'Precisely then, my lord.'

'When she returned to your house, were you angry with her?'

'Very, my lord.'

'Did you take any action against Fraulein Kavanagh that you think may have hardened her position against you and the Alliance?'

Ormonde hesitated. *Now*, thought Kit, *now he will lie.*

'Yes, Honoured Judge. I freely admit that I beat her for her disobedience.' Ormonde looked at his beringed hands where they lay in his lap, the hands that had struck her. 'I see now that I should have treated her with kindness. I was just so angry.' He drove a fist into his palm. 'I felt she'd jeopardised an opportunity to break the dreadful stalemate in the peninsula, and that more men, men like these' – he gestured about the court – 'would perish because of her.' There was a sympathetic murmur from the assembled soldiers, and Kit felt their ranks of hostile eyes upon her.

'I think we can all sympathise with your position, my lord,' said the judge. 'You had the greater good at heart.'

'Always, Your Honour,' said Ormonde, sincerely.

'To recapitulate,' summarised the Elector, 'your contention is that you trained Fraulein Kavanagh to spy for England, and after her first visit to Mantova and the discovery of her husband's body she decided to spy for France.'

'Yes.'

'What next, my Lord Ormonde?'

'I decided to take her to the name-day ball of Prince Eugene of Savoy, at the Palazzo Reale in Turin.'

'An odd place to take someone who is a friend of France.'

'Forgive me, Honoured Judge, I was not clear – these events have only become crystallised in my reflections in recent days – if I cast my mind back over our whole acquaintance, I can only see *now* how and when the change was wrought.'

'I see. So you took Fraulein Kavanagh, in her alias as the Comtesse Christiane Saint-Hilaire de Blossac, to the prince's ball.'

'Yes.'

'Now tell me – and I want you to think very carefully about your answer – was she in your employment that night?'

Ormonde frowned slightly. 'I do not understand the question.'

'I am happy to elucidate,' said the Elector benignly. 'In fact it is my duty to ask you this question with great care for your answer will be germane to this case. Did you charge Fraulein Kavanagh, that evening of the prince's name day, to *work* for you at that ball; was she told to gather any information that night?'

'No,' replied Ormonde. 'Why would she? All those gathered were our allies; the Prince of Savoy and his noble deputies. It was, more than anything else, a practice; a mere outing for her persona, if you will.'

'Let us have clarity – *all* those gathered were allies.'

'Yes.'

Kit heard the emphasis with misgiving – where did such pointed questions tend?

'We now come to our first piece of evidence; and now I believe I must offer a little explanation to the court.' The Elector held up an object with the air of a conjuror completing his trick. 'This fan was found in your cell upon your arrest.'

Kit looked at the fan and her heart gave a leap.

'No . . . no . . . that's not right,' she protested. 'I left it in my chamber in the Palazzo Borromeo – upon the dressing table . . .'

'So you admit it is your fan?' asked the Elector.

'It is the fan that was given to me by the Duke of Ormonde.'

'Let the court understand that I have it upon the testimonial of two Imperial guards that the fan was found on the floor of the prisoner's cell.'

'It must have been planted there! I swear that . . .'

The Elector interrupted loudly, talking over her. 'You have already sworn once and once will be sufficient. Remember you are constrained to tell the truth in the name of God. Please limit yourself to answering my questions and my questions only. Look at the reverse of the fan.'

Kit's heart began to thump with dread.

'Is this your writing?'

'Yes.' It was a whisper.

'Would you please read to the court, loudly and clearly, what is written on the reverse of the fan, beginning from left to right?'

She held the fan before her face in order to read the faint pencil scrawl. In the language of fans that Ormonde had taught her, she was telling the observer that she was being watched. And she was – every eye was on her, every ear straining to hear what she would say. Her hand shook, fluttering the fan slightly. Reluctantly, but in a clear voice, she read what was written there.

'Victor Amadeus of Sardinia – Became Duke of Savoy aged nine. Remodelled the Palazzo Reale. Put down his rebellious citizens in the "salt wars". Persecuted the Vaudois (Savoyard Protestants). Married to Anne Marie d'Orléans.'

'Go on,' urged the Elector.

'Prince of Anhalt Dessau – ninth of ten children, introduced the iron ramrod to the Prussian corps, married to Anna Louise Fohse, an apothecary's daughter from Dessau.'

'What else?'

'Count Wirich Philipp von Daun – born in Vienna, son of Field Marshal Wilhelm Graf Daun, one son named Leopold.'

'That will do.'

She folded the fan slowly, handed it back to the clerk and glanced murderously at Ormonde. What a quicksilver mind he had! How clever he'd been to find the fan in her chamber and use it against her! He sat forward, feigning shock; his fingertips pressed the corner of his kerchief to his mouth, a waterfall of lace falling to his lap.

'My Lord of Ormonde, you knew of this writing?'

'No,' he said, wide eyed. 'Not a word.'

'Can you think of a reason why Miss Kavanagh would have collected information on *Alliance* generals, rather than the French?'

Ormonde spread his hands wide, one of them still clutching the lace kerchief.

'Lies!' shouted Kit. 'You tutored me like a schoolmaster and they were my subjects. I learned about the Alliance generals as a practice – you said so yourself! You said that if I was safe at Turin I would be safe in Mantova.'

The Elector brought his hand down upon his lectern. 'The accused *shall* stay silent unless directly addressed, or she shall be clapped in chains.'

Kit sat down, her heart racing, her blood boiling.

'So,' continued the Elector, 'after Fraulein Kavanagh had passed the evening in Savoy's company without detection, you thought she was ready to enter the French court.'

'I did think that, yes, Honoured Judge.'

The Elector raised his hand – a paper fluttered in the fingers. 'I have here a signed and sworn testament from the aforementioned Brigadier Panton. He writes of a visit to the Palazzo Borromeo immediately following the siege of Mantova. He says that following the failure of that siege and the heavy losses sustained by his men, he agreed to help you to feed Fraulein Kavanagh into the French court. He details the somewhat *unorthodox*' – he spoke the word fastidiously – 'method of infiltration, which involved a corpse playing the part of the Vicomte de . . .'

'Not a corpse!' Kit interjected. 'He breathed right enough before Panton killed him.'

'Fraulein Kavanagh, for the last time, there will be no interjections from the accused. Your turn will come.' Then the Elector checked himself. 'You are suggesting that an officer of the crown murdered an innocent in your cause?'

'Not in my cause, Honoured Judge. But in Ormonde's, of that I am sure.'

'It is true the unfortunate man was very lately dead, my lord,' interjected Ormonde smoothly. 'He was an English foot soldier, who had been killed by a French outrider that very morning.'

'An Englishman, you say?'

'Yes, Honoured Judge. We could not risk a French body, lest someone in the French court of Mantova recognise the man.'

'Did this poor unfortunate have a name?'

'I'm sure he did, Honoured Judge, but I never learned it.'

Kit snorted. So this man, her counterfeit husband, who had made the supreme sacrifice for Ormonde's cause, was to remain nameless.

'But Fraulein Kavanagh, you actually believe that a brigadier in the English Army would murder one of his men in cold blood?'

'I know he did,' said Kit stubbornly.

'Did you see this dreadful crime committed?'

Her colour rose. 'I, that is, not directly,' stammered Kit. 'Panton had pinned me in the carriage and was blocking the window with his back.'

'Then I suggest you do not pursue this matter further, unless you want to compound your charges by accusing the brigadier of murder?'

Kit's heart sank. Everything she had planned to say, about Panton and the corpse, had already been supplied. Ormonde and his creature had well and truly stolen the wind from her sails. She pursed her lips and shook her head.

'And now to Mantova. And here, I suppose, we must hear from the accused. Fraulein Kavanagh, is it the case that during your stay at the court there, you discovered the French plan to lay siege to the city of Turin?'

'Yes,' she said, beginning to see a way out.

'And what did you do with such information?'

'I escaped, placing myself in great danger, and conveyed the information to Ormonde, as I was instructed.'

The Elector turned to Ormonde. 'My lord?'

Kit also turned to the duke, one eyebrow raised. Now what would he say?

'She arrived at my house dressed as a coachman. But it is my opinion that the French let her go, knowing she would come to me with whatever they had schooled her to say.'

'And what did she say?'

'She told me that the French were retreating to the Po valley, under the Duc de Vendôme.'

'Lies!' she shouted. 'I told you the French were to attack Turin, and you refused to warn Marlborough, so I did it myself.'

Ormonde shook his head, sad and sorry. 'Poor lost child – she lies like the devil. It is no use, Kit.' He addressed her directly for the first time. 'We know the unhappy sequel to these events.'

'What did happen next?' asked the Elector.

'She escaped from my house again, and was next seen by Panton at the gates of Turin. The city was virtually undefended, watched only by a single regiment of dragoons. She exhorted those men to open the gates, so that the French could walk right in.'

'How would she do that?

'She is acquainted with one of the captains. His name is Ross.'

'How would she know this gentleman?'

Ormonde looked directly at Kit with his hooded eyes, of indeterminate colour, his expression eminently readable. 'She danced with him at Prince Eugene's name day.'

The Elector glanced at his clerk. 'Call the captain to appear tomorrow.'

He shuffled his papers together efficiently. 'We will conclude our business for today and take the prisoner back to custody until tomorrow, when we will hear the testimony of Captain Ross.

'My Lord of Ormonde, I see no need for us to trespass on your time tomorrow. You are excused, with the thanks of this court. Have you anything further to say?'

Ormonde turned to the judge and spread his hands, his eyes wide, his expression guileless. 'Only this, my lord: that I sheltered this poor slut, and made her into a lady. I gave her a priceless Rockingham mantua which I have never seen again. The fan, also of great price, she defaced, as you have witnessed, and,' he looked directly at her with eyes like awls, 'a coffer of diamonds disappeared on the same night as she.'

Kit froze.

The Elector nodded to her guards. 'Has anyone searched the prisoner?'

'Not yet, Honoured Judge,' answered one.

'Then do it.'

She stood, helpless, while the rough hands tore at her bodice. She had wondered, in her cell, why she had not been searched; now she knew why. Ormonde was orchestrating this – he had waited for this moment – the audience all seated and the torches lit, ready to *oooh* and *aah* from their benches and boxes at the climax of the impresario's drama. The guard's meaty fist emerged from her lacings, dripping with diamonds, and the audience gasped, just as she'd known they would.

Chapter 41

Oh me and my cousin, one Arthur McBride . . .

'Arthur McBride' (trad.)

Alone in her cell, the diamonds she'd rightfully earned returned to Ormonde's pocket, Kit thought of the following day.

Whatever came to pass she would see Ross again, even if it was to be for the last time.

She asked for some water and some tallow soap and some oil of olives – and the guard complied with a readiness that made her afraid. She took the wig from her head, put the sorry thing on the floor and shook out her own hair, caked in powder, grey as a crone's about her shoulders. She washed her face of every trace of powder and paint and patches; she would greet Ross clean and fresh faced, as he had seen her every day on the campaign – the 'pretty dragoon' who could not yet coax a beard. After an hour the guard took the candle away and even its small warmth was denied her. She let her hair dry unbound – her scalp chilling in the dank winter dungeon, the hair turning into whispering snakes as it froze. As she shivered, curled up in a ball under her travel gown and cloak, she clamped together chattering teeth and thought of Maura's stories – the princess in the dungeon, with hair of ice.

Anxious to get to court in the morning, she had been waiting since the grey dawn crept like a spectre through her barred window. She wanted nothing else but to get warm. She had tucked her shining hair into the dreadful wig, to keep her only card in her sleeve, for now; and she was grateful for the horsehair, as good as a hat. All through the night, when her cheek froze to the cold stone floor, only her heart had burned within her, holding in the deepest core of its fires the thought of Ross and the last piece she had to play, a last gambit on the chessboard.

She was taken to her seat in the hallowed courtroom, her fingers and toes thawing painfully. Almost at once she saw Ormonde seated in the crowd – so he had come to court a second time; no doubt to see her safely condemned. Then Captain Ross was called and walked into the great chamber in answer to his name; and she forgot Ormonde.

He sat opposite her – and looked about him with the confidence that had been bred into his bone. Not for him the fallen glances of Ormonde. He looked at her directly with the hostile blank stare of a raptor, as if he did not know her. *Dear God*, thought Kit, *what have they told him of me?*

In all other respects he was absolutely correct – his uniform neat, his dark hair dressed and tied, his cheek clean shaven. With a strange sense of pride, she thought as she had before that he was any man's equal; and even the Elector seemed to detect his quality, asking for his name and his oath with something akin to deference. Kit could hear the familiar cadences of her captain's voice, but his words were indistinct to her – he might have been speaking another language for at his side – she took a breath – hung her father's sword. The blade gave her courage.

'Captain Ross,' the Elector began. 'Do you know this lady?'

Let him not be another St Peter. 'Yes.' Kit felt an irrational relief.

'Where did you first see her?'

At the lighthouse in Genova, thought Kit. *He pushed me into the ocean because I stank like a civet after a fortnight at sea.*

'I met her at the Palazzo Reale in Turin, at the name day of Prince Eugene of Savoy.'

'And how much time did you spend in each other's company?'

'Perhaps an hour? No more.'

'And how did you spend this hour?'

'As most guests at a ball spend their time. We had a conversation of no consequence and we danced.'

'How did she introduce herself?'

'As a French countess. I know now, of course, that that was not true.' His blue gaze went through her like a sword.

'You said your conversation was of no consequence.'

'Light acquaintances in company talk of small things.'

'Did you?'

The captain shifted in his chair. 'No.'

'So you spoke of weighty matters?'

'Yes. She told me she had lost her husband.'

'So she elicited your sympathy.'

'I suppose she did, yes.'

'Did she ask you, at any point, about military strategy?'

'No.'

'And if she did not ask, what did you tell?'

A silence.

'Captain. Did you say anything to the accused about the strategy of the Grand Alliance?'

'No.'

'Did you talk of military matters at all?'

'Yes.'

Kit sat a little straighter, a chill travelling down her spine. The Elector's questions had taken a dangerous turn, but not only for her; she now feared for Ross. She prayed, now, that he would lie – but she knew he would not – it was not in his nature, any more than you could ask a bird to swim or a fish to fly.

'I expressed my discontent with certain elements of the Alliance command.'

'Which particulars?'

Captain Ross cleared his throat, and looked about him at the gathered uniforms. 'I expressed my . . . disquiet that we were being asked to make repeated sorties to besieged cities, incurring vast Alliance losses, only to lose the land gained the very next day. I also strongly deprecated the vast expense of the prince's ball, when that very week I had been told that we could not purchase new flints for our muskets, as the army was out of funds. I lost a good man because of it.' A murmur of agreement ebbed and flowed around the court from the redcoats. 'We also spoke of a man of mine who had disappeared before Mantova, leaving me his sword.'

'Deserted?'

'I suppose you could call it that.'

'Wouldn't you?'

'No.'

Kit's heart warmed at this single syllable of denial. He thought that there was still some honour, then, in Kit Walsh.

'Anything else?'

'Yes. We spoke of love.'

'*Did* you.'

'Not the love of a man and a woman – that is, we spoke of such things a little; but mostly we treated on the love between soldiers, of men of honour. The love that means you will defend a fellow of your regiment to your last breath, and put yourself in harm's way every day for one of your colour.'

Kit watched the faces about him, sober, serious, entranced, and patently on his side. She saw then that Ross had the qualities of Marlborough – men would follow him anywhere, just as she had.

'And how did the "countess" react to your opinions about the army?'

'She was sympathetic to my views.'

'Do you think she may have felt, from the opinions that you expressed, that she had found an ally? That you might be induced to change sides?'

'I would refute any such suggestion with my dying breath,' said Ross, with some heat.

'But you accept that expressing such views about your superiors is insubordination.'

Ross sat a little straighter. 'I have followed every order given me to the letter, whatever my private feelings.' And Kit remembered, when he had visited her the night before her flogging. *I have never wanted to disobey an order until this one.* 'I can only account for such a slip by saying that I had drunk overmuch of the prince's wine; the wine that was bought in place of a score of matchlocks for the dragoon's muskets. And I'll wager that I am not the first man to have his tongue loosened by a beautiful woman.' Kit hugged the word 'beautiful' to her, to keep her warm.

'Indeed,' said the Elector drily. 'And tell me, Captain, how did you take your leave of the countess?'

'I expressed my resolution to stay alive, and she promised to do likewise.'

'Did that strike you as odd?'

Ross drew his dark brows together. 'In what sense?'

'Well, you are a serving soldier; you live your life on the battlefield. She is a countess, her life is lived in salons and theatres. Did her saying so not give you the notion that perhaps she had a more dangerous task at hand than to take tea and attend the play?'

Captain Ross shook his head. 'It never crossed my mind.'

'Did you form the impression, from that leave-taking, that you would meet each other again?'

'I must say that I did.'

'Hoped?'

'Yes.'

'And you did see her again, did you not?'

'Yes.'

'Captain Ross, would you please tell the court about the second time you met the accused.'

Ross shifted in his chair. 'It was in very different circumstances. It was at the Palatine gate at the city of Turin, at the commencement of the French siege. The dragoons were defending the gates alone, and had repelled the outriders, incurring some loss of life. Before the greater part of the French forces could fall upon us, my Lord of Marlborough descended from the hills and took their rearguard, drawing the French fire and attack. The forces turned upon him, and we were able to withdraw through the gates and secure the city, along with the Hessian forces who had entered the city from the rear.'

'But you were on the battlefield when the accused met you?'

'I was.'

'Why were you there, at great danger to your person? Your place, surely, was within the walls of the city with what remained of your men. I put it to you, Captain, that you were waiting at the gate for the countess – you knew she would be there because you had arranged a rendezvous.'

'No!' Kit and Ross exclaimed the word together, caught each other's eye, and uncomfortably looked away. 'No,' Ross went on, moderating his tone with a visible effort. 'I had gone out again to turn the bodies and look for survivors.'

'You did not wish to leave such an office to the seekers, who are paid to carry out this grim task?'

'No. They are my men, until their last breath.'

The Elector stroked his long nose. 'A manifestation, no doubt, of that brotherly love of which you spoke.'

'Yes.'

Again, a murmur of approval rippled about the court. *They love him*, she thought. *They hate me, but they love him. They will not let him be taken in irons.*

'And then you met the accused.'

'Yes.'

'Was she riding or on foot?'

'She was on foot. I saw no horse.'

'So it might be reasonable to assume that she had arrived with the French cohorts?'

'I always find assumptions to be dangerous.'

'Answer the question.'

'She might, I suppose.'

'And how did she greet you?'

For the first time, he dropped his blue gaze. 'She embraced me.'

There was a sensation about the court.

'How exactly?'

'She . . .' He shifted again, sighed. 'She kissed me on the lips.'

The men cheered, with as much approval as they had disapproved of Ormonde.

The Elector quelled his court with a look. 'A very familiar greeting, surely, for someone whom you had met but once before? Or were you better acquainted than you own?'

Ross's face went suddenly still. 'What are you suggesting?'

'*I* ask the questions, Captain Ross,' said the Elector, all courtesy gone. 'What happened after she greeted you in this way?'

'I told her a battlefield was no place for a woman, and led her to safety.'

'You led her through the *gate*.'

'Yes.'

Kit went cold – if she could sense the danger, could not Ross?

'And how did you gain ingress?' asked the Elector grimly.

'I spoke the password.'

'Which was?'

Ross looked about him. 'It cannot matter now. It was the dragoon's motto – *Nemo me impune lacessit* – No one touches me with impunity.'

The Elector clasped his hands together with great care and placed them on the lectern. He spoke clearly and distinctly. 'Captain

Ross. Let me be absolutely clear. You met a woman you believed to be a French countess, on a battlefield in the middle of a French attack. She embraced you, and in return you led her through the city gates?'

There was silence in the chamber. When Ross spoke, he spoke low. 'Yes.'

'Captain Ross,' said the Elector. 'I put it to you that you sold Turin to the French for the price of a kiss, and if Brigadier Panton had not had the presence of mind to arrest this woman, she would have opened the gates that night to a stealth attack from French reinforcements. By dawn they would have taken the city and every dragoon and Hessian would have been dead in their beds.'

Ross looked ashen.

'At worst, you were this woman's accomplice. At best, you were her dupe. In either case, the consequences for you will be dire.' He gestured to his sentries. 'Put him in irons.'

Kit stood. 'No.'

'Fraulein . . .'

'No! I must be heard.'

'And shall in time.'

'Now.'

'Very well,' said the Elector testily. 'Let us hear you. What signals had you planned to bring the French forces to Turin once the city was sleeping? What torches would you light in the windows, what pennants would you fly from the battlements? What blades had you sharpened for the throats of the unwitting sentries at the postern?'

'I made no such plans!'

'You bewitched this foolish captain into giving you the password.'

'I knew it already!' protested Kit.

'Do not try to protect your *amour* – it does you little credit.'

'I am no *amour* of hers,' protested Ross.

'Come, come, man! She bewitched you – why else would you take her through the gates with you?'

'Was I to leave her on the battlefield?'

'Why not?' cried the Elector. 'She was an enemy and an alien. Why take such a person through the gates?'

'Because you do not leave a man behind!' It was a shout.

There was total silence in the court. Precisely, carefully, the Elector steepled his hands together, fingertip to fingertip. He spoke softly and dangerously. 'But Captain,' he said. 'We do not speak of a man. The *comtesse* was not one of your dragoons, to whom you are so devoted, of whom you spoke so eloquently in terms of brotherly love. So I ask you again; why did you take her though the gates of Turin?'

Ross pushed the balls of his palms into his eyes. 'I do not know,' he said, low voiced, despairing. 'I do not know why I took her through the gates.'

'I do,' said Kit into the silence, gentle and clear. She stood up tall and straight; straight as a soldier on parade. 'He let me in because he knows me.'

Slowly, slowly, Ross took his hands away from his eyes, and looked up at her.

'That is the court's very contention,' said the Elector, exasperated. 'Are you admitting, then, that he plotted with you?'

'No, not that. He aided an old friend – I have known him for a full year.'

A gasp whispered around the assembly.

'Explain yourself. This plot between you has been a device of long standing?'

'No,' said Kit. 'He was and is the most loyal of the queen's soldiers.' She looked Captain Ross in the eyes. 'And so, once, was I.'

She slid the matted wig from her and shook out her red hair so it fell about her face. She spoke to him in her strong Dublin brogue, breathy and low, just as she'd done when she had been his dragoon. 'Don't you know me, Captain Ross? I am the brother that you lost. And that is my father's blade that you wear. I am Sergeant Kit Walsh.'

He looked at her, the colour draining from his face, his eyes burning blue.

'Fraulein Kavanagh, what are you saying?'

'I am saying,' said Kit clearly and loudly, 'that I am as loyal to the Grand Alliance as any man here. I fought for a year as a dragoon in the Royal Scots Greys.'

There was another gasp about the room, and a rising tide of chatter. She stared defiantly at Ormonde – he gazed at her from beneath his hooded lids, his face curiously immobile. One man in the place, then, believed her.

'Fraulein Kavanagh,' bellowed the Elector over the commotion, 'I must remind you where you are. This is the Imperial court, held under the aegis of Prince Eugene of Savoy. And before that, this place was a house of God. You have placed your hand upon the Bible and sworn to tell the truth in his name. It is true, you are in dire straits, but your dishonesties have taken us to the realms of fantasy.'

He might as well not have spoken. She fixed her eyes upon Ross. She spoke to the captain directly.

'Do you remember now? I fought alongside you at the Abbey of San Columbano, where the French fought in monks' clothing. I cut the warning bell from the rope and you gave me a chalice. I buried the babes with you in the valley below. I froze with you in the mountains of the Adige, and we slept cheek by jowl.' Rising tears tightened her throat. 'You told me what we were fighting for. You drew a boot in the mud and told me about the countries of Europe. You told me everywhere has a horizon, and you had to ride for it before the enemy. Then I took a musket ball in the hip at Luzzara. I was decorated by Marlborough himself, given five pistoles by his own hand.' Ross seemed to be in a waking dream, he did not respond at all. Kit turned to the Elector in appeal. 'Marlborough – Marlborough knows me. I rode straight from the Palazzo Borromeo to warn him of the French attack. Marlborough ordered a fast-rider to warn the dragoons.' She felt it would not be tactful, in this company, to tell of the Prince of Savoy's plan to leave the dragoons to be taken by surprise. 'I took it upon myself to be Marlborough's fast-rider. I rode to warn the dragoons,' her voice cracked at last, 'for they are my regiment.' She looked at Ross, who was still and pale, his eyes as blank as a statue's. 'I was doing my commanders' bidding, as I always have. My loyalty to the Grand Alliance is beyond question. Marlborough saw me, talked with me on Superga hill, he will vouch for me if the captain will not.' She could not keep the reproach from her voice.

The Elector tapped his fingers on his lectern, impatiently. 'The Duke of Marlborough,' he said in carefully measured tones, 'is currently mobilising his troops for the Low Countries. Here the battle may be over, but the war is yet to be won, and is waged on many fronts.'

'Now the battle is over?' echoed Kit, in a dream – repeating without understanding; Ormonde's parrot.

'Yes, over,' said the Elector with relish. 'Your compatriots have withdrawn from the peninsula, returned to France and left you behind.'

She blinked as she digested this. So the stalemate had been broken, the chess pieces returned to the box for now. But they were to be taken out again, and dusted off, and repositioned on the board for another game elsewhere.

'I see this is news to you. They have abandoned their tool. It would behove you now to confess, then the court might be merciful and grant you a quick death.' Only then did she understand the true seriousness of her situation. She saw Ross, even in his stupor, flinch at the word 'death' and turned back to him in a final desperate plea. 'At Cremona . . .' she paused, took a breath, 'at Cremona, when you took a musket ball of your own, I carried you beneath the aqueduct. Do you remember now? I sang to you then a certain song . . .' Because she could never separate words from music, and because the rhymes had been marching through her head all night, she sang into the silent courtroom. Every limb was stilled, every tongue silenced, even the snow fell noiselessly outside, loath to break the spell. Her voice rang around the old stones, as the monks' voices must have in days gone. Her voice, sweet as a bell's chime, singing the secular little tune, for that moment as glorious and godly as any plainsong:

> Oh me and my cousin, one Arthur McBride
> As we went a walkin' down by the seaside
> Now mark what followed and what did betide
> It being on Christmas morning . . .

As she sang Ross stood, as if he had woken from his dream, his eyes holding hers. It was working. She sang on, joyfully, giving the simple little ditty her all. Ross's skin was as grey as a spectre's. His mouth was working, and she ceased her song to hear him. No sound came, until he mumbled out; 'Honoured Judge, may I be excused for a time?'

The Elector nodded, and Ross rose and descended from the stand, not once looking at Kit.

'But Captain . . .'

Ross stopped but did not turn.

'Hold yourself in readiness,' said the Elector. 'You will have charges of your own to answer.'

Ross did not reply, but, back straight as a ramrod, walked from the room.

Kit swallowed cold bile, a chill stone of disappointment sitting in her stomach, sickening her. How could he not know her? She could not be so changed. She was still Kit under the skin; she had given Ross proof enough, God knew, of their acquaintance – she had told him things that no other living soul would know. Granted, other dragoons might have told her of the battle in the abbey or the bundling at night, but at Cremona they had been alone, and no other man alive had heard her sing 'Arthur McBride'.

She swallowed back tears. What chance had she now? She had revealed herself at last, and for what? Ross had not come to her rescue. At least Ormonde had acknowledged their acquaintance, for all his lies; it had been Ross who had not.

When he was gone, the Elector turned to her.

'Now, let us get to the bottom of this fantasy. Are you actually suggesting that you were a soldier in the queen's army?'

Kit was suddenly deathly tired. There seemed little point in persisting with this examination. 'Yes, Honoured Judge. For over a year and four campaigns.'

'Disguised as a man.'

'Yes.'

Now the Elector rubbed his weary eyes with the pads of his fingers. 'I must own that your story seems unbelievable. Have you anyone who can corroborate your story?'

Her eyes stung. The very man that could have done it had just walked out of the door.

'How did you assume this new identity?'

'I enlisted in Dublin, and was issued a uniform.'

'But how was it possible to manage such a deception? To live among men?'

She shrugged – her male gestures returning. 'We were never without clothes along the road. And I was careful. I bought a false prick.'

There was laughter from the throng.

'A what?'

'A false prick, wrought of silver.'

'Wherever did you find such a thing?'

'I bought it in Genova.' Not for worlds would she give up the name of Maria van Lommen.

'And do you still have this strange appendage? It might constitute evidence in your defence.'

'No. It was taken from me in hospital – when I took my injury at Luzzara.'

Then it dawned upon her. She struck the carved arm of her chair sharply. 'There *is* one who can vouch for the truth of what I say. He knows I fought as a dragoon, for it was he who discovered I was a woman.'

'Who is this person?'

She took a deep breath. 'Doctor Atticus Lambe, army surgeon to the Scots Grey Dragoons.' Atticus Lambe. He had always wanted to expose her. Well, now he had his chance.

The Elector nodded. 'Very well.' He leaned heavily on his lectern. 'I will be candid with you, Fraulein Kavanagh. The complexion of this trial has changed somewhat following your revelations. It is up to you to prove the veracity of your story, for what is now on trial here is your loyalty to the Alliance's cause.' He called for his sentinel, and the man entered the room with a rapid step, fresh snow upon his shoulders, ruddy of cheek, short of breath. He looked agitated.

'Call Doctor Atticus Lambe of the Scots Greys to appear on the morrow.'

'Yes, Honoured Judge. But, my lord?'

'Yes?'

'There is something more.'

'Well?'

'Captain Ross has absconded.'

Chapter 42

I'll cut off your heads in the morning . . .

'Arthur McBride' (trad.)

Atticus Lambe trained his pale grey eyes on Kit. She could see he knew her at once.

'I have never seen her before in my life.'

'Are you sure?' asked the Elector.

'I am confident of it, Honoured Judge.'

'Bear in mind, if you will, that she is now in woman's attire. This female claims that she fought with the dragoons, dressed as a man.'

'That is not possible, Honoured Judge.'

'Not?'

'In my medical opinion? No.'

'Could you tell the court why?'

Atticus Lambe adjusted his pince-nez on his nose, his eyes never leaving Kit. 'They have not the physical strength nor the mental acuity for the task. Their limbs are soft and weak, their humours erratic. They are plagued by (saving your honourable presence) monthly discharges of their bodily fluids. The woman's state at war would be insupportable.' This speech was directed straight at Kit, and the surgeon delivered every word like a blow.

Kit gazed at him with contempt; the Elector inclined his head. 'So much for the general objections; now to the specific. The accused claims that she was treated by you following the Battle of Luzzara, in the fortress of Riva Garda.'

'I did indeed establish my field hospital in that barbican, but anyone may have known that.'

'It was common knowledge?'

'Yes.'

'The accused maintained that, in the person of Kit Walsh, she was injured in the hip, and you were obliged to operate upon her person, thus revealing her – ahem – woman's parts.'

Atticus Lambe laughed, a sound she had never heard. 'Ridiculous.'

'Did you treat a patient by the name of Kit Walsh?'

'Yes. He was a redhead, but that is as far as the resemblance goes. He took a musket ball at Luzzara. A peevish fellow and a coward; I cured him only for him to desert shortly afterward.'

Kit could not hear herself so described. 'I escaped not through cowardice, but a certain knowledge that if I were stripped for the lash my sex would be revealed.'

The Elector waved away her interruption. 'And this Walsh. He could not have been the accused, concealing her sex? She spoke of a false phallus; did you ever see such a thing in Walsh's possession?'

'Never. And, if I may add, I have never heard of such a thing in all my years as a doctor. Of necessity I saw Walsh without clothes, for I had to lay him open; and I can assure you,' the pale eyes turned upon Kit again with undisguised malice, 'he was made as all men are made.'

'Then how do you account for the assertions made by the accused? That she was this man Walsh?'

'Medically, I would say she is suffering from some hysterical episode – to which females are prone – leading to a delusion of the middle brain. In practical terms I would say that she happened upon Walsh somewhere on the road following his flight; befriended him, perhaps seduced him, learned his story, and now uses his identity to mitigate her crimes.'

Kit threw up her hands and laughed hopelessly, slapping her palms smartly back down on her knees.

The Elector turned to her, his iron-grey brows raised to join his wig. 'Something amuses you?'

'To be accused in my female persona of seducing myself as a male is singular indeed.'

'I am much surprised at your mirth, for the situation in which you find yourself is calamitous. The good doctor does not know you. The captain did not know you. Can you produce any other officers that can vouch for you?'

She could not. The surgeon had confounded her at last. He himself could not take her life, but if the Empire condemned her, her blood would not fall upon his hands. Yes, Lambe had had his revenge – she had served it to him as surely as he had dined on her plate of pork.

The pig – the pork. 'Taylor,' she blurted. 'Sergeant Taylor. He would know me. He hated me, but he would know me.'

The Elector sighed. 'Then I suppose we must call him.'

'Honoured Judge?' Atticus Lambe spoke, diffidently. 'If I may?'

'Yes, Doctor Lambe?'

'I regret to inform you that Sergeant Taylor of the Scots Greys is dead, by his own hand.'

'I see.'

'He lost an eye in a knife fight with Private Walsh, and later lost the use of his arm in a duel with the same miscreant. Such a man is no more use in a battle than a woman.' Lambe flashed a pale glance at Kit. 'Fighting was his life, and once he could do it no more he made an end. He broke into my store of laudanum, and drank his last draught.'

Kit glared at Lambe. '*Broke into your store of laudanum*,' she said, low and scornful. 'Indeed, for you were jealous of your precious drug. I'll swear you locked it up good and tight. You would never let so much as a jorum go without purpose. I've no doubt that if Taylor took such a draught it was you who prescribed it to him, aye, and helped him drink it down.'

'Be silent!' said the Elector. 'Such heinous accusations do nothing to aid you, but rather prove your guilt. Thank you, Doctor. We will trespass on your precious time no further.'

Lambe stalked from the room like a man in a hurry, but not before he could look to Ormonde in the onlookers and give a tiny, almost imperceptible nod.

'And here we must make an end,' said the Elector. 'Kit Kavanagh, have you anything to say?'

She looked at Ormonde too. 'I am guilty of mistaking a fiend for an angel, nothing more.'

'Unhappily, this court cannot agree. I find you guilty of spying upon the commanders of the Grand Alliance on behalf of the Franco-Spanish command of the Two Crowns.' The Elector flattened his hands upon the lectern, and pushed himself to a standing position. The gathered soldiers, as one, stood with him.

'The court is adjourned, and will reconvene tomorrow for sentencing. Take the prisoner down.'

A priest came to hear her final confession. He introduced himself as Father Bonifacio, and was cheerful and sanguine about her impending death. He spoke of her hanging with palpable envy, his face shining with devotion, clearly piqued that she would beat him to paradise. 'You are almost as high as heaven here,' he said, in heavily accented English. 'So not too far to go. And this abbey of San Michele was built by an archangel.' He spoke the words with a beatific smile.

Kit said nothing. 'The archangel Michael brought the materials up the mountain himself, on his great wings.' He fussed in his robes, bringing out his Bible. 'So, there's a good chance that the angels may save you. All is not lost – if you make your confession and your peace with God the angels will carry you heavenward. Now.' He sat opposite her. 'I'm sure you have done some good, and your good deeds God knows already. Now is the time to speak of the evil you have done to others – think of it as balancing a ledger. We are speaking now of your debts to mankind.' Dully, she raised her head at last; all she could think of in the debtors' column was the death of Sergeant Taylor. She remembered that when she'd enlisted, right at the beginning of her journey, her recruiting officer had asked her, in lieu of training, *Have you two arms and two legs and two eyes in your head?* When she'd taken Taylor's eye, albeit in self-defence, and lost him the use of his arm in their duel, she had condemned him to ruination and despair. It was, at that moment, the only thing for which she was truly sorry. She spoke of Taylor's fate to the priest, who listened and nodded and pronounced the Benedicite over her with a profound air of disappointment. He'd hoped, she was sure, for more meaty sins.

When the priest had gone, leaving his Bible for her to read in her last hours, she was given a candle, and a fine cut of meat. She could not eat the meal. She leafed through the pages of the Bible and turned to the chapter of the babes. *'The fruit of the womb is a reward. Like arrows in the hand of a warrior, so are the children of one's youth. How blessed is the man whose quiver is full of them; they will not be ashamed when they speak with their enemies in the gate.'* She read the verses over, remembering Ross saying them when they had buried the newborns in the valley – one of the episodes in their shared life that Ross did not, or would not, remember. He had denied her like St Peter.

She shut the book. God would not send his angels to save her. She had ignored him since she had left behind her mass-going Dublin days. He would not hear her now. Instead she prayed to God's mother, conjuring Mary in her mind. She did not picture Her in her dimensional plaster incarnations, nor her flat portrayals on the church walls, thin as paper and haloed in gold. She prayed instead to the Madonna della Fortuna, carved of wood and cleft from a ship, as much a fraud as she was herself.

Chapter 43

And so to conclude and to finish disputes . . .

'Arthur McBride' (trad.)

Kit watched her last sunrise from the window of her high tower. It was fitting that it should be the most beautiful she had ever seen. The craggy mountains were painted rose-gold, from peaks to valleys; the snows smoked on their peaks as if they were the fiery mountains of the south. The cultivated lands below, cross-hatched by the plough, and the wild lands with the tares, showed a thousand colours of earth like the patchwork of a quilt. No: the squares of a chessboard. Everywhere has a horizon, Ross had said. This was the last one she would see.

She wore her red hair loose, and it tumbled now to her shoulder-blades. She wished she had a soldier coat, for as a soldier she could face what was to come – as a woman, she was not sure.

At the hour of nine they came for her and she hoped, as she descended following the bronze and black backs of the Imperial guards, that the Elector would be merciful – would commute her sentence to imprisonment or labour. But as she crossed the courtyard she saw the scaffold – three wooden steps up to a gibbet and a black looped noose swinging gently in the wind. The snow whirled about the rope, around and through the noose. The wind whipped her red hair about her face, the only colour in the place.

She entered the crypt and a hush descended on the press of redcoats that had gathered there. Billeted on the monastery, with little to do until they descended upon the Netherlands, they had gathered here every day as if this were the playhouse. But this drama was short – to Kit, now that her heartbeats were finite, everything happened so fast. The Elector entered, sat at his lectern, placed a black cap on his head and extinguished all hope.

'Kit Kavanagh,' said the Elector. 'You are sentenced to death by hanging. You shall be taken from here to the courtyard of the Sacra San Michele above, where you will be executed in the eyes of the army and in the name of the Prince of Savoy. Have you anything to say?'

She had so much to say, but there seemed little point in any of it. There had been so many words spoken in this room and most of them falsehoods. That a house of God should play host to such lies after centuries of truths spoken under these vaults seemed, somehow, the greatest tragedy of all. So she raised her head, and spoke her own family motto to the court. 'Truth relies on its own arms,' she said. She looked at the blank, uncomprehending faces, searching among them for Ormonde; but like the Devil himself, he had vanished. So she would die here, in this infernal, holy place, far from home, with not one familiar face to turn away in sorrow as the rope snapped taut and the noose tightened. She closed her eyes in despair.

Just then the great doors cracked open, banging back against the stone pillars, and an avenging angel rode through them on a horse of steel grey. The horse reared in a maelstrom of white snowflakes that had blown in from the courtyard. The archangel wore a cowled cloak, and she recognised the horse before the figure. It was Flint. Then the angel threw back his hood – it was Captain Ross, wearing the scarlet of the Scots Grey Dragoons.

Kit was dreaming, or dying, she was hanged already and swung from the noose, her breath stolen and her eyes changed. Ross slid from the horse and dropped the reins, and Flint trotted straight to Kit and laid her heavy head on her mistress's shoulder, nuzzling her ears and mouthing at her bodice. Flint, whom she'd left on the battlefield, whom she'd meant to collect but was prevented by her arrest, had stayed faithful to the end.

'I found her wandering outside the gates of Turin, when I ran from you like a coward the other day,' said the captain. 'Her presence confirmed to me what I already knew in my heart, that you were who you claimed to be.'

Kit stroked the mare's nose. '*She* knows me.'

'She has been the most faithful friend of all.' Ross took her hands, drew her to her feet. 'You are right to chastise me,' he said, 'for this dumb beast knew all along what I could not acknowledge. I knew the truth of what you said here; in some way I always knew you, even when we met at the ball: the same eyes, the same voice. I just could not believe that the man who was my brother could inhabit the person of the only woman to draw my eye since my wife.' He raised one hand to her cheek. 'I'd thought I could never feel again until I came to Genova and knocked you into the sea.' He smiled. 'Many nights along the road with you I stayed awake, worrying I'd caught Lambe's complaint. You see, I'd fallen in love with Kit Walsh.'

She laid her hand over his, on her cheek. 'But I am Kit Walsh.' She smiled.

'Yes,' he said. 'And, man or woman, I cannot be without you again.' He gestured to the bench. 'But even these shallow fools divined my affection. I knew I could not be the only witness to vouch for Kit Walsh. I needed to bring another testimonial.'

She raised her brows. 'Flint?'

Ross smiled and shouted a command. Through the open portal, in formation, marched a regiment of foot. Kit looked closer; they were dragoons without mounts. Her hands flew to her mouth as she recognised each face: Southcott, Hall, Book, Wareham, Swinney, Rolf, Noyes, Crook, Page, Dallenger, Kennedy, Lancaster, Farrant, Gibson, Laverack and Morgan.

'They would all come,' said Ross, 'and all of them have broken their charge. Once a dragoon, always a dragoon. I told them of the good offices you'd done, riding to save us. They are here to swear to your identity.' He turned to the men. 'Regiment, present to Sergeant Walsh.'

He raised his arm.

'We swear.' They shouted as one.

'What is the meaning of this?' The Elector rose to his feet. 'Captain Ross, you are a wanted man; your testimony is unreliable. And furthermore, not one of these men who claim to know the accused is an officer, so the Imperial court cannot accept their testimony.'

'Hold, Honoured Judge,' said Ross, in the voice of command she remembered so well. 'There is one who will yet be heard, one who is neither foot soldier nor cavalry.'

The Elector, apoplectic, glared at Flint. 'Am I to hear the testimony of a *mare*? You shame these proceedings, Captain. Take that animal out of here. I will not hear you. The court does not recognise a horse.'

'Perhaps the court will recognise *me*.'

There on the threshold, filling the doorway, stood the Duke of Marlborough. A hurrah went up, and Kit realised she had never once seen him when he was not accompanied by cheers – he spent his life with applause ringing in his ears. He wore a golden cloak over ermine and a half-armour of gold, and on a wig so white that the snowflakes did not show he wore a golden tricorn. He was magnificent.

He strode to the lectern, stripping off his gloves a finger at a time. He went straight to the bookman and slapped his hand on the Bible.

The Elector, utterly confounded, slipped his wig from his head in befuddlement, to reveal a shaven grey pelt. The clerk dropped his quill with an ugly splatter.

'You may take down my testimony – Clerk, pick up your pen. Quills may do as much harm as swords. You may as well rend your other pages. Time for the truth.' He winked at the gallery, preparing them for a jest. 'From the horse's mouth, what?'

It took less than a ring of bells to free Kit. Marlborough detailed the whole of their acquaintance in his booming tones, and the poor clerk had to scratch like a housecat to keep up. Flint, happy to be near her mistress, stood as still as if she was on parade, snorting occasionally to punctuate the duke's testimony. When he'd had enough, the duke rose, made a brief nod to the Elector and held out his gloved hand. 'Come along, Kit. I am sure Captain Ross will convey you safe.'

She took Marlborough's hand, and let him lead her out to the courtyard, where Ross and Flint waited for her. The dragoons had not been idle – they were busy dismantling the scaffold and smashing it to matchwood. Marlborough put Kit's hand in Ross's, and called his servant. His man helped the duke to mount his white charger, but before he spurred his horse Marlborough reached into his saddlebag. 'We met a knave along the way, masquerading as the Duke of Ormonde. It transpired that he'd neglected to settle his bills with you. But between myself and the good captain here, we persuaded him to pay the reckoning.' And he threw down a glittering handful of diamonds in a graceful arc, falling upon her like the snow. She caught the stones in her skirts like a milkmaid and laughed up at him.

'If you speed your nuptials,' said the duke, 'I will officiate at the wedding.'

'Wedding?' Kit asked, a laugh bubbling through the word.

'Well? There is no profit in delay, is there?' He pointed at Ross. 'I shall need a man like this back by my side soon, so take your honey month while you may.' He smiled, doffed his gold tricorn and rode through the great gate.

Kit looked at Ross shyly. He looked at her hands. 'You once said your wedding ring was your most prized possession.'

'That was a lie,' she said. 'It was base metal – a false ring for a false husband, worn by a false countess. But I swear I will never lie to you again.'

'I have nothing to give you, base or otherwise.'

'We will have a ring wrought in Genova,' she said, smiling to herself. 'I know a silversmith there.'

'But for now . . .' He plucked a strand from Flint's mane and twisted the wiry hair about her first finger. She looked at it as if it was made of diamonds too. 'But I do have something to give you, or rather, to return.' Ross took Sean Kavanagh's sword from his sheath with a metallic ring. She held it to the light – old-fashioned in style, heavy in the hand, but the blade still keen.

'You once told me it was your dearest possession,' she said.

'That was the truth.'

She handed the blade to him. 'Then take it back again.'

'But it is yours.'

'Ours,' she corrected. 'We will hang it over our hearth.'

He smiled and handed her up on to Flint's back, vaulting up behind her. He gathered the reins.

'No,' she said, turning her head to smile at him. 'She knows me. I'll take the reins.'

Ross returned the smile, handed over the reins and took her about the waist.

'Hold on tight,' said Kit.

Chapter 44

And always lives happy and charming . . .

'Arthur McBride' (trad.)

Kit and Ross were to be married the next day on Superga hill, before the little marble chapel.

The snow had left off, and the sun shone, and Turin, stronghold of the Empire, shone below.

The bride had been given the use of the Duke of Marlborough's own tent in which to ready herself. She had no fresh linens, not even a shirt or a sheet to make a shift. She wore the tattered and soiled travel gown she'd worn since she'd fled from Ormonde, made worse for wear by her days spent on the road and nights spent in a cell. Her wig was long gone – she had washed her face and hands in Marlborough's ewer, had rinsed her hair and combed it as best she could with her fingers, but could do not more. She had her diamonds but when she fastened them in her ears and wrists with the help of the small vanity glass in Marlborough's pavilion, they looked ridiculous next to the shabby gown. 'Like pearls in a pigpen,' she said to her reflection. She took them off again. Kit studied herself. Her face was very pale, her freckles very pronounced, her eyes very green. She looked, with her wild red hair and shabby gown, like a lunatic woman wandering abroad. She shook her head at her reflection. How could Ross take her thus?

She paced, biting her lip, waiting for her summons as if she awaited the battle bugle. When Ross came to fetch her, she ignored the large parcel in his arms and launched herself on him.

'Is it right?' she asked. 'I am not long widowed. Everyone knows my story now. Everyone knows I came to seek a different husband and he is not long cold. Will they not say that the cow that lows most after her calf goes soonest to bull?'

He held her cheek in his hand. 'Not long widowed,' he said, 'but your husband has been gone from you a long time.'

She kissed the hand. It was true. Richard, her Richard from Kavanagh's, had not been hers for some years. He belonged to the widow from Rovereto; he was hers to mourn.

'That is the past. Time for the future.' He handed her the bundle that he held, wrapped in brown paper and string, and she nearly buckled under the weight of it. She tore off the paper to reveal a bale of red cloth. She shook it out; it was not a uniform, but a gown. It was dragoon red and trimmed with snowy white fur. There was a tricorn too, trimmed with a plume of white feathers, fastened with the dragoon cap badge of the eagle and laurel. Ross pointed to the full skirts. 'See; the tailor's paper is still pinned there.'

'So it is.' She drew out the pin, and took the paper from the folds.

'Why don't you read the bill,' urged Ross. 'It will gladden you, I'm sure.'

She opened the folds and read the bill over. 'Received with thanks – 100 guineas.' Private Southcott – one guinea. Private Hall – one guinea. Privates Book, O'Connell, Wareham, Swinney, Rolf, Noyes, Crook, Page, Dallenger, Kennedy, Lancaster, Farrant, Gibson, Laverack, Rees. One guinea, one guinea, one guinea for each. One hundred names, one hundred guineas.

Kit looked up from the paper, tears pricking her eyes. 'They paid for it. They all did.'

'Yes,' he said, 'with their army wages.'

She could not speak. Ross kissed her gently on the forehead. 'Better hasten,' he said. 'The Duke of Marlborough waits.'

As the chapel bells rang Kit emerged from the tent, resplendent in the red gown.

She had no maid to help her, so she had dressed her mass of red hair as best she could, plaiting a trio of braids to wrap around the rest as she had done in the alehouse, leaving the long curls to tumble to her left breast. She wore the red hat cocked to the right as the dragoons wore theirs. The gown fitted as if it was made on her. Now she looked quite different – her mass of hair coiled neatly, glowing carnelian against the red of the gown and the white of her bosom, her cheeks pink with pleasure, her lips deep rose where she'd bitten them until the blood came. Now she could fix Anne of Austria's diamonds in her ears and at her wrists – now they fitted the picture. Her neckline was bare – she touched the place between her heart and her throat where the diamond collar should sit, and smiled secretly at her reflection.

Outside in the low winter sun Ross waited for her, resplendent in his dress uniform, his shadow a dark knife-strike cutting the crown of the hill. Marlborough stood with him, back in his armour, fidgeting from foot to foot as if he could not wait to be gone and take up swords again. The duke performed the function of a priest, standing before them and taking a hand apiece.

She took Ross's other hand and smiled – he squeezed her fingers and her horsehair ring pressed into her hand; her doubts vanished. Marlborough took two golden swords from his ensign and laid them crosswise on the frozen grass as if they were to dance the Mattachins. He straightened, and waved his regiment's kerchief above his head, signalling the commencement of the camp marriage. 'Jump, rogue!' he shouted, and Ross jumped nimbly over the two swords, his boots hopping between the blades.

'Follow, whore!' cried the duke, and Kit hoisted her skirts and hopped likewise, taking the ritual in good part. Then she stood with Ross again, he buried his hands in her red curls, took her in his arms and kissed her hard, and the dragoons cheered themselves hoarse, casting their tricorns into the air.

In Marlborough's vast pavilion of billowing crimson silk, Kit sipped at her marriage cup of genever. The sack-posset had been eaten, the stocking thrown; the duke himself had left directly after the marriage, anxious, she knew, to assume his position on the chessboard. For hours it seemed she had drunk and talked, been hammered on the back, been obliged to recount her adventures over and over again to the men she had fought beside. She had seen them treat her with chivalry and deference at the beginning of their discourse and, by the end and another cup or two, revert, unconsciously, to their former camaraderie. She was glad to see it, glad to see that though her clothes had changed she had not changed in essentials. And for as many dragoons as she greeted, she must tell her story again to certain of Marlborough's officers, who found her story incredible, and prompted her to repeat the particulars of her adventures again and again. At length she had a chance to stand in a private corner with her husband and clink her goblet with his; she had been generous with her time, as had he, for they knew that tonight they would be together, and every night after that.

'Renewing old acquaintances?'

'And making new ones. But there is one man to whom I have not yet been properly introduced.'

'And who is that?'

She laughed up at her husband. 'You! I still do not know your Christian name.'

He looked down at her fondly. 'Would you like me to own it?'

She considered. 'No,' she said. 'You will always be my Ross.

Quondam captain, present husband. And henceforth I shall be Mother Ross – it will suit me very well.'

He smiled. 'Another name for your collection. Yet you will always be Kit to me.'

'Just Kit.'

'Not just . . .'

He studied her closely, touching her constantly with lips or fingertips.

'I am real,' she assured him, 'and I am yours.'

But he could not leave off his inventory. He traced each eyebrow, ran a finger down her upturned nose, counted each freckle. He pushed at the miniature diamond chandeliers hanging at her earlobes, so they swung back and forth. His fingers moved down to caress her collarbone and the notch a musket had once made.

Then he frowned. 'What became of the diamond collar? Did that rogue Ormonde keep it?'

'I sent it to a friend,' she said. She had sent it, by Marlborough's fast-rider that very morning, to Bianca Castellano in Rovereto for the care of herself and Christiana. The price of the gems alone would keep mother and babe in comfort for the rest of their days. She pictured Bianca, in the Gasthof, opening the canvas roll at one of the little wooden tables, the necklace falling out on to the pine, Bianca reading the letter rolled with it with gaze widening, the bright gems reflected in her eyes.

'It does not matter, does it?'

'To me, not at all,' said Ross. 'Besides, when we are in England we will find something to adorn you here, so my Lord of Marlborough tells me.'

'England?'

'London. For a very particular reason.'

She sensed that he was teasing, but a little in earnest too. 'What might that be?'

'I told you,' he said playfully. 'To fit you with a necklace.'

She shook her head. 'I may now be a woman, but I have no need of necklaces, and the other accoutrements of fine ladies.'

'You will be the first lady to wear a necklace of this sort.'

Chapter 45

When a trusty shillelagh came over their heads . . .
                                    'Arthur McBride' (trad.)

Kit felt the cold metal necklace settle on her collarbones.

She lowered her eyes from the glory of St James's court, looked down and touched the collar with her fingertips – the metal warmed quickly to her skin. Fine gold knots alternated with enamelled medallions showing a rose wreathed by a garter. From the collar hung a golden pendant of a knight on horseback battling a dragon who was wreathed about his horse's legs. This was St George. He looked like a dragoon.

Then she looked up at the queen – Queen Anne, infirm, bloated, her face so full as to have not a wrinkle upon it, smooth as a babe despite her age, but as full as a melon. Her teeth were worn snags, her eyes sunken, her expression earnest, as if she had much to say to Kit.

The yeoman of the guard whispered in Kit's ear that she was to fall upon her right knee, and repeat the vow of the Garter – she spoke the vows but could not remember a word of them either then or afterwards. For a moment she could not rise, whether from the emotion of the moment or the old wound in her hip she could not be sure, but she found herself assisted by the queen's own gloved hand. Infirm as she was in other particulars, her Majesty's grip was firm and strong.

'Arise, Mistress Ross,' said the Queen, 'Lady Companion of the Garter.'

Kit smiled shyly – of all the names she had assumed in her life, this was one she could never conceive of getting used to.

'And now we have done with the happy business of the day, I have something of a more private nature to say to you. In recognition of your extraordinary service in our army, it will be my care to provide for you, in the same manner in which I would look after any retired officer of the male sex.' Kit felt such a pang at the term 'retired' that she almost missed the pertinent points of the queen's benefice. 'Therefore you may apply to the Earl of Oxford at the exchequer for the order of fifty pounds, which I am pleased to give you as a pension; in addition my Lord Treasurer Oxford shall pay you a shilling a day subsistence for life.'

A handsome sum. The fifty pounds would keep her well, in addition to Ross's fortune and income. The shilling she had no need of, but she had a happy thought; she would direct the treasury to send it to Bianca each month for baby Christiana. The thought pleased her so much that her gratitude was effusive. 'I thank you, Your Majesty, with all my heart.'

'And furthermore,' said the queen, 'I would like to make you a promise. I hear you are recently married, for which I congratulate you. If you should be delivered of a son, I will give him a commission to the army as soon as he is born.'

Kit smiled involuntarily, and heard herself thank the queen, but the pang she already felt spread through her core. Her overwhelming sadness, that there would never be a son to receive such a commission, was tinged with pity; pity for the great lady who stood before her, for it was well known that the queen had worn out her body with seventeen pregnancies and seventeen stillbirths. That Anne of England had the grace to make such an offer to another woman was truly touching and made Kit admire her very much.

The queen gestured to her footman to take her arm. She turned once, looking back as if her neck pained her. 'Come and see me,

Mistress Ross,' she said. 'Come and see me and tell me your histories.'

'I will, Your Majesty,' Kit promised.

'You see,' said the queen, low voiced, 'I know a little about a woman in a man's profession.' She smiled wistfully, and hobbled from the room.

Outside, the sunshine on the Mall seemed dimmer than the gilt of the throne room. Ross, smiling proudly, touched the little gold figure at her throat. 'He's a dragoon!' he said, just as she had thought. 'So might our son be one day.' He bowed from the waist and missed her frozen expression, then offered his arm. 'Might a humble captain escort you, my Lady Companion of the Garter?' She covered her cares with a smile and a curtsy. 'Gladly,' she said.

They walked home to Ross's house in Charles Street by way of the park, enjoying the pleasant afternoon sunshine, and the children with their hoops on the paths and their boats on the lake, the gentlemen with their smart horses and their even smarter carriages, the calls of the birds and the piemen. Kit felt, all of a sudden, that she was now a part of those paintings she had seen in the palace – those scenes of pleasure gardens or pastoral fantasies where people were secondary to the landscape. Just dots, commoners. Kit was nothing now – she was a smear of paint in the larger scene, the canvas that was London.

Some fellows in regimentals saw the collar, recognised it, stared. She smiled and walked on, pleased and proud, feeling that perhaps she was not invisible after all. Their conversation turned, as it always did, to the past; and soon she and Ross were reminiscing about their campaigns with the Scots Greys. Where other newly-weds would discuss the future, and build their fantasies of what their lives together would hold, they did not; and nor did they, at that time, realise that anything was amiss.

At the barracks in Green Park, there was a great muster, and

Kit and Ross stopped to watch. 'Viscount Galway's men, from the banners,' said Ross. 'Heading out to Spain as soon as they may. Almansa, in the east.'

Almansa, thought Kit; it sounded so exotic, so exciting, like a clash of blades.

'Galway fights to keep the Bourbons out of eastern Spain. Yet another battle front for the endless Wars of the Spanish Succession.'

Kit said nothing, but she remembered meeting Philip of Orléans in the Palazzo del Te in Mantova. The prince who chewed on a chicken leg under a fresco of grappling giants, offering her his priest to say mass for her dead husband. It seemed another world, and she'd been another person. She'd been at the centre of the conflict; now she was at the edge, looking on.

They could see the battalions gathering, the soldiers, the pioneers, the engineers, the sappers, the workmen; the cavalry horses lining up, rearing and skittering. The equipages of guns and cannons, their iron and brass noses glinting in the setting sun, squatting next to seige machines that stood tall like giraffes. Pyramids of cannonballs, boxes of shot in their wool wadding, glittering flints tied on strings like shark's teeth. The fascines, the gabions, the tents, the palisades. All the accoutrements of Captain and Mistress Ross's former life.

They watched, silent, smiling wistfully, their expressions oddly alike, until it was quite dark.

At home Kit took off her hat and rang for a dish of tea. But instead of taking her place by the fire, as she'd done every evening since she had become mistress of this smart townhouse, she stayed standing, touching her father's sword where it hung over their mantel. The blade was warm from the fire, as if it had just been taken off, as if it still spent its days hanging next to a warm body. Then she took the heavy collar from her throat and placed it carefully in the box the palace had given her, with a blood-coloured velvet cushion. She arranged the gold knots and the medallions in a neat circle, and in the centre little St George, who looked so like a dragoon. Then she closed the lid on him.

Kit tried her best – her very best – to fold herself into the society in London. The coffee house, the play, the Vauxhall pleasure gardens. Thanks to the Duke of Ormonde she had all the knowledge of manners and music and social niceties that the beautiful wife of a handsome young officer could require. She and Ross were a popular couple, invited everywhere. Her celebrity and her story made them universally welcome, and in the recounting of her histories, with fond interjections from Ross, she was able to spend most of her evenings back on the field of battle with him. It was at those evenings in their mutual reminiscence, and the nights in their hot sweet bed, and the days riding Flint and Phantom through Hyde Park, that they were happiest. (The truth was that even riding in Rotten Row was too sedate for them, and the thrusting young couple garnered many a disapproving glance as they galloped across the turf at an indecent speed, and even jumped the manicured hedges of yew and myrtle.)

The rest of society's pleasures left Kit cold. Once she saw Lucio Mezzanotte performing at the Covent Garden; as she listened to him in the honeyed dark, his voice transported her back to the Palazzo Borromeo on Lake Maggiore. She could see, from her seat in the circle, that he still wore the Prince Rupert's drop about his neck. He was still a lapdog on a leash. She looked about the gilded theatre for his master, but could not see him. Perhaps Ormonde kept to the shadows, as he always had. The duke had not the power to fright her now; not when she had so powerful a protector as the queen herself.

The couple took pleasure trips that spring, to ease the relentless social round. They went to Dublin to visit Aunt Maura, and found the redoubtable lady running Kavanagh's as she always had – a little whiter of hair, a little more crooked of back, but still strong. She was delighted to see her Kit safe and sound, nodded sagely when she heard of Richard's fate, and, against Kit's expectations, became fast friends with Ross. Kit realised that, charmingly, Ross was treating her aunt as he might one of his fellow officers – he had decided, apparently, that running an alehouse was not unlike running a regiment. 'You chose well this time, girl,' said Maura, as she bade her niece goodbye. 'That look you always had in your eye, he has it too.' Maura stoutly refused their help. 'I wouldn't give the bar back to you now, Kit, if you fought me for it,' she said. 'I swear it is the only thing keeping me alive.' They said their farewells under the swinging Kavanagh's sign, with its motto *Virtus Ipsa Suis Firmissima* emblazoned under the lion and crescents. Truth relies on its own arms. Kit left with a barrel of stout and a link of Dublin sausage in exchange for a promise to visit as often as she might.

Their visit to Ross's Scottish estate was less successful – it rained relentlessly and in the cold grey manor the white-haired Lord of Ross and his lady looked down at Kit, long noses pinched with cold, sorrowing inwardly that their beloved son had married some army hoyden, with neither name nor property. Ross, in respect of his lady, cut the visit short.

At home once more, Kit renewed her intention to be the perfect wife and content herself. She spent her first afternoon back in London baking pies, something she had not done since Kavanagh's, and was pleased with the result. She laid the pies on a pitching board outside the door to cool for Ross's dinner, but soon heard a commotion. She opened the door to find several young fellows taking the pies in their hands and kicking the board to the gutter. Without hesitation she took up a stick from the woodpile and chased them into the street, just as she was, with sleeves upturned and floury hands. She caught all three of them in the alley, and laid about them, young as they were, handling the stick like a sword. When they'd scattered, crying for their mothers, she marched back to the house, trying, without thinking, to sheathe the stick at her side. Recollecting herself, trying to slow her breathing and her heart, she thrust the stick back in the woodpile. She glanced at her father's sword where it hung above the mantel, sidewards and shamefaced, as if she was not worthy to look directly at it.

At another time she went to purchase one of the new-style hoop petticoats from the tailor's. She had resolved to follow fashion and dress in the manner befitting a captain's wife; although in truth she found nothing duller than her fittings at the tailor's and could summon no interest in the accoutrements of women. Walking home from the tailor's by Knaves Acre, she happened to walk through a narrow alley, and a fellow coming the other way accidently bumped her, by reason of her voluminous petticoat, and shoved her against the wall. Winded and shocked, she immediately gave the fellow an uppercut that felled him to the ground. She landed on him, knee to chest. It was easy – she was much the stronger, and had the advantage of surprise; he could never have expected such an adversary dressed as she was. She let him up, only to knock him down again, thrashing him with such force that the fellow begged to be clear of her. Breathing hard, she stood as he took to his heels, looking after him without seeing. Shaking, and white, and tingling in every muscle, she hurried guiltily home. She was horrified at her actions, and even more at the sensations she had felt. She had not felt so alive since she returned from the theatre of war. She sat herself on her fireside chair and tried to master her feelings with some lavender water; but soon she was up again, and pacing, and could not be still.

Some days later a new uniform arrived for Ross along with a letter from the High Command. Ross pocketed the letter without a word, but Kit knew what it would say. She took the heavy bundle of red cloth upstairs and cut the string with the paring knife she kept, out of habit, in her shoe.

She did not call for the valet but laid the clothes out herself in Ross's wardrobe. The crisp shirt and stock, the jacket with the snowy white facings, the tricorn and the cap badge of the dragoons, and the coat – oh, the red coat – with the bright buttons. She laid it all out, and even stood the boots up before the wardrobe ready to step into. She stroked the fabric of the coat, feeling the familiar nap under her hand. She stood back and looked at the uniform for a long, long time. Then she shut the door.

That night, over their night-cup, she asked Ross directly.

'When?' she said.

He did not dissemble; or ask her, in mock confusion, what she meant. He cradled her cheek with his hand and looked at her with a pitying gaze she could not stomach. 'Soon,' he said.

That night, she could not sleep. She rose silently from the bed, and pressed her lips to the warm curve of Ross's back – just to be sure he slept. She lit the lamp and tiptoed to his dressing room. Then, slowly and methodically, she put on the uniform.

Her fingers remembered what to do – they buckled the buckles, buttoned the buttons and tied the ties without thinking. The coat and boots were too big, the hat fell over her eyes, but when she pushed the mass of her hair into the brim it sat as it always had. She lifted the lamp and looked at herself in the glass. There she was. It was Kit.

The door creaked behind her and she spun about, guiltily. Ross stood there, naked to the waist, his hair rumpled, his blue eyes hardly open. Then his gaze snapped wide. She read there a gladness, a recognition, as if he greeted an old and dear friend. 'Kit!' Then the gaze dropped. 'What are you doing?'

She could not reply, but took off the tricorn, and loosened the stock at her throat. She laid the things in the drawers again, carefully and deliberately. One sudden movement would shatter the fragile tension between them, like a Prince Rupert's drop, and then everything would be in smithereens. But Ross spoke. 'You miss it, don't you?'

She turned, defensive. 'I'll tell you that if you'll tell me another. Do you miss *him*?'

Ross pushed his hands through his bed-rumpled hair. 'I do not understand you. Miss whom?'

'Aye, you understand,' she said, without heat, but with sadness. 'Kit.'

He looked back at her with an inscrutable expression, part love, part pain, part she knew not what. He did not reply but turned and left the room, just as he'd left the abbey courtroom when faced with a revelation he could not countenance. Frozen to the spot, she heard, a few moments later, the front door bang.

Kit, wide awake on her pillow, heard him come home much later; but he did not return to their bed. It was the first night they'd spent apart since they'd wed.

Ross's commission papers arrived the very next day. And now she knew. He was going and she would lose him, and she would face life in this alien city, going alone to the coffee house and the play, while he fought on the fields of Spain, perhaps to fall in the mud for the last time, with no friend or lover to run to him, and turn his body over, and close his eyes.

She would not be a coward this time – she would ask him, straight out. He opened the papers and she saw him smile a smile of pure joy. Her heart sank. It was no good his pretending – he could not wait to be abroad, and from her side. On horseback, in battle, that was where he lived.

'Dearest,' she said, 'tell me what is in the letter.'

'You may read it yourself,' he said, cock-a-hoop; and passed the paper to her.

By the Order of Henry de Massue, 2nd Marquis of Galway, and in the name of her Majesty the Queen, Captain Ross is hereby given commission to report to the barracks at Hyde Park to recommence his active service as Captain of the Royal Scots Grey Dragoons at dawn on the fifth day of April in the year of our Lord seventeen hundred and seven.

Furthermore, it is Her Majesty's personal request that Mistress Kit Ross, quondam Sergeant of the Royal Scots Grey Dragoons, shall also report at that time, and shall be employed by the regiment as a Sutler, to be present in the lines for any and all such manoeuvres which shall be required of the division. She is to be equipped with the same arms and accoutrements of her fellows, for the Queen is well aware that there may be occasion for Mistress Ross to defend herself in the field, and Her Majesty would by all means prevent harm befalling such a well-beloved subject.

Yours etc, Sir William Windham, High Commander of Her Majesty's Army

She looked up, her face aglow. 'It is a commission.' She read the paper over. 'For *both* of us.'

He nodded, his blue eyes wary.

'You did this! Last night, when you ran from me.' She should have trusted him – he spoke with actions, not words, as a soldier should. When he'd left her at the courtroom at San Michele he'd gone to fetch Marlborough. Last night he'd gone to petition the High Command.

'Not I. I merely made the request. It was the queen who made it so. And here – I had the measurements from your tailor.' He passed her a heavy bale, wrapped with paper and string – she cut the twine with her paring knife and her new uniform sprang forth from its bonds, as if it was alive and could not wait to be worn. She hugged it to her, eyes shining.

'We ride at dawn,' he said. 'But for tonight,' he smiled, 'we shall stoke our last home fire with your detested hooped petticoat. I think the cane will make a capital blaze.' He could not finish the sentence, for his wife launched herself at him and, as they embraced, the letter and the uniform fell to the floor.

At dawn two cavalrymen reported to the Hyde Park Barracks, to ride for Almansa to augment the forces of the Duke of Galway. Both wore the red of the dragoons, both were mounted upon grey mares. There was little to choose between them. One was perhaps a little taller than the other, and although the taller wore a shining new blade, the shorter wore a sword whose metals were dimmed with age, and whose blade, though keen, seemed to be smithed in the old style. Only the most observant bystander, peering closely beneath the tricorn hat of the shorter fellow, might have his attention caught by a set of very comely features, by the subtle curve of the body beneath the coat, and the coil of red hair tied at the nape; and remark that there rode a very pretty dragoon.

The two men mingled with the company, and were lost to sight as they greeted other dragoons who appeared to be as dear to them as brothers. Somewhere someone played a violin, a merry air from Galway, in honour of their commander. Then the herald sounded, the banners streamed and the outriders rode forth.

At the vanguard Kit and Ross turned to each other at the sound of the trumpet and shared a smile of pure joy. Perfectly in accord, perfectly happy, they spurred their horses towards another horizon.

Epilogue

When Kit saw herself, quite clearly, crossing the Figure Court, she knew that she was very near the end now.

Most days now the quadrangle of the Chelsea Hospital would be peopled with the dead, walking on the neat green squares of grass, or down the loggias, or under the cupola, but she'd never seen herself before.

So many old friends she saw there who had passed into the hereafter; Marlborough, in his flowing wig and his half-armour, Marlborough, who'd been attainted by Parliament for embezzling army funds, disgraced by the Whig Party, but was mourned by the whole of England when he died.

Sometimes she even saw Queen Anne herself, hobbling about the precincts of the hospital with her gouty gait, long dead and succeeded since by two King Georges. And Ross, of course, her Ross whom she'd lost two years ago, after a lifetime of happiness. She saw him often, riding on his old horse Phantom, trampling the manicured lawns. She always saw him riding away from her; young again, dark haired, laughing over his shoulder. She saw him as she had first known him; Ross before the wig and the gout and the colonelcy and retirement to the Chelsea Hospital. But she saw him riding away. Always riding away.

She never saw the Duke of Ormonde, Ormonde, who had achieved his desire to replace his great rival Marlborough, as the commander-in-chief of the army. But he could not quit his scheming – attainted for treason, and stripped of his titles, he'd fled to Spain to plot his next design. He'd outlived Marlborough, and the queen, and would outlive her too. She smiled – she'd forgiven Ormonde long ago. If he had nine lives, like the cat she'd always thought him, then she wished him the joy of them.

She knew her own life was ending as soon as she saw herself walking the lawns – her own figure, in a saffron gown, and no bonnet on her red hair. This woman had her stance, her way of walking, and her hair had just Kit's curl to it as she stopped one of the old, scarlet-coated soldiers and he pointed to her rooms.

Kit watched her younger self walking up the Long Ward. She had not walked like that for years – now she could not manage ten yards without help. Her ghost approached. She was not afraid. She was ready. Ross, she thought, I'll be with you soon. But when the spectre knocked and entered, Kit was surprised to see that the figure did not, after all, have her face.

The woman took Kit's old hand in her younger one. On closer inspection she was not so young as she'd looked at a distance. Her hands were worn, and a starburst of fine lines radiated from the outer corners of her green eyes, and wrinkled in an attractive manner when she smiled.

'I have come a long way to find you,' she said in an accent Kit recognised from somewhere, some country where she'd been, and fought.

'Who are you?'

The red-headed woman untied the ribbons of her cloak and laid bare her throat. There she wore a collar of diamonds, with some of the stones gone like missing teeth. Kit vaguely recognised it.

In return, Kit showed the lady Sean Kavanagh's sword, now old and rusted. She wanted her to know what she once had been. She recited the names of the campaigns she and Ross had fought together like a litany (she had never been one for prayer). She liked the music of the words: Carpi, Cremona, Luzzara, Turin, Almansa, Oudenarde, Malplaquet.

Then she showed her guest the 'Great George', the collar of the Order of the Garter in its faded box, the corners softened and worn with age. She looked again, at the saint on horseback, invited her to touch the little gold figure. She remembered Ross touching it thus. 'So might our son be one day,' Ross had said. He'd said the same when she'd worn it each year at the Garter ceremony at St James's, or on her name day, or at Yuletide. Until, one year, he'd ceased to say it, and never said it again. 'I never had a child,' Kit said, tears choking her voice.

The red-headed woman took her hand. 'Yes, you did. You have always had a child. I am your daughter.'

Kit smiled. 'That cannot be.'

'Don't you know who I am? You should, for I bear your name.'

Kit looked at the lady with her old eyes – and saw her tiny, wrapped in a shawl with only a kiss curl of red hair. 'Christiana?'

She reached out and cupped the lady's cheek. Christiana took the hand and pressed it to her flesh, to her bone.

'Christiana,' repeated Kit, her tears falling now. 'I never thought to be a mother.'

Kit could feel the smile under her hand, the cheek she held bunching to the shape of an apple. 'Say a father instead – for you supported me by placing yourself in daily danger. You paid for my childhood with a diamond collar, my adulthood with an army pension. You may not have suckled me, nor wiped my nose, but you raised me as much as any other man did, and for that, Kit Walsh was my father.'

'How is your mother?'

'She is a little infirm these days, but well in essentials. She lives in Venice, in a house she bought for us with your diamonds. She married a salt merchant, is now widowed.' Kit nodded. Bianca the butcher's daughter, now a dowager of salt; the princess of victuals.

'And are you happy?'

'I married an Englishman. A quartermaster in the navy. We have lately moved to Portsmouth. He is in London buying sail canvas in Spitalfields. I begged to come with him.' She smiled. 'He calls me Kit.'

Kit smiled too and nodded, suddenly deathly tired. She closed her eyes. Christiana rose quietly. She stooped and kissed the old lady's papery cheek.

'I'll come again,' she said.

Kit watched Christiana walk away and looked beyond her to Ross, riding away from her as she always saw him. There would be no need for her to come again.

For today it was different. Another figure rode beside him – a red-headed beauty, young and lithe, a red pigtail flowing out beneath her tricorn. *There's a horizon everywhere you go*, he'd always said. And as they rode, over the hills and far away to where the earth meets the sky, Ross held out his hand, and Kit took it.

THE END

Acknowledgements

For a while I had a vague awareness of a remarkable female soldier who had fought as a man, but I only really became acquainted with her many names and her story when I read Daniel Defoe's book *Mother Ross: The Life and Adventures of Mrs. Christian Davies, Commonly Called Mother Ross, on Campaign with the Duke of Marlborough*. This contemporary account opened my eyes to Kit's extraordinary experiences in the British Army, and was an invaluable source for my novel. I had great fun reading *Swearing: A Social History of Foul Language, Oaths and Profanity in English* by Geoffrey Hughes, and was able to pepper my book with some good barracks language! I learned a great deal about sailors' votive shrines in Genoa from an article in *The Oxford Historian* Issue XI entitled *Spectacular Miracles* by Jane Garnett and Gervase Rosser. The other source which deserves a mention is a work of fiction; *Shield of Three Lions* by Pamela Kaufman was one of my favourite books growing up, and, as it features a heroine who dresses as a boy to go on Crusade, deserves a mention as the inspiration for this book.

There were other sources for this novel besides written ones. I must mention two films; *Farinelli* (1994) which is so informative on the experience of the *castrato*, and *Le Roi Danse* (2000) which allowed me to see the *Ballet de la Nuit* as it would have been performed, when the young Louis XIV danced the role of Apollon. Both films were directed by Gérard Corbiau. I must also mention Dublin-based band *Lad Lane*, who, through both their recorded and live performances, opened my ears to the lively loveliness of traditional Irish music.

Thanks also to Cecil Sharp House, home of the English Folk Society. It was in the library there that I managed to track down *Arthur McBride*, the folk song which is the touchstone of this book.

I needed many names for my dragoons, and at a Remembrance Day ceremony at my local war memorial I had an idea. So all the dragoons in this book – bar Ross, Kit and Taylor who are real characters – are named after the fallen on the war memorial at St. Mary's Church, Abbey Road. A very small tribute to a very great sacrifice.

And finally, my thanks must go to all the lovely people who helped me with this book. Martin O'Grady was very helpful in giving me the Dubliner's history of Kavanagh's – the Gravedigger's pub. And I had the great honour to meet a real-life Chelsea pensioner, IP Derek 'Yorky' Layton, who was most informative about the Chelsea Hospital's first female resident. At Hodder I must thank my editor Kate Parkin, who was there at the inception of the book and gave the go-ahead for Kit's story to be told, and was there too in the final stages to give me the benefit of her fantastic editorial skills. Thanks also must go to Francine Toon for managing the production of the novel and Ian Paten for his eagle-eyed copy edit. As always, I am indebted to my agent Teresa Chris for her unfailing guidance and support.

And, last but never least, my thanks to Sacha, Conrad and Ruby, who are always on my side.

Historical Note

Kit Kavanagh (also known as Christian Walsh, Christian Davies or latterly Mother Ross) was a real person. In this novel I have augmented and embellished her adventures but her own life was no less remarkable.

She was born in 1667 and ran an alehouse in Dublin with her husband Richard. When he was pressed into the British Army she followed him to war dressed as a man, and enlisted in the army too. Initially she was shipped to the Low Countries, where she further disguised her appearance by having a false penis made out of silver.

Kit served as an infantryman and then as a dragoon in the Scots Greys. She fought several campaigns under the Duke of Marlborough. She was known to the duke personally, and he rewarded her for her bravery in action. She accepted the paternity of the daughter of a woman she met on her campaigns, rather than admit her true sex. Kit eventually found her husband Richard, but he was already married to another woman. Kit continued to fight, but her sex was revealed when she took a musket ball in the hip and was operated on by the field surgeon. Upon her return to England she was commended by Queen Anne, who gave her a handsome pension and a pledge to give a commission to Kit's first-born son.

Kit married Captain Ross and every man in her regiment made a contribution to buy her a wedding gown. After her marriage she enlisted again as a sutler in the army and served for many more years. She ended her days in London's Chelsea Hospital – the first woman to be admitted there as a pensioner. Kit died in 1739 and was buried at St Margaret's church Westminster. Some years later the Duke of Ormonde was buried next door in Westminster Abbey.

Arthur McBride

Oh me and my cousin, one Arthur McBride
As we went a walkin' down by the seaside
Now mark what followed and what did betide
It being on Christmas morning

Out for recreation we went on a tramp
And we met Sergeant Knacker and Captain Vamp
And a little wee drummer intending to camp
For the day being pleasant and charming

Good morning, good morning the sergeant did cry
And the same to you gentlemen, we did reply
Intending no harm but meant to pass by
For it being on Christmas morning

But says he my fine fellows if you will enlist
It's ten guineas in gold I will slip in your fist
And a crown in the bargain for to kick up the dust
And to drink the King's health in the morning

For a soldier he leads a very fine life
He always is blessed with a charming young wife
And he pays all his debts without sorrow or strife
And always lives happy and charming

And a soldier he always is decent and clean
In the finest of clothing he's constantly seen
While other poor fellows go dirty and mean
And sup on thin gruel in the morning

Says Arthur, I wouldn't be proud of your clothes
You've only the lend of them as I suppose
And you dare not change them one night or you know
If you do you'll be flogged in the morning

And although we are single and free
We take great delight in our own company
And we have no desire strange places to see
Although your offer is charming

And we have no desire to take your advance
All hazards and danger we barter on chance
and you'd have no scruples to send us to France
Where we would be shot without warning

And now says the sergeant, I'll have no such chat
And I neither will take it from spalpeen or brat
For if you insult me with one other word
I'll cut off your heads in the morning

And then Arthur and I we soon drew our hods
And we scarce gave them time for to draw their own blades
When a trusty shillelagh came over their heads
And bade them take that as fair warning

As for their old rusty rapiers that hung by their sides
We flung it as far as we could in the tide
To the Devil I pitch you, says Arthur McBride
To temper your steel in the morning

As for the wee drummer, we rifled his pow
And made a football of his row-do-dow-dow
Into the tide to rock and to roll
And bade it a tedious returnin'

And we haven't no money to pay them off in cracks
And we paid no respect to the two bloody backs
For we lathered them there like a pair of wet sacks
And left them for dead in the morning

And so to conclude and to finish disputes
We obligingly asked if they wanted recruits
For we were the lads who would give them hard clouts
And bid them look sharp in the morning

Oh me and my cousin, one Arthur McBride
As we went a walkin' down by the seaside
Now mark what followed and what did betide
It being on Christmas morning